THE SONS OF MOUNT CARMEL

By R. Jay Alvarez

For Maryann, my love and my muse

"Before I formed thee in the belly I knew thee; and before thou camest forth out of the womb I sanctified thee...

Jeremiah 1:5

PROLOGUE

SUNDAY MORNING

Milton Iglesia had taken a window seat in the last row of a Trailways bus way before the birds began their morning chorus. There would barely have been enough room for even a small child to squeeze in next to him. It was pitch-black outside. The bus picked him up at the nearest bus stop to the Tekakwitha Home for the Emotionally Disturbed at three a.m. sharp in the sleeping host town. It was located at the remote northwest edge of New York State, an eight-hour drive from New York City, not far from the Canadian border. The locals preferred the guests of Tekakwitha to go back to where they came from in the middle of the night.

When he got on the bus it was empty. The driver didn't utter a word when he stepped up, nor did he make eye contact with the big man. Milton pressed into the rear seat. He could see the blotches of grey in his own bearded, burly reflection in the window among the passing lights on the Thruway.

The authorities thought he could go back to New York City — to society — on his first pass. And after twenty years under the care of the Tekawitha psychiatric team, and no signs that he would commit violence again, the state pronounced he was ready for the outside. He'd only been sixteen when he committed that one evil act.

Over the course of the long silent ride through the dark rolling hills of the Adirondacks and Catskills, the light started to ease through the nighttime mist finally bringing the green into full view. Passenger cars started to join the bus on the road. For half the trip the thruway seemed restricted to only buses and tractor-trailers.

Each car the bus passed the big man leered deep down into its interior, hoping to grab the sight of a woman's thighs. It didn't matter if the unsuspecting woman was a mother traveling with her child sitting at her side. It did not matter at all. He captured the image and saved it.

Tekakwitha notified Father Manuel Gonzalez, pastor of Our Lady of Mount Carmel Church in the South Bronx — Milton's half-brother — during one of the priest's monthly visits, that he would be released in thirty days. The state also notified the Upper Westside precinct where he would temporarily live, but it was not that police precinct that could have benefited from the information. As a registered sex offender, the precinct notified the local community board, but the people who lived in the area where he would take a room — residents of the Upper West Side — had not much to fear from the big man. As it turns out he would quietly check into an S.R.O. hotel on West 73th Street, and come-and-go, without disturbance.

But it was Bronx detectives that could have used that information. Especially Detective Toni Santiago and Lieutenant Ryan Condon of the Bronx Homicide Squad, but they hadn't been told. There was no reason to notify police in the borough in which he formerly lived and committed his one crime, or so it was thought.

The Manhattan skyline climbed into view. The big man's face had been so close to the window that circles of eager mist momentarily obstructed his view with each vulgar breath. The bus barreled through the Lincoln Tunnel emerging in front of the big city's obese Port Authority bus terminal. Milton grabbed his backpack from the rack above his seat and lumbered off the bus and into the bustling lobby that Sunday afternoon, and took it all in. She was there to greet him. Just as she said she would be.

CHAPTER 1

"What's cooking?" Detective Toni Santiago said into her iPhone.

She noticed the time on the screen read 6:42 before she answered. She'd been running on the tree-lined campus of the College of Mount St. Vincent not far from her apartment in North Riverdale. Holding the phone to her damp ear with one hand she listened and walked; dripping in her blue and gold — Fighting Irish — t-shirt and shorts, and held her bulldog Vita's leash with the other. The dog had a lock on Toni's empty bottle of Poland Spring between its slobbering teeth.

"A priest?" Toni said and stopped walking. She swiftly swiped sweat from her ear, put the phone back, and continued to listen.

"In the face?" She said, and started to walk again as she listened, Vita waddled alongside her.

"For crying out loud," she said. "Crime Scene there yet?" She stopped again, didn't budge, Vita stopped again too.

"Good. All right, I'll be there in forty-five."

Toni made it to Our Lady of Mount Carmel Church by 7:45. *Channel 7 Eyewitness News* and *New York 1* news vans were already parked across the street, with others pulling up. A few of the reporters were using the backdrop of the church as they spoke into their mikes.

There was yellow crime scene tape across the front steps leading to the entrance of the rectory. Barricades had been set-up on both sides of the rectory steps to keep parishioners and passersby from blocking the entrance.

Two uniformed cops stood like Corinthian columns on either side of the rectory door. One held a clipboard and took-down the ID's of everybody who stepped up into the rectory: EMT'S, Crime Scene Unit investigators, Medical Examiner personnel, Night Watch and Bronx Homicide detectives; names, ranks/titles, shield numbers. Toni showed her gold detective shield to the officers, as did her partner, Detective John Geddes. After their ID's were noted, Toni and Geddes ducked under the yellow tape and entered the threshold of the murder scene.

As soon as they stepped into the rectory, a couple Night Watch detectives pointed them to the kitchen without comment. In their walk down the narrow, dark, hallway, Toni noticed one still candle under a clear, red, cover that washed the walls in just a whisper of flickering red light. When they reached the doorway of the kitchen they stopped and took in the spiritless, bloody body of Father Manuel Gonzalez in the rear. The back of his head had landed on the hard, linoleum floor near the sink. A stew of blood radiated around the priest's head like an aureole.

Toni turned back to look at one of the night watch detectives. "Anybody else here?"

"Priest in the office back by the front door," the detective said and nodded in that direction. "Father Gribbons."

"Okay, thanks."

"You need us to stick around, or you got this?"

"No, we got it now. Thanks for the response."

Toni stepped into the rectory office where the priest was sitting on an upright wooden chair in the far corner like he was being punished.

"Father Gribbons," Toni put out her hand to the priest, "I'm Detective Santiago. I've been assigned to lead this investigation." Toni pulled up another wooden chair nearby without letting the priest's hand go.

Toni only stood a little over five-two but sounded taller.

—

"Thank you, detective," Gribbons said and shook Toni's hand. Toni held his hand a little longer than she would have normally. She was struck by how soft the priest's hands were. Not that this should have surprised her considering his line of work. But she had no illusion, not for one second, that those soft hands couldn't pull a trigger, if necessary.

"Can you tell us what you know, Father?"

Father Gribbons was a tall, lanky priest in his mid-fifties. He'd been assigned to Our Lady of Mount Carmel right out of seminary like Father Manny Gonzalez only Gribbons had arrived ten years before.

"Well, I just got back about 6:30 this morning. I was at a weekend retreat. When I came in I first found it strange that the lights were not turned on. It was completely dark, except for the one candle in the hallway that's on all day and night. Father Manny woke up at five-thirty each morning and would head downstairs to the kitchen to make a pot of coffee, and would leave the lights on in the rectory office before going back upstairs to shower. Often he would go out for a morning run in the park—

"Mount Carmel?" Toni said.

"Yes, Mount Carmel Park," Father Gribbons said. "He'd always leave the lights on, except, recently he'd stopped going."

Even in the rectory office, the scent from the decades-convergence of burning candles and dark wood walls was robust.

"Do you know why, Father?" Toni said. "Why he stopped going?"

"No, I'm afraid I don't. I asked him several times if everything was all right, and he'd say he just needed a change."

"Okay," Toni said. "Please go on."

—

"Well, I turned the lights on and I could hear the running water in the kitchen and started to go down the hallway. When I arrived at the doorway to the kitchen, I saw him on the floor, and all the blood."

The kitchen had two windows facing the back of the rectory into the garden with a fire escape. There was a crucifix hanging on the sliver of wall between the windows. In the center were an oak table with six chairs and a half-filled cup of black coffee with a lipstick mark. There was also a shattered coffee cup on the floor. The water was still running into the stainless steel sink.

"Did you walk into the kitchen, Father?"

"No. I stopped at the doorway, saw his body and came right back here to the office and dialed 911," Gribbons said. "I knew he was dead."

Gribbons took off his glasses and wiped his eyes with a handkerchief.

Toni watched the priest for an extra moment.

"When did you leave for retreat, Father?" Toni said.

"Friday afternoon," Gribbons said. "You know, detective, the entire congregation over the years always eagerly awaited his words at mass. They had a deep affection for Father Manny. All those dark and light faces with sparkling brown eyes. All those eyes not knowing Sunday would be his last."

Toni wondered too if Father Manny had had any idea it would be his last as she sized Father Gribbons up. She then wondered if Gribbons had had any idea it would be Father Manny's last.

"Where was the retreat, Father?" Toni said.

John Geddes walked into the rectory office and joined the interview. Geddes stood about six-four and had recently turned forty. Half of his almost eighteen years in the department were spent in Bronx Homicide.

"The sarge coming?" Toni said.

"Outdoor range."

9

Toni introduced Geddes.

"Where was that retreat, Father?"

"Massachusetts, Clarence, Massachusetts. The Clarence Abbey," Gribbons said.

"Oh, really," Toni said. "What religious order is that?"

"Cistercians," Gribbons said. "They're Trappist monks."

Toni nodded.

Father Manny's bloody body had been found spread between the sink and the table. She thought the priest would have turned when his attention was drawn to the shooter, maybe surprised and unable to focus at first, or maybe the figure had just had a cup of coffee with the priest. But whether he was surprised to see the figure or not, Toni imagined that when Father Manny turned — before seeing the gun in the shooter's hand — he captured the settled glint in the eyes looking back at him, and with a gasp blurted, "Mercy..." as a solitary bullet shattered his glasses, pierced his left eye, and expelled from the back of his head.

Geddes said, "Father, what was Father Manny's normal Sunday like after mass?"

"After mass, his day was usually full. He'd meet with various members of the congregation for lunch and others for dinner most often here in the kitchen until he retired to his private office to write in his journal before going to bed."

"He kept a journal?" Toni said. "Where is it?"

"He kept it on the top of his desk. His office is on the second floor. And you know — Gribbons stopped, and looked up at the ceiling — it's odd but his office door was open."

"On the second floor?" Toni said. "Why's that odd? He just always kept it closed?"

"Yes, but it's not only that," Gribbons said. "When I got back after I found Father Manny's body and called 9-1-1, I went upstairs quickly just to put my bag in my room and that's when I noticed his office door was open. And I paused, just for a moment, and looked in and noticed several of the draws to his file cabinet were open."

"So, it felt like somebody other than Father Manny had been in there?" Toni said.

"Yes, I think so," Gribbons said. "I'd never seen his file cabinet draws left open like that."

"Okay," Toni said. "Back to this journal. You said it's on his desk."

"Yes, it should be there." Father Gribbons said raising his eyes to the ceiling again. "It's red."

"What about an appointment diary?" Toni said. "He must've had one."

"Oh, yes. That's right here." Gribbons slowly rose up and stepped behind the desk in the rectory office. There was a table behind the desk with a printer/fax machine, and up against it was a green hardcover diary. Father Gribbons handed it to Toni.

"Have you looked at this since you found Father Manny's body, Father?" Toni said as she leafed through the diary?"

"No, I haven't. I thought it was best I not touch anything until you arrived. I've learned not touching anything always seems to be very important to arriving detectives."

Toni looked at the priest.

"I watch 'Law and Order' re-runs on occasion."

Toni kept leafing through the diary.

"I see his last appointment yesterday night was at 7:30 with a Mrs. Samantha Cohen." Toni looked up. "Do you know her?"

"Oh, yes, of course," Gribbons said. "She was one of Father Manny's closest friends. They grew up in this neighborhood and first met, I believe, here at Mount Carmel or maybe it was high school. No, maybe not high school, maybe they met at college. I'm not sure really, but I know she attended Georgetown and, and of course, Father Manny went to seminary. She's a very fine personal injury attorney."

"Do you have her number?" Toni said.

As Gribbons peeled off Cohen's business card from the ancient rectory Rolodex, Toni thought about Gribbons' odd reaction to bring his bag up to his room—just after seeing Father Manny's dead body and calling 9-1-1.

Their attention had then been drawn to huffing sounds of heavy lifting rebounding off the walls of the hallway. Medical Examiner personnel were squeezing the dead weight of Father Manuel Gonzalez down the narrow hallway in that all too familiar temporary secular vestment to death investigators: a body bag.

"Are you all right, Father?" Geddes said.

Gribbons nodded his head as he again wiped his eyes.

Toni placed her hand on his shoulder. "I'm sorry for your loss, Father."

Gribbons nodded again as he put his handkerchief in his pants pocket.

"Detectives, I don't know if you're aware that Father Manny was a very good friend of a lieutenant in your department. He's a detective too. They too were childhood friends."

"Is that right?" Toni said. "Who's that?"

"Ryan Condon."

"Lieutenant Condon," Toni and Geddes said together.

"Yes," Gribbons said.

Toni looked over at Geddes, closed her notebook and said, "Let me give Tazzo a call." She stepped out of the office and strolled down the hallway. Two minutes later she was back.

"We have to leave, Father," Toni said. "When we get back we need you to come down to the medical examiner's office to formally identify his body. If we have time—when we bring you back—we want to see Father Manny's office upstairs and that red diary. Will that be all right?"

"Yes, of course."

Before leaving the rectory, Toni asked the Crime Scene team to do a complete survey of Father Manny's second-floor office: video; photographs; the collection of potential DNA evidence, the works. And to shut the water off in the kitchen after they lifted any prints from the faucet knob. She imagined the running water was the only sound that resonated throughout the rectory until the single shot was fired and the coffee cup shattered.

CHAPTER 2

Normally, a direct call to the lieutenant — or sometimes just a text — would have been enough of a notification, even a high-profile murder like a priest — to just give him the basic details as his squad of detectives worked the case until either he or Tazzo got there. But this wasn't normal. Toni spoke to Sergeant Tazzo who was out at the outdoor range for his annual firearms requalification. Tazzo confirmed that the lieutenant and Father Manny had indeed been longtime, childhood friends.

Toni and Geddes pulled up at Lieutenant Ryan Condon's home. He was mowing his patch of lawn. It was his day off. It was the first time Toni had been to his home in the two years she'd been assigned to the Bronx Homicide Squad. He lived in a modest two-story brick house in the Throgs Neck section of the Bronx with his wife of twenty-two years. They had no children.

Ryan looked up at the unmarked, black-walled, department car. Toni knew Ryan could see it wasn't good. He shut off the mower and it yawned to a stop. Ryan kept hold of the lawn mower and waited for them to approach him.

"What's up?" Ryan said before they were fully out of the car. A cool breeze, on which was the fragrance of fresh-cut grass, brushed their faces. They were within a couple feet of him in the middle of the lawn before they spoke up.

"It's about Father Manny, Loo," Geddes said.

"Father Manny?" Ryan said with focused eyes; fists still gripped to the lawn mower. "What about him?"

"He'd dead, boss?" Geddes said.

Ryan didn't reply for a moment.

"What? What was the cause? Heart attack? What?"

Toni couldn't tell Ryan that his friend's face had been broken open as easily as he'd broken the Eucharist during Mass. Ryan shifted his gaze from one to the other.

"What?" Ryan said again as he took a step away from the mower; placed his hands on his hips and blurted, "Ahh, no, you got to be kidding, don't tell me homicide."

Toni reached out to touch him, but he turned away. He started to walk in a circle on his lawn, hands still on his hips, shaking his head. He then stopped, turned to them. "Where'd it happen?" His voice cracked.

"The rectory," Toni said.

"How?"

"He was shot, boss," Geddes said.

"Shot?" Ryan said. "Where? Where was he shot?"

"Loo..."Toni paused, "...Loo, he was shot in the face."

Ryan stood still for several moments, then doubled over; both hands on his thighs as if he was in a football huddle; then he raised up with both fists clenched at the simmering sun when one long wordless burst of heartache rang out from him.

The screen door to his home flung open: a woman rushed down the steps, out onto the lawn and reached for Ryan.

"What is it?" the woman said. "What's happened?"

It was the first time Toni had seen Ryan's wife. A deep piercing pang struck Toni's chest. She was not what Toni expected. His wife looked to be about Ryan's age only very tired. She looked older than her years. Yet, Toni could see she had once been very beautiful with her long red hair and long legs. Toni wanted desperately to hold Ryan right there on his lawn too.

"Manny's dead, Jocelyn," Ryan said as he straightened up.

"What?" She said. "How?"

"I'll explain inside," Ryan said.

Ryan held his wife's shoulders and guided her back into the house without replying, then twisted back to his two detectives. "Who caught this?

"It's mine, Loo," Toni said.

_____

15

"Is Father Gribbons there?"

"Yes, sir," Toni said.

"All right. I'll see you back at the office," Ryan said. "You taking Gribbons down to the M.E.'s office for the I.D.?"

"That's our plan," Toni said.

"All right, I'll be in the office by three. Call in the rest of the squad."

"You got it, boss" Geddes said.

Toni stayed still as she watched husband and wife step up into their home. It was the middle of summer and Jocelyn Condon was wearing an oversized flannel shirt with the sleeves rolled up. Toni did not miss the thick scars on the inside of her wrists.

Toni whipped the car out from in front of Ryan's home.

"Did you see her wrists, Geddes?"

"What about it?"

Toni looked over at Geddes and turned back to face the windshield. "I had no idea."

CHAPTER 3

After they brought Father Gribbons to the M.E.'s office to identify Father Manny's body, by mid-afternoon Toni and Geddes showed up at the midtown Manhattan office building housing the law offices of Brown, Whitehead, and Cohen. They found out from the managing partner of the firm that Samantha Cohen would not be in due to a family emergency. Toni had already done a quick DMV check for Samantha Cohen's home address on her iPhone. They shot over to her residence on Sutton Place unannounced.

The rotund Puerto Rican concierge called up to the Cohen apartment before they were pointed to the elevators. Toni took in the lobby. It reminded her a little bit of the lobby of the Surrogates Court in lower Manhattan: all marble and frescoes.

"Do you know who was working the desk here last night for the four-to-twelve and twelve-to-eight shift?" Toni said before they stepped away.

"Sure, sure, detective," the concierge said with a big smile for the pretty Latina detective. "I work the day shift with Willy, and we relieved by Hector and Mike. We switch between who is doorman and concierge. They was relieved by Hernan at midnight. Only one concierge on duty overnight. We relieve him this morning at eight."

"They on duty tonight?" Toni said.

"Yeah, they are, unless one goes sick or something."

"You have CCTV here?" Toni said looking up at the cameras scattered in different corners of the concierge and lobby area.

"Of course," the concierge said, and looked back to the backroom of the concierge desk. "Look." Toni could see one huge flat screen T.V. with multiples boxes of CCTV indoor and outdoor views.

Toni nodded and stepped away with Geddes.

"Thanks, Amigo," Geddes said.

17

Samantha Cohen opened her front door.

"You said you're from the Bronx Homicide Squad?" Samantha Cohen said after she invited them in. She had no make-up and her eyes were bloodshot and swollen, holding a tissue in each hand. She was wearing a white terrycloth bathrobe, collar-up. "You're here because of Manny?"

"Yes, Mrs. Cohen," Toni said and handed her an NYPD business card. "We're investigating the murder of Father Gonzalez. I'm Detective Santiago, this is Detective Geddes."

Toni was struck at how beautiful Samantha Cohen was, and how obviously Latin was her DNA. She had short, French-cut, jet-black hair with deep brown eyes. When Geddes had pulled into the parking space, Toni' took another look at the DMV check information she'd pulled-up on her iPhone. She was forty-three years old but looked to be in her mid-thirties. She kept herself fit. Toni wondered what facial cream she used: Lancôme Absolute L'Extrait, Toni figured. Toni had to settle for a L'Oreal facial cream, the bastard-child of L'Oreal products. And she was more than a few inches taller than Toni, which was another shot in the gut.

They followed Cohen into the living room. "Can I offer you something to drink? Coffee, tea—

"No, thank you," Toni and Geddes replied together.

Toni took a look at the vista of the East River before sitting down. A vast window spanned almost the whole length of the apartment's eastern view. Two door-like windows, which reached up to the ceiling, were swung open and an East River gust made the vertical blinds clap. It pays to be on the twenty-first floor, Toni thought. It gave her a welcomed shiver. There had not been a hint of breeze down on street level when they'd arrived.

"We were told you knew Father Gonzalez well, Mrs. Cohen?" Toni said.

"Yes, I knew him very well. We were very close friends."

"Father Gribbons told us you both grew up in the Mount Carmel area," Toni said. "How did you meet?"

"Yes, that's right, we grew up in the same neighborhood. But it was a long time ago, detective. I can't be sure. I probably met him through somebody else." Cohen paused before she continued. "You think knowing how I met Father Gonzalez would help you find his killer?"

Interesting, Toni thought. Her childhood friend has been murdered and she can't resist playing lawyer. Of all people, a lawyer knows — or should know — how important relationship details are in a murder investigation. She wondered if Cohen would continue to play lawyer.

Geddes cleared his throat. "Can you tell us when you last saw him, Mrs. Cohen?" Geddes said.

"I was supposed to see him last evening. We were going to have dinner at the rectory together, but he called me late yesterday afternoon. It was actually almost six. He said something had come up and had to cancel. I asked him if everything was all right, and he said everything was fine."

Cohen grabbed a tissue from the box on the glass coffee table. There was a pile of crumpled, used, tissues up against it. She didn't seem to care.

Geddes said, "So, he didn't tell you why he canceled?"

"No, not at all. He didn't sound great, but I wasn't surprised by that since he was sick."

"Sick?" Toni said.

"Yes, he'd been diagnosed with pancreatic cancer about two months ago and it was progressing very quickly." Tears eased from her eyes, but her face remained strong. As if there was no connection between her face and the tears running from it. She swiped another tissue.

"Why had you planned to see him last night?" Toni said. "Was it just to see how he was doing?"

"Well, actually no. He'd called me earlier in the week and invited me to come over last night. He said he had something to discuss. I asked him what it was about and he said it was nothing urgent and could wait until I came."

"Okay," Toni said. "So, when had you seen him last?"

"I saw him about three weeks before right here. He came for dinner. That's when he told me about his cancer."

Toni listened.

Geddes said, "Mrs. Cohen, when did you find out he'd been killed?"

"This morning on *New York 1*," Cohen said. "Have you any idea who did this yet?"

Toni and Geddes didn't reply right away. Toni actually appreciated how effectively Cohen changed the subject. Toni thought she could learn a few things from this lady lawyer.

Geddes said, "No, Mrs. Cohen. That's why we're here speaking with you. Can you think of any reason someone would want to hurt him?"

Cohen shook her head.

"Do you live here alone, Mrs. Cohen?" Toni said as she scanned the abundant apartment; one disfigured female nude by Picasso and one Freda Kahlo self-portrait occupied one wall. Could they be the real thing? Nah. If it wasn't for the introductory art history course Toni had been required to take last semester as she worked on her B.A. in Criminal Justice part-time, she wouldn't have known a Kahlo painting from a Vermeer.

"No, I live here with my daughter. She's sixteen. Her father and I are divorced."

"Is she your only child?" Toni said.

"Yes," Cohen paused and held Toni's eyes, "She's my only child."

What the heck was that all about, Toni wondered. If she only had a daughter, she only had a daughter. What's with the hard look?

"What's your maiden name, Mrs. Cohen?" Toni said, half expecting her to reply, "How would knowing my maiden name help you find Father Manny's killer?"

But she didn't. She stood up, tightened the belt to her robe and looked out her opened living room window, the same vast window overlooking the East River, her back to Toni and Geddes and said, "Morales."

Toni deftly swiped one of Cohen's used tissues from the coffee table and put it in her pocket.

"If you don't mind my asking, where were you from 6 p.m. yesterday evening until 6 am this morning?" Toni said.

Cohen turned to face them, holding herself tight with her arms. "I was here at home."

"With your daughter?" Toni said.

"No, she'd spent Sunday night at her father's."

Toni and Geddes gave her a moment to continue.

"She's volunteering this summer at the ASPCA on 92nd Street, and her father lives on 89th and East End. She can sleep a little later and walk to work."

"I see," Toni said. "I guess she takes the bus to work when she stays here."

"Yes, right, the York Avenue bus."

"Mrs. Cohen, I need to ask you," Toni said, "Can anybody confirm you were here at home last night? Did you have any company or have any conversations on your home phone that we can verify?"

"Am I a suspect?" Cohen said.

Toni paused before answering and wondered what was really up with this broad. There she was playing lawyer again.

"No, Mrs. Cohen, you're not. These are routine questions that we'll be asking anyone close to Father Gonzalez."

Cohen paused before answering too. "Well, I'm sorry. I was alone and didn't use the phone," Cohen stepped over to them on the sofa. "Do you have any other questions?"

Toni and Geddes took a moment before they stood up.

"No. We appreciate your time." Toni said, and they started to walk to the apartment door. Cohen followed.

Toni turned to her before leaving with Geddes and said, "I'm sorry for your loss."

"Thank you," Cohen said.

Just before she closed the door behind them, Toni said, "Mrs. Cohen, just one last question. By any chance do you know Lieutenant Condon?"

Cohen held the door open but didn't respond.

Toni continued. "I was just wondering. Father Manny and Lieutenant Condon knew each other as kids, and you knew Father Manny. You know he's the commanding officer of the Bronx Homicide Squad. He's our boss."

"Yes, I knew that," Cohen replied.

"You did, well, I just thought you maybe knew Lieutenant Condon too when you and Father Manny were in high school."

After a long pause, Cohen said, "I haven't seen or spoken with Ryan Condon in over twenty years,"

"I see," Toni said.

"Is that all, detective?"

"Yes, Ma'am.

CHAPTER 4

Toni and Geddes were accelerating on the Cross-Bronx Expressway en route to Bronx borough headquarters — also the home of the Bronx Homicide Squad; both housed in a police precinct stationhouse built in the '1970s. Father Gonzalez was thought to have been shot at the rectory sometime after 6 p.m. Only one shot had been fired. No other spent shell casing or bullets were found: only the round that exited from Father Manny's skull. They blew past the chain of tenement buildings that lined the Cross-Bronx Expressway.

Toni grew up in a pre-war elevator building on the Grand Concourse in the Fordham section of the Bronx and went to public schools. In those days, she was called by her actual name, Antonia. She was named after her grandmother — her mother's mother.

She'd always been a bright kid but didn't do well in school. Except for athletics and music she was a poor student. It may have had something to do with the unmanageability of her home life. Her father had progressively surrendered to alcoholism after her mother's sudden death due to a brain aneurysm: she was only four years old. Her high school teachers always told her she had tremendous potential, but she wouldn't or couldn't apply herself. That all changed when she barely graduated from high school and enlisted in the United States Marine Corps.

Toni Santiago excelled as a Marine. She proved to be a fast learner and took to military life with ease graduating number one in boot camp out of a platoon of over sixty other women. This earned her the honor to pick just about any military occupational specialty she wanted. She chose the military police.

Being an M.P., as it turned out, was another natural fit for her. She no longer had trouble focusing. She had found nurturing and sustenance within the disciplined lifestyle of the Marines. In fact, she'd thought seriously about making the Marine Corps a career, but about a year before Toni had been discharged—while stationed on Okinawa—she fell in love and became engaged to a Marine from Helena, Montana. She believed she had every intention of relocating to Montana when they were both discharged, except, when that day came, he broke off the engagement and fled back to Helena without her. She hadn't heard from him since, which turned out to be okay. Deep down she always knew (and maybe her Montana marine knew too) that she would become a New York City cop, just as her father had been.

Minutes after they'd gotten back, Toni watched Ryan walk into the squad room. He was showered and shaved. Toni recalled again that she'd recently come to intimately know her forty-three-year-old boss. He was almost six-foot, with a still lean athletic frame, natural tan, and short cropped curly dark hair, with just a touch of gray at his sideburns. She winced.

There were about twenty-five detectives milling about: speaking on the phone, speaking with each other, typing up reports—a blur of movement and sound. Normally the squad would have had six detectives covering the shift, but the entire Bronx Homicide Squad had been called in—which amounted to twenty-four detectives, a sergeant, and a lieutenant—and put on overtime. Not that the promise of extra money drove them. They would do whatever it took to track down Father Manny's killer.

Through the partially open horizontal blinds of Ryan's glass-encased office, the hefty silhouette of the Chief of Bronx detectives could be seen: Deputy Chief Buddy King.

"The chief just got here, Loo," Toni said as she and Geddes approached him from behind.

Chief Buddy King was the image of the prototypical big-city chief of police. He was six-four, about two hundred and seventy-five pounds, with a gut that projected out about half-a-foot from his rib cage. The way the chief's gut stuck out always looked unnatural to Toni like a breast implant the size of a basketball.

Ryan and King had been radio car partners twenty years earlier when Ryan was first assigned to a Harlem precinct as a rookie. Buddy King had about ten years on the job at the time and broke Ryan in.

"What's the crime scene look like?" Ryan said to Toni.

"Doesn't look like robbery."

"Nothing stolen?" Ryan said, as Chief King stepped from the office and waved him in, leaving the door open and took the seat at Ryan's desk.

"Nothing so far," Geddes said.

Toni said, "We got to get back to do a detailed inventory. We wanted to check-in with you first. Crime Scene should be wrapping up, so, now we'll have the run of the place."

"You caught this, Toni?"

Toni knew how scattered Ryan must still be from the shock of Father Manny's murder. She'd told him—as they all stood on his lawn—she'd caught the case. She wondered if he'd asked just to confirm she'd caught it through normal rotation and had not been specially assigned to it by Sergeant Tazzo, his second-in-command. Ryan had the authority to change whoever caught any given homicide. She wondered if he wanted her on it or not. Toni had half as much time in the department as the next junior detective—with eight years— and only two years in Bronx Homicide, but she proved to be one tenacious investigator.

"Yeah, it's her case, boss," Sergeant Vic Tazzo replied for Toni walking up to them. Tazzo was a dapper second-whip. Clean-shaven, well-groomed, single man in his late 30's. He had a couple Armani suits.

"All right," Ryan said, pointing to his office. "Let me talk to the chief first."

Tazzo held Ryan's arm for a moment and said, "Sorry about Father Manny, Loo."

"Thanks, Vic."

"Nobody's leaving until we break this."

"Thanks, Vic," Ryan repeated and stepped in the direction of the kitchen. "Let me grab a cup of coffee before I head in."

Toni could tell Ryan needed an extra couple seconds to cut off the sudden sting building-up in his eyes.

Ryan stepped into his office.

"How you holding up, Ryan?" King said as he stood up from Ryan's desk and came around the front.

"I'm all right, Buddy," Ryan said, as he stepped around the chief and behind his desk. Chief King patted him on the back as he passed.

"A terrible shock," King said. "Just terrible."

Ryan absently took a moment to leaf through the messages on his desk as if he was alone. The chief then stepped over to the brown leather sofa in his office—leaving the desk chair for Ryan. The sofa, everybody in the squad knew well, was a Godsend after putting in the first twenty-four hours to break a fresh homicide, and there was no hope of heading home anytime soon.

Chief King dropped into the sofa.

The whoosh-sound of a substantial adult male, dropping into a leather sofa seemed to announce that their exchange could begin.

"When'd you see him last?

"Yesterday," Ryan said, "at Mass. I came down with Jocelyn and caught the eleven o'clock mass with him. We spoke with him for a few minutes after. He seemed tired to me, but in good spirits."

Ryan looked down at his shoes.

"Listen, Ryan, there's something I gotta talk to you about."

Ryan's head shifted up quick, and with a loud voice said, "Don't even think about it, Buddy. I know where you're going. My squad has this case and I run this squad."

Toni's head — as well as the civilians being interviewed in the squad room, shifted to the volume of Ryan's voice, but the other detectives pretended to not hear a thing.

Chief King stayed put and patiently looked at his former patrol partner for a few seconds, then stood up and went to look out the second-floor window with his back to Ryan. Ryan had that view memorized. A string of five-story tenements with a African-American hair salon, Hispanic bodega, Chinese take-out, and Korean dry cleaners on street level. And if you squinted you could see deep into a narrow alleyway — between two of the buildings. There was always laundry hanging from a few of the fire escapes even though there was a laundromat around the corner.

King turned to face Ryan, "The Padre was your close personal friend. You two were buddies as kids. This is too important. We need to keep our emotions in check. You know what I mean; we can't let ourselves get jammed up and make mistakes."

"Listen, Buddy, what's this 'we' crap?" Ryan said and pushed his office door shut.

Ryan walked up to face Chief King at the window. "It's 'I' need to keep my emotions in check, and I will. You think I'm going to let anything mess this up? This will be done by the numbers, I guarantee you that. I'm not going to let his killer walk on this. Not a chance."

Toni deliberately sat right outside Ryan's office door and had no trouble hearing every word.

"All right, all right, Ryan. Just remember that he was a priest. Nobody cares except us that he was your friend. All that anybody out there cares about is that he was a priest. That's all the Archdiocese cares about, that's all the Mayor cares about, that's all the Commissioner cares about, that's all the public cares about. We can't afford to fuck this up."

Ryan looked at the chief carefully for several moments himself and said, "All right. I understand that, Buddy. And I understand your position. All right. You can take my word on this. I can handle it."

"All right," King said, and both sat silently captured by their own thoughts.

Ryan finally spoke up.

"You know, he loved being a priest, just loved it. And he was great at it, Buddy. The school reading scores were in the top ten percentile of the Archdiocese for three years straight. The only South Bronx Catholic school with that record. He was real proud. Real proud of those kids."

King nodded.

"Did I ever tell you how I first met Manny?"

"No, Ryan," King said and shifted in the chair to get comfortable. "How'd you guys meet?"

Ryan was sitting in his third-grade class at Mount Carmel School and Manny was introduced as their new classmate and assigned to sit next to him. During their milk and cookies break, Ryan heard that Manny had moved into a building on the west side of Mount Carmel Park. Ryan lived on the Southside. Manny's parents had brought him to school first thing after arriving in the middle of the night from a seventy-two-hour hike that had started in Miami. Manny was still in the clothes he'd traveled in, not yet suited up in the traditional Mount Carmel Catholic School uniform: of a white shirt, sky blue tie with the school's emblem, and navy blue pants.

Manny looks at Ryan with these panic-stricken eyes —
he hadn't washed the sand from his eyes — and a milk film
smeared across his upper lip and said. 'Aren't you scared
living across the street from a cemetery?'

" 'That's not a cemetery,'" Ryan told Manny. 'That's
Mount Carmel Park.' "

Ryan grinned. "Manny thought the park was a
cemetery. That's the first time we met."

Toni would've taken the case away from Ryan without a
second thought. She knew it was a mistake to keep any
detective personally acquainted with a homicide victim
working the case. Except it wasn't her place to say so. But she
wondered how Ryan could stay detached. If it wasn't because
the chief and Ryan went back so many years, he would be off
the case, post-haste.

But whom exactly did she think she was to have an
opinion on that anyway, she thought, closing her eyes shut for
a moment. She was more than personally acquainted with her
boss. Didn't that affect her ability to do her job?

Ryan opened his office door and waved Toni, Geddes
and Sergeant Tazzo in, looked back at King and said, "I got
this, Buddy."

Ryan went back to the sofa. Toni, Geddes, and Tazzo
took the three rigid department issue chairs in front of the
desk.

Ryan addressed the group. "What do we got?"

Before Toni got it started, she'd noticed Bronx
Homicide number 147 had been added by the squad's *civilian
administrative aide* to the bulletin board on Ryan's office wall:
Gonzalez/Manuel, M/H/43.

"No forced entry, as far as we can tell so far. But we're
heading back to do a full scan of the rectory."

"Anybody have anything to say?"

"We talked to the other priest at Mr. Carmel," Toni said. "Father Gribbons,"

"Where was he?" Ryan said.

"Retreat," Toni said. "Returned to the rectory about 6:30 a.m. He found the body and called 911."

"Kind of early to get back from a retreat," King said rhetorically. "Where was it?"

"Massachusetts," Toni answered. "Clarence, Massachusetts."

"Clarence, Massachusetts. I know that place. It's a Trappists monastery. I went to a couples retreat there myself about ten years ago with the wife. That's about a four-hour drive. He'd have to leave at 2:30 in the morning to get to the rectory by 6:30 a.m."

Toni nodded.

"Except," Chief King said, looking up at the ceiling, "it's possible if he left right after their early morning prayers." King looked back down at the others. "Their morning prayer is at 2 a.m," King said. "It's a hell of a thing. Those Trappists wake up in the middle of the night, go to the chapel and chant a few prayers then go back to bed until five-thirty or so when they get up to start their day. I made those prayers once over the weekend. Jen, my wife, didn't budge from bed."

King shot Ryan a nondescript look. The kind of look Toni deduced one partner would toss the other in a how-about-that kind of way, sipping on a couple of Dunkin Donut coffees in a patrol car. Just catching up on the mundane details of each other's lives at the start of the tour before shit on the street happens.

"Hell of a schedule," King said.

Geddes said, "Maybe he left Saturday afternoon or evening; made the trip back but stayed with a friend or something for the night."

"Yeah, could be," Toni said. "But why didn't he just tell us that?"

"Don't know. But I wouldn't read to much into it."

30

"All right. It's important to get it straight for the record," Ryan said. "Who else?"

"We interviewed a Samantha Cohen about an hour ago," Toni said.

She picked up Ryan's face change a shade. Nobody else may have picked it up, but she did. Like a schoolboy pretending to be unimpressed by the pretty girl who's trying to talk to him in the schoolyard, but the fleeting flushed face betrays him.

"Who's Samantha Cohen," Sergeant Tazzo said.

"Lifetime friend of Father Manny's," Geddes said.

King looked at Ryan. "You know her, Ryan?"

"I met her through Manny over twenty years ago. I haven't seen her since."

King looked back at Toni, "So, what's her story?"

"She was Father Manny's last appointment Sunday. She was in his book for 7:30 p.m. She said he called late yesterday afternoon and canceled, said she had no idea why but he seemed okay to her over the phone."

"What's she do?"

Geddes answered. "She's a personal injury lawyer. We spoke to her at her apartment on Sutton Place."

"Sutton Place, very nice," King said with genuine appreciation. "How do you read her, Toni?"

"Well, she looked like she was broken up about his murder. She heard about it on *New York 1*. I don't know if her reaction was real or show. She started to play lawyer with us. Nothing major. Just a little resistance. But I found it strange. I asked her how'd she met Father Manny and she wouldn't say. Or claimed to not recall. I don't buy it. You know what I mean. We all remember how we first met a person that became important to us down the road. We may not remember a lot of the details during the relationship, the times and dates are sketchy, but we remember that first meeting and how it happened. It just didn't make sense that she wouldn't answer."

Toni looked at Ryan, but he averted her eyes.

"Anybody confirm where she was last night?" King asked.

"No," Toni said. "She said she was home alone. We need to talk with the doorman or concierge on duty, see if they corroborate what she said. Take a look at their CCTV."

Ryan looked at Toni. "Is that it?"

"No. There was a lipstick marking on a half cup of coffee sitting on the table in the rectory kitchen above the priest's body," Toni said.

"Lipstick?" King repeated.

"Yes, sir," Toni said.

"Crime Scene send the cup to the lab?" Chief King said.

"Yes, sir," Toni said and pulled out a clear plastic bag with a tissue. "I grabbed a tissue Cohen blew into while we were there when she wasn't looking. We should get the results in a couple of days."

Chief King grinned. "Good."

Ryan said, "Is that it?"

"Just one other thing," Toni said, holding Ryan's eyes for a moment then looking to Chief King. "Samantha Cohen said Father Manny had been diagnosed with pancreatic cancer about two months ago."

"Did you know about that, Ryan?" King said.

"No. No, I didn't."

"Shame," King said, shaking his head. "Fighting cancer and then murdered."

The office was silent for a few moments.

"All right, so you've got this Samantha Cohen and Father Gribbons to follow-up on, and that lipstick," King said and looked at Ryan. "What's your gut tell you about this Lieutenant?"

Toni again looked at the small-framed photograph on the second shelf of Ryan's bookcase — ironically in front of a collection of homicide investigations books. The photograph was of two young effervescent men in their early twenties, taken many years earlier in front of the police academy in Manhattan, one arm over each other's shoulder. It was Father Manny and Ryan Condon at his academy graduation. He was in his new, dark blue police officer's uniform with a shining shield on his left breast. Manny was in a black suit and white collar with a cross hanging from his neck.

Ryan finally said. "What I'm wondering right now is did Manny know he had this enemy before he got shot? Or was he a stranger to him? And if he did know this guy was a threat to him, why didn't he tell me?"

After Chief King left, Toni, Geddes, and Tazzo got up to leave, but Ryan told Toni and Sergeant Tazzo to stay for a minute.

Geddes said, "You want the door closed?"

"Yes," Ryan said.

As soon as the door was shut Ryan said, "I don't want you talking to Samantha Cohen again without my okay."

"Is there a problem?" Toni said.

"There's no problem. Just don't speak to her again without clearing it with me first."

Toni held his gaze, looked at Sergeant Tazzo, then back at Ryan and recognized why he'd invited Tazzo to stay. Ryan was laying down the law, and he wanted Tazzo to be a witness. He was cutting her off from having complete access to the principles in her investigation. He was establishing something new between them. But why? She wondered. So he met Samantha Cohen twenty years ago through Manny. Cohen herself said she hadn't seen Ryan in over twenty years. So why wouldn't he want her to speak with Cohen again without clearing it with him? What's it to him?

CHAPTER 5

Toni Santiago first met Ryan two years before when she was a patrol officer in a Spanish Harlem precinct. Her sector car had been called to a triple homicide at a social club at E. 105th Street and First Avenue in the early morning hours of a frigid Friday night. There was snow on the sidewalk, and a cardboard sign outside the entrance to the club that read in black magic marker, "NO GUNS ALOW INCITE."

Nobody would identify anybody. All they would say was that a black male walked up to the three Latino male victims sitting at the circular table draped with a red tablecloth and opened up on them with what looked like a Mac 10 machine pistol. The Manhattan North Homicide Squad was responsible for interviewing all the patrons. Toni and the other uniforms were responsible for making sure nobody tampered with the crime scene or left without being identified and interviewed.

It was during that time that Toni noticed a pretty, shapely young black women dressed in a skin-tight white dress, no more than twenty years of age, standing off to the side where the D.J. booth was set up. Toni watched her carefully from across the dance floor. She would catch her ever so slightly shake her head and quickly wipe a tear from her eye. She did not want to be noticed.

As the sun was peeking above the frozen East River, Toni watched her secretly compose herself and sit down to be interviewed by one of the Manhattan North homicide detectives. Like all the others, she said she couldn't identify the shooter and didn't know the victims. The detective took her name, address, age, cell phone number, and let her leave with his card in the palm of her hand. Toni wanted to talk to her.

When the crime scene wrapped-up, Toni jumped into her jeans at the precinct, shot up to her apartment building in Riverdale (the same building her aunt lived in) and picked up her bulldog. She walked and fed Vita, grabbed a coffee and toasted corn muffin from the Riverdale Diner, then shot down to the Castle Hill projects with her dog in tow.

Castle Hill was a collection of eight-story buildings managed by the N.Y.C. Housing Authority. And like most box-shaped New York City projects, it was constructed of that distinctive reddish-brown brick. Toni always thought two things about the projects: first, the City must have gotten a very good price on that revolting reddish-brown brick, and, second, the projects always looked more to her like a prison compound than a place for families to prosper.

Toni kept the car running that cold Saturday morning as she sipped her coffee, worked on her muffin, and watched the entrance of the twenty-year-olds Castle Hill building.

After listening to Vita snore curled up on the front seat for a few hours, Toni's eyes were about ready to shimmy-down, when the young woman stepped out of her building, now wearing a long, black, down coat, and trucked through the snow to a liquor store three blocks away. The street and sidewalk had still not been cleared.

Toni waited for her to turn the corner from the liquor store and stepped right in front of her with Vita on a leash.

"Do you know who I am?"

The woman stopped cold. Toni pulled out her shield and I.D. card.

"I was there last night, and I know, you know, who shot those three guys."

The woman's eyes were wide, but she stayed quiet.

Toni pointed at the bag she was carrying. "Who's all the booze for?"

The young woman held Toni's gaze for a few long moments until her eyes started to water and trickle down her cold cheeks. She agreed to jump into the car with her and Vita.

That was one of the upsides to having your bulldog along on a stakeout; nobody would make Toni for a cop. And it made the informant more comfortable too. It wasn't exactly department policy, but it worked for her, and she was on her own time anyway.

From the age of six on, her father would sometimes take Toni on surveillance, and she loved every minute of it. Her Dad would lie in the back seat, his partner would be driving, and she would be sitting up front with hands stretched to reach the dashboard flashing a big smile. Whenever whoever they were tailing looked through their rearview mirror, all they would see was the head of a man behind the wheel and a smiling little girl. All teeth. The view she offered was just as effective: the flat face of an English bulldog.

Toni pulled into the back of an abandoned BP gas station a few blocks away. The snow-covered and stagnant gas pumps reminded Toni of a couple scarecrows she'd seen on a deserted stretch of Kansas plain as she drove cross-country to her first Marine Corps duty station in Camp Pendleton, California when she was nineteen.

The young woman told Toni that she had no idea her boyfriend was going to shoot those three guys. She said she had never been to the place before, but that he wanted to bring her there. He said the dancing and Latin music was great. She said they were dancing Salsa when he looked in the direction of where the three guys had just sat down. He left her on the dance floor, walked to them and shot them dead. No words were exchanged between her boyfriend and the victims. She said she was shocked. She then added that her boyfriend had also shot a rival dealer a couple weeks before on White Plains road and promised her it wouldn't happen again.

"Is he in your apartment now?" Toni said.

The young woman nodded.

Toni put in a call to Bronx Homicide with the information and the commanding officer — the first-whip — Lieutenant Ryan Condon, and his cavalry of detectives descended on her and picked up the shooter. She would never forget how exhilarated she'd become when she watched Ryan Condon pull up in his unmarked car, chauffeured, of course, by one of his detectives, as all New York City Police bosses are from the rank of sergeant and above. He approached her in his long black cashmere-looking overcoat and sky blue tie, gave her a warm professional handshake and she got a direct look up into his remarkable light-brown eyes for the first time.

"Wow," was all she thought.

Following that arrest, the triple homicide in the social club in Spanish Harlem was cleared, as well as the murder in the Bronx on White Plains Road. About a week later, Toni got a call from Sergeant Tazzo, who said that Lieutenant Condon was impressed with her initiative and asked if she'd be interested in coming up to Bronx Homicide for an interview. Within ninety days she was transferred to the Bronx Homicide Squad, and within her first year she was formally promoted to detective and received her father's gold shield.

The Father Manny Gonzalez murder was her case. She'd caught it.

She had to be present to witness Father Gribbon's formal identification of the body at the ME's Office; she had to observe the autopsy; all supporting detective investigative reports were forwarded to her; she maintained the case file; she'd be the one to submit affidavits to a judge for a search warrant; she'd be the one to testify before the Grand Jury when they made an arrest; she'd be the primary detective to testify in court if it went to trial; she'd be the one the media would most often identify in connection with the investigation.

Other detectives — over time — would be reassigned to other cases, but she'd be the one detective on this case until it was broken and beyond. Not Sergeant Tazzo. Not even Geddes.

Other than her, only Ryan would be as consumed by — and have access to — every element of the case.

Did Ryan know she would back off, she wondered. That she was in no position to take him on. She'd been with Ryan. She'd had sex with this married man. Her boss. Her stomach sank with that realization again. Now, she knew she was up against the very real consequences of her choices. She knew being with him would catch up with her, and it now had. It didn't take long.

Silently she continued to stand in front of Ryan and Tazzo when there was a sudden knock on the door. Geddes — leaning on the doorknob — pushed open the door before being invited in. They each shifted their tense gaze at him.

"What's up?" Ryan said.

"We just got a call from the lab. It looks like the bullet recovered from rectory kitchen matches a round recovered at a bank robbery in the Lower East Side this morning. The perp fired a shot into the wall behind the bank manager's desk and threatened to put the next round into his face. He took off with a little over three grand."

"You're kidding," Tazzo said. "What's Manhattan Robbery have to say?"

"They've got a description, but the guy was wearing a black wool cap over his face. They looked at the bank video. Can't see the guy's face at all. The witnesses say he's a male Hispanic, five-six to five-eight, slim build. The bank manager noticed a small red tattoo on the back of his hand. Looked like a heart to her."

"What caliber?" Ryan said.

"Nine millimeter…just like ours."

"What'd he sound like?" Toni said. "Accent?"

"He had a lisp. Spanglish accent. One of the tellers said it sounded just like a guy she went to high school with. Manhattan Robbery has an I.D. on him. His name's Ernesto Cruz. Turns out he's got a rap sheet."

"What's his last known address?" Toni said.

"Parole said he's at an S.R.O. somewhere on the Upper West side. He got out of Dannemora about a month ago. He did twelve years for a bodega robbery and attempt murder. He shot the owner behind the counter," Geddes said.

"Manhattan Robbery sitting on his last known address?" Toni said.

"Yeah, they are," Geddes said.

"All right," Ryan said. "I want you and Toni sitting on that S.R.O. with Manhattan Robbery,"

"Wait a minute, Loo," Toni blurted. "We need to get back to the rectory and do a thorough search. We told Father Gribbons we'd be back to do that."

"Why didn't you do it while you were there this morning?"

This is not good, she thought. What's going on here?

"For one thing we wanted to notify you about Father Manny in person, so we left the scene sooner than we wanted to," Toni's voice started to rise. "Plus we thought it would be important to talk to Cohen as soon as possible since we were told she could've been the last person with the priest before he was shot."

"Toni," Tazzo said and gave her the boss look.

The office was quiet for a few long moments.

Ryan spoke up. "I want you and Geddes with Manhattan Robbery, got it."

39

"Ryan…I mean Loo," Toni caught herself. The unwritten protocol in the NYPD was a boss could refer to a subordinate by their first name, but a subordinate never used the boss's first name unless they had a personal relationship of some sort, and, in any case, never in the presence of others, if they did. You could get away with the slang for the rank: Sarge for Sergeant or Loo for Lieutenant, but not their first name.

Toni continued, "We can't keep Father Gribbons and his staff from going into Father Manny's office indefinitely. If we don't get back there to do a search, we got to release it."

"Then release it," Ryan said. "You're not going to find anything about his murderer in his second-floor office anyway."

"Wait a minute…" Toni blurted.

Toni knew one thing she'd be looking for in Father Manny's second-floor office was the journal he would write in before going to bed as Father Gribbons mentioned. Gribbons said it should be on his desk. There could be something in his personal journal that would put some light on what his concerns were and who the killer could be. There was no way she'd tell Ryan about the journal now. Something had spooked him and she couldn't trust him. This is not good, she thought.

"Wait a minute…" Toni started to say again, but Geddes held her elbow and said, "We got it, boss," as he guided Toni out of the office.

After Toni stepped out of Ryan's office and closed the door behind them, Geddes looked down to Toni. "What's up Bulldog?"

Straightaway she wondered what Ryan would be up to while they waited for Ernesto Cruz with Manhattan Robbery. She had no doubt Ryan put her on the stakeout to keep her out of the picture for a while. Ryan could've put anybody to sit and wait for that suspect to show up.

It didn't make sense for the detective who caught the case to waste hours waiting for one guy while she should be doing a thorough search of the Mount Carmel rectory and Father Manny's second-floor office. But Ryan knew just what he was doing, Toni figured.

Geddes sometimes called Toni "Bulldog" after one afternoon — one year earlier — when it is alleged that as Detective Toni Santiago window-shopped with her then two-year-old English bulldog down the commercial strip of Fordham Road, she'd spotted a wanted shooter getting out of a livery cab. The story goes that she turned the dog leash over to a security guard in *Victoria's Secret*, told him to call 911, and confronted the muscular bad guy.

Regrettably, she'd chosen not to carry her off-duty automatic that day so she snuck up on him, driving every inch of her five-foot-two, one hundred twenty-pound athletic frame into the guy's back like a professional linebacker, and announced, "POLICE, DON'T MOVE!"

She knew then she was in real trouble because he didn't move, in fact, he didn't budge, and replied by swatting her away as he went for the .38 in his back pocket. But Toni recovered quickly, leaped up, and lunged for his gun hand, and bit down on his thumb, practically severing it.

When the uniforms arrived the gun had been tossed into the middle of the street, and Toni Santiago was found wrapped around one of his legs with part of his calf muscle in her mouth. The bad guy was dragging Toni down the sidewalk as he squealed, "You crazy lady! You crazy!"

Her colleagues in the Bronx Homicide Squad affectionately dubbed her, "The Bulldog of Fordham Road."

Toni always denied it happened that way. She said it was her bulldog that had broken away, and almost severed the bad guy's thumb, and had a hunk of his calf in her mouth.

"You hear me bulldog?" Geddes repeated. "What's wrong?"

41

"Nothing," Toni said to Geddes, picked up the phone and called Father Gribbons. She asked him to go through Father Manny's office thoroughly and if he discovered anything that he thought would help with their investigation to let them know.

"Good idea, Bulldog?"

"What choice do I have, Geddes?" Toni said as she grabbed her jacket. "Let's go. It's starting to stink around here."

CHAPTER 6

By 5 p.m., there was another knock on Ryan's office door. Sergeant Tazzo stepped in. "Loo, Samantha Cohen's outside."

Ryan's head rose straight up and erect, mouth slightly parted, eyes wide, like someone about to leap for a skydive.

"Samantha Cohen?" Ryan repeated as he tried to make her out through the horizontal blinds in his office. He'd thought he'd reach out to her since Toni brought her name up, but each time he picked up his Blackberry and started to dial he'd end up punching delete.

Tazzo nodded.

Ryan stood up as soon as Samantha stepped into his office. It was hard to believe how beautiful she still was. The last time Ryan had seen Samantha was when they were all twenty, the summer before their senior year of college.

"Hi, Samantha. Have a seat," Ryan said, as he pointed to one of the chairs in front of his desk. Samantha looked at Ryan with a warm smile and hesitated to sit.

"Hello, Ryan."

It appeared to Ryan that she thought he would give her a warmer greeting, but he didn't come from behind his desk until she sat down. Ryan then walked to the blinds behind her and opened them wide.

She pulled a pack of cigarettes from her pocketbook.

Ryan was surprised to see her smoking. It was true he hadn't seen Samantha in over two decades. His last image of her was when they were both twenty. And when they were twenty, Samantha wasn't a smoker — as far as he knew. She was an honors student at Georgetown University, and an NCAA tennis champion, as well as a modern dance protégé of sorts. Ryan had attended Fordham University in the Bronx; Manny had attended St. Joseph's Seminary in Yonkers.

Samantha was wearing a black pants suit with a silver brooch of a vine affixed to her lapel. She seemed to have the same slim dimensions and the same radiance. She no longer had long, straight black hair. It was now short. She wore deep, red lipstick, her barely tanned complexion a delicate sheen.

"I'm here because of Manny," Samantha said,

Butterflies percolated in Ryan's stomach as he captured the detailed memory of the only time they'd made love.

They'd both been so nervous. Ryan had had enough sense to bring a condom, but he'd never had sex before, and in his rattled state he put it on the wrong way — inside out — so it covered only one-third of his inheritance. He tried desperately to draw it completely down by pulling from the inside of the greasy item with his index fingers, but it didn't work out. It never occurred to him to pull it off and try it inside out. They were so rushed kissing and fondling each other. They could not hold themselves back any longer, so Ryan slipped off the condom completely. Samantha never knew.

"Of course," Ryan finally said, taking a moment to get focused, snapping out of his reverie.

He wondered why she'd decided to drive through half the Bronx to see him at the precinct. She'd already given Toni and Geddes her statement. If it became necessary for him to speak with her directly, he would have met her in Manhattan — with his detectives. There was no point to her making that trip through the Bronx. It seemed to him a phone call would have done the job. He waited for her to speak up, but she continued to fumble with the pack of cigarettes. He didn't want to make small talk, but he did.

"How're your parents, Samantha?'

"Okay, well," she finally stopped wrestling with the cigarette pack, "my father passed two years ago..."

"Oh. I didn't know. I'm sorry. I'm very sorry to hear that," Ryan said. "He was a tough old guy."

44

Samantha smiled. "Yes, he was," she said, and finally pulled a cigarette out of the pack. "But my mother is fine. She's still on Cedar Avenue, you know. We can't get her to move," Samantha broke another smile, and Ryan's breathing picked up again. "That's her neighborhood and she's not leaving."

"How about that, she's still there," Ryan said. "And your sister, Elizabeth?"

"Oh, Liz is doing great. She's down in Florida. Boca Raton with her husband and two girls."

"That's great," Ryan said. "Please give them my best."

Manny had always stayed in touch with Samantha. Hearing she'd become a successful personal injury attorney did not surprise Ryan at all. When she was eleven, her father had had an accident at the record factory where he'd worked. He'd pounded through an unstable staircase that had been reported to management months before, but the company never got around to having it fixed. It severed his spinal cord leaving him paralyzed from the waist down.

It was a grueling turning point for her father and her family. All their lives turned upside down. Enormous sacrifices were made to care for her father. And what made it worse was how pathetic her father's compensation was for having lost the use of his legs. Outrage always simmered in Samantha over that. She always said she'd get justice for her father one day, and she did.

Fourteen years later, after she'd received her NYU law degree, she took her father's former company to court and won a huge settlement. This finally covered the extreme medical bills they'd acquired over the years, as well as making it possible for his life to dramatically improve because they could finally afford to make their modest apartment paraplegic friendly.

"I will," Samantha said. "Okay if I smoke?"

"Go ahead," Ryan said and handed her a half-empty Coke can for the ashes, disregarding the no smoking in department buildings policy.

She offered him a cigarette but he shook his head and she lit up. "Did you know I have a daughter, Ryan?"

"Yes, I did," he said. "How old is she now?"

"Sixteen. She attends the Langston School."

He knew the school: a private school for wealthy Upper East Side kids. Years earlier he'd been a detective assigned to the Upper Eastside precinct—before he'd been promoted to sergeant—and was called to investigate the theft of a Dell laptop from the main office. The school staff suspected the Croatian maintenance man. It turned out the thief was one of their students. The school refused to press charges.

Samantha took another puff. The smoke hung above them like a memory. Ventilation wasn't the best in Ryan's office, but he didn't mind inhaling her second-hand smoke.

"What's her name?"

"Vanessa."

They paused for a few moments and looked at each other, expressionless.

"And your husband, Samantha, how's he doing? He's a lawyer too isn't he?"

"Yes, he is…well…my daughter's father's an attorney. We're no longer married. We were divorced a few years ago."

"I'm sorry to hear that, Sam." Ryan immediately realized he'd called her by her nickname. His face heated up.

"What about you, Ryan? Kids?

"No."

They held each other's eyes.

"And…and…how is Jocelyn…Jocelyn isn't it?" Samantha asked as she nervously took another puff. Blue smoke swirled around her face.

"She's great," Ryan said.

Ryan had met Jocelyn at a Hofstra/Fordham football game the fall of their junior year at the Hofstra field. Ryan was the quarterback of the Fordham team. At six-one, one hundred-ninety pounds, a spear-throwing arm, and wicked quick on his feet, he was exciting to watch, but Fordham lost by a field goal anyway.

Jocelyn was a cheerleader for Hofstra. As he walked back to the bus for the certain-to-be silent ride back to the Bronx, Jocelyn ran up in front of him and blocked his way.

"You're really a good, QB. QB."

Ryan was tongue-tied for a moment looking into the steady blue eyes of this tall, lovely lady with waist-length red curly hair, who didn't budge.

"Well, thanks," Ryan said. "Thanks a lot."

"Tough loss," she said.

During the course of the year that followed Ryan made a few trips on the Long Island Rail Road to see Jocelyn Hart in Nassau County. Except, the truth was, he didn't see how it would work with a redheaded beauty that lived in a house with a two-car garage from Valley Stream. Out of shame, it took him awhile before he brought Jocelyn to his South Bronx neighborhood to meet his parents. It's not that he was ashamed of his parents, that wasn't it at all. He was ashamed of his streets. But that's when Ryan got how much Jocelyn truly loved him. He could have been from Yemen, it didn't matter to her; she just wanted him.

Jocelyn and Ryan saw each other throughout their junior year until his fling with Samantha Morales the following summer. Jocelyn always believed Ryan had spent the summer working as a counselor at an instructional football camp in Vermont, which had been his plan, at least, until Samantha eclipsed his affection for Jocelyn. But when Samantha dumped him, he needed Jocelyn more than before.

He thought he'd never tell Jocelyn about the fling, rationalizing that there was no need to hurt her. But he couldn't bring himself to go on with Jocelyn if she didn't know. She forgave him, and at first seemed to be unaffected by it. So, soon after Ryan graduated from the police academy, and Jocelyn became a special needs teacher, they were married. The wedding ceremony took place at Mount Carmel parish. Father Manuel Gonzalez was the officiate.

The last thing Samantha wanted to do was ruin Ryan's wedding day, and she'd promised Father Manny she would not attend. But when that day came, she could not stay away. She had to see her beautiful young man. She had to see her love — the love of her life — make the commitment to love and cherish — another — 'til death do they part.

Ryan was not to ever to know that Samantha had been in attendance on their wedding day. Father Manny urged her not to go, but she just could not — not be there. She knew that it would've been a terrible mess if either Ryan or Jocelyn had noticed her, but she took a chance of secreting herself in a pew in the rear, right corner — the groom's side. She'd disguised herself with a black kerchief, dark sunglasses, and a battered black trench coat. She looked like a homeless person who'd routinely spent hours in church for shelter.

Her disguise worked, or, so Samantha had always thought. Ryan hadn't noticed her at all, but it didn't escape Jocelyn. And, after two miscarriages — during the first three years of their marriage — and the need to finally remove her fallopian tubes, rendering her barren, his one summer experience with Samantha would often come up and she'd become very agitated, accusing Ryan of meeting with Samantha again and again which wasn't true. The accusations would often lead to Jocelyn tearfully slapping Ryan several times before he could calm her down. And when he couldn't calm her down, he'd dial 9-1-1 and she'd be taken to the hospital again.

They sat there in silence while Samantha took a couple more drags. When she was done, she dropped the cigarette butt in the Coke can.

"I can't believe what's happened," she said. Her eyes brimmed with tears.

Seeing her tear-up brought him back again to that one summer. They'd been dating for eight consecutive inseparable weeks when Samantha abruptly broke it off. She just closed the door of her third-floor apartment on Ryan's face one crushing afternoon. Her eyes had that same build-up of tears. It was the last time they'd seen each other—as far as he had known.

"I know, Samantha," Ryan said. "It's a huge tragedy. He'll be missed for sure."

"You have to find who did this?"

"I will," Ryan said.

They sat quietly for a few more moments, both with dazed expressions. Both chose to look away, up and out the same high small window of his office. The window faced the front of the precinct, and if you stood up and looked out of it, you were again faced with a string of fire escape-draped tenement buildings across from it. But if you were sitting and looked up and out the window—on a clear day—you had a distant view of the water tower on the roof of a tall housing project several blocks away.

The water tower stood out because the large square box that encased it. It was composed of intermittent smaller squares with gaps that gave it the appearance of a chessboard. Ryan often found he'd unconsciously look out at the water tower and imagine chess moves before he returned to the conversation or report that had previously held his attention. He wondered whether Samantha was doing the same at that moment. They had once been shrewd chess combatants.

"Any idea who it could be?" Samantha said, as she declined Ryan's offer of his handkerchief, and pulled a package of tissues from her bag.

Sergeant Tazzo stood up from his desk — which was directly outside Ryan's glass-encased office. The letters Commanding Officer stenciled in a blue arc across the upper glass portion of the door. He held a phone receiver in his hand and motioned to Ryan he had a call. Ryan waved him off.

"So, you'd planned to meet Manny," Ryan said. "But he canceled."

She stopped wiping her nose. "That's right."

"They said you told them Manny had cancer. Is that right?"

"Yes," Samantha said. "Did you know?"

"No I didn't. I don't understand why he didn't tell me."

Another thing Ryan never completely understood was why Samantha stayed in touch with Manny over the years. It was true they were all from the same neighborhood, but it was not as if they'd ever gone to school together or anything, like he and Manny. And it was actually Ryan who had introduced Samantha to Manny. The truth was he didn't know when Manny and Samantha had become such good friends. And there just never seemed any point in asking. Samantha had to stay history for Ryan, so he asked no questions.

"He only told me about it a few weeks ago. I'm sure he was planning on telling you, Ryan."

"When did you see him last?"

"About three weeks ago in my apartment," Samantha said as she pulled out another cigarette. "That's when he told me about his cancer."

"I see," Ryan said as he leaned back and stroked his face. "I saw him yesterday at Mass." Ryan paused. "He seemed fine to me though…tired, but otherwise fine."

"Did you mention he looked tired to you?"

"No, I didn't. I wish I had. Maybe he would've opened up to me then. About the cancer or if he had any idea he was in danger. Except, Jocelyn was standing with me. He may not have wanted to bring it up in front of her."

Samantha was silent.

"There's something else…" Samantha began to say but stopped.

Ryan wondered what was on her mind. What did she know? And again he could not stop thinking how lovely she still was. Even with the occasional puff on her cigarette, she was still the image of class. But the confidence she exuded in her youth had been tampered with. He couldn't put his finger on it, but something changed. He could see it in her eyes. But who doesn't change over two decades? Yet, it seemed to go deeper than just the passage of time.

"Samantha, if you know something that could help us…"

Samantha didn't respond.

Ryan couldn't help wondering what the day-to-day details of her life had been over the years. When had she finished law school and gone into private practice? What were her rookie lawyering years like? How did she negotiate the various halls of justice and the transient assortment of characters that passed through them? How determined an advocate for the disenfranchised had she become? And when she met her husband, did she know he was the one? And if that was true, what happened? Or did she never really love him, and only married him because she needed to. It was just time. So what curves were thrown at Samantha that led to their divorce?

There was a sudden knock on his office door. It startled them both. Sergeant Tazzo needed a minute in private. Ryan stepped out of his office, closing the door behind him, and listened to what Tazzo had to say and stepped back in.

"Everything okay?" Samantha said, looking up at Ryan with wide eyes as he'd closed the door and returned to his desk, but remained standing.

"Good," Ryan said. "Do you have a ride home?"

"Yes, Ryan, I have a car waiting for me out front."

"Good, I'll have one of my detectives walk you out. I'll give you a call when we have something."

He would have walked her out of the building himself, but he knew it was not a good idea. It was as if his cells were jumping in his bloodstream craving for a fix. "For crying out loud, what a feeling," he shuttered inside.

She stood up slowly and said, "I appreciate that, Ryan."

Ryan walked her to the door when she turned to face him but didn't speak.

"Is there something you need to tell me, Samantha?"

She looked up at him for several moments. "I need to speak to you in private sometime."

He held her gaze.

"Sometime soon," she continued. "There's something I need to explain to you."

"About Manny?"

"Yes, I don't know, maybe. Yes, maybe."

Ryan looked at her.

"Tell me now," Ryan said, as he started to close his office door again.

"Not here, Ryan," she said, and gently touched his arm. "I would rather not talk to you about it here. I don't know if it will help you find Manny's killer. I just think it's important you know. Can we go out for a drink or something to eat?"

Ryan didn't answer.

"Can you break free for a while?" she persisted.

Ryan felt a sudden shot of resistance, hard, absolute resistance—but then it was smashed with exhilaration, absolute exhilaration. He couldn't believe it, exhilaration smashing up against his resistance: like he was being torn in two.

"I can't get away now!" he blurted and stumbled back a step, then back behind his desk.

"Okay," Samantha persisted calmly. "Maybe later?"

Ryan looked at her for several long moments.

"No, I can't do it. I got too much going on here."

52

"Maybe tomorrow?"

"I don't know," Ryan said. "I'll give you a call if I can."

"Okay, Ryan, thank you." Samantha handed Ryan her card. "My cell number's on the back."

Ryan didn't reach out to take the card and she left it on his desk.

"Is that diner on One Hundred Thirty-Eighth Street still there?" she said.

"The Silver Bay? Yeah, it's still there."

The Silver Bay was the neighborhood diner where Ryan had taken Samantha a couple of times when they'd dated as teens.

"I hope to hear from you, Ryan," Samantha said and left his office.

Ryan closed his office door and stood still without moving; he then slowly stepped over to his window. He couldn't deny that each time he stood to look out his office window it brought him right back to Samantha's teenage bedroom window — especially if it was late at night. He'd recall how after the first and only time they'd made love, lain side-by-side, under her white, damp sheets, sealed with their youthful aromatic juices, looking out her open bedroom window, both mesmerized by the glow of the white streetlamp as if it were a luminous moon.

Except, the background was not the deep, dark, infinite sky, spotted with stars, but a column of mundane, fire escape draped brick buildings. And, yet, since all the windows facing them reflected that solitary streetlamp, an incandescent white glow was vibrating in the center of each windowpane. He imagined it was applause.

It was then, on that early summer morning, when they'd been seized with true love and joy for the first time in their young lives.

CHAPTER 7

Throughout late Monday afternoon, into the late night, two Manhattan Robbery detectives, including Toni and Geddes, sat on an ancient single-room occupancy hotel on the Upper Westside. It was one of the few S.R.O.'s left in that neighborhood that had transformed over the last forty years from a high-crime area — partly because of all the S.R.O's — to a gentrified area of renovated tenements that had been turned into co-ops along with a steady buildup of high rises. That S.R.O. had the distinction of providing shelter for former and active convicts.

Finally, by 5 a.m. Tuesday, as a private garbage truck was hauling a few stacks of empty crates from the front of the Jewish deli next door, a wobbling Ernesto Cruz dripped out of a black private cab. There was no problem recognizing him from the photo his parole officer had texted the detectives the day before. He was in all-black: black collared shirt, black slacks, and black, pointed shoes. He looked like a flamenco dancer, except for the white fedora resting on the back of his head like a 1940's newspaper reporter.

As he swayed in front of the cab driver's window fumbling through his handful of bills, the four detectives walked calmly up to him without fanfare or excitement.

"Police, Ernesto, don't move," Toni said, and like synchronized vices, they gripped his arms and guided his elastic body and forced his chest and face down onto the hood of the black cab. Toni took off his fedora and emptied his pockets into the hat onto the hood of the car. In addition to a few vials of crack, it looked like he had about $1,500. in cash. Geddes gave him a good toss, inside his waistband and between his crotch: No gun.

Toni pulled out her pen flashlight and pointed it at the back of Ernesto's hands. "There's the red tattoo, just like the bank manager said."

"What's your name?" She asked.

A slurred voice answered, " Ernesto Cruz."

By about 9 a.m. Tuesday, Toni and Geddes left Ernesto Cruz in the cell of the Manhattan Robbery Squad On West 13th Street; shot down to Manhattan Criminal Court, and picked up a search warrant for Ernesto's room at the S.R.O. They found a Glock, with one round in the chamber and eight rounds in the ten-shot magazine resting between the mattress and box spring of his single bed. The serial numbers had been scraped from outside and inside the automatic, but the ballistics examination determined that the Glock was the same gun used to murder Father Manuel Gonzalez, and used to fire a round into the wall behind the bank manager's desk.

At noon, Toni and Geddes were back at the Manhattan Robbery Squad. Ernesto had slept off some of his drunk and was ready to talk. Present during the formal videotaped interview was Toni, Geddes and two assistant districts attorneys from Manhattan and the Bronx, respectively.

Toni gave him his Miranda warnings, and he waived his right to an attorney. Toni figured (in Ernesto's jailhouse lawyer mind) he knew the bank robbery charge was a keeper because of the eyewitnesses, especially the bank manager, but he didn't want anything to do with the murder of a priest. Without hesitation, he admitted to robbing the bank, and firing the shot into the wall over the teller's head, but said, "I did not kill no priest!"

He said he bought the gun from a drug dealer on the corner of E. 110th Street and Lexington Avenue sometime after 1 a.m. Sunday night—long after Father Manny had been shot.

"Where were you from six p.m. Sunday until six a.m. Monday?" Toni said.

"I was in my room," Cruz said as he took a sip from the can of coke she had given him.

"You were home from six p.m. on—you weren't out that night and came home later?"

"Oh, yeah. I was at a club on Eleventh Avenue. Until almost one o'clock, then I left."

Toni and others looked at each other for a moment.

"Listen, Ernesto," Toni said. "We don't want to ask you a hundred questions to get all the details. We found the gun that was used to kill a priest in your room. You hear what I'm saying? In your room. Now concentrate. Tell us exactly where you were and who you were with from six p.m. Sunday until six a.m. Monday. You got it?"

Ernesto's eyes opened wide and explained that at 6 p.m. Sunday night he was at a Latin seafood place where his cousin worked as a bartender on City Island. He'd gotten there about 5:30 p.m. alone. He had a few drinks and a steak sandwich at the bar. He had more drinks after his meal. While he was there he spoke to his cousin on-and-off, and the owner, whom he'd known since before he went to jail too. His cousin owed him a thousand dollars, and he went there to collect, which he did. He said he left about 9 o'clock for a club on W. 44th Street and 11th Avenue.

He'd met a young woman at the club whom he spent the night with on Riverside Drive and 158th Street. Around 4:30 a.m. on Monday she called a private car service for him and went home, back to the S.R.O

"So you went to her place. You didn't make any stops?" Toni said, prompting him to recall what he'd said before the formal interview that he had purchased the Glock.

"Oh, yeah, yeah, yeah," Cruz said, as he rubbed his dripping nose with the palm of his cuffed hands. He bent over and wiped his face again on his black pants. Geddes handed him a box of tissues from the top of the file cabinet and pulled the wastebasket from the corner of the room and placed it next to him.

"Thanks," He blew his nose over and over again. Geddes gave Toni a look and motioned an imaginary spoon to his nose. They waited.

"Did you make any stops when you left the club?" Toni said again.

"Yeah. We stopped by One-Tenth Street so I could buy the gun."

Being locked-up for the last twelve years, when he looked to buy a gun, none of the guys he knew were around. Some junkie told him that the word was this crack dealer had a gun for sale. Killing two birds, he paid three hundred dollars for the Glock and another three hundred dollars for the crack. He said he didn't know the dealer's name, and never saw him before.

"Did she know what you were doing?"

"No, no, no. She thought I made the stop just for crack. She didn't know about the gun. But she felt it in my waist when I got back in the cab."

"She didn't get out of the cab with you," Toni said, "to buy the crack?"

"No, no. She stayed in the cab."

"What time did you leave the club with her?"

"About one."

"What's her name?"

"Cancun."

"Her real name?"

"I don't know her real name. That's the name she give me."

"So what did you do after picking up the gun and crack?"

"We went to her place in the Heights."

"Washington Heights?" Toni said. "Where exactly?"

"One fifty-eighth and Riverside."

"What time did you get to Riverside?"

"I say it must've been like one-thirty. Something like that."

"And you didn't step out again?"

"No, no," Cruz said. "I stayed there 'til I left like I said maybe six."

57

"What kind of cab did you take from the club?"

"I don't know. That Uber shit I think."

"But the same cab that picked you and her from the club took you to one-ten and Lex. and then to her apartment?" Toni said.

"Yeah, yeah. It was the same cab."

"What's her building number on Riverside Drive?"

"I don't remember. I didn't look up."

"What about the phone number? Don't tell me you don't have her phone number," Toni said with one eyebrow raised for effect.

"No, no, detective. I don't have it."

Geddes said, "Come on, Ernesto. Didn't you want to see her again?"

"I don't care," Cruz said, looking at Geddes's serious face.

"What does she do for a living?" Geddes said.

"She's a dancer," Cruz said.

"What kind of dancer?" Toni said.

"A stripper," Cruz said as he sat back in his chair.

"This club on forty-fourth—where you met Cancun, is a strip club?" Toni said. "She's one of the strippers? She works there?"

"Si, detective," Cruz said with a grin.

"So, you leave her place about six and go home. What did you do then?" Toni said.

"I went to sleep. I got up like noon and went to the bank."

"To do what?"

"I robbed the bank, detective," said Cruz. "You know that.'

"Did you fire the gun?'

"Yeah, detective, I fired the gun into the wall," Cruz said. "I was just trying to scare them, but I didn't kill no priest. I ain't even ever been to that church in the Bronx, I don't know no Father Gonzalez."

CHAPTER 8

When Toni and Geddes found the Glock in Ernesto's SRO, Ryan was sitting in a booth at the far end of the Silver Bay Diner waiting for Samantha to arrive. He'd just gotten word from Geddes about Ernesto Cruz's statement. Toni wanted to confirm Ernesto was with that stripper when Father Manny was shot and killed, and Ryan gave them the green light to check-it-out. He'd also given them the green light to take Ernesto to Manhattan North Narcotics to look at photographs of people recently arrested for dealing drugs in East Harlem. Toni wanted that drug dealer who sold him the Glock.

When Samantha walked-in, a line of cab drivers at the counter turned to check her out. It didn't look to Ryan that any of them had actually noticed her enter. Yet they all turned. They'd been guided by their male intuition to look. No words were exchanged. Yet, somehow it was conveyed that a stunner had entered. Maybe they all just snatched a whiff of her perfume and turned. But Ryan recognized that wasn't it either. It wasn't a blast of perfume that caused that reaction, but silence.

The silence occurred when the first of the cabbies at the corner of the counter — closest to the door — suddenly stopped chewing his BLT. This caused another at the counter to sense the sudden absence of chewing when the front door opened-and-closed at his back, so, he turned from his bowl of tomato soup; which led to a series of neck twists to flutter down the counter, and a collective and respectful quiet washed over the diner as if royalty had entered.

She wore dark, round sunglasses even though it was overcast. She scanned the diner, dipping her glasses halfway down the bridge of her nose, spotted Ryan, took the glasses off and marched directly to him. Watching her approach made Ryan's breathing quicken.

59

Ryan stood up as she slid into the booth to face him. It had been so many years since he'd last sat with Samantha in a restaurant booth. Not only had they often gone to the Silver Bay for a cheeseburger and fries, but there was another place, a Cuban-Chinese place, a few blocks away they also liked going to. There you had a choice of the Chinese staples: fried rice and spare ribs; shrimp lo mein, orange chicken; or, the Spanish staples: yellow rice and red beans with a Spanish steak or pork chops and fried plantains.

They'd been about seven weeks into their romantic immersion, sitting in the Cuban-Chinese place one afternoon, when Manny happened to walk in. It was the very first time Manny had met Samantha, and it had been the last time — until the present — that Ryan and Samantha had faced each other in a restaurant booth. Ryan had told Manny about Samantha many times over the summer, but Manny had not yet met her. Ryan recalled how proud he was of having this beautiful, bright, Latina at his side and how genuinely delighted Manny was for them both. He had that priestly glow even then, while he was still in seminary. A glow Ryan missed very much.

"Have you ordered, Ryan?"

"I was waiting for you."

"Thanks," she said, and placed them on the side of the table. The waiter approached. They decided to just start with coffee.

"Any developments?" Samantha said as they waited for their coffees to arrive.

"My people are following up on a few things, but nothing worth talking about," Ryan said, cutting to the chase.

"I'm here. What did you want to talk about?"

She paused and looked at Ryan as the waiter put two mugs of black coffee on the table without saucers, a single napkin apiece and teaspoons. The odor of hamburgers and onions was heavy. The whole wall behind the counter was covered with stainless steel diamond-shaped tiles. At the grill was one man in a white apron and white, long-sleeve shirt partially rolled up holding a spatula. It was parallel to where Ryan and Samantha sat in the back.

"Ryan, do you ever think about that one time we made love?" Samantha said.

It was the July 4th weekend—six weeks prior to his twentieth birthday—when he first met Samantha; they were both nineteen. They'd met through her cousin, whom, for barely a flicker, Ryan had dated four years earlier. Her cousin was five years older than Ryan and when she found out that he—at five-ten and one hundred seventy-five pounds—was only fifteen, she let him go. But four years later—at almost twenty—the same cousin introduced him to Samantha as the three by chance jumped on the same downtown-bound subway car at the Cedar Avenue station. He was on his way to the 42nd Street library to return a copy of *Crime and Punishment*.

There was a public library blocks from his Bronx walk-up, but he liked to take the solo-ride on the subway, and come up into the midtown light, under that striking building on 42nd Street and Fifth Avenue, where the two lions waited to greet him. To be permitted to sit and read in that vast third floor reading room of the New York Public Library, which seemed to be the size of Mount Carmel's ball field, with frescoes of blue skies and clouds, spread across that vast high-ceiling, like Fernando Botero sculptures, suspended over him, gave him hope. He could dream there.

Ryan had an instant crush on Samantha. She had long black hair and a slim figure that she carried with a grace that reminded him of a little dancer in an Edgar Degas painting. The noise and rumbling of the subway car made it impossible for him to hear her tell him her name at first, but she stood up on her toes, put her face up to his, and with sensational, dark brown eyes repeated herself slowly, "SAAA-MAAAAAAN-THAAAA." His heart skipped a beat. The next day Ryan called her cousin and asked if he could have Samantha's number.

By the end of July, anyone who saw them together would say Samantha and Ryan were love struck. They were inseparable. If you caught them walking down the block or catching the occasional summer apartment party, concert or baseball game in Mount Carmel Park or just sitting on the stoop in front of Samantha's five-story walkup for hours on end, they were always together.

After weeks of cuddling that escalated to heavy petting — more often than not in Mount Carmel Park — they were ready to take the ultimate, intimate plunge, but they were both at a loss in coming up with a suitable place. Neither had a car nor did any of their close friends in the neighborhood. As inner-city college students, they both still lived at home and their mothers were home all day long. Then in a tongue-and-cheek way, after a blistering and heart palpitating petting episode that Samantha reluctantly brought to a halt, she supposed their only hope was for him to visit her in the middle of the night. She was not at all serious since she lived in a three-bedroom apartment with her younger sister, Liz, and her parents.

As it turned out, the thought of making love to Samantha so inspired Ryan he was convinced it could be done. Samantha did not think it was possible, even though she had her own bedroom. After all, she appealed to Ryan, her family was on all sides of her, and the walls were paper-thin due to her tenement's renovation a few years earlier. When the buildings were constructed sixty or more years earlier they were practically sound proof. South Bronx renovations guaranteed the cheapest sheetrock was used to separate the rooms. But this did not throw cold water on Ryan. Not even a little bit.

He believed he could climb the fire escape — which faced the front of the building — and which was providentially attached to her third-floor bedroom window (not her parents or sister's window!) He proposed that he leap onto her fire escape sometime between three and five in the morning and pay her a visit. Samantha didn't take him seriously but promised to let him in if he appeared on the fire escape. She let him go with a long, deep, penetrating kiss, and a smile that said, "You're a piece of work, Condon." He returned the smile.

Samantha underestimated Ryan Condon. When he tapped on her fire escape window at 4:17 a.m., (according to her digital clock) with his "How could you doubt me smile," her whole body flushed with joy, but she hadn't prepared for him. She didn't think he would do such an insane thing, so, when she fell asleep hours earlier with a smile just imagining his visit, she hadn't cleared away the blockade of stuffed animals on her window-sill. Still half-dreaming, and gasping for breath, she quickly snatched at each one like she was clearing a battalion of bowling pins.

Ryan had slipped out of his fourth-floor apartment at about 3 a.m. not able to sleep a wink. His mother hadn't heard him leave, and his father was working the midnight to eight shift at La Guardia Airport as a security guard. Ryan trolled Samantha's block for almost an hour waiting for the right moment and gumption to go for it. It was a hot summer night so there were constant obstacles: an occasional couple and drunk wobbling down the street; people looking out the windows sporadically; cars and gypsy cabs driving by, including the occasional radio car on routine patrol. The thought of getting grabbed on the fire escape before making it into Samantha's bedroom made his legs rubbery. Yet the thought of being with Samantha generated such a state of rigid focus in him that it steadied his wobbly legs.

"I don't want to talk about that, Samantha," Ryan said. "What else is on your mind?"

There was a long pause as they held each other's eyes.

"I need to do something that is long overdue, Ryan. I want to be honest with you and apologize to you."

"Apologize?" For what?" Ryan said, but he knew this could only be about one thing.

"For how I broke up with you, and finally tell you why I did."

Harsh sizzling and smoke rose up from the grill as a couple burgers were flipped. Ryan didn't know what to say. Yes, it was on his mind too, it had always been on his mind: it had been on his mind for over twenty years. Yet, it seemed strange, under the circumstances that she would bring that ghost up now. He wondered whether she was a little unmoored. She called that morning and again insisted that he meet her; that she wanted to talk about Manny, and yet she'd brought up the one time they'd been together.

He couldn't deny that that was the happiest night of his life, but that was not the end of the story. He'd been carved up pretty good when she dumped him, but that was the past and this was just not the time. He had only one purpose now, and that was finding Manny's killer.

"Forget it, Samantha, it was a long time ago. We were kids. It happens. Forget it."

"I've never forgotten how I hurt you, Ryan, and I never stopped loving you."

Ryan sat stunned for a moment. Then took a slow sip of coffee.

"Listen, Samantha. I'm not here for this. I said to forget it. I'm not interested. You hear what I'm saying?"

Ryan couldn't deny he felt it was irrational for her to bring something like that up, but he also could not deny that he was exhilarated that this woman — who broke his heart when they were college kids — now claimed to still be in love with him. Who's the deranged one here, he wondered — her or him?

"Do you follow what I'm saying?" He said, trying to get anchored. "I'm not interested."

"Ryan, listen —

"Come on, Samantha," Ryan said, cutting her off, "I'm not listening to this." He took another quick sip of his coffee, tossed a couple of bucks on the table and started to get up.

Samantha held his wrist with both her hands, looking up at him. "Ryan, please just listen to me. I don't know if what I need to tell you will help you find Manny's killer, but you must listen to me."

Ryan stood over her for several long moments. Then finally she let his wrist go, and with a deep sense of foreboding he sat back down. He could feel himself sinking.

CHAPTER 9

Toni and Geddes put Ernesto Cruz in their car and worked their way up to Manhattan North Narcotics. If Cruz couldn't pick out the dealer he'd bought the gun from, then they would cruise the streets with him in the department car and see if he could pick the dealer out from amongst the usual congregants.

Toni led Cruz into the offices of Manhattan North Narcotics. This was her turf. In her eight years on the job, she'd spent her first two years right out of the academy as a narcotics-undercover, followed by four on patrol, and her last two in Bronx Homicide.

"Who you got there, Toni?" one of her former narcotics partners shouted across the office. "Not another *desperado*?"

"Shaft, my man" she replied. "You know it. Have *desperado* will travel."

The black detective had a hearty laugh. His name was actually Corwyn Washington. But his nickname was attributed to the 70's movie character of a Harlem private detective who had an affinity for wearing long black leather coats. Toni's Shaft was a long black leather coat man too, so the name stuck. But he didn't have the slickness of the movie Shaft. Her Shaft was a big, jovial guy, always reminding her of the comedian, Cedric the Entertainer, but he was one dynamite narcotics detective. There was no better detective in Manhattan North in infiltrating drug gangs. Getting them to trust him first, he then followed up with several buys of real weight and then tossed out the net and brought in his catch. He was a true fisher of men.

Toni left Ernesto in another room with Geddes. She gave Shaft the background on him and the homicide details.

"How do you know he ain't the shooter?" Shaft said as he backed over to the coffee machine in the corner. He offered Toni a cup.

"No, thanks," Toni said. "We're not sure he isn't yet. But he's got an alibi we're going to check out. He says he was in the sack with a stripper when the priest got shot"

"Where's she strip?"

"Place on West 4-4 and 11th."

"The Golden Dolphin?"

"Yeah. That's what he says."

"They've got incredibly hot chicks in that place."

"How the hell would you know? You're a father of twin girls for crying out loud. I don't think Mrs. Washington would like to hear this."

"One of my informants, Toni, one of my informants" Shaft winked. "Detective is only as good as his information. Right?"

"Yeah, right," Toni said and started toward the photo room. "Let's get in there," Shaft followed with his cup of coffee.

There was barely enough room for the card-size table in the photo room that was positioned in the center. Against the cinder block walls—circling the table—were file cabinets with countless photos of people (male and female) arrested for buying and selling drugs. There was a time when a detective would pull out one of the long, narrow, metal, drawers from one of the file cabinets; and based on the general description of the perpetrator: height, weight, race, age, slap it onto the table, and the witness or victim would flip through hundreds of photos by hand, one at a time. It was rare to get a hit. But now, sitting in the center of the desk was a Mac.

"What area you want to cover?" Shaft said, sitting in front of the blue screen with the bold white letters "N.Y.P.D. NARCOTICS DIVISION" traveling across it like circling news reports on that building in Times Square. He dragged another seat over for Toni.

"Make it One-Ten and Lex. Our guy said he bought the gun from a dealer on One-Ten and Lex. If we come up empty we can always broaden the search. How about over the last two years?"

Shaft grabbed the mouse, hit the icon he wanted, entered the coordinates and presto, fifty-four citizens had been arrested on drug dealing charges in the last two years on East 110th Street and Lexington Avenue.

"You can call your guy in now," Shaft said. "All you got to do is let him hit the enter button after each photo; the next set will pop up. If you need any help, just give a shout."

Toni kept a hold of the mouse and hit the enter button after she was satisfied Ernesto had taken enough time to look at each photo.

Toni was again dazed by how many faces she recognized. Not just because she'd made buys from some of them during her narcotics undercover days, but because of the four years she'd spent in East Harlem.

She'd recognized too many of their faces from her patrol time: watching them trudge to school; going to *La Marqueta* dragging a shopping cart with their mothers or swimming at the Parks Department pool on 115th Street. It was alarming to be reminded of how many kids when they became young adults, were grabbed for selling or buying drugs on 110th street. She knew she shouldn't have been surprised seeing so many familiar faces. But the truth was she was often thrown by some of the faces she saw. She just wanted to believe that more kids dodged the dead-end heroin/cocaine scene in El Barrio than what appeared to be true. Again, it saddened her.

"That's it from One-Tenth Street, Ernesto," Toni said, clicking the last photo on the screen. "You sure you didn't see the guy?"

Ernesto vigorously rubbed his nose and eyelids with his handcuffed fists, "No, Santiago. I don't see the guy. I know him if I see him, no problem."

Toni thanked Shaft and told him they might be back to do a broader search, but they would take a ride up to E. 110th Street and Lexington Avenue — see if Ernesto could pick-out the dealer off the street. When Toni, Geddes, and Ernesto got back into the unmarked car, Toni texted Ryan to let him know what they were up to.

Ryan read Toni's text and said to Samantha, "I'm listening."

Ryan's hands were clenched around his Blackberry on the table. He held Samantha's eyes. He continued to feel a stirring in him that he tried to keep under control.

"Ryan, I never told you why I had to break it off with you," Samantha said as she gently placed her hands over his. "I know it's a long time ago, but you need to know."

Ryan didn't say a word, and slid his hands out from under hers and placed them in his lap.

It had happened the last week in August. Just before the Labor Day weekend. That's when Samantha told him she didn't want to see him again.

They'd gone to afternoon Sunday Mass at Mount Carmel the day before and had decided to head downtown to see "Forrest Gump" on 42nd Street afterward. They'd stopped at Carvel for ice cream, walked north through Central Park, and picked up the 6 at 86th Street and Lexington Avenue for the ride back to the Bronx. He'd gotten her home about 10:30, went home and stayed home. No more late night visits. They would not let that happen again. They were soul mates and knew it.

When he dropped her off he told her that he could not see her the rest of the week. His mother's sister and two cousins were visiting from Ft. Lauderdale on Monday. Ryan had to drive out to his other aunt's house in Suffolk County first thing in the morning with his parents, and wouldn't be back until Saturday. It was absolutely the last thing he wanted to do.

That Monday afternoon Samantha was at her summer part-time job at the Gap store on Third Avenue. She worked two days a week: Monday and Wednesday. It had become their summer routine that when she left her job — usually about 8 p.m. — she'd walk down bustling 149th Street to the north side entrance of the park where Ryan would always be waiting. They'd walk through to the south side of the park — hand-in-hand — to her block: Cedar Avenue.

But he wasn't there to meet her that night.

When he got back to the Bronx on Saturday, he wasn't able to reach Samantha by phone. He called and called Samantha's home again and again but nobody would answer. For the next couple of days, he kept calling, going back to her block over and over again — but he didn't see her, or her parents, or her sister, or the visiting nurse who stopped by daily to assist with Samantha's father. All the shades had been drawn, day and night. It was as if a massive drone had lifted the entire family up-and-out of their tenement.

He had trouble eating and sleeping. Black rings started to appear under his eyes. He had the depleted, expired look of one of the junkies down the block. He wondered then whether she had gone on a trip — maybe she'd returned to Georgetown early. Maybe the whole family had gone to drive Samantha back to Georgetown, but why would she not have told him? It didn't make any sense.

By Wednesday, he'd decided to take a chance and knock on her apartment door, even though the shades were still drawn, and he knew — in his heart — there was nobody home. He was stunned when her mother answered. It was clear to Ryan that Samantha's mother had been crying. He never quite understood that then. She told Ryan to wait, without completely shutting the door. After several long minutes, Samantha came to the door.

"Yes," Samantha greeted him in her terry bathrobe, barely making eye contact. It was about three in the afternoon. Her eyes were bloodshot, her straight black hair tangled. She was pale. She'd been crying too.

"What's wrong, Samantha?" Ryan asked with alarm and concern, hands and arms opened wide. "Why haven't you called me back? Is your father okay?"

Samantha didn't respond.

"Is Elizabeth okay?"

"I can't see you anymore," she finally said weakly. Her eyes started to brim with tears.

"Why? What's wrong?"

She didn't reply.

"What's happened?" Ryan said, as his insides started to collapse. "Why are you doing this? Did something happen? Did I do something? Tell me what it is?"

Still, she stayed silent. He wiped a strand of her hair that had dropped over her eyes with his fingertips. Her head faced down at Ryan's feet.

"Please, Samantha, tell me what's going on," Ryan said, reaching out for her hand holding the door.

She pulled her hand away. "I just can't see you anymore," she said, still without raising her eyes, shaking her head. "It just can't work."

"What can't work?" Ryan said, "What do you mean it can't work; it's been working!"

Samantha stayed silent.

71

"Please, Sam. I love you." He reached out to touch her hand again. "Please don't do this."

She yanked it back that time and looked directly into his eyes and held them, "It's over! I don't ever want to see you again! Understand!" She slammed the door in his face.

He remembered how he stood there in front of her apartment door. He couldn't move. He had a tense grip on the doorframe with both hands as if his fingers had been screwed in. He stared into the peephole, trying to see right through to her, which gave him the feeling his body was tumbling deeper and deeper into an abyss.

He became dizzy — black spots flickered past his eyes. He hung his head. He could feel an eruption building in him. He knew he should move away from her door before it burst, but he could not. So, he stayed attached to her doorframe. The wave began in his stomach and then fired down his legs to his toes, as if needles were simultaneously stabbing him, rippling from his midsection, then to the lowest part of his body until the feeling rose and blew up and through the top of his head. He'd never known that kind of pain.

He slid down to a squat, and it started. The tears started to drip, in silence. He tried with all his will to stop, but he could not, he tried to just leave, but still could not.

At the time, it seemed it would never end, but, of course, it had — hours it seemed, as he remembered that day, but, in truth, it must have been only minutes.

He eventually stood up and stepped down and out of Samantha's tenement building and her life. A puddle of his agony was what he left for her.

He'd never known — that at the very moment — Manny had been sitting in the living room consoling her family.

"We were very happy together that summer, weren't we?" she said.

"Samantha, I don't want to get into that. It's old news. We were kids, and we were only together for a summer. Now, if you've got something to tell me just tell me."

He could not let this get drawn out. Yet, he hoped she would not get to the point too quickly. He did not want their conversation to end, their business to be concluded, for them to part.

"You know I came back for you?"

Ryan's eyebrows furrowed, "Came back for me. What are you talking about?"

"I know you never knew that. But it's true. After I finished at Georgetown and moved back to New York to attend law school I came looking for you because I loved you. But I spoke to Manny and that's when I found out you were getting married. Manny didn't think it would be wise for me to contact you. And I knew he was right. You'd made a commitment to another girl, and as much as it broke my heart, I admired you for it."

"Broke your heart?" Ryan said. "What is that, a joke?"

Samantha paused, "Remember the day I left you, at my door."

Ryan stayed silent.

"Well, that day I'd been to a doctor," she said. Tears began to build in her eyes.

Ryan felt as if a calloused hand was choking his heart. He stayed quiet but his expression changed from exasperation to pained focus.

"The doctor thought I could be pregnant," Samantha said. "He turned out to be right."

Ryan looked at his watch. It felt like he'd been at the Silver Bay diner longer, but only fifteen minutes had passed. His head was spinning. What was the point of her bringing up that she'd become pregnant? Was it because of that one experience? So that's why she shut the door in his face? It didn't make sense. It was so long ago. But he remembered very well that he had forsaken protection. What the hell was he doing there with her anyway? What the hell was she talking about and why? What could this have to do with Manny's murder?

"Who?" Ryan said, his hands still on his lap.

Samantha dropped her gaze, then looked up at Ryan and said, "It wasn't you, Ryan."

At first, Ryan was relieved, but to his consternation, it hit him hard. He'd thought he was the only one with her that summer. He instantly felt bludgeoned with the thought that he'd been an ass, a cuckold.

"I didn't mean to hurt you, Ryan."

"What's the point of bringing this up now?"

"I was only with one other man that summer, Ryan," she said and looked deeply into his eyes as. "Only once with one other man."

Ryan waited for her to tell him who it was, but she'd stopped. He was getting aggravated. A few moments passed and she still wouldn't answer, until finally, she shook her head.

"That's some routine you had there, Samantha. You know, you were some kind of player."

Ryan gave his coffee a vigorous stir, splattering some of it onto the table soaking his napkin then tossed the spoon on the table like he was tossing a set of dice. This sent an irritating clang through the diner. A few of the cab drivers turned to glance at them. Ryan and Samantha sat silently for a few minutes, not sipping their coffees, holding each other's eyes.

"I've got to go," he said and began to get up.

"But there's something else, Ryan. Please give me another minute."

"I got to go," Ryan said and walked out.

CHAPTER 10

Toni and Geddes were in the area of E. 110th Street and Lexington Avenue. That corner was a popular hangout for criminals. There was always sure to be a cluster of four or more mostly male drug-dealing citizens on each of the four corners. Those males dealt most any illegal narcotic a customer could want. A variety of different colored pills; cocaine and heroin in neatly packed glassine envelopes clearly marked with the brand logo of the respective drug gang responsible. And marijuana for those not committed to the addictive options.

On the southwest corner stood a brown brick fourteen-story apartment compound. Its dismal, square construction shadowed over the illegal deals at the intersection: the life-depriving deals, the escape-filled deals, the shame-based deals, the dead-end deals.

Deals in front of the twenty-four-hour bodega on the northwest corner with flashing Budweiser and Michelob signs; deals in-front-of the twenty-four-hour candy store on the southeast corner that did not open the door but sold through a slot in it; deals in front of the twenty-four-hour bakery on the northeast corner that sold coffee and Latin sweets through a thick plastic box with a turntable that effectively barred the customer on the outside from the delicacies on the inside.

It was common knowledge with precinct cops that if a tour of duty was coming to a close without an arrest, just keep circling One-Ten and Lex., and it wouldn't be long before the officer either personally observed or was directed to a crime in progress. Often it was robbery: one dealer putting a gun into the face of another dealer and taking his product, or an upper eastside customer getting snatched like a lamb by one of the assorted wolves concealed in a narrow doorway.

Ryan had sent another eight detectives in four unmarked cars. He'd told them all to dress down. He wanted four on the street and four on the roofs of the tenement buildings on both the south and north sides.

Most of the buildings on the block connected, so if the bad guy bolted into one of the buildings and figured he could disappear into an apartment before the police caught up, one of the detectives on the roof would come flying down and intercept him in the hallway before he ducked into an apartment. Or if the bad guy tried for the roof itself, thinking he'd hurdle over a succession of roofs and exit from another building, he would be greeted on the roof.

But the most important reason for putting a couple of detectives on the roofs was to keep knuckleheads from tossing things down at the police as they were taking action. It was not unusual for a brick or a Ziploc bag of piss to land disconcertingly close.

Ryan sat in his department car alone monitoring Toni's and Geddes's transmissions over the radio. He welcomed the chance to sit back and try to process what Samantha had been getting at. What's this business about her being pregnant? And why'd she feel the need to tell him then?

And, how could this have anything to do with Manny's murder? He wondered.

What had Manny known all these years? He must've known Samantha had gotten pregnant. Maybe that was the catalyst of their twenty-year friendship. But why would Manny have kept it from him? Sure, he was a priest and he needed to protect Samantha's privacy, but this all happened a couple of years before he entered the priesthood. Not that somebody needs to be a priest to protect a confidence. But Manny knew how completely in love with her he'd been. How could he not tell him?

Now he was at a loss. How could Manny have kept it from him? The only reason Ryan felt made any sense was that Manny somehow believed if Ryan had found out how Samantha had become pregnant, it would have shattered their friendship. But why would it have that effect on their friendship? Why would that have affected him and Manny? Ryan knew he was reaching out into perplexing territory for answers.

All he knew without any doubt was that his friend, Manny Gonzalez, had been a man of intense moral courage. The Manny Ryan knew would not have kept that from him without a very good reason. The Manny Ryan knew would have shared it with him, not out of a failure to respect Samantha's privacy, but from the deep recognition of how devoted Ryan was to Samantha. Yet, he did not, or could not, because other lives would be affected, Ryan reasoned. But what other lives could have been affected by Samantha's pregnancy? It didn't make any sense.

He knew he should have given Samantha another minute to tell him all she felt she needed to, but he just couldn't hear any more. That had been enough for him. But he wondered who was the father of her child? She broke it off with him after she'd seen the doctor? Ryan's mind was spinning again. So what became of the pregnancy? Did she have the child? Did she have an abortion, God forbid. If she had the kid, where is the child now? Was it a boy or a girl?

The hours crawled by as Toni, Geddes, and Ernesto waited for the dealer to make an appearance on the corner. Up to that point they'd alternated between circling the block, or, fixed on the corner for extended periods of time. Ernesto hadn't seen the guy. The only thing their stakeout accomplished was to temporarily slow down drug dealing activity in the area.

Toni didn't think for a second that all drug dealing stopped; all crime stopped because they were in the area. Not on 110th Street at least. It was too notorious a corner.

Drugs were the lure to that corner, but it was also a place to catch-up with brothers and sisters in crime. It was a prominent East Harlem corner in which to muster when you were released from Rikers or dropped anchor on the city again from upstate and needed some quality time to plan your future before your next collar. And for those who mustered on 110th Street, there was always the next collar, unless you overdosed and died or were taken out by another of those mustering.

They all knew the police were looking for somebody, but they were resigned to the reality that that could be any one of them. There would be no point in alerting their *amigos* wanted for one thing or another because most (if not all of them) were wanted for something: from not paying a ticket for drinking in public or urinating on the street, to drug sales, robbery, and murder. They just hoped it wasn't them this time.

As for the dealer who sold the gun used to kill Father Manny, he could be the shooter or he just had no idea the Glock had been used to murder a priest. Toni hoped that when they had him, he would turn out to be Father Manny's killer, but she knew that it could go either way.

At 9:30 p.m. Ernesto shouted, "Look, Santiago, that's him, that's him," and pointed to the southeast corner.

"Okay, Ernesto, *suave*, okay, which one? What's he wearing?" Geddes said as cool as could be without taking his gaze from the street and using one of the few Spanish words he picked up during his eighteen years working in the Bronx.

"He's got the Yankee cap on, man," Ernesto said, still pointing, not being able to contain his excitement. "He's got that shopping bag in his hand."

Geddes said to Toni, "You see his face before he turned?"

"No," Toni said. "He turned his back as soon as Ernesto spotted him."

"I didn't get a look at him either."

"All right," Toni said. "I'm going to get out and approach him. Slim chance he'll make me before I'm on top of him. Geddes, stay with Ernesto here and let the boss and the guys know to move in as soon as they see I'm a couple steps from him."

Toni didn't wait for Geddes to acknowledge what she'd said. She started to jump out of the car as she pulled her gun from her holster, hiding it inside her right jacket pocket, finger on the trigger guard. She walked slowly toward the congregation on the corner careful to not make eye contact with any of them.

As soon as Toni got to the corner — just before she was about to yank out her gold shield from the chain around her neck and announce, "Police, Don't Move" — their Yankee hat suspect glanced over his shoulder, peeled away like a subway rat, and dived down the staircase into the 110th Street train station — his shopping bag flapping in the wind. One place they hadn't considered he'd dive into. But Toni was on him.

When Toni bolted down the two flights of stairs, she could see the dealer fleeing down the platform in the direction of the tunnel. She howled, "Police Stop! Police Stop!" The dealer must've heard her screeching voice, but he wouldn't turn in her direction even one degree. His untied Reeboks echoed through the station as he pounded down the platform like a Pamplona bull.

There was no way out in the direction he was going, Toni knew as she ran just fast enough to keep him in sight. But as the dealer approached the tunnel, which only led to the next station, it hit Toni hard, "Holy shit, he's going to run through the tunnel."

A cold rod of fear ran right up her back with that thought; she knew what it would mean if she chased him into the tunnel. If she slipped and hit the third rail, she'd become the equivalent of a pillar of salt.

Or, if she fell onto the tracks and couldn't get out of the way of an oncoming train, more than her spirit would be crushed. Not to mention how things would go—if she survived the tunnel—when she caught up with him. She hoped the guy wasn't carrying another gun.

All those thoughts flashed through her mind in a flicker as her legs unconsciously pumped faster and the dealer got swallowed up in the long dark tunnel. The bottom line was she just couldn't stop herself. She just couldn't.

Toni burst into the tunnel after him. She felt sure Geddes would have notified the Transit Authority to cut off the power when he watched her chase the dealer down into the station, but she knew very well it would take some time before power would stop.

The dealer was making good time on the two-foot-wide gang walk and was putting more and more distance between himself and Toni. He'd been through that tunnel plenty of times before, Toni figured. And Toni could see from his silhouette that he was no longer carrying the shopping bag. He must've dumped it in some familiar hiding spot in the tunnel.

She tried to pick up her speed about a quarter of the way through but then plunged into some solid obstruction sticking out of the wall about stomach height that sent her tumbling down into the middle of the tracks gasping for breath.

She picked herself up and tried to run, but fell again on the slop that layered the narrow center trough of the tracks. She jumped up again, started to run, and plummeted again. Geddes suddenly heaved her up like a rag doll, which utterly spooked her, and she screamed.

"What are you doing here!"

"What am I doing here?" Geddes said, as he gave Toni a moment to get her balance before he let go of her jacket, which he used to hold her up. "I'm yanking you off the middle of these tracks. That's what I'm doing here."

81

"Who's got, Ernesto?"

"The lieutenant's got him."

"Get out of here, Geddes. You're going to get hurt. You got bad knees. Go back out. Get them to block him off at the next station," Toni said and continued running, finally able to maintain her footing.

She could see the Yankee cap about the equivalent of two city blocks ahead of her; she was gaining on him, running with focus down the now dry subway trough. The express train then blasted past them on the center track wreaking havoc on their eardrums and lapping them with a hot mechanical breeze.

When the dealer got to the platform he started to walk as if he'd just stepped off a train that had just pulled into the station. It was obvious to Toni he didn't know he'd been chased clear through the tunnel. She was only a few feet from the platform and about leap up onto it when she heard another train coming from a distance and looked back. Sure enough, it was the uptown local just pulling out of the 110th Street station. It then occurred to her to look back again and was stunned when she spotted Geddes's black silhouette about a half city block away from the foot of the platform where she stood on the tracks.

"John, for crying out loud, John, the train is coming!" she screamed as if Geddes couldn't hear the train himself. "Move your ass!"

Geddes trudged down the middle of the tracks with his bum knees, the gift of another foot-chase through a back alley years before. It was going to be okay, Toni thought—Geddes would make it in time, but then his knees gave out and Geddes' belly flopped into the trough.

Toni ran back to him, yanked her big partner up under his shoulders like he was only spirit, not flesh, and pushed him to continue as she followed behind.

82

She was pumped up, she twisted to look back; the train was bearing down on them both. The motorman had just spotted them and was yanking the cord to his mega-horn, blasting, blasting, and blasting; piercing sounds bouncing off the underground walls. "BLAAAAAAAAAAA! BLAAA! BLAAA! BLAAAAAAAAAAAAAAAAAAA!"

They'd just made it to the foot of the platform when all the power on the tracks suddenly shut-down, and the shrill sound of steal subway car wheels — locked in place — began to fill the tunnel. The eight-car train slid on the tracks; sparks flying from its undercarriage as if engulfed in flames. Geddes heaved himself up onto the platform first, twisted back to Toni, shot his arm out and yanked the former woman Marine off the tracks. The two detectives rolled on the platform like kittens, colliding with the wall. They were safe.

Toni made direct, wide-eyed contact with Geddes for a moment and said, "Wow!"

But without skipping a beat she shot up and resumed her pursuit of the Yankee cap. There was a mix of about a dozen people waiting for the train at the station. Toni yelled, "Stop that guy! Stop that guy!" Nobody moved. Toni couldn't blame them. The dealer finally looked back. He'd apparently still had no idea he'd been tracked. Or that two detectives almost got clipped by the screeching train in the process. He became a running-man again and rushed for the exit turnstiles: there were no other cops in sight. In her mind's eye, Toni could see the running man making it out onto the street and wondered where and how it would end.

Then, seemingly right out of the platform wall, a uniformed transit cop and several of her Bronx Homicide colleagues jumped out and blocked the dealer's path to the turnstiles. Without pausing for a second, the dealer jumped onto the tracks.

The screeching train continued to barrel down the track still unable to stop. They watched the Yankee cap in horror. The dealer momentarily froze in the trough of the track, like the pause button on a DVD player had been pushed; he faced the nose of the train fully upright with his hands raised up. But, the train miraculously came to a stop, inches from the brim of his cap, dropping the dealer on his back in anticipation. To everybody's surprise, he jumped up from the trough and continued to bolt for the other side. Up to that point, the dealer hadn't lost either of his untied sneakers or his Yankee cap.

Without missing a beat Toni jumped back down and dived for the dealer before he could get across the express track: just catching one of his ankles and a Reeboks sneaker. Toni had a vise grip on his T-shirt with one hand and the unoccupied Reeboks with the other hand, but in her lunging apprehension somehow ended up buried under him. Geddes and a uniformed transit cop carefully climbed down to the tracks and pulled the guy off Toni.

The transit cop said, "You're out of your mind detective."

"You bet your ass," Toni said in beaming acknowledgment and pointed down to the third rail on the express track. "Can you grab that Yankee cap over there for him?"

After they pulled the dealer and themselves up to the platform, Toni and Geddes carefully walked back into the tunnel and retrieved the shopping bag. Geddes then radioed Ryan.

"Loo, we got him," Geddes said, still breathing heavy.

"What's he got?"

"Toni's giving him a toss now," Geddes said.

Seconds later. "A lot of cash, and a lot of heroin. He wasn't packing."

"He's the guy, he's the guy, he's the one I got the piece from!" Ernesto said with excitement in the back of the unmarked car with Ryan, overhearing Geddes's broadcast.

"All right, Ernesto. Take it easy," Ryan said. "You did good. You did good."

"Loo," Geddes suddenly called out over the radio. "You still on the air?"

"Yeah, go ahead."

"This guy's got a cop shield," he said. "A silver shield, number 6-7-0-2."

"What!? A silver shield!?"

"That's right, number 6-7-0-2."

"What?" Ryan said. "What was that number again?"

Ryan could hear Geddes ask Toni, "What's the shield number again?"

"6-7-0-2," Toni said in the background.

"6-7-0-2," Geddes repeated into the radio. "6-7-0-2."

CHAPTER 11

Around 10 p.m., Toni and Geddes were on their way to the precinct with the handcuffed dealer sitting in the back seat with Geddes. Toni was driving. Ryan had assigned two other detectives to bring Ernesto back to the squad office.

"Where do you want him, Toni?" said the detective who walked in with Ernesto.

"Where's the lieutenant?"

"I don't know. He said he had to take care of something."

"Put him in the cell," Toni said and started to head to the interview room. "Thanks."

There was nothing outstanding about the drug dealer. He was a clean-shaven, thick-bodied man of medium height; with full, straight black hair combed back under his Yankee cap. He didn't look typically Hispanic to Toni; he looked more Japanese or Samoan. He reminded Toni of a compact version of a sumo wrestler. To the non-discerning eye, he might appear to be a fat-body, but Toni knew better. She'd been buried under him on the tracks for a few too many seconds. He was solid muscle. If he wasn't handcuffed he could toss Toni's tiny body like a shot put.

Toni told the dealer his rights as they traveled up Third Avenue from 116th Street.

"What's your name?" Toni said, in the rear-view mirror.

"Mateo,"

"Mateo what?"

"Mateo."

Toni and Geddes looked at each other.

"Your first and last name are Mateo?" Toni said.

Mateo Mateo nodded.

By the time they started the formal interview back at the Bronx Homicide Squad, they knew who he was. They had a copy of his adult rap sheet that noted one conviction for drug possession and two arrests for robbery without conviction. After checking with the Manhattan District Attorney's office, they found out that the victims of Mateo's two robbery arrests declined to prosecute. They had also received his unsealed juvenile record from the liaison NYPD officer assigned to Family Court. It contained a report of his juvenile history prepared by his probation officer for the court.

Mateo Mateo was twenty-four. He'd emigrated from the Dominican Republic with his family when he was twelve years old, moving to Washington Heights. His father found a job as a scrap factory worker in Williamsburg, at less than minimum wage. Mateo was the oldest of six siblings and was pressed to find a job.

He'd been enrolled in the local public school where he wasted no time making a name for himself. He started by robbing his classmates of their lunch money. In the two years Mateo attended J.H.S. 133, he managed to pick up a fair amount of cash, which he shared with his family. His parents thought he'd made the money delivering groceries at Fairway on the Upper West side.

It wasn't until Mateo's final month of his final year at J.H.S. 133 that the dean of discipline got wind of his strong-arm talents. A few friends of students, who had been victimized by Mateo, whispered into the dean's ear, but when the dean approached the student-victims they weren't willing to identify him, so he moved on to high school. Mateo was expelled from high school within a month of being arrested for robbing a classmate in the bathroom as the vulnerable student was moving his bowels. After almost a year in the Spofford jail for juveniles, he was released and never returned to school.

Although Mateo Mateo was focused on things other than academics during his brief school experience, there was one subject he seemed to have an aptitude for: Mathematics. Turns out he was not only proficient at terrorizing his schoolmates, but also had a head for numbers. This had apparently served him well as an up-and-coming Spanish Harlem drug dealer.

Mateo admitted giving the gun to Ernesto on Monday about one o'clock in the morning just as Ernesto had said. But he wouldn't admit he took any money for it. In his travels through the criminal justice system, he knew "sale" was always more serious than possession. Just giving Ernesto the gun didn't seem too serious to him. Toni knew that according to the New York State Penal Law the charge of criminal "sale" of a firearm didn't require money to be exchanged. Giving the gun to another was enough to be charged with "sale." But, at this point, it didn't matter to Toni or Geddes whether he gave or sold the gun. What mattered was: Had he killed Father Manny before he passed the Glock to Ernesto?

Mateo said he'd been hanging out at a bar on E. 105th Street and 2nd Ave: Carlito's Place. There was a tall, lean, guy in his early twenties, at least six foot two, wasted at the bar. He was clean-shaven, dark brown eyes, short hair cut military style. Mateo said he followed the guy into the men's room. The guy almost didn't make it—he was wobbling all the way in. The guy threw up in the toilet and wobbled out of the bar without grabbing his money on the bar. Mateo saw he had a blue blazer on when he went into the stall, but came out without it. Mateo went into the stall where the blazer was hanging and searched it; that's when he found the Glock without a holster. He'd never seen the guy before.

"Where'd you get the shield...the badge?" Toni said.

"From the same guy. From his jacket. It was in the outside pocket."

"What did you do with his jacket?"

"I put it back up on the door. On the hook."

"Did you think he was a cop?" Toni said.

"No, I don't think so. He was very fucked up. He looked to me like he had been knocking them back for a straight twenty-four, maybe more. If he was a cop, he was a very fucked up one. Worn out," Mateo said. "He looked too young to be a cop anyway."

"How old he look to you?" Toni said.

"Nineteen, twenty, tops."

"Did you see an I.D. card at any time," Toni pulled her I.D. card out to show him. "A card like this?'

"No, no. I didn't see no I.D. card. Just the badge."

"What about a shield...badge case like this?" Toni showed him the black leather wallet-like case that held her I.D. card and her gold detective shield.

"No, no. He didn't have no wallet. Just the badge by itself in his jacket."

As Ernesto Cruz had done before him, Mateo Mateo denied he knew Father Manny or where Our Lady of Mount Carmel Church was even located. Toni and Geddes stepped out of the interrogation room and put Mateo in the temporary holding cell.

It was almost midnight when Toni was then told she had a call. She stepped out of the interview room and picked-up. It was Father Gribbons.

"Yes, father."

"I hope I'm not calling too late, detective?"

"Not at all," Toni said. "These are normal working hours for me, but I'm surprised you're up so late."

"Well, I came across a folder with an exchange of letters between Samantha Cohen and Father Manny and I thought I should let you know right away. I think you might want to see them. And a newspaper article."

"All right, Father, thanks. We're busy right now, Toni said. "Can you give me some idea of what's in the folder?"

"It looks like Samantha Cohen had another child," Gribbons said. "Out of wedlock."

89

"Really?" Toni said.

"It seems so."

"Okay, well, we can't get there until tomorrow morning."

"No worries, detective. I'll have folder here in the rectory office for you."

"Thank you."

When Toni stepped out of the stationhouse, the pungent smell of garbage perfumed the hot early morning air. She looked east to see if she could get a glimpse of the sun, but it was out of sight. Obstructed by the massive beams of the Cross Bronx expressway high overhead. Oddly enough, the detached steady hum of morning traffic heading to, or coming from, the George Washington Bridge was comforting to her—the assuring, unceasing flow of life regardless of what was happening below.

As Toni jumped into the late model unmarked Ford she noticed a stray white—or off-white—mangy dog in the parking lot of the stationhouse sniffing for whatever it could find. The dog had a blackened rope around its neck that had once been white. She wondered why the stray wasted its time in the police parking lot when the streets overflowed with South Bronx delights.

She hung her suit jacket on the hook over the rear driver's side door and started up the Ford. As she waited for Geddes she just sat still in the scorching interior as hot air blew from the air conditioning. Slowly the interior temperature began to drop. She pointed the jets at her wet face and blouse, which started to very slowly cool off.

When Toni and Geddes showed-up at Mount Carmel, Ryan was on his way to Sutton Place. They pulled in front of the Gothic church for the second time; it had a "NO PARKING ANYTIME" sign. Geddes tossed the official police business placard on the dashboard, and they both got out. Toni looked up the block and spotted a tiny, dark Latin man pushing a white *coquito* cart on the corner.

"You still like *coquito*, Geddes?" Toni said, looking up at her tall, blue-eyed partner as they walked toward the cart.

"Hey, I've been a Bronx cop my whole career. I've sucked on many a *coquito-ice* in my day since I was a rookie. I'll always take a *coquito* ice when offered." Geddes said. "Or maybe you just think that a white boy has no long-term appreciation for anything ethnic."

Toni ordered two *coquitos* in Spanish.

"Hold on now, I didn't say that," Toni snickered, as she paid the vendor and was handed two coconut-ices in white Dixie cups. "And I don't know that a *coquito* ice is all that ethnic."

The two detectives stood on the corner. Toni welcomed the frigid coconut ice slithering down her throat. Geddes loosened his tie and looked up at the darkening sky. Toni was grateful for the soothing breeze that swarmed around them, although she thoroughly enjoyed the heat. She always figured her affinity for the heat had something to do with her hot-blooded Puerto Rican roots, even though she was born and raised in New York.

Toni sighed quietly. She was doing just what she was meant to do. She was in the business of hunting killers by pulling together bits and pieces of information one way or the other. That's what she did, and she did it well. Standing there out in the open with her partner, breathing in the hot morning air on a high-crime street in the South Bronx, about ready to enter Mount Carmel Church to draw more pieces, delivered her to a state of sublime peace. She wondered how many of her colleagues felt the same about their work. She chose to believe many of them did, except she didn't know that for a fact: they didn't talk about it.

Toni wanted to check in with Mother Theresa at the school before speaking with Father Gribbons. They found her in the school gymnasium, with a tribe of screaming youngsters, running basketball practice in full habit with a crucifix around her neck and a whistle in her mouth. Pattering running-shoed feet stomped and skidded on the wooden court; the bouncing ball echoing off the walls.

The mother superior was in her early 70's and had been at Mount Carmel for fifty-two years. She'd been one of Manny's and Ryan's grade school teachers thirty-five years earlier. When Toni asked if she had any idea who would have wanted to hurt Father Manny, she didn't answer right away but drifted into a place of reflection keeping her eyes on the kids.

She recalled for Toni and Geddes how when Ryan and Manny were altar boys they sometimes argued over who would ring the bells during the Mass.

"Who rang the bells was especially important on the days Father Javier happened to be the celebrant of the Mass," Mother said with a grin, then yelled at one of the kids on the court, "James you should have taken a shot there. Don't be afraid to shoot!" Then looked back to Toni and Geddes.

"So, whoever was not assigned the bells would then be responsible for holding the Bible under the priest's face as he read from one of the Gospels, and Father Javier had notorious breath."

Toni remembered her own first communion: the Bishop had breath that smelled like rotten eggs. Toni imagined how that kind of odor must've tormented penguin-draped Ryan or Manny, as it whirled around, between and through the sacred words of the Gospel, and up their nasal passages as they tried to keep up the Bible. They must've been rendered practically unconscious until the reading was completed.

"It was not until Father Javier snapped the Bible closed that the altar boy was catapulted out of his trance. The altar boy should have been paying attention and should have closed the Bible right after Father Javier stopped reading, but the truth was their attention had been momentarily incapacitated," Mother said with a hearty chuckle, then blew her whistle. "You could've have blocked that Maryann. Jump. Jump!"

"Anyway," she continued, "providentially one of the reasons Father Manny aspired to become a priest, he always said, was the example of Father Javier. You see, Father Javier was a very small, old priest, a frail priest. He was in his seventies and late eighties as Ryan and Manny were growing up, yet he delivered homilies that were unpretentious and spirited, lacking any sense of self-consciousness."

Mother Theresa explained that Manny and Ryan had attended Mount Carmel through the end of junior high school. Father Manny went on to Cardinal Spellman High School and Ryan attended Cardinal Hayes. Yet, they'd both come back to attend Sunday Mass regularly at Mount Carmel to listen to Father Javier's sermons." In Manny's junior year in high school, he heard Father Javier's homily on one particular summer Sunday that resonated deeply with him.

"Father Javier started slowly, building up his intensity as he went along. That day was a celebration of the memory of St. Mary Major, who had been canonized because she caused it to snow in the middle of summer. " 'It's a miracle!' " Father Javier proclaimed. The trouble was it would often take him several seconds after a spirited pronouncement to remember what his point was and how to proceed," Mother was beaming. "Madeline, dribble, dribble, this is not football. You're not a running back for the Dallas Cowboys!"

"Anyway, as I was saying, it was not unusual for Father Javier to lose his place too as he recited the Mass, and the entire congregation would say the next word. For example, he would hold the cup of wine up as he read and say, "When I take this…" and he would get stuck, having lost his place, and the congregation would reverently announce, "Cup!" Geddes eagerly volunteered.

"Yes, but on that particular Sunday — and I was there — Father Javier captured Manny's imagination when he expressed in his homily how proud he was to be a Catholic because of Catholicism's rich history.

" 'Others don't have what we have!' he'd announced with vigor. Then in his endearing way, he pulled out a tiny tour guidebook of Rome he had picked up on one of his visits, turning it toward the congregation, the pictures, of course, too small for anyone to see from the pews. But then Father Javier asked the congregation to pray for more men to enter the priesthood. He announced, 'We need more priests! Pray that more young men of Christ are willing to give up sex and that other stuff and enter the priesthood!' " Mother chuckled heartily.

"But this did it for Manny," Mother Theresa said. "To witness this frail, ancient priest who'd been carrying the message to his flock for over sixty years sputter those words of commitment and sacrifice required of priests with wide eyes of love and devotion and enthusiasm, well, Manny sensed the priesthood was his calling, too."

Suddenly a crew-cut headed boy about eight years old ran up to Mother Theresa, "Dorothy keeps pulling my tie, Mother. Tell her to stop."

"Dorothy, stop pulling on Jose's tie," Mother said, then snuck a peek back at Toni and Geddes. "Dorothy likes Jose."

Toni tried again. "Mother, any idea who would have wanted to hurt Father Manny?"

"No, I'm afraid not, my dear."

"Mother," Toni said, "Did Father Gribbons and Father Manny get along?"

Mother Theresa paused before answering with one raised eyebrow and took the whistle out of her mouth. "Well, yes, of course, dear. Father Gribbons and Father Manny were together for twenty years here. They were like brothers."

"I know Father Manny was about ten years younger than Father Gribbons and had been at Mount Carmel ten years before Father Manny arrived. I mean as a priest that is," Toni said. "You think he ever resented Father Manny since he was the pastor? Or maybe Father Gribbons never had any ambition to be pastor?"

"Well, no, actually when Monsignor Cannaughton retired almost ten years ago, Father Gribbons was disappointed that he wasn't appointed pastor..."

"...Since he'd been at Mount Carmel long before Father Manny arrived," Toni repeated.

"...Yes, true, but Father Gribbons is a devoted servant of God and the church and he embraced Father Manny's appointment without reservation. I'm certain of that."

Toni and Geddes nodded.

"I wonder how Milton is taking this? Father Manny always protected his little brother?"

"Father Manny had a brother?" Toni said. "Where is he?"

"Oh, dear, it's very sad," Mother Theresa, said. "He's upstate at an institution for the mentally challenged. He's been there for over twenty years."

"I see," Toni said. "Did he go to school here too?"

"No, no, dear. He attended a public school. He needed special care."

"You said Milton, Mother? Milton Gonzalez, I guess?"

"I suppose," Mother Theresa said, shrugging her shoulders. "You will find out who did this, detectives, won't you?"

"We will, Mother," Toni said.

"Terrible lost soul, terrible lost soul, who did this, terrible lost soul," Mother Theresa said, then pranced onto to the court to show them all how to do a lay-up.

CHAPTER 12

"Coffee, detectives?" Father Gribbons asked as he led them to the rectory conference room. Toni was about to decline since they'd just had two coconut-ices less than an hour before, but Geddes said he would.

"That would be terrific, Father," Geddes said. "If it's not any trouble."

"Not at all, just give me a minute," Gribbons said and stepped out.

Toni took in the conference room. The walls had framed photographs lined up of each archbishop of New York, including the current one—John Cardinal Keenan—all the way back to the first one appointed in 1820, including a photograph of Pope Francis.

Gribbons returned with three black coffees on a tray, milk, and sugar on the side. Toni and Gribbons took theirs black. Geddes took four sugars and enough milk to effectively obliterate the taste of the coffee. Toni raised her eyebrows slightly, which she couldn't help doing each time she witnessed Geddes's exercise in wrecking a wholesome cup of coffee.

Toni got to it. "Father you said you found a folder with a few letters?"

Gribbons handed Toni the yellow folder, letting them know he had to leave to visit a parishioner at Calvary Hospital. They could stay in the rectory as long as they needed to.

"Before you leave, Father, just a few questions," Toni said. "You found this folder last night?"

"Yes."

"Did you know about this folder before last night?"

"No, detective, I didn't."

"And you read through the folder's contents for the first time last night?" Toni said, gesturing with the folder in her hand.

"Yes."

"Thank you."

The first item in the yellow folder was a twenty-three-year-old, *Daily News* article on August 7th with the headline, "CO-ED RAPED-MOUNT CARMEL PARK."

The story read, "An out-of-state college student home for the summer was raped and beaten in Mount Carmel Park as she was returning home from her summer job at a neighborhood clothing store, police said yesterday. The victim was spotted by police officers in the park at 1:45 a.m. and taken to Jefferson Hospital. She was found in a desolate area of the park, on the other side of some large rocks in a semi-conscious state," police said. "The name of the victim was not released."

The story continued, "The victim's family notified police about 10:30 p.m. since, they said, she normally would have returned home by 9 p.m. at the latest. Officers conducted a search directed by the precinct commanding officer, Captain Patrick Harnett.

" 'The search area covered a ten-block radius with emphasis on her route from the clothing store to her residence, Harnett said. 'Initially, it did not include Mount Carmel Park since the family of the victim was certain that she would never walk through the park at that hour by herself. But by 1 a.m., we extended our search to include the park.' " The article wrapped up with, "The victim is in serious but stable condition. Police have no witnesses or suspects at this time."

Toni eerily felt she'd seen that newspaper headline before, but how could that be? She was only eight years old then.

"What was the victim's name," Toni said and handed the article to Geddes not expecting an answer from him.

She then noticed a copy of a birth certificate for a Jeremiah Francisco born on May 21st, at Georgetown University Medical Center in Virginia. The birth certificate indicated his mother's name was Samantha Morales.

———

"And she said she had only the one daughter," Toni murmured. "No wonder she gave me that direct look when I asked if her daughter was her only kid. Father unknown. Hmm..." Toni started to get a bad feeling.

The first letter was dated August 29th.

Dear Manny,
I am at such a loss. I don't know what to do. I am just so sad that I am pregnant. The thought that I was impregnated is tearing me apart. I cannot have this child, Manny. I feel my only recourse is to have an abortion. I know this will upset you, but I just cannot have this baby. I just cannot do it. Thank you for all your help. I know it hasn't been easy for you either. I'm leaving for school tomorrow. I'll be in touch.
Samantha

"Holy Toledo, Geddes, Samantha Cohen was the rape victim," Toni said. "So, Father Manny was in touch with her right after she was raped, interesting. But what's this " '...I know it hasn't been easy for you either.' " "What's that mean? How was her rape tough on Father Manny?" Toni said and handed that letter to Geddes too. "So Samantha Cohen must be the mother of this kid born in Virginia, Jeremiah Francisco. The rapist's kid. What a mess."

September 17th
Dear Manny,
Thank you for your kind and considerate words. You're not judging me for my thoughts on having an abortion is greatly appreciated. I still cannot make a decision. I'm just so confused. I understand what you've written about the child growing within me is also a child of God, but thoughts of having this child are very, very upsetting. I also fear how the child will react if he one day learns how he was conceived. I pray constantly for guidance. Please pray for me.

99

Samantha

October 19th
Dear Manny,
Thank you for keeping me in your prayers. I respect your point of view. I feel that God would want me to have this child, but I just cannot bring myself to make that decision. I know that as time passes, it will be more difficult for me to have the abortion. If I had this child, I could not raise it. God forgive me, but I could not bear to look at this child's face. I'm sorry, Manny, but that's how I feel. God have mercy on me
Samantha

November 20th
Dear Manny,
Thank you for your continued kind words and prayers. Thank you for reminding me that God loves me. Manny, I've decided to have the baby. Your suggestion that the child could be turned over to the Franciscans Orphanage of Putnam County is what I want to do. Thank you for exploring this option, and for your gentle guidance throughout this ordeal. I could not have come to this decision without your help. I have resigned myself to it.
I intend to stay here in Georgetown and continue my studies. I expect that the baby is due sometime toward the end of my semester in May. I am seeing a doctor here who is affiliated with Georgetown University Medical Center where I will have the baby. I will contact you periodically as the day approaches. Have a peaceful Thanksgiving.
Samantha

Toni then started to read the copy of a letter dated May 25th, the following year, from Father Manny when he was still a seminarian to the Director of the Franciscan Orphanage.

Dear Father Joe:

As a follow-up to our conversation on May 12ᵗʰ, I want to inform you that a healthy baby boy was born on May 21st. The child was 9 lbs., 1 ounce. The mother has chosen to turn her child over to your orphanage. She is a loving young woman of God; however, under the circumstances in which the child was conceived, she does not believe it would be in the best interest of the child for her to raise him. It is her wish that the child does not know the identity of his parents, but be told that he was delivered to the orphanage after his parents were killed in a car accident. It is also her request that her child's family name be changed to one of your choosing.

I have assured her that you and your fellow brothers and sisters will provide him with the love and nurturing that any child of God deserves. Please let me know when I can deliver the child to your care and love.

The mother has named the child Jeremiah after the Old Testament prophet whose message brought her consolation during this very difficult time.

One With You in Christ
Manuel J. Gonzalez,
St. Joseph's Seminary
Yonkers, New York

May 29th
Dear Manuel:

I am in receipt of your May 25ᵗʰ letter. We are anxiously awaiting the arrival of Jeremiah. You may bring the child as soon as is convenient for you and his mother. Although it is not our custom to deceive a child delivered into our care when he comes of age, we do understand his mother's concerns and will respect her wishes.

Thank you for assuring her that her child will be provided with an abundance of love from all our brothers and sisters. Please inform her that she is always welcome to visit her son should she have a change of heart.

The child's family name will be Francisco, Jeremiah Francisco. Named after our St. Francis.

One With You in Christ

Father Joseph Egan
Director, Franciscan Orphanage of
Orange County

Toni and Geddes rose to leave. She carried the folder.

As soon as she got back in the car, she ran the name Jeremiah Francisco and date of birth on her iPad. It came back to an address on Pelham Parkway in the Bronx.

But the information that followed startled her: Under his name, date of birth and address was an asterisk.

"Whoa!" she blurted to Geddes. "Cohen's kid's on the job. He's a rookie on our job."

Following the asterisk were the initials: M.O.S. [Member of the Service]. Appointed to the department nine months earlier.

Toni and Geddes had taken a ride up to Jeremiah's place on Pelham Parkway. She rang his bell but there was no answer. They canvassed the area for his car but didn't spot it so they sat on his building for hours until finally giving up. Toni hesitated to call headquarters to find out where Jeremiah was assigned. She was afraid it would get back to Ryan.

CHAPTER 13

It was almost 10 p.m. Toni and Geddes were on their way to the strip club on West 44th Street. After four years as a Marine Corps M.P. and eight years in the department, not to mention being raised by her widowed-detective-father, Toni had developed a knack for sizing suspects up, and neither Ernesto Cruz nor Mateo Mateo gave her a flicker of that thing—that guilt thing—that either one was the shooter. They'd talk to the stripper Ernesto said he was with Sunday night, and check out Mateo's alibi anyway, but she knew neither one was her shooter. She just knew it.

When they pulled up in front of the Golden Dolphin, the street was quiet. The block was a strip of loading docks with trucks pulled into each of the bays for the night. The truckers started their day about 4 a.m., and quitting time for some would be as early as 2 p.m. This was the perfect time to grab a Budweiser at the Golden Dolphin and watch some female flesh prance in darkness to the sounds of music and imagine being with them.

There was always that chance, but most only managed to stagger home to seize the flesh of their unsuspecting wives and girlfriends (if they had someone to go home to) obsessed with the goddesses they'd watched just hours before. The loneliest ones slipped down to purchase the flesh of another or resigned to seizing their own flesh.

Toni led the way through the two golden doors into the vast, dark, air-conditioned space. The voice of Barry White flowed from the sound system massaging the audience. White, red and blue lights flashed and rotated, mirrors reflecting each other into infinity. A Latin beauty was dancing with her breasts exposed and the bottom half of her leopard design bikini intact. She was gyrating around a pole. A foul-pole, Toni thought. There were about sixteen men sitting at the horseshoe bar all coupled off.

It was a curious phenomenon to Toni how the mass of men that frequented strip clubs found it necessary to go with a buddy to sit with. Somehow, sitting alone to watch an exotic looking woman rotate her body seemed a little too needy and dysfunctional for these men, but going with another guy was like attending a sporting event. And she wouldn't be surprised if at least one or two of the spectators were off-duty cops allegedly working off the stress of the job.

Toni stepped to the bar and told the busty bleached-blonde barmaid in a white, see-through blouse, no bra and very short, tight jeans (jeans that were cut up so high the bottom third of her milky-white buttocks were exposed) that they were detectives and needed to speak with the owner or manager. The barmaid gingerly wiggled away on her four-inch, white stilettos to the back of the club. Nice shoes, Toni thought. A minute later she was back and told Toni and Geddes that the owner was in his office and would speak to them back there.

It turned out the stripper in the leopard bikini bottom — having an aerobic workout with the pole — was Ernesto's dancer, Cancun. The problem was they couldn't interview her until she got off at 11 p.m. Toni figured they could interview her at home the next day since it was expected she would only corroborate Ernesto's story, but Geddes thought it would be a better idea if they waited.

"Suddenly interviewing the stripper's urgent, Geddes," Toni said, with squinted eyes.

Geddes looked away.

There was no way she would hang out in that alleged "Gentleman's" club for ninety minutes.

"I want to go downtown," Toni said. "Follow-up on the original rape report and the shield."

"Go ahead, I don't need the car," Geddes said. "After I interview her, I'll take a cab home."

Toni took her partner in for an extra couple seconds.

"Yeah, sure," she said. "I'll be back," and slipped out en route to police headquarters in lower Manhattan.

Geddes kept Cancun under surveillance.

About twenty minutes later, Toni walked into One Police Plaza, clipped her I.D. card to the outside of her jacket, and took the elevator up to the N.Y.P.D. Criminal Records Division. She sat in front of a stand-alone computer and waited a couple of minutes for the *police administrative aide* to send her the file with all complaints received in the 51st Police Precinct twenty-three years earlier. Fortunately, she didn't have to look through all the complaint reports, which numbered over a thousand, thanks to the newspaper clipping in the folder Father Gribbons had given them. The date of the rape was Monday, August 7th.

She'd held the cursor down on the arrow to the right of the big screen, and each complaint report had flashed by in a blur from January 1st of that year. It gave her the same sensation she'd get traveling on the number 4 express not able to catch a clear look at the vanishing commuters on the passing stations. She slowed down when she got to the end of June, slowed down even more as the July complaints rolled by, and stopped — when she'd arrived at the first 51st precinct complaint for the month of August.

Cautiously, she scrolled until the first complaint report of August 7th, appeared on the screen scanning each one: Burglary 2nd Degree, Grand Larceny Auto; Assault 2nd degree, Assault 2nd degree again, Assault 3rd degree, Robbery 2nd degree, Child Endangerment 1st degree, Burglary 2nd degree; Arson 2nd degree, Manslaughter 1st degree; Criminal Mischief 2nd degree, then, there it was: Rape 1st Degree. She stopped.

The complainant/victim information read: "Samantha Morales, age 20, 440 Cedar Avenue, Bronx, New York 10454. The brief narrative: "At above time in Mount Carmel Park the above victim was allegedly raped by an unidentified male."

Unidentified male, Toni thought. So, she didn't know the rapist.

Toni knew the report submitted by the officer was purposely brief. The investigative follow-up reports would have details. The initial reporting officer's role had been to document that an alleged rape had occurred, get the victim to the hospital, and notify the detectives who were in the park because of the search, as noted in the report: "Detective Schimmel, 51 Squad on the scene; Captain Harnett, 51 C.O. on the scene; alleged victim transported to Jefferson Hospital via EMS."

The notation she read next really got her thinking. "Detective follow-up reports sealed as per court order."

Sealed?

After leaving the Criminal Records Division on the second floor of One Police Plaza with a hard copy of the rape report, she jumped on the elevator and shot up to the ninth floor to visit the Shield Desk. Although it was called a "desk," in fact, it was an office that kept a record of all shields issued to each of the thirty-eight thousand police officers in the N.Y.P.D., as well as I.D. cards.

The Shield Desk also was an archive of sorts concerning police shields history. In addition to identifying the name of the current holder of a particularly numbered police shield, it could also give the chronological history of which officers were assigned a specific shield over the previous hundred years or more. And, it kept a record of shields permanently retired because they'd been assigned to NYPD officers killed in the line of duty.

Toni pulled the silver-colored shield, commonly referred to as a "white shield," #6-7-0-2, (taken from Mateo Mateo) from the clear plastic evidence bag. The first thing she needed to know was whether it was an official shield or a duplicate.

"Did you know, detective, that duplicate shields are most commonly given to police officers upon their retirement by the various police unions at their monthly retirement dinners, regardless of rank," the gray-haired and sloth-like police administrative aide said, as if she was addressing a member of the community and not a member of the department."

"Really?" Toni said.

"That's correct. When an N.Y.P.D. police officer retires, his or her official shield is returned to the department. The retirement shields look exactly the same as an official shield, including the number, except the retirement shield is slightly smaller by as little as an eighth of an inch."

"Is that so?"

"That's correct."

The police aide put the white shield # 6-7-0-2 into a regulation shaped mold for white shields.

"Each police officer rank in the N.Y.P.D. had a different shaped and sized shield," the aide continued. "Most other police departments throughout the country issue the same shaped shield or badge with only the different ranks designated to each."

"How about that," Toni said.

It turned out shield # 6-7-0-2 was not regulation size; it was a duplicate. Toni then needed to know whether or not shield # 6-7-0-2 was actively assigned.

The Shield Desk aide tapped the four digits into her large-print keyboard. It turned out it shield # 6-7-0-2 was not currently assigned. Toni thanked the aide and was about to walk out the door when she turned around and said,

"Who had the shield last?"

The aide lumbered to a file cabinet and returned with an antiquated index card that listed each and every police officer ever assigned shield # 6-7-0-2. The last person it had been assigned to was a Police Officer Shawn Tripp who'd resigned from the department two years earlier.

"You know," the aide began, "a shield can be returned for several different reasons."

"Really?" Toni said. "What are the reasons?"

"The officer resigned, retired, was promoted and issued a different shield, died in service of natural causes, or, killed in the line of duty. No exact period of time needs to pass before reassigning it to a new police academy graduate."

"How about that."

"Yes, often a shield that had been returned would sit in the Shield Desk office for many, many years before being reissued."

"Really?"

"Oh, yes, it is also very common for a retired member of the department to call us here and request his or her shield be put on hold if a family member was joining the department or was on a promotion list, in which case that family member would be issued the very same shield at his or her academy graduation or promotion."

"Well, that's nice," Toni said.

"It is," the aide said. "And it is not uncommon in the N.Y.P.D. to have the same shield passed on for three or four generations of police officers within the same family: great-grandfather, grandfather, father, son or daughter."

"You don't say?"

"That's correct."

When Toni Santiago was promoted to detective, she'd been assigned the very same detective shield her grandfather and father had carried: Shield # 6-6-4.

Toni could not help asking to see the card herself. On the top of the index card, which had once been white but had turned a light brown over the decades, was the number 6-7-0-2 in bold letters with the following handwritten entries:

Robert Billheimer-Issued: 1/25/32: Retired: 2/14/53

Joseph Reinertson-Issued: 7/7/55; Promoted Detective: 3/6/67...

Eric Wilson-Issued: 3/19/69; Resigned: 4/3/70

Robert Mast-Issued: 7/6/71; Retired: 8/1/91

Ryan Condon-Issued 9/5/95: Promoted Sergeant: 6/29/05

"Holy shit," she whispered. "Ryan..."

CHAPTER 14

It was at the Cedar Avenue entrance to Mount Carmel Park where rookie cop Jeremiah Francisco met with her for the first time. It was very late that night. He'd been off-duty the last two days and was in jeans, a sweaty white polo shirt, and a blue blazer.

He wanted Samantha Morales-Cohen to show him where he'd been conceived. He wanted her to look him in the eye and detail how it happened. He wanted her to explain why she hadn't had the courage to keep him. And after she spilled her guts to him, he looked forward to telling her to go to hell, just as she'd once done to him.

That humid Wednesday had progressed into another sweltering South Bronx night. At first, not a leaf twitched on any tree in the park. But as he'd driven down the long hill of tenement-lined Cedar Avenue, the comatose leaves began to stir and suddenly the sky turned black and opened up, delivering a barraging downpour.

Some in the park didn't react to the sudden signs of torrential rain coming as if they could wish it away, but when pounding sheets reduced them to soggy forms, they barreled out too. The sweeping rain also drove everyone on the fire escapes off, except for one white-bearded old man who opened his arms wide to the elements, like Noah.

Jeremiah noticed the black, four-door BMW pull up on the park side with its wipers flapping away what it could, but the door didn't open until the downpour stopped as abruptly as it had started. It was then that Samantha approached him with a warm smile and brimming eyes. Jeremiah's heart yanked hard as he watched this mature, pretty woman in jeans, running shoes, and a Georgetown University sweatshirt gracefully walk up to him. He could hear her running shoes squeak in the wet pavement with every step. It was the first time he'd laid eyes on his mother.

But then she stopped cold as she scrupulously looked at his face from a few feet away. Tears had then begun to leak from her eyes. It took a few moments for her to get her composure so he gave her his handkerchief. After a few more moments she put out her two hands to take his, but Jeremiah stuffed his hands deep into the back pockets of his jeans like a baseball manager.

"Are you Samantha Morales?"

She slowly put her levitated hands down and said, "Yes, Jeremiah, I'm Samantha Morales. I'm your mother."

They stood looking at each other for several long moments before either of them spoke up again. Jeremiah was confused by her reaction to seeing him. It's not as if she couldn't have found him if she'd wanted to see what he'd looked like. "So, here I am," he thought. "Your bastard son."

"Are you going to tell me what happened?" Jeremiah said.

"Yes, of course," Samantha said as she looked around. "Can we go someplace else to talk Jeremiah? Do we have to stand out here in the open? It's late. Maybe we can talk in my car."

"No, right out here is good. We'll talk right out here," Jeremiah said with a dead stare. "This is where it all began, right?"

In that neighborhood, if someone mentioned he was going to Mount Carmel, he may need to say which Mount Carmel. The Mount Carmel of the Old Testament was named after a location in present-day Israel — said to have been a favorite place of the Old Testament prophet, Elijah. Some thought it was fitting that the park was named after Mount Carmel. Mount Carmel was said to mean "park" or "fertile ground." Except, many would say Mount Carmel Park was fertile ground for wickedness.

A patrolling precinct sector car stopped about a half a block away on the soaked street. Jeremiah knew they'd be running the license plate of the BMW. The cops would've learned that the BMW was registered to a Samantha Cohen, her age, address, that it had not been reported stolen, and that she had no outstanding warrants. The sector car then slowly came closer and from diagonally across the street continued to observe them. It then rolled up on them. The passenger side window went down.

"Everything okay?" the cop said.

Jeremiah didn't speak. Samantha's back was to them and hadn't noticed them pull up. She turned and in a friendly way said, "Yes, officer, we're fine. This is my son. We're just talking."

Jeremiah had parked his SUV a block away in a bus stop on Cedar Avenue. He'd walked to the Cedar Avenue park entrance and waited. Samantha had arrived fifteen minutes after he'd spoken to her on the phone. He'd found her number in the dead priest's Rolodex. She was shocked to hear his voice. She thought it was someone else at first but then knew who it was. She gasped when she had realized who it was.

When he said he wanted to speak to her at Mount Carmel Park, she did not hesitate. She said she lived in midtown Manhattan but would leave right away. She would be right there. She said she was glad he contacted her. That she should have reached out to him a long time ago. Yeah, sure, he thought.

The cops took in each of them — from one to the other and back again — without saying a word for a few moments; the one who asked the question looked away from Samantha and took a long look at Jeremiah, then looked back at Samantha.

"Your name, *Senora*?'

"Samantha Cohen," she said to the cop.

"Cohen?" the cop repeated.

"That's correct, officer," Samantha said. "Do you want to see my identification? I have it in my car."

The cop paused.

"That won't be necessary, *Senora*, but thank you."

The officer then looked back at Jeremiah and asked, "Do I know you?"

Without hesitation, Jeremiah said, "No, you don't."

"You look familiar to me," the same cop said.

Jeremiah did not reply but held his gaze.

Samantha spoke up again, "Officer." The cop abruptly turned to Samantha again. "I told you this is my son."

The officer paused and then nodded without another word.

Samantha and Jeremiah watched the red taillights of the sector car as it slowly rolled away down the slick, shining street.

Samantha then looked back at him. "I don't blame you for being angry with me."

Jeremiah did not reply. He took in a deep breath of the clean street and recently watered trees and grass, which delivered a comforting freshness.

"So are you going to show me where it happened?"

Samantha looked at her angry son; her only son.

Jeremiah noticed Samantha gazing at him, "Listen, I don't have all night."

"I see," she said and paused again.

Samantha's eyes began to fill. She crossed her arms and looked down at her sneakers. "Except..." she began and then stopped. Jeremiah waited for her to finish what she was about to say.

"Except what?"

She didn't respond right away. "Nothing, Jeremiah. I'll explain to you later."

Jeremiah turned away from her, walked into the park and said over his shoulder, "Show me where it happened."

CHAPTER 15

By the time Toni made it home, it was just after 1 a.m. It was never too late to pick up Vita at her aunt's apartment two floors below her own. Her aunt would be on her comforter listening often to Brahms as she waited for her detective-niece as she'd often waited for her detective-brother. Toni had called her on the way.

When Toni's mother died, her aunt had taken her place. She didn't know what she would have done without her aunt over the years. If it hadn't been for her *Tia*, she never could've dealt with the changing hours of the police work and kept her dog. And Toni knew she needed her dog. Aside from her aunt, it was the only other long-term relationship she had. Good thing for Toni that her aunt loved her forty-five-pound bulldog as much as she did.

And Toni wasn't a bad piano player because of her aunt. Her aunt had been a concert pianist with the Puerto Rico Symphony Orchestra, having performed all over the world: Geneva, Tel Aviv, Rome, Istanbul, Madrid, and New York's Carnegie Hall.

Fortunately for Toni, when she was growing up her aunt worked at home giving piano lessons. She'd never had children of her own and never married. So it was a joy for her to take care of Toni for her widower brother who worked those erratic police hours. And now her aunt was delighted to take care of Vita. Toni imagined if she ever married and had a daughter she would love for her aunt to teach her child to play too. Except, marriage was still nowhere in sight. Her pattern of disappearing from available men needed some maturation. Her misguided fling with Ryan Condon drove the point home.

It's not that Toni was promiscuous—far from it. In fact, before getting caught up with her boss, she hadn't been on a single date for almost a year. And the truth was her crossing that line to having sex with Ryan was not her pattern. She'd typically date a guy for months before having sex.

But also typical of her pattern was her need to move on as soon as the guy showed genuine interest in her. She would run for the hills. She would get frenetically lost in her cases; work horribly long hours—often unpaid hours—just to avoid whatever she was trying to avoid. Since the Montana Marine left her (eight years earlier at age twenty-two), she'd only dated two guys with huge chunks of time between where she didn't date at all.

Toni's aunt opened her apartment door. Her aunt was in her mid 70's. She was wearing a housedress.

"I'm sorry, *Tia*."

"Ay, child, it is no problem. You know that."

Vita was grunting, shaking and twirling at seeing Toni. "How's my big girl!" Toni said and bent down to hug her wiggling dog. Vita was a ball of activity as she tried to lick Toni's face.

"I feel like half a PB & J, and a cup of tea, how about you, child?" Her aunt said. She was her father's older sister by fifteen years. She'd been like a second mother to her father too.

Toni stood up.

"Sit," Toni said once, and Vita froze in the sitting position head locked, looking up at Toni with complete focus. "Yes, *Tia*, that would be great. *Gracias*."

Her aunt went into the kitchen and Toni took a seat at the dining room table. After leaving headquarters, Toni had gone back to the strip club to hook back up with Geddes and interview Cancun. She was satisfied Ernesto was with her at the time of the shooting and dropped Geddes off at his apartment after the interview.

115

From the dining room table, Toni watched her aunt grab two plates, open a loaf of wheat bread, pop two slices into the toaster, pull out a jar of Skippy peanut butter and strawberry jam from the refrigerator, prepare their sandwich, cut it in half, then into quarters, pull two boiling cups of water (both with the NYPD logo) from the microwave, dunk the Lipton tea bags a few times, and brought it over to the table. This was one of their comfort foods.

As they sat quietly munching on their half sandwiches and sipped their tea, Toni noticed the Monday *Daily News* sitting on her aunt's coffee table in the living room. She stared at the headline, "PRIEST EXECUTED' IN MOUNT CARMEL."

"So how is your work, child?" Toni's aunt was an amateur sleuth. She was a devoted fan of Agatha Christie mystery novels. And, in many ways, she did remind Toni of one of Christie's main characters, "Miss Jane Marple." She loved talking to Toni about the cases she worked on, which was not a surprise to her. When Toni was a little girl, she remembered how often Toni's father would sit at the dining room table with his big sister, drink coffee, and talk about his cases. And her aunt was never spooked by the details. Toni always figured that was because she'd had a lot of practice. Not only was her brother a detective but her father — Toni's grandfather — had been an NYPD detective too. When her grandfather had been discharged from the Army after WW II, he joined the NYPD, and her aunt was a curious little girl who'd always been bewitched by murder investigations. And she got a special thrill from discussing Toni's cases with her and offering an occasional insight that could be helpful. For Toni, it was the next best thing to having her father to talk through cases with.

Toni tipped her head to the *Daily News*. "That's my case, *Tia*."

Toni grabbed the newspaper from the coffee table and placed it on the dining room table for them both to see. After a few moments, she opened the paper to page three. There was a photograph of Father Manny taken when he was first assigned pastor of Mount Carmel years earlier. Toni started to read the story when something familiar about the headline struck her again.

"What a shame," her aunt said. "He had a nice face."

Toni flipped back to the front of the paper and focused on the headline again. What was it that was familiar about that MOUNT CARMEL rape headline she'd seen back at the rectory?

"I feel as if I've seen a headline like this before, *Tia*," Toni said. "I saw the same kind of MOUNT CARMEL headline earlier today for a rape that happened twenty years ago, and there was something very familiar about it. But how could that be, Tia? I was only eight when it happened. And I don't remember if I even knew if there was a Mount Carmel park or church in the Bronx at that time."

"Ah, huh. Ah, huh," she uttered. "Is that rape in that headline connected to the priest's murder?"

Toni looked at her for an extra moment. "We don't really know, Tia."

"Do you have a motive for the priest's murder?"

"Well, *Tia*, we're pretty sure it wasn't robbery, no money or property is missing, as far as we know. But there was one file cabinet left open, but we're not sure what if anything was taken.

"Could the shooter have planned to rob the rectory but panicked when he saw the priest and left after shooting him without taking anything?"

"Yes, *Tia*, but what robber wouldn't expect a priest or two to be in the rectory between 8 and 11 o'clock on a Sunday night?" Toni said, then looked at her aunt. "That's the estimated time of death."

"I see," her aunt said listening.

"We have the murder weapon," Toni said.

The time of death essentially eliminated Ernesto Cruz as the shooter. Toni and Geddes followed up on the times he claimed to be at the restaurant on City Island with his cousin and the owner. They both confirmed he was there during the evening.

Cancun the stripper admitted she'd noticed him come into the Golden Dolphin about 10 p.m. About 1 a.m. — after her last dance — she went to E. 110ᵗʰ Street with him before they went to her apartment. She said she thought he got out of the cab just to buy crack but was surprised when he came back with a gun in his waistband.

She was sure he didn't have the gun before they got to E. 110ᵗʰ Street. She'd had her hands all over his body on the way and there's no way she wouldn't have felt the gun, she'd said. The car service they'd taken from the Golden Dolphin to E.110ᵗʰ Street then to her apartment had a record of the pickup, drop-off, and stops. The driver was shown a photograph of Ernesto and confirmed he was the passenger and was with a woman who fit Cancun's description.

Mateo Mateo, on the other hand, had not as yet been able to give a reliable alibi for the time of the shooting. He claimed he was alone at his hi-rise apartment on E. 102nd Street and First Avenue from 6 p.m. until he walked over to E. 110ᵗʰ at 10:30 p.m. He said he'd made a few phone calls from his landline at home, which they'd be able to verify when they subpoenaed his Verizon records. But, Toni recognized, all that would prove was that calls were made from his apartment, not that he made the calls himself. But it was all he had. Speaking with whomever he claimed to have spoken to was on Toni's list of things to do.

He'd stolen the Glock from a drunk in the bathroom stall of an East Harlem bar between 11 p.m. and midnight. So, who was this tall clean-shaven drunk whom Mateo Mateo claimed he'd stolen the gun and shield from?

"So you have the murder weapon, but you don't feel you have the shooter," her aunt said. "Not yet, anyway."

Toni smiled at how much her elderly concert pianist aunt sounded like a cop herself. Her police detective inheritance had rubbed off on her quite a bit.

"That's right, *Tia*."

"Child," her aunt began. "What if the priest wasn't killed because of anything in his current life? Could it be he was killed for something that occurred a very long time ago? Something deep in his past that nobody in his present circles would have known about?"

That was exactly where she was afraid the investigation would lead.

"*Tia*," Toni said, "my boss, you know, Lieutenant Condon, grew up with the priest. They were lifelong friends."

"Really," her aunt said with wide eyes. "Such a small world."

"And, *Tia*," Toni continued, "He's taken more control of the investigation. I'm not sure if he wants me to dig deep into the case. It's the first time he's ever tried to put the brakes on me. I'm little worried where that's going to lead."

"I see," Toni aunt's said pensively.

"I wonder how *Papi* would have handled it?" Toni said.

Toni's deceased father had been a police officer for twenty-eight years, twenty-three as a detective. He'd had a reputation as one of the sharpest first-grade detectives on the job. Detective Joe Santiago cracked many a high-profile case in his day. He was tenacious. But what really made him dangerous—inside or outside the department—was his integrity and courage. He could not be influenced. Not by political connections or money or the threat of violence. He was formidable.

But what was also true — Toni and her aunt well knew because they lived it — was that he was a drunk. Very few knew that about her impregnable father. He was a very controlled drinker. Would not drink on duty ever, but when he signed-out, oblivion would find him. They didn't know that her father would sometimes splash a few with one or more of his partners after work, but then he'd call it a night and drift away to some dive to drink in the way in which he needed.

From her early teens on, Toni would sometimes get a call from a bar owner letting her know her father couldn't make it home on his own. She'd throw on a pair of sweats, grab a cab and walk into the bar to retrieve her old man. Often the owner would hand her his loaded .38 being held for him behind the bar. Invariably when she tapped on his shoulder to rouse him from his cave of escape, he would say, "Toni! My baby girl!"

As disappointed and secretly ashamed of her father's condition she was, she loved hearing him say that. She loved him deeply.

Three years earlier, at the age of fifty-four, after he'd been retired only a little over a year, Joe Santiago was killed by a hit-and-run driver one early morning as he swayed to another bar just before closing time. The killer was never identified.

"*Tia*, there's something else," Toni said not able to look into her aunt's eyes. "I've been with my boss. I've slept with him. I've been in Bronx Homicide for two years," Toni looked up at her aunt, "and two weeks ago I slept with him. I had too much to drink. But that's not really it. That's not the real reason. I always found him such a good-looking man and such a leader. I think I put him up on some pedestal like he was some kind of Greek God or something."

Toni had made a murder arrest of a senior-citizen numbers-man. He'd been wanted for killing a Bodega owner he thought shorted him of his fair share of the policy action the owner had taken-in over time. There were no witnesses, but Toni had gotten a call from a mentally challenged man named Rudy whom (a few months earlier) she'd seen getting mugged at knifepoint on a side street alleyway as she'd been heading back to the precinct. She terminated the robbery with her Tazer, and Rudy was very grateful.

As it turned out Rudy sometimes mopped floors at the social club the numbers-man hung-out at and was mopping the back room when the numbers-man bragged about taking out the Bodega owner to a few of his crew. It was a good collar for her and another clearance for the squad.

After she'd dropped the prisoner off at Bronx Central Booking and drew up the murder complaint with the A.D.A. on duty, it was about 4 a.m. when she'd got back to the squad room to sign out. It was quiet and desolate, except for one person who'd decided to stick-around: Lieutenant Ryan Condon.

Ryan had been with Toni when she made the arrest. To both of their surprise when the numbers-man walked out of the social club about 1 a.m., and they approached, instead of just letting them take him, which is what they expected from a senior-citizen numbers man — even one wanted for homicide — he ran. And when Toni and Ryan chased after him and turned the corner he'd just turned down, the number's man fired one shot at them. To which Toni could not help shouting in bafflement,

"What the hell are you doing?"

With Toni's outburst, the numbers-man suddenly dropped the gun as if he'd just come to his senses.

So when Toni got back, they were both still hyped from almost getting shot three hours earlier. Ryan invited Toni for a drink. Trouble was it was already after 4 a.m. and the bars were closed. So, they decided to pick-up a six-pack and cruise around in Ryan's department car. They bantered about the arrest, with the windows of the Ford wide-open, and breathed in the humid neighborhood. It was another sultry night; the early morning hour did nothing to cool off the streets.

They found themselves, at first, driving around Toni's childhood Fordham neighborhood, ironically like they were on patrol. Toni pointed out the elementary and junior high schools she'd attended. Within forty-five minutes they had each drunken three beers, grabbed another six, and knocked those off too.

Toni was feeling euphoric as they replayed over, and over again how stunned they were when the numbers-man shot at them.

Ryan thought they should jump on the Bruckner Expressway and head to the Northeast section of the Bronx, the Pelham Bay area; go to Orchard Beach and watch the sunrise. By 5:15 a.m. they were cruising through the tunnel of trees on the Pelham Bay Park roadway when Ryan confused Toni and bore right following the sign to the NYPD Pistol Range on Rodman's Neck, instead of the beach.

"Where you going, boss," Toni half-slurred. "You heading to the range?"

Ryan didn't say a word; he looked at Toni and smiled warmly with his brown, eyes, and kept driving. A smile she'd never seen before. Within minutes he'd pulled into one of the many open parking spaces about 100 feet from the police booth, at the gated entrance of the range, manned by a uniformed cop twenty-four hours a day.

He shut off the engine and kissed Toni. She pushed him back, looked at him for several long moments, then pulled him in and kissed him back. Within minutes Ryan straddled Toni, and the rest is history. Little did the cop in the booth know that he'd provided the security, and the dark provided the privacy for a Budweiser-induced muster of a couple of New York's Finest.

The following late afternoon, when Toni signed-in for her 4:30 to 1 a.m. tour, she went right for the coffee maker and poured herself a cup. She breathed in its aroma hard hoping it would help clear her still fogged-up head. Ryan stepped out of his private office, put his mug out in front of her, looked down at her. His look seemed to say, "Sorry about that."

When it was almost to the rim, he looked at her again, which distracted her, and it spilled over his hand. He switched the cup to his dry hand and walked back into his office shaking off his wet hand without another word.

If it weren't for that small acknowledgment, Toni wouldn't have been sure anything happened the morning before. And if they'd never ever talked about it, that would've been okay with her. She wanted to pretend it hadn't happened.

She knew time passes too quickly to waste it with a married man, a married man she could not trust; a deceptive married man. But what married man who cheats on his wife isn't deceptive. And if deception is the number one trait of a man who cheats on his wife, what is the number one trait of the woman with whom the man cheats?

Shame, she'd thought to herself. Shame.

"That was a big mistake, *Tia*. I don't know how to handle this. And he's married, *Tia*. I must've been out of my mind."

"You want to know what I think your *Papi* would say?" her aunt said with a forgiving but determined gaze. "I think he would say to use caution, but there was no doubt you must find out more about your superior's relationship with the priest. I think he would tell you that it might be messy, but wherever the chips fall is where they fall. He would tell you not to draw any conclusions, just search for the truth. He would remind you that that is what a detective really is—a seeker of the truth."

Toni broke a smile. She had loved listening to her father talk about his work. He would describe the detective's role in a simple and clear way.

"I think he'd remind you that as the case detective it is your responsibility to bring the murderer to justice, whoever it is."

Toni continued to listen.

"He would recommend, I think, you share your thoughts with no one, including your partner for the time being. Sometimes, you remember, your *Papi* would say, the pursuit of the truth is a lonely business.

"Remember when a detective in your *Papi's* very own detective office was hired to commit a murder in Denver, Colorado, by a Brooklyn drug dealer. How surreal it must've been when the detective got off the plane at JFK and saw your *Papi* alone waiting for him. How their eyes must've locked, the detective instantly knowing that your *Papi* was there to arrest him. Most any other policeman would have let those people in Internal Affairs make the arrest, but not your *Papi*. He got the call, and a killer was a killer as far as he was concerned."

Toni nodded, finished her sandwich and washed it down with her tea.

"Thank you, *Tia*."

Toni got up, went to the kitchen sink and started to wash her plate.

"Leave that child," her aunt said. "You don't have to do that."

In fact, each time Toni ever began to wash a dish or glass or a cup her aunt would always say that same thing. And Toni's answer would always be the same too.

"I don't mind, *Tia*." It was their ritual.

"By the way," her aunt said to Toni from the dining room table. "I think your *Papi* had a case in Mount Carmel Park some years ago. I think a young girl was raped."

Toni froze. "Really?"

CHAPTER 16

Toni took Vita for a short walk before she raced back to her apartment building.

So her aunt thought her father had a case in Mount Carmel. When could that have been? What kind of case was it, if he had? It couldn't have been the rape of Samantha Cohen. He wasn't a detective yet then. But he was on patrol in the same precinct at the time of the rape.

She found herself repeating over and over the two headlines in her head:

"PRIEST EXECUTED IN MOUNT CARMEL;
CO-ED RAPED-MOUNT CARMEL PARK;
PRIEST EXECUTED IN MOUNT CARMEL;
CO-ED RAPED-MOUNT CARMEL PARK."

She started to again feel overwhelmed with the sense she'd in fact seen the headline before. But when? Where?

Then it came to her with a rush.

Sometime after her father's funeral — three years earlier — she was working through his things when she'd found a shoebox he'd kept with some mementos of his police career. Amongst other stuff, the box contained some newspaper articles. One of the headlines had the words, Mount Carmel. She didn't think anything of it at the time and sure wasn't ready to read any articles her father had saved.

Vita finished her business and Toni pulled her stocky body back into the building; jumped on the elevator and up to her fifth-floor apartment. As soon as she stepped in, Vita slopped up some water from her bowl, went to her basket, and curled up. Toni absent-mindedly reached to put Vita's chain on the hook by her front door, but it clattered to the floor without her noticing, and trotted to her bedroom.

She yanked her bedroom closet door open and stared up at the shelf that easily had forty pairs of her shoes. Four rows, ten boxes per row, which almost touched the closet ceiling. The boxes were red, gray, green; each marked with a handwritten label announcing what type of shoes were enclosed: "Black Pump w/Buckle Strap," "Funky Mid Heel," "Low Black Ankle Boot," "Fabulous Black Stiletto Slides w/White Piping on Top," "Low Black Italian Loafer with Tassel."

She grabbed a stepladder and pulled down the boxes one row at a time. She started with the row to the extreme right. She knew the box she was looking for, plainly marked "PAPI," was at the corner of the closet. She just couldn't remember which corner.

After pulling down about twenty pairs of shoes, which now filled the oval carpet on her bedroom floor, she found the box she was looking for. Toni pushed boxes away to make room, sat down and crossed her legs. She had not opened that box since her father was killed. She again thought about his killer.

Toni wanted the hit-and-run driver who robbed her father's life to be brought to justice, but she couldn't shake the thought that her father may have been more at fault than that driver. She imagined in the early morning hours of that fateful night her father was stumbling from the bar into the street, and the happenstance driver didn't see him. Could she blame the driver for taking off? You bet! In a perfect world, the driver should have stayed until the police arrived. But if the driver had waited for the police, his life would have been thrown into a tailspin too, especially if he'd had a few drinks himself.

She couldn't deny the findings of the Accident Investigations/Reconstruction Unit or the Medical Examiner's toxicology report. Her father had been struck with such force that his body had been boosted into the air, and plunged like a javelin over the top of the unidentified car and landed on his head in the middle of that midtown Manhattan Avenue. His skull had been crushed.

No ambulance could have saved him. His blood/alcohol level was 0.28. It was a typical alcoholic's death. Woefully, one she'd feared would come to her father one day.

But what did gnaw at her badly, real bad, real, real, bad…was that the driver never called 911 for an ambulance after he'd fled the scene. He didn't even make an anonymous call. He just took off and left her bleeding and mangled father on the street.

She carefully took the lid off the box. It not only had newspaper articles but other mementos of her father's police career and military service. The duplicate gold detective shield #664, which was given to him when he retired, a collection of his activity logs stacked neatly on one side of the box; various police medals including the Police Combat Cross; 5-1 Precinct and DB (Detective Bureau) collar brass for his uniform shirts; his dog tags from his two tours in Vietnam with the U.S. Army Special Forces, plus a Purple Heart and two Silver Stars.

She placed the medals and other mementos on the coffee table and began to pull out the newspaper articles, which were neatly folded, one at a time. "THE GIRL IN THE CARDBOARD BOX" was the headline of the first she grabbed. The petite victim was found in a cardboard box and dumped on a deserted industrial South Bronx street. A couple of days later a follow-up article had a picture of her father and his partner walking the handcuffed murderer into the precinct.

128

Another headline, "OFF DUTY DETECTIVE FOILS BANK ROBBERY." Another, "ROOKIE COP'S PERSEVERANCE SOLVES 20-YEAR-OLD MURDER."

Another article was titled, " INSIDE THE BROOKLYN BRIDGE, A WHIFF OF THE COLD WAR. It had something to do with fallout shelters set up in the City during the Cuban Missile Crises.

She lifted another article, unfolded it. There it was! "CO-ED RAPED-MOUNT CARMEL PARK."

Then it all came back to her. She was indeed only eight years old at the time. It was a weekday summer morning, she was still on summer break, and her father was still a uniformed cop. He'd just gotten home from working a midnight to eight shift at the 51st precinct. Her dad had brought home the Tuesday morning *New York Post* and was lying on his stomach, head at the foot of his bed, arms hanging over, reading the paper spread out on the wood floor. Toni climbed on his back, as she had since she was a very little girl, and looked at the paper over the top of his head. It was the first time the headline of a newspaper covered an incident that happened in her father's precinct — but on that morning it had.

" 'Where's Mount Carmel Park, *Papi*' " she now distinctly remembered asking.

" 'Far from here, Baby-Girl.' "

"Wow! Isn't this something?" Toni now muttered as she held the article in her hands.

Her father must've been involved in some way, but he said nothing as she was sprawled on his back that morning. It was not something he wanted to discuss with his eight-year-old daughter. But he must've been involved in some way, she thought again. Why bother saving the article if he hadn't. She had never read the article. She just remembered being captured by the headline.

There was a notation in her father's handwriting on the edge of the clipping. "Victim…Georgetown University."

She went back to her living room gripping the article and slumped into her sofa. Absently she stared at a framed copy of Norman Rockwell's "Runaway." It hung above the mantle of her apartment's pseudo fireplace.

It depicted a state trooper with his high, shiny black leather boots sitting at the counter of a diner alongside an eight-year-old boy-runaway upon whom he was looking down to with sage eyes. The runaway was looking up at the trooper with wide eyes. Both their backs were to the viewer. In the background, the diner counterman in his white shirt smiles down at the youngster. The broad back of the trooper always reminded Toni of her father's broad back. Her father had hung the Rockwell in her bedroom soon after her mother's sudden death when she was four years old. It made her feel safe.

It then struck her that when she'd pulled the rape complaint report at One Police Plaza that night, she'd never bothered to check who the reporting officer was. At the time it didn't matter. She knew that whatever uniformed cop took the initial complaint would only be a formality, and would likely not have any bearing on the investigation. It was whatever detective worked the case that would have mattered most, and the follow-up investigation. But, curiously, there were no follow-up investigation reports in the database.

She then grabbed her copy of the report from the case folder scanning down to the very bottom to see who took the report.

"Holy crap," she whispered, but Vita's head shot straight up anyway. The report had been prepared by P. O. Jose O. Santiago, shield # 7623.

"*Papi* took the report. *Papi* was there."

Toni leaned back again, deeper into her sofa and looked back up into the Rockwell, falling deeper and deeper into thought. It was just after 2 a.m. when her iPhone rang.

"Hello?"

"It's Sergeant Tazzo."

"What's up sarge?"

"We got another homicide. Mount Carmel Park. Crime Scene—

"In the park!" Toni said, cutting Tazzo off.

"Yeah, female victim, that's all I know. Crime Scene, the M.E., and the lieutenant are on the way. Give Geddes a call. I want both of you over there. I'm on my way too."

"You got it," Toni said.

She slowly placed the phone down on her coffee table and whispered, "Holy shit!"

CHAPTER 17

When Ryan arrived at the homicide scene in Mount Carmel Park, Vic Tazzo was there; he'd gotten there about fifteen minutes before. Tazzo walked him over to the body behind the rock and told him the deceased was an apparent female but her face was smashed beyond recognition. Her jeans found a few feet away did not contain identification. Ryan looked down at the figure and recognized a strawberry shaped birthmark on the inside of her left thigh.

Ryan turned away from the body, stepped a few feet away, bent over, and threw-up.

"I got to leave. You've got this Vic. I'll give you a call on the cell."

"You all right, Loo?" Tazzo said and leaned down to Ryan still bent over.

"I'll give you a call on the cell."

Ryan jumped into his department car and pulled out of the park.

As soon as Toni pulled up over the curb through one of the south side entrances to Mount Carmel Park in her Jetta, she could see the glittering police lights firing from over a hill to the west. There had been a torrential downpour a couple hours before, and the lights glistened against the glass-like asphalt path, and silver-drop leaves and grass. It looked to her as if it could be mistaken for dusk just after the sun lulls behind the horizon, except the lights, gave a staccato rhythm, not a steady orange or red glow.

She slowly drove down the wide path to another narrower passageway, with a steep incline in the direction of the lights. When she got to the top, she could see the emergency vehicles below that generated all the lights. Marked and unmarked police cars, an ambulance, a Crime Scene van, and a police Emergency Service truck the size of a fire truck that delivered a massive beam of white light illuminating them all. She decided to get out of her gunmetal gray Jetta on top of the hill and walk down to the crime scene.

As she went down the narrow, fenced path, she noticed the back of a wide, glacier-like rock that began low and rose up very high like a miniature ski slope. She could still not see any of the police or medical personnel on the scene or the victim because they were all obstructed by the massive rock.

"This mutt knew how to pick his spots," she whispered.

She'd thrown her running shoes on when she'd left her apartment, which was a good thing because she had to jump over the fence onto the wet grass and mud to get down to where the others were mingling behind the glacier rock.

She got to the corner of the rock and took in what she saw before stepping up to the others. A crime scene detective was flashing photographs. A group of uniform cops was assembled in a column, slowly inching forward, sweeping the white-beams of their flashlights over the ground for physical evidence. The victim had a slim figure and was nude from the waist down; her jeans were crumpled a few feet away to one side, her white running shoes tossed nearby, as were her panties. Toni wondered if the victim had rushed out of the house to meet someone as she just had.

The victim was wearing a white tank top; her face was up against the bottom of the flat side of the rock; only a small amount of blood could be seen. After the crime scene detectives took enough photographs of the victim in that position, the medical examiner slowly turned the muddy body over.

The victim's face had been crushed against the rock; flattened and caked in blood and mud.

Toni surmised that the killer had grabbed her hair and repeatedly smashed her face against the rock until her body submitted to his desires. Toni walked slowly, closer to the victim and looked down on her. The stench of that corner of the rock struck her first. It was not from the crime victim herself, she knew that right away, but from the saturated dirt against the rock that had been steadily urinated on over time. The downpour earlier had no freshening effect on the stench. Toni let out a breath of sadness over that human being's face being ground into it.

Her blood had poured down onto the front of her white tank top turning it burgundy. Toni then noticed one of the crime scene detectives lean down and pick up a sweatshirt a few feet away, and hold it up like he worked in a cleaner, turning it from one side to the other, to get a better look at it. The letters on the front of it read: "GEORGETOWN UNIVERSITY." A chill went up Toni's back.

"What do you think?" a voice behind her said.

Startled, Toni turned, "Oh, hey sarge."
"Patrol found her about an hour ago. Unidentified female called 911 said there was a woman's body behind a rock. Said she thought she was dead and hung up."

"Where's the Loo?" Toni said.

"He had to leave," Sergeant Tazzo said and walked to the other side of the body.

"Ah huh," Toni said. "No I.D. on her?"

"No," Tazzo said. "You see the sweatshirt: Georgetown University. Not a lot of Georgetown sweatshirts being worn in the South Bronx these days, don't you think?"

Toni got that bad feeling again. She remembered her father had scribbled on the old *Daily News* article that the rape victim attended Georgetown University.

"No, I guess not," Toni said, keeping her eyes fixed on the body.

Crime Scene detectives continued to take photographs and video of the scene and collected the physical evidence they'd discovered or whatever the uniforms brought to their attention. They used rubber gloves to retrieve and deposit the items into plastic, or, paper bags depending on the evidence, then sealed and marked the bags, and logged each one in.

"Rape for sure, maybe robbery too," Tazzo said. "Maybe he took off with her purse if she was carrying one."

"Did the lieutenant seem okay when he was here?" Toni said, looking up at the sergeant.

"Yeah, fine," Tazzo said, without looking at Toni.

A uniform cop handed him a Dunkin-Donuts coffee with a lid. "You want a cup?" Tazzo said to Toni.

"No thanks."

"So, what do you think?" Tazzo said.

She looked around before speaking and then said, "Raped for sure. Or somebody wanted it to look like rape the way he threw around her clothes and underwear."

"We'll know after the autopsy," Tazzo said.

"Right."

One of the Crime Scene detectives approached and showed them a clear plastic evidence bag that had two spent shell casings.

Tazzo said, "What caliber?"

Nine millimeter," the detective said. "We missed them at first. They were hidden in a grass patch a few feet from the body."

Tazzo nodded.

The deputy medical examiner: a short Asian man in his thirties with glasses, approached.

"What's it look like, Doc?" Tazzo said.

"Two shots: One to the front of the kneecap, the second to the bottom of the back of the head, exited out the front of the face. The shot to the knee went clean through and out the back. It appears the assailant shot the deceased in the knee first to disable, then committed an assault."

The M.E. squinted as he adjusted his glasses.

Toni found it interesting how the M.E. referred to her not as "her." It was: 'one to the front of the kneecap', not 'her' kneecap, 'exited out the front of the face" not 'her' face. Toni figured everybody had his or her own way of staying detached. Toni half expected the M.E. would refer to her as an 'it" next, instead of the deceased.

"Or at least that's a possibility," the M.E. continued. "I'll let you know if she was sexually assaulted after the autopsy. But then the assailant—either before or after the possible assault—struck her face up against that rock innumerable times then fired that final shot into the back of her head."

Toni said, "What about the spent rounds?"

One of the Crime Scene detectives displayed another plastic bag containing one mangled spent round.

"We dug this one out of the dirt under her head. Looks like the shooter just popped her as she laid flat. Probably unconscious after taking that pounding against the rock like the doc said. The round she took to the knee we haven't come up with."

"If she was standing with her back against the rock when the shooter fired," Toni said, "it probably shattered against the rock after going through her knee."

"That's what we're thinking," the Crime Scene detective said. "We'll take another look in daylight."

"Good," said Tazzo.

They all remained silent for a couple of seconds—eyes fixed on the body—as if they'd agreed to take a moment to reflect on the tragedy of the deceased's demise or maybe say a private prayer.

The M.E. and the Crime Scene detectives then drifted back to their work.

Toni spoke up. "Robbery's possible, but I don't think so. Maybe the perp. took her purse or whatever she was carrying, if she was carrying anything, as an afterthought, but it wasn't his main thing," Toni said.

"And not very likely she would have been dragged into the park from the street without somebody noticing. It was still too early; must've been a few people on the street even though it was pouring a short while before. Someone would have seen something. Looks like she was in the park willingly. Since she's probably not from the neighborhood, looks like she came here to meet someone and it just went bad. Somebody she knew and maybe even trusted."

"Drug deal?" Tazzo said.

"Maybe," Toni said. "You know Samantha Cohen was raped in this park twenty-three years ago," said Toni.

"What?" Tazzo turned to Toni. "The lawyer?"

"Yeah. My old man worked out of this precinct back then. He took the complaint report. She was attending Georgetown at the time."

"You sure about that?" Tazzo asked.

"It was Samantha Cohen all right; then Samantha Morales. I picked up a copy of the initial report at Criminal Records a couple hours ago."

"Hmmm," Tazzo said.

"What sarge?" Toni said.

"Nothing." Tazzo looked away in thought as the M.E. personnel then slowly lifted the body—now with a tag on its toe—and placed it into the long plastic bag and zipped it up.

They both then turned when they sensed someone approach.

"How's it going, Sarge?" a disheveled Detective John Geddes said when he finally arrived on the scene, breathing heavy.

"Hey, Toni," Geddes said, sneaking a glance at her.

137

She greeted Geddes, but Tazzo just looked him over. One hour passed since Toni had gotten there; two hours since she had notified Geddes.

"Sorry I'm late," Geddes said as he fidgeted with getting his shirt back into his jeans.

That was always a challenge for Geddes, Toni knew very well, even when he hadn't just rolled out of his First Avenue studio apartment. After all, they'd been partners for the last two years and when you work that long with the same partner you get to know more details of their lifestyle than you really need.

Geddes was captivating to many women because of his tall, chiseled physique and deep blue eyes, but he never did anything for Toni. She couldn't get around his absent-minded nature and general sloppiness. But she loved the big lug, nevertheless, no doubt about it, the way a little sister loves her big brother. And when he wanted to be, he was one sharp detective.

When Toni had called Geddes at his Upper East Side studio apartment to let him know that they were being summoned to another crime scene, Geddes's response had been, "Shit!" which meant to Toni—reading between the lines—that he probably had one of his assorted flight attendants in the sack with him, which mildly surprised her. She didn't think Geddes had had enough time to pick up a new hostage from Mickey's in so short a time.

Mickey's was the bar embedded on street level in the four-story walk-up in which he lived, and a popular hangout for New York's Finest and their groupies. And, as she thought about it, he didn't mention he was meeting anybody after work, which he would routinely share with her.

When they'd gone off-duty about three hours earlier—after talking with the stripper Ernesto Cruz had spent the night with in Washington Heights, and after making a couple other short- stops and she dropped him off at his place—he said he was calling it a night.

But when it came to targeting a temporary occupant for his bed he was the self-proclaimed master. Ever since Geddes's divorce nine months earlier, after fifteen years of marriage, just about anything resembling hips had the potential for him.

Toni could not help but squint whenever she imagined lumberjack Geddes looking up at the butt of his latest conquest as she stepped gingerly up the ladder to his cozy loft bed. Then she had a semi-staggering thought. Don't tell me he invited Cancun home: Ernesto's stripper.

"I had a little trouble getting out of the apartment," Geddes said with wide eyes.

Tazzo turned his attention from Geddes and said to Toni, "All right, that's it for tonight. Zero-800, M.E.'s office. You're catching this homicide too Toni. You all right with that?"

"Yes, sir."

He then shifted his attention back to Geddes. "You think you can make it to the office by eight, Geddes?"

Geddes was mum; he stood there looking down on the sergeant with his puppy dog expression.

Geddes then found his voice. "Oh, yeah, sure, Sarge, listen I'm sorry, Sarge, but—

Sergeant Tazzo gave him a look of hopelessness and walked away.

Toni and Geddes watched him jump in his department car and pull out of the park.

Toni then headed to her Jetta without uttering a word.

Geddes was left standing there.

"What?" He shouted to Toni's back. "What?"

Toni turned and waited for him to catch up to her and said, "Geddes, Geddes, you dog, you dog. You really need to be crated."

"What?" Geddes repeated.

"The stripper!"

Geddes did not reply.

139

It was 5 o'clock the same morning. Ryan was sitting at home in the darkness of his quiet study surrounded by a collection of photos and mementos of his police and family life. He'd just put away his seventh bottle of Budweiser.

A white light from the street lamp squeezed through the uneven spaces between the dangling tree leaves on his property, and spread over the wall of plaques—with the NYPD logo—for outstanding police service and acts of heroism like blotches of mud.

On one bookcase shelf was a framed photograph of him and his squad of detectives (including Toni) at their last Christmas party; a photograph of him and Jocelyn in St. Peter's Square in Rome taken during their honeymoon; a rosary given to him by Manny hanging off the corner of a photograph of him and Manny in their fourth grade school uniforms at Mount Carmel school.

He couldn't believe Samantha was dead. He'd been with her the evening before. How had he let himself get caught up in such a doomed situation? Why did he ever agree to have coffee with her, to begin with? He knew—deep down he knew—it could lead to disaster. That all he'd been trying to hold onto—his marriage, his career—could vanish, but he just couldn't help himself. Every part of his mind was telling him to stay away from her, and every other part of him longed to be with her.

The mistake he'd made with Toni at the range was because of booze and loneliness in both of their cases. He knew that. He believed Toni knew that. Toni was a mistake, a huge mistake. And, in fact, it was the first time he'd ever been with another woman since his marriage to Jocelyn.

But Samantha, for him, was something completely different. He just couldn't help but accept Samantha's invitation to go to her apartment, even with the almost certain knowledge that it could destroy all of their lives. He couldn't help texting back, " 'ok' " when she asked him to promise not to change his mind. He just couldn't resist her pull. He just couldn't wrench himself out of her spell. He was at a loss.

Where the hell does such a drive come from? That damned drive that leads to only one place.

"Sam's dead," he whispered, shaking his head. "Sam's dead."

Jocelyn wasn't home. She'd left a note for him on the kitchen counter that she would be spending the night at her mother's home in Valley Stream. She would never know that he'd been with Samantha. Ryan knew she couldn't have imagined he'd do that to her. If she ever found out, she'd never forgive him. He knew that.

"Mercy, Father, Mercy," he repeated from where he sat in the dark corner, curled forward, elbows on his knees, face in his hands. He picked up the eighth bottle of Bud from the wood floor and guzzled long and hard, put the empty bottle back on the floor, and leaned back into the thick, leather chair.

"When did I become so weak?"

He looked at the plaques on the wall directly across from him and watched the blotches of mud dance over them for a long time.

He looked up at the ceiling and whispered, "Show me the way, Father. Help me find Sam's killer. Help me to find Manny's killer. Please show me the way." He stayed seated without moving for some time, both arms stretched out on the arms of the chair.

Finally he slid onto his knees, in slow motion, like a camel, working his way down, hands clasped together, forehead landing on the wood floor with a soft thud, and after several minutes said, "Please forgive me. Please forgive me."

Toni cruised up the Henry Hudson Parkway, headed back to her North Riverdale apartment absorbed by the image of the female body with the Georgetown sweatshirt that had been pummeled and shot up against that glacier rock.

Once Crime Scene and the M.E. rapped up, and the body was removed, Toni knew Sergeant Tazzo wouldn't keep her or Geddes out any longer. They could all try to get a couple of hours of sleep before the investigation kicked into high gear at 8 a.m. As the case detective, Tazzo directed Toni to start her day at the M.E.'s office on First Avenue to identify the body, and witness the autopsy.

She knew it was a long shot to think the victim was Samantha Cohen just because of the sweatshirt, but she couldn't help herself. And if it was, she wondered, what the hell would've driven her to go back to the same place she'd been raped twenty years before; and late at night, no less. It just couldn't be, she thought. But Ryan had to suddenly leave the scene. Not that it was against department procedure to leave a sergeant in charge of a crime scene, but a rape and murder in a city park of an unidentified woman was major news. He was the C.O. of the Bronx Homicide Squad, for crying out loud.

Why did he leave? Did he recognize the body? Why didn't he tell Tazzo he wanted Geddes or another detective in the squad to catch the case: not her. Especially after Ryan put limits on her with the priest's homicide. But if he was in shock — potentially recognizing it was Samantha Cohen crushed against that rock — it just dissolved from his mind. And Tazzo, the ranking detective supervisor on the scene, recognized a possible connection between the Mount Carmel rectory and park murders, and made the decision. Toni was glad he had.

CHAPTER 18

Toni got to the M.E.'s office at 7:55 a.m. Wednesday morning. The body of Samantha Cohen was exposed on the stainless steel table, under the bright fluorescent lights, ready to be further undone. The layer of blood and mud caked to her body had been washed away. The odor of antiseptic death engulfed the classroom-size room. The deputy medical examiner — the same doctor who was on the scene a few hours earlier — was at the large stainless steel sink off to the side washing his hands.

It made Toni wonder for a second what the point of that was. He wasn't about to do surgery. It wasn't as if contaminating the body could make things worse. He was just going to invade her body, invade her body as if her body hadn't been invaded enough. Toni didn't think that clean hands were all that important. She suddenly shook her head hard, like Vita would when a fly found its way into her ear. It stopped that non-detached interior monologue cold.

"You okay, detective," the doctor said looking up and over his half-moon glasses.

"I'm fine, Doc. Do your thing."

In her two years in homicide, Toni had seen enough autopsies to gain a well-developed professional detachment to it all. It's not that it had become routine, but like any other homicide detective, whenever she had to identify a body (as the one she'd observed stabbed, or shot, or bludgeoned to death, at the crime scene the night or day before), over time she'd lost interest in watching. All she needed to know was the cause of death. Except, this morning she'd chosen to watch.

The masked deputy medical examiner did his excavation with precision, slicing cleanly and efficiently, as he removed this or that, cutting here and there, as he spoke into the mic suspended above the body. Flashes of light occasionally reflected off the scalpel into Toni's eyes.

Toni had heard all those routine pronouncements before, and wasn't interested, but she finally heard part of what she needed to:

That semen was discovered inside the victim's vaginal cavity that would be submitted for DNA analysis. Whichever living and breathing monster matched it could be the killer. Except, there was one problem: the deceased's vaginal wall had no signs of trauma.

Interesting, Toni thought.

One hour later, Toni was driving north on the FDR Drive back to Our Lady of Mount Carmel to attend Father Manny's funeral. Traffic was light heading northbound at that late morning hour, but southbound traffic was still tight as the final battalion of cars piled into Midtown and lower Manhattan.

Toni's iPhone rang, "Yeah,"

"Toni, it's Bill Gordon over at the I.D section."

"Yeah, Billy, what's up?"

"We compared the print taken from your deceased in the park last night with the fingerprints on record with the New York State Bar. It's confirmed, comes back to attorney Samantha Cohen of Sutton Place."

"Ah, huh. Okay, thanks."

As she passed a lone white sailboat with its yellow fin-like sail standing tall, basking in the sunlight, breezing north on the dark and rocky waters of the East River, she tossed over and over in her head the nexus between the Father Manny and, now, Samantha Cohen's murders: Ryan Condon. He had been acquainted with both victims twenty years before; had put limits on her investigation, and miraculously his shield number—6-7-0-2—ended up in the hands of one of the suspects.

Again she wished her father had been around to run this all by.

Our Lady of Mount Carmel had been built in Gothic style in 1926. When she'd looked up at the façade of the church, she caught a glimpse of the Virgin Mother above the doorway comfortably sheltered in a carved out space. Several neighborhood pigeons were resting at her feet.

Toni noticed the buildup of dark gray heavy clouds, too, which she hoped would break during the Mass. Her white-bra was already damp under her navy blue pants-suit, and fresh white blouse. The collection of swiveling fans attached to the walls on each side of the church only circulated the heavy air. But, it was still standing room only. The congregation had come out in force to bid their beloved pastor — Father Manuel Gonzalez — farewell.

The first few rows were filled with an assortment of clergy including the Archbishop of New York. But what was also striking to see was the delegation of uniformed New York City police officers of all ranks in their dress blues and white gloves that filled the rows as well.

"So, why was Father Manny shot dead?" Toni thought as the kneeling congregation of civilians and clergy and police officers, with heads bowed, chanted those prophetic words:

"Lord, I am not worthy that you should enter under my roof, but only say the word and my soul shall be healed." At that moment she looked up at the green-red stained glass windows above the majestic fresco of the Mount Carmel countryside high above the altar, and felt she could almost see those words rise up high into the pointed arches and ribbed vaults.

When Geddes and Toni stepped out of the church she noticed Ryan and his wife speaking with Father Gribbons at the top of the steps. Toni watched them carefully. She deeply regretted her involvement with Jocelyn's husband. Toni knew that if she'd seen Jocelyn just once before her involvement with Ryan, it would have been all she needed to keep from crossing that line — drunk or not.

She watched the couple as they went down the steps. Ryan held her elbow and walked her to their car. She had a bandage wrap on her right hand and wrist. There was a clear vulnerability to her, Toni recognized again. He opened the door for her, and guided her into the passenger seat as if she was much older. They drove off.

Before heading back to the squad office, Toni stopped by her apartment to walk Vita. She got back to Bronx Homicide just before 1 p.m. Ryan was already addressing about twenty detectives scattered around the office. Some sat behind desks, others on desks, and still others leaned against walls, or the wrought iron bars of the single squad room cell all with pad and pen and iPhones in hand. Geddes picked a file cabinet to lean against. It was standing room only.

It was a real mosaic of an N.Y.P.D Homicide Squad: mostly white men, with a smattering of African Americans and Latino men, including two women: one German/Irish, the other, Toni. Homicide was still a men's club.

Ryan shot off a list of things he wanted to be done: Canvass all apartment buildings surrounding the park for witnesses with special attention to apartments whose windows faced the park; get a record of all parking tickets issued and CCTV footage within a five block radius of the park from 6 p.m. to 6 a.m.; show up at the park at 6 p.m. and stay until 4 a.m., find out if anyone was in the park the night before and noticed anyone suspicious, or, size them up as possible suspects; interview city bus drivers on the route going past the park, and token booth clerks working during those hours; contact Parks Department and find out what (if any) baseball teams were playing in the park, speak with the team managers, get names of players, find out if they all left together or did any of them decide to stick around; get a record of all arrests made in Mount Carmel Park the day before and within the previous 30 days: disorderly conduct; public intoxication; urinating in public; drugs, everything. The list went on and on.

She looked at the lines on Ryan's face very carefully — like a palm reader — and wondered for a split second if she could detect indicators of any involvement with the two murders. She wasn't serious about anything being disclosed, but she looked hard anyway. He was clean and pressed in his white long-sleeved shirt, sky blue tie, and dark blue suit pants. Anybody walking into the Bronx Homicide Squad would know he was the commanding officer just by taking one look at him. There was no mistaking he was the police executive commanding that squad. Except, his clean-shaven face was not unmarked that morning. He had a bandage on his chin.

Toni knew Ryan was trying to look like he had it together, but he looked worn-out. What would you expect? She thought. Most anybody else would be weary after being called out to a homicide crime scene at 2 a.m. as she had. Except, Ryan hadn't stayed at the scene until 4 a.m. as she, Tazzo and Geddes had. He'd taken off.

But there was something more than just the fatigue of being hung-over etched in the lines of his face. And it was more than sadness. It seemed more like remorse. And it wasn't just in his facial lines. It was in his voice. It was in the tone of his voice. No, it wasn't really the tone, or not just the tone, it seemed to Toni, as she watched him take a few steps back and forth on the dull black tile floor as he addressed the troops, there was a quaver in his voice; and a faint, faint, barely detectable, shortness of breath: Like someone recovering from a heart attack.

Toni wondered if Ryan had really not seen Samantha Cohen in over twenty years.

"Toni," Tazzo called out startling her.

The meeting had broken up only a few minutes before. Detectives were animated: Some getting on the phone, others getting on their computers or iPhones, or grabbing their notepads and jackets and heading out the door.

"Come on in." He waved her over to Ryan's office.

When she stepped in, Tazzo closed the door behind her. Ryan had just sat back at his desk holding a steaming cup of black coffee. It was in a cup with a Chicago P.D. logo, one of a stack Bronx Homicide got from visiting police detectives over the years. Tazzo was sitting on the couch. Toni took the seat in front of Ryan's desk, crossed her athletic legs and flipped through her notepad looking every bit the professional female detective in her pants suit and white blouse, her shining straight black hair flattened against her scalp into a ponytail.

She picked up the familiar scent of Ryan's Aqua Di Gio aftershave mingled with the excretion of a profuse amount of beer.

Being raised by an alcoholic, Toni had acquired such a sensitive sense of smell that she not only captured the slightest hint of the morning-after effects that oozed from a person who'd knocked down a river of booze, but also whether it was a river of beer or hard liquor. With her father, it got to the point that she could even figure out if he'd been drinking White Label and water or Vodka and grapefruit or Bacardi and Coke.

Tazzo started. "What'd the M.E. have to say?"

"Doesn't look like Cohen was raped," Toni said. "The M.E. found semen, but there was no trauma to the vaginal cavity. M.E. figured she'd had consensual sex within a few hours of her death. Maybe they got into a dispute after they had sex in the park or something."

Ryan was straight-faced.

Toni continued. "The M.E. also thinks the victim may have bitten the perp. He couldn't be sure, but one of her teeth was broken in a way that's not consistent with her head being bashed into the rock. He's going to do a lab analysis on what was in her mouth. He thought he might come up with particles of the perp's flesh or blood for DNA analysis also.

Toni took a hard look at that bandage on Ryan's chin. "How'd she end up back in the same park murdered where she was raped as a kid? The killer has to be someone she knew or somebody that at least knew about the rape. It sure can't be a coincidence. One thing for sure is it rules out the perp. being a stranger."

There was silence.

Toni continued. "I mean she lived on Sutton Place for crying out loud. What the hell is she doing in Mount Carmel Park!"

A beam of South Bronx sun filtered through the office window. Particles of dust danced in the light. File cabinets deflected the rays from landing on either Ryan or Toni, directly, but it spread across Ryan's desk, and, from the knee down, lit up Tazzo's finely creased pants.

149

Toni uncrossed her legs, flipped another page of her notepad and then brought up duplicate white shield # 6-7-0-2.

"I went to headquarters to check on the dupe shield."

"Who's it assigned to?" Tazzo said.

"It's not," Toni said. "Last cop it was assigned was a P.O. Shawn Tripp. He resigned two years ago.

Ryan shifted in his big leather chair.

"I got to talk to this ex-cop. Find out if he had a dupe of his shield made at some point and maybe gave it to somebody, or just lost track of it."

"All right," Tazzo said. "But you know how it is with dupes. They're not that tough to get made."

"Yeah, but I want to find out what he's been doing since he left the job," said Toni. "I also want to know who this female caller to 911 was. Was she just somebody that likes walking through the park in the middle of the night, or maybe she was with the perp, who knows, and was feeling guilty."

Tazzo nodded.

"Anyway, I want to bang out a request for the tape for you to sign, Loo," she said, acknowledging that requests for 911 tapes needed to be approved by the commanding officer.

"I'll take care of that. What else you got?" Ryan said, and took a sip from the mug.

She paused, then her mind started to move fast. Here we go again, she thought. Why wouldn't Ryan let her pick up the 911 tape? She focused on him; he leaned back in his chair, expressionless.

There was silence.

As Toni looked back and forth between her two bosses, it seemed they were both lost in thought, listening to the muffled rumbling of activity in the squad room. Man, do they know more than they are telling me, or what? But why? Why was Ryan holding back? Why wouldn't he admit shield # 6-7-0-2 was his cop shield? Get it all out in the open. And now he won't let her pick up the 911 recording, or, volunteer whether or not he knew Samantha Cohen had been raped twenty years ago. What is he not saying?

"You feeling okay?" Toni said to Ryan.

"I'm fine."

And Tazzo, what's up with him? Is he covering for the lieutenant? Damn, this is becoming a real mess fast, she thought. If they're trying to cover something up here, they know they have a problem because she's working the case. Her thoughts were running fast and furious. Maybe Tazzo put her on it because he was feeling unsettled too about the lieutenant's potential involvement.

"Listen, one other thing," Ryan said. "Don't bother heading down to the ME's office for Cohen's report. I'll take care of that too."

Toni didn't reply and stayed seated. Tazzo then stood up and opened the door.

"Did you know Samantha Cohen was raped in the park twenty-three years ago, lieutenant?"

Ryan remained silent.

"The lieutenant knows, detective," Tazzo said. "And you got a few things to follow up on with the Father Manny homicide, don't you? You've got to speak to that priest at Mount Carmel again, and any office staff, right?"

"I want to see the CCTV at Cohen's apartment building. See if she had a visitors."

"I'll take care of that too," Ryan said without looking up at Toni. His eyes fixed on some paperwork on his desk.

Tazzo jumped in again. "All right, Toni, grab Geddes and get at it. The boss needs to do a few things."

Toni stood up and looked down on Ryan without moving to the door.

"All right, Toni," Tazzo said again, as he guided her out the door and stepped out behind her. After the door closed, she looked at Tazzo without a word.

"What's on your mind, Toni?"

Toni looked up into Tazzo's eyes and paused before answering. "Nothing," and walked to her desk.

One of the other detectives announced she had a call. She took it without sitting down.

"Listen, it's me," the male voice said. Toni remained silent.

She had no interest in talking to him there and then. That damn one-night stand. Would she ever learn? She turned and looked over at Ryan's office through the partially opened blinds and could see him standing behind his desk, on the phone, looking back at her. She looked away.

"What do you want?" Toni said.

"We need to talk."

"You're right about that."

"Can I come over to your apartment tonight?" he said.

"No, you cannot!"

"Please don't jump to conclusions about anything."

She was told she had another call.

"Why don't you check with Chief King: see if he'd jump to conclusions!" Toni said, hung up, and took the other call.

Ryan was revolted with himself. He didn't want to hold back on Toni, but if she knew he'd been with Samantha only a couple hours before she ended up dead in the park, he'd never have a chance to find her killer.

All those years he hadn't known anything about the rape. He'd been away with his family the week the rape happened, not that it really mattered he'd been away. Living in their South Bronx neighborhood wasn't like living in Middle America where everybody hears everything. Violent crime was so common in their neighborhood that unless you were personally involved, or, happened to be a passerby, you'd often never hear about it. Not that you didn't sense the impact of the shootings, stabbings, robberies, burglaries, and rapes. You did. Everybody did. But once the blood was washed off the sidewalk, there was no story to tell.

The truth was, as fast as things moved for them the previous afternoon, there hadn't been time for her to explain. He seemed to have been holding his ground when he left the diner — fighting his impulse to be with her again — but then he received her text and suddenly, without a second thought, he returned it. She'd asked him to come to her apartment on Sutton Place so she could finish what she had tried to tell him. He knew he shouldn't do that, but he couldn't say no either. The fight was over.

They held each other and deeply kissed. They were in a ceaseless state of lovemaking that entire evening. The theme of what they shared was clear: their love had never died. They were content once again, just as it had been when they were both college-age. Seized in the divine.

At about 10 p.m. they'd finally had something to eat. As they lay in bed and ate the pasta dish Samantha had whipped together, they still had not talked much.

153

He shuddered at how raw and extreme his emotions had been. It was a force that overtook him, the collision of joy and suffering. His whole body, mind, and soul were spinning with elation one moment, and the next he was swimming in crushing sorrow — elation over having his arms wrapped around her once again, elation over consuming her scent, elation over being deeply within her, elation over the prospect of being with her forever, then sorrow over not having been with her all those years, sorrow over how she could have stayed away from him for so long. Finally, sorrow over what he was doing to his wife, and what it would mean.

After they finished eating he was standing at her living room window with only a towel wrapped around his waist. He felt like he was in a dream looking down at the shimmering East River from the twenty-first floor. He was lost in thought as he watched a massive oil tanker travel up the narrow river, clearing the Ed Koch Queensboro Bridge.

Samantha came up behind him; he was startled for a moment; she held him tight. Her arms wrapped around him, her hands flat against his chest pulling tight. The side of her face pressed against his back, he could feel the moisture of her tears.

He swung around with a blast of guilt that blew open his chest and sharply announced he had to leave; he held her away; he scurried to get dressed.

He couldn't stop to even look at her — he just had to go. He raced around her apartment grabbing his stuff scattered on the path to her bedroom: boxers, slacks, shoes, shirt, tie, gun, and holster. He talked fast, not sure what he was saying. As he grabbed his suit jacket from her carpeted floor by the front door, she tried to stop him. She'd said she needed to tell him something very important before he left.

He couldn't stop to listen. "Tomorrow, Sam. I've got to go. We'll talk tomorrow."

She took his hands and held him still. After a long moment, she kissed his hands, looked up at him. Complete confidence leaped from her eyes that tomorrow — for them — would come.

When he left Sutton Place he jumped into his department car and headed for the Bronx, but he didn't go home. He took the exit that led to their old neighborhood. He couldn't bring himself to go directly home. On the way uptown, he stopped at a bodega on Third Avenue in Spanish Harlem and picked up a few Budweisers. He found himself cruising around Mount Carmel Park sucking down the beers with the police radio crackling in the background.

He stopped on the south side of the park and stared through the fencing into the baseball field all lit-up by the bright lights high above, and reminisced about all the years he'd spent on that field — the place where so many so-called glory days of his youth happened. Little League baseball, Pop Warner football. Game-winning home runs hit and touchdown passes tossed. His so-called glory days were now over, he knew that with certainty. As he looked out at the two late games still in progress on the illuminated diamonds, he could see the names of the teams playing: *Utuado vs. San Cristobal*; *Umacao vs. Boca Chica*. Teams named after various towns in Puerto Rico and the Dominican Republic; players offered opportunities for glory.

He knew there was no glory in what he'd just done. No glory at all.

CHAPTER 19

After hanging up on Ryan and taking that last call, Toni grabbed her suit jacket from the back of her seat, flung it over her shoulder, grabbed her notepad, walked over to Geddes — who stood by the coffee machine about to pour himself another cup — took his still empty cup from his hand, placed it on the countertop and said, "Let's get out of here. I'll be in the car."

It was noon when she stepped out of the stationhouse and was met with a wall of South Bronx summer heat. She winced at its force, and over the exchange, she'd just had with Ryan. She walked slowly to the parking lot in the back, jumped into the unmarked department Dodge Charger, started the engine, and turned the air conditioning on full blast.

She took Geddes for a run over to the Communications Division in Brooklyn determined to listen to the voice of the 911 caller who reported spotting Samantha Cohen's body in Mount Carmel Park. She wasn't about to let Ryan stop her from listening to that recording.

She didn't know how much to tell Geddes. With only a couple of years from getting his twenty to retire, she didn't think he'd want to get caught up in being charged with insubordination. No way she could let him know. Not yet anyway. She couldn't take the chance of letting him in on why she was doing what she was doing. She had to take a chance on keeping him in the dark and hope he didn't get blindsided by any questions from either Ryan or Tazzo

When they pulled up in front of the Metro Tech facility in downtown Brooklyn — the home of the N.Y.P.D. Communications Division — she asked Geddes to wait for her outside using the excuse that there was no parking anyway. "I'll be right back, Geddes. I just need to drop off this CD."

"What CD?" Geddes said.

"It's an old case," Toni said. "You know how it is with Communications. If you don't use the tape, and it's not vouchered as evidence, they want it back."

Geddes looked at Toni with a baffled expression.

"Yeah, I know, but I mean, we came all the way down here to drop off a CD when we got these two fresh homicides cooking? I figured we came down to pick up a 911 CD for last night's homicide in the park."

Toni jumped out of the car as Geddes was speaking, "No, the lieutenant said he'd take care of that."

"He'll take care of it. What the hell does that mean?" Geddes said still puzzled. "He's coming down here to pick up the CD himself?'

Toni shrugged her shoulders and was about to close the car door but Geddes went to pull out his iPhone, "Let me give the boss a call, see if we can pick up the CD since we're down—

Toni leaned back down into the car, holding the door open, and cut him off, "No, Geddes." She knew she sounded a little too excited. "I got the feeling he just wanted to take care of it himself like he had his own reasons."

Geddes still looked puzzled.

"Listen, he said he was going to pick it up himself. He told me not to pick it up. So, I'm not going to pick it up, but I want to listen to it."

"What's going on here?" Geddes said.

"Nothing, nothing," Toni said. "At least nothing, not really, not yet."

"Ahh huh," Geddes said and looked away.

"You all right with that for now, big man?" Toni said still holding the door open.

Geddes took a few moments before he looked back at Toni. "I guess you don't have a request form?"

Toni looked away, "Well…"

"All right, bulldog. Do what you got to do. But, be careful."

Toni marched into the building, hit the elevator banks, and shot right up to the seventh floor where the office that duplicated 911 tapes office was located. She didn't have a request form signed by her C.O., she had something better: a cop buddy in that office who'd been in the same academy class with her. Her friend set her up in a room with a headset.

"Operator 272, where's the emergency?" The female 911 operator answered.

A female voice said, "There's a woman in Mount Carmel Park..."

"Yes, what about the woman?"

The female voice hesitated. "...She's dead, I...I think she's dead."

"Where exactly in the park is the woman?"

The female voice fell silent.

"Hello, ma'am, are you there ma'am?"

"...She's behind a big rock." The line went dead.

Toni listened to the recording over and over again. There was something about the voice that unsettled her. It sounded like a mature woman. No accent. Not a teenager or somebody elderly. But there was still something odd about the voice. It sounded slow. It sounded like someone who was either mentally challenged or, under the influence of drugs or alcohol. That was it, wasn't it? It sounded like a medicated voice. She wondered if the caller was a late night passerby that had just stumbled onto the body while getting buzzed in the park, or, had the caller been with the killer, and, after the deed had been done, and she'd parted ways with him, it was, yes, an attack of guilt that drove her to make the call.

As it turned out, there was no caller I.D. information to trace. And Toni wouldn't be surprised if the caller used a 'burner" phone—disposable and untraceable.

Ryan parked his department car on a meter in front of the Metropolitan Restaurant on First Avenue off E. 53rd Street. Samantha's sister had picked the place. It was only a few blocks from the Sutton Place apartment. In the thirty-forty minutes, it took him to drive from Bronx Homicide to the restaurant in East Midtown Manhattan, the heat had ratcheted up another five degrees.

She'd suggested he come to the apartment to speak with her, but Ryan prophesied it would be better to meet somewhere else in case there was any press waiting around. In truth, he didn't want to speak with her in the same apartment he'd made fervid love to Samantha only hours before she'd been killed. He couldn't afford to have the concierge or doorman place him there. Not that he really thought any of the same crew on duty the night before would be working during the day, but he didn't want to take that chance.

The restaurant was a wide-open space with wood floors and red brick walls. A glistening bar to one side tables neatly draped with white tablecloths, each prepared to seat four: water and wine glasses and white cloth napkins with glittering silverware at each place.

The slim, model-like hostess in a white, summer dress, holding several menus, asked if he'd had a reservation.

"I'm meeting a Mrs. Rivera," Ryan said as he scanned the restaurant not knowing if he'd still be able to recognize Samantha's kid sister. It had also been over twenty years since he'd last seen Elizabeth, and, at that time, she was only fifteen years old.

The hostess asked him to follow. She walked him over to the corner table in the rear where the only woman in the restaurant was sitting alone. Elizabeth sat up straight as they approached, eyes opened wide, hands on her lap.

"Ryan?" Elizabeth said as she stood up and gave him a hug. His heart suddenly squeezed tight as he looked at this woman who bore a remarkable resemblance to her sister. She was several inches taller, but she had Samantha's long, fine, black hair held back with a black headband just as her sister had often worn it when they were all young. What a beautiful woman she'd become, Ryan thought as he held her. Samantha's kid sister; his heart squeezed tight.

In that instant, he also recognized the shock and grief he'd seen so many times before on the faces of other loved-ones of murder victims trying to be brave. But, in this bizarre case, he needed to be brave too.

"Thanks for coming down to meet with me, Ryan," Elizabeth said as she sat back down, and he pulled a chair out to sit.

The waitress approached and asked if he wanted something to drink. He could see that Elizabeth was having ice tea.

"Just water please," Ryan said to the waitress then turned back to Elizabeth. "So, you live in Florida now?"

"Well, yes, I live in Boca Raton with my husband and two girls. How did you know?"

"I think Manny mentioned it."

"Oh, my God. My God. Father Manny too."

Ryan nodded.

"Do you have any idea what happened to my sister?" Elizabeth said as she took her hands from her lap and clinched them on the white tablecloth, looking directly into Ryan's eyes.

"No, we don't, at least not yet."

The waitress brought a bottle of Perrier and poured Ryan a glass full.

"Ryan, what do you think could've happened?"

"I don't know. Not yet. But we have a whole squad of detectives working on it. We'll find out who did this, Elizabeth."

"Oh, please call me Liz. Everyone calls me Liz these days."

"Sure, of course," Ryan said. "When did you speak to Samantha last?"

"Last night. I called to say hello. She told me, Vanessa, her daughter—did you know my sister had a daughter, Ryan?

"...ahh, no..."

"...well, she's a beauty, just like her mom, sixteen years old. Sweet sixteen."

Ryan stayed silent.

"...well she said Vanessa was staying at her father's. She was very upset about Father Manny, you know. She told me detectives came to her home yesterday morning."

"Yes."

"I found one of the detectives' cards in her apartment, a Detective Santiago," Liz said. "And Mommy told me you came to tell her about Samantha. Thank you for doing that, Ryan. Thank you for doing that yourself."

When he'd thrown-up in the park after seeing Samantha's body and left so abruptly, he'd gone directly to Samantha's mother's apartment and stayed.

"When you spoke to Samantha on the phone—what time was that?" Ryan said.

"Oh, it was a little after eight. Her daughter stayed at her father's...oh...I already said that."

"Aside from her being upset about Father Manny, did she say anything else?"

"No, not really. She said she was tired and planned to get to bed early."

"Liz," Ryan said, "did you know about Samantha being raped?"

Liz held Ryan's eyes for a moment before responding.

"You know about that? Poor Samantha." She pulled out a package of Kleenex from her bag. "It's just terrible what happened. First that horrible rape, now this."

The waitress approached again. Ryan shook his head.

161

"Can we continue?" Ryan said.

Liz nodded.

"So, you were fifteen when it happened?" Ryan said. "The rape, I mean."

"Yes, it was a terrible, terrible night. My parents were never the same after it. Samantha was so strong. She was strong for them, she always was. She knew how terrible it was for my parents to live with what happened to her. It was just a terrible time. Samantha always blamed herself for walking through the park so late. She was so used to walking through the park with you. When we picked her up at the hospital — my Mom and me — of course, we asked her where you were? You always walked her through the park, right?"

"Yes," Ryan said.

"She told us you were with your family and she started to cry-and-cry again, 'Don't tell Ryan. Don't tell Ryan,' "Liz said.

They sat in silence for several moments, both lost in their own memories.

"Do you know how it happened, Ryan?"

"No. No, I don't."

"It was terrible, Ryan, terrible."

"Do you know if anyone was ever arrested then?" said Ryan.

"No, no." Liz looked down at the table again wringing her hands.

"What is it?"

"Oh, God, I haven't spoken about this in such a long time."

Ryan waited.

"I'll tell you something I never told anyone. Samantha always said she couldn't identify the rapist."

Ryan took that in for an extra moment. "And she could?"

"Yes."

Ryan sat up straighter. "She knew who raped her. It wasn't a stranger. She recognized him?"

"Yes, but she never told the police she knew. And she never told my parents. To this day my mother still doesn't know. And my father's gone."

"Liz, do you know who the rapist was?"

She shook her head. "No, I don't, Ryan. She never told me. She said it would hurt too many people if she identified him."

"Did she ever say what people?"

"No, she never said."

"I see," Ryan said. "Liz, was Samantha impregnated from the rape?"

She closed her eyes for several seconds.

"Ryan, I promised I would never speak to anyone about it." She stopped. "But I suppose it doesn't matter anymore. Samantha had a son. He was born in Virginia when she went back to Georgetown that summer."

"Where is he?" Ryan's heart started to beat hard.

"She turned him over for adoption as soon as he was born. She never saw him again. It was a horrible, horrible, situation. Horrible for everybody."

"Do you know what adoption agency or any anything at all?"

"Father Manny arranged for the adoption, through a Catholic agency. I never had any details."

"Manny? Really?" Ryan said. "Do you know what the child was named?"

"Oh, Ryan, this is so hard. I've held this secret all these years as Samantha asked me to." She paused again. "He was named Jeremiah. Jeremiah Francisco."

"Jeremiah Francisco."

"Yes," Liz said, and continued to wipe her nose,

"Do you have any idea where he is now?" Ryan said.

Liz shook her head.

"She was so generous and kind to me. She was the best big sister anybody could have. I loved her very much," Liz said, then put down the tissue and looked into Ryan's eyes. "And she always loved you, Ryan.

Ryan was silent.

"You think there's some connection with her murder and the rape?" Liz said.

"We don't know," Ryan said clearing his throat. "But all this background information will help us find out."

"It's strange, isn't it, how she was murdered in the same place she was raped," Liz said. "My poor sister."

"Yes, it is."

"And right after poor Father Manny," Liz said.

"Yes."

Liz seemed to fall into deep reflection.

"Liz," Ryan said, almost in a whisper. "We need a family member to identify her body. Would you be up to it? Is it okay if we drive down to the medical examiner's office as soon as we're done here?"

Liz fixed her gaze on Ryan without answering. More tears dripped down her cheeks. She nodded.

CHAPTER 20

After Ryan dropped Liz at Samantha's Sutton Place apartment, he took the Third Avenue Bridge over the Harlem River and back into the Bronx. He stopped by the 51st precinct detective squad. He wanted to find out why the investigation never led to the identification of the perp. and a subsequent arrest.

He talked shop with the detective squad commander, Lieutenant Bill Hullihan, for a few minutes, then he got to the point of his visit: He wanted to see the over-twenty-year-old rape case file. As he'd expected, it was buried in the basement and would take some time to find. Hullihan told Ryan he was leaving for a week's vacation to Block Island in a couple minutes with the family, but would have one of his detectives contact him as soon as it was pulled.

"What about the arrest log, Bill, before you head out?" Ryan said. The detective squad arrest log would give him some basic information right away, such as the name, address, and date of birth of the defendant and the disposition of the case.

"Sure, it's right over here," Hullihan said. They both walked up to a small table leaning against a filing cabinet. "If there was a collar made, it should be in the log. It goes back to the '50's."

The Arrest Log was bulky, three-inches thick, green, hard-covered, 17x21 sized book with categories written horizontally across and vertical lines running down. Hullihan broke it open and leafed back through the heavy pages back to the 90's and spotted the entry.

"Here it is," Hullihan pointed to it and stepped to the side so Ryan could take a closer look.

The entry read:
Date of Occurrence: August 7
Time of Occurrence: 2200-2400
Place of Occurrence: Mount Carmel Park

Charge: Rape/Assault
Date of Arrest: August 8
Arresting Officer: P.O. J. Santiago, shield # 7263
Time of Arrest: 0430 hours
Perpetrator: Name removed. Records sealed. Authority
Bronx Supreme Court, Judge Burton Jones.
Age: 16
Race: Hispanic
Disposition: Closed

"So, they did make a collar," Ryan said. "It was a kid."

"Looks that way," Hullihan said. "We need a judge to release the folder, Ryan."

Ryan glowered over the entry. Samantha's family never knew about it. Ryan wondered if Samantha ever knew a suspect had been arrested.

Ryan's cell phone rang. "Yeah."

"Loo, it's Vic, you still at the 5-1 Squad?'

"Yeah, I am."

"Good, good," Tazzo said. "Listen, boss, the canvass, the guys came up with a witness, said she looked out her window about 11 o'clock last night. She faces the main entrance of Mount Carmel Park, on the south side. She saw a male and female talking to each other. Said there was a black car parked near them. Figured it belonged to them since there were no other cars parked on the park side at the time. There's no parking on the park side of the street after 10 p.m."

"Only the one car?" Ryan repeated, not to clarify but to hear himself say it.

"Yeah, that's what she said. Only one car. Maybe they arrived together."

"Or maybe he drove over in his own car and parked somewhere else." Ryan was thinking out loud.

"Yeah, could be. Said it was a fancy sedan. She had no clue what make or model it was. A radio car pulled up on them and it looked to her the couple was talking to the uniforms. The woman was doing most of the talking. The cops didn't get out of the car."

"Description?"

"She didn't have the best view," Tazzo said. "She's on the top floor of the building, the fifth floor, but, she said, the guy was tall, early twenties. The woman looked older to her and slim like a dancer she said." Tazzo paused. "She was in jeans, sneakers, and a sweatshirt."

"Could she read the sweatshirt?"

"No. She could see letters, but couldn't make it out. Said after the radio car pulled away the couple walked into the park, she lost sight of them. She stepped away from the window too at that point. About twenty minutes later she looked out the window and saw the black sedan was still there."

"Is it still there now?" Ryan said.

"Yeah, it is. Black, 2017, BMW," Tazzo said. "Registered to Samantha Cohen."

"All right."

"Listen, boss, since you're down at the 5-1, maybe you can check with the desk officer…"

"No problem. I'll find the radio car team that pulled up on them?"

"If they worked the four-to-twelve they got off at midnight, they should be coming in soon for today's four-to-twelve," Tazzo said.

"Unless they were swinging out and off the next couple days," Ryan said. "I'll take a look at the roll call and get the names and numbers of the cops working it last night."

"Probably no more than fourteen, I figure. Seven radios cars during the four-to-twelve max. "

"Right, "Ryan said, "Make sure Crime Scene dusts the car. Talk to you later."

At 3:45 p.m. there was a knock on the 51st Precinct Squad Commander's office door. A street clothed cop in his mid-thirties stuck his head in, "Lieutenant Condon?"

"Yeah," Ryan said and raised his head from the arrest log. "You, Nee?"

"Yes, sir. You wanted to see me?"

"Come on in. Close the door behind you." Ryan watched the stocky, prematurely bald cop as he did. "Grab a seat."

The officer took the seat placed in front of the desk. "You had Sector Henry last night?"

"Yeah, I did, we did," he said. "I was riding with P.O. Velazquez.

"Any chance you guys pulled up on a couple speaking together last night between eleven and twelve in front of Mount Carmel Park? Woman in her early forties, the guy younger?"

"Yeah, yeah, we did, just before we made this Nike store collar on a-hundred-forty-ninth street. Guy does a smash and grab. Shatters the window with a hydrant cap, tip-toes in, grabs the hi-tops of his choice, and walks into our arms."

Ryan waited. "And the couple?"

"Oh, yeah, yeah. We pulled up on the park block with a couple coffees to make a few entries in our books. Saw a woman in a black BMW drive up on a guy standing at the Cedar Avenue entrance," the cop said. "Why, boss? Is something up?"

"You could say that," Ryan said. "Did you run the plate?"

"Yeah, we did, it came back to a...wait a second, I got it in my book." The cop looked in his activity log and said. "Yeah, it came back to a Samantha Cohen, which we found kind of strange, this Cohen lady standing outside the park talking to this young guy."

Ryan nodded.

"What's up boss?"

"The Cohen lady was killed in the park last night."

"Ahh, no! Damn! Damn!" The officer said. "You know we knew something wasn't right about those two standing there."

"What do you mean?"

"I mean what a place and what a time to shoot the shit. I mean it wasn't that late, but it was kind of late to see a couple that looked like them hanging out outside the park. Tell you the truth we didn't know what to think. My first thought was drug deal, but when we pulled up on her and I spoke to her she was very polite. And the guy she was with didn't look like a typical neighborhood bad guy. He was dressed neatly, jeans, blue blazer, clean, white polo shirt. He did look tired though like hung over. Like he hadn't had any sleep for a while, but he didn't seem high on drugs or booze or anything, at least not when we saw him."

"What about height and weight?"

"Six-one, six-two, I'd say. Lean, muscular build, had an athletic look."

"Could you recognize him?" Ryan said.

"Oh, yeah, no problem."

"Describe his face for me."

"Clean-shaven, dark-brown eyes, short curly hair, handsome fella. You know—the officer said and stopped suddenly.

"What?"

"Well, I got to tell you—Nee said, and stopped again.

"What? " Ryan said. "What is it?"

"Well, I got to tell you, the guy looks a lot like you."

"You mean built like me?"

"No, well, yeah, you both have a similar build, but I mean the guy looks like a young version of you, I mean his face. I mean you got a little gray around the ears, and he's a little taller, but aside from that, I mean, he looks like he could have been your kid brother or something."

Ryan fell silent for a moment then spoke up.

"Well, that's not the first time somebody looks like somebody else. When I was a rookie, one of my first collars was a bodega stick-up. I put one of our cops in a line-up with a robbery suspect and the woman picked the cop out instead of the bad guy; he looked so much like that guy."

"Yeah, I know what you're saying, Loo, but this guy last night looked a whole lot like you. I mean—

"All right," Ryan waved his hand to cut him off. "Listen, I need you to head up to Bronx Homicide for about an hour. Any problem with that?"

"No problem at all, boss. Anything I can do," Nee said, "As long as the desk knows."

"No problem. I'll let the desk sergeant know. Head up, see Sergeant Tazzo. I'll let him know you're on your way up. I want you to look at some photos."

The cop rose from the chair, "Can I go up like this or do you want me in the bag."

"No, no, you don't have to be in uniform for this. I'll let the sergeant know."

Ryan watched Nee as he stepped to the closed door to leave the office. The officer then turned as he grabbed the knob and said, "Oh, listen, I forgot to mention that the Cohen lady said that guy was her son."

Ryan took a ride up the Grand Concourse to the Bronx County courthouse area on East 161th Street and stopped by the district attorney's office. His plan was to ask them to draw up a request to unseal the juvenile record of Samantha's rapist and present it to a judge. Ryan knew there wouldn't be any trouble getting the request drawn up, but what wasn't so certain is whether or not a judge would authorize it. He'd have to convince a judge that in view of the fact that she'd been murdered in the same park she'd been raped by the juvenile years earlier, they needed the juvenile's identity to find out his whereabouts at the time of the murder in order to either eliminate or consider him a suspect.

What he couldn't admit was that the true reason he ached for the identity of the rapist was personal. Liz said Samantha recognized her attacker. If Samantha recognized him, maybe he'd know him too. He just had to know who the rapist was. He hoped the judge would take the position that it was more important for the Bronx Homicide Squad to know the identity of the then juvenile rapist than to further protect his identity.

CHAPTER 21

Toni was only four years old when her mother died at the age of twenty-six. She didn't really remember her, but it was clear from all the album photographs (her father had compiled and always kept) that her mother was a beautiful woman. At the Bronx apartment where she'd been raised, one photograph always rested on her father's bedroom night table in a frame. It was their wedding picture. The photograph on her childhood night table was of Toni at six months sitting on her mother's lap as they looked into each other's eyes. For as long as Toni could remember, those two framed photographs never collected dust.

She died of a brain aneurysm. Her father found her mother lying on the floor by Toni's bed, where Toni had been sleeping soundly on her stomach.

Toni vaguely remembered one day she was living in a house in the country, and, another day—shortly after her mother's death—she was living in a walk-up apartment building on the fourth floor in a place called the Bronx. The country, she later found out, was a suburb thirty-five miles from New York City in Rockland County.

She'd seen pictures of their former home. It was a one-story yellow ranch, with a deep green lawn. A bunch of colored flowers were planted in the long flowerbeds in front of the house: a rich collection of pinks, yellows, and violets. Her father told her that her mother had planted all the flowers. That she had loved flowers. The truth was Toni had no real memory of life in Spring Valley. Except for her four years in the Marine Corps, the Bronx was the only home she'd ever known.

After leaving the Communications Division in Brooklyn, Toni and Geddes headed back to the Bronx and shot up Webster Avenue, an avenue said to have featured, at one time, the warehouse/headquarters of the 1920s "Bronx Beer Baron" otherwise known as Dutch Schultz. It was a two-way, four-lane tenement, warehouse, and housing project lined route. Trees were in very short supply. Toni wanted to get over to the Crime Scene Unit and see the video and photographs taken of both crime scenes: Father Manny's and Samantha Cohen's. Plus she wanted to see what forensic information they'd come up with.

They made it to Webster Avenue and Fordham Road (diagonally across from the sprawling Fordham University campus) where the N.Y.P.D. Crime Scene Unit was located. The Crime Scene Unit wasn't located in a precinct, but a twelve-story office building. Even though the N.Y.P.D. had seventy-six police precincts scattered all over the five boroughs, there still wasn't enough space to house all the specialized units.

Toni and Geddes got off the elevator on the top floor of the office building. The floor was completely inhabited by the Crime Scene Unit. Either direction you took — stepping off the elevator — led to a crime scene unit desk or office. The layout was a square. A series of desks, file cabinets, computers, detectives and forensic civilian specialists sitting out in the open, with private offices for the bosses: one lieutenant and two sergeants assigned to each borough, and the commanding officer, a captain. Toni greeted, shook hands, or hi-fived many of them as they made their way around to the lieutenant in charge of the Bronx.

"Well, if it isn't the super-gumshoes of Bronx Homicide," Lieutenant Kleinheidt announced when they walked into his office. Kleinheidt offered them a cup of coffee. Toni declined; Geddes accepted. Geddes always accepted.

"Help yourself, Geddes. You know where the pot is."

The lieutenant handed Toni the Crime Scene report folders on both homicides that included the usual: written report, photographs, diagrams, lab report results, and two DVDs.

"It's only draft reports, the finals won't be signed-off on for a few more days. If you want to see the DVD while you're here, pop it in over there." Kleinheidt thumbed to the DVD player on a stand under a framed photograph of the Chief of Detectives. "I'll be right outside if you need a hand."

Toni leafed through the Father Manny report, first, "Holy shit!"

Holy shit?" Geddes repeated.

"Yeah, holy shit! Two sets of prints were lifted from the file cabinet. One belonged to Father Manny, the other's unidentified. They eliminated Gribbons, the housekeeper, and the two office staff women. Maybe our shooter belongs to those unidentified prints."

"Could be."

"Hey, look at this. They've got two sets of shoe prints coming into contact with the blood. One set is an eleven. Had a boat shoe sole. Who wears boat shoes in the South Bronx for crying out loud?" Toni looked up at Geddes but he didn't reply.

Toni continued, "They've got the size-eleven going into the rectory and out. Another footprint, a running shoe, size seven—a little *hombre*—just going out."

"Maybe they belong to the first cops on the scene," Geddes said without looking at Toni.

She felt a rise with that comment and almost snapped her neck to look at her partner. "You're killing me, Geddes."

"Just a thought."

"I don't remember any cops at the scene wearing running shoes and boat shoes, do you?"

"Nope," Geddes said, with half a chop-busting chuckle.

"We got to find out what Cruz and Mateo's shoe sizes are."

174

"Ah huh," Geddes kept reading the Cohen report.

"Wouldn't it be a pisser if it turns out Ernesto Cruz is the size seven, waited for Father Manny in the rectory, shot him and took off, and Mateo is the size eleven; showed up at the rectory to make sure the job was done right. That would explain the size eleven's entry and exit."

"Didn't you tell me you didn't think Cruz or Mateo was involved?"

"Yeah, yeah, all right," Toni said, and handed the Father Manny report to Geddes, jumped up, and popped in the dvds.

She didn't notice anything beyond what they'd already seen at the Cohen park homicide scene, but the Manny rectory crime scene made her freeze on a frame when the camera made it into Father Manny's second floor private office.

"You see that?" Toni said and pointed at the bottom corner of the monitor. "That looks like the journal Gribbons said Father Manny wrote in every night."

"What?" Geddes replied, without lifting his head from the report. Toni didn't answer.

She started to go through the photographs of Father Manny's soulless body on the kitchen floor taken from various angles and distances. It gave the flawed perspective that he'd posed in different positions for the camera. She then moved on to study the photographs of Father Manny's second-floor office. The photographs captured the whole room, taken of each of the four walls from top to bottom. One wall had two windows facing the backyard like the kitchen, another was completely covered with a bookcase from floor to ceiling, the third wall had a Spartan-like cot against it and a crucifix above it, and the final wall was where his desk rested with a file cabinet with five drawers just to the left alongside it.

Toni focused on a couple of photographs taken of the items on top of Father Manny's desk.

"Look at this, Geddes," Toni said, as she pointed to what appeared to be a journal on Father Manny's desk. "That looks like a red-journal, doesn't it?"

Geddes looked at it closely and shrugged his shoulders.

Toni pulled another photograph from a slightly different angle and a close-up that clearly showed it was a journal. "Look here, it's clearer in this one." She handed the photograph to Geddes.

"Yeah, I can see it," Geddes said. "So what?"

"So what?" Toni said, with a twinge of exasperation. "Maybe Father Manny made a few entries that will tell us something."

"Yeah, that's possible, or maybe not," Geddes said, and got back to another photo he was looking over. Geddes had been in Bronx Homicide for over nine years and was long past getting too excited by first impulses.

"Hmm," Toni said. "Yeah, yeah, I know. All right, let's get out of here."

Toni abruptly stood, snatched the photograph from Geddes' hands, threw it on the lieutenant's desk and started to walk out the office. Geddes sat with his hands suspended as if he was still holding the photo.

"You coming," Toni said and stopped to look back at him from the door.

"Yep," Geddes said, rising and slowly shaking his head.

Toni and Geddes were waiting in the rectory when Father Gribbon's returned after placing the monstrance on the altar for 3 p.m. adoration of the Blessed Sacrament.

"Oh, I'm sorry, detectives. I hope you weren't waiting too long."

"No, father, we just got here," Toni said, and wasted no time." Let me ask you, was Father Manny's appointment book always kept by this fax machine?" Toni pointed to it.

"Yes. It's was always kept there or sometimes our secretary would have it."

"He didn't keep it in his office on the second floor?" Toni said.

176

"No, never. Most of the time it was our secretary who entered appointments in the books. In fact, my appointment book was often kept at the secretary's desk too. That's what worked best for us. The secretary would prepare a daily list of appointments for us each day based on the entries in our appointment books. It made the most sense for the books to be kept down here."

"But Father Manny always kept his journal in his office upstairs?" Toni said.

"Yes, his private office. There would be no reason for his journal to be down here."

"Can we go upstairs?" Toni said. "We want to see his office."

"Of course."

Toni and Geddes followed Father Gribbons as he headed in the direction of the staircase. Halfway up the steps, Gribbons turned and glimpsed down on them. "You know, as you would expect, I often saw Father Manny as he ascended these very steps." Gribbons continued up the steps. "He'd always pause to gaze at this crucifix hanging on the wall at the top of the stairs here." Father Gribbons touched the feet of the crucifix.

"He did this each and every day—touched our Lord's feet as he passed. You'll notice the feet of the crucifix has faded over the years. Then he'd continued down the hall to his office before going to bed."

As soon as they stepped into the office behind Gribbons, Toni scanned the top of Father Manny's desk. In the photograph, there was a red journal-looking book at the top, left corner. It was no longer there. Toni caught Geddes's eye quickly.

"Where's Father Manny's journal, Father?"

Gribbons walked to the desk and looked it over. "It's not here. I don't understand. He usually kept it on this corner" and placed his hand on the left front, corner. "Maybe it's in his desk." Gribbons then abruptly went behind the desk and started to pull out draws.

"Hold on Father," Toni said, and she methodically pulled out all of the desk draws, and also went through the bookcase. No red journal.

"Maybe he brought it into his bedroom?" Gribbons said.

"Let's go," Toni said.

After they'd come up empty in the bedroom too, Toni said, "Any other place you think it could be, Father?"

"No," Gribbons said shaking his head. "No, I can't think of any other place."

Toni then pulled out the color crime scene photograph of Father Manny's second-floor office.

"Father, you see this is a photograph of this office?"

"Yes."

"Right here on Father Manny's desk, this appears to be a journal of some kind." Toni pointed at that area of the photo." "A red journal."

"Yes, I see. It does look like a journal. Is that Father Manny's journal? Yes. I believe it is. That's his journal."

"Well, this photograph was taken by our Crime Scene photographer the morning of the murder right?"

"Yes."

"Before they left Monday morning, they took this photograph," Toni said again.

"Yes," Gribbons repeated.

"Well, there's no journal on this desk," Toni said, pointing at the left front corner of the desk with the photograph.

"No, there isn't," Father Gribbons said.

"Well, where is it?" Toni asked.

178

Father Gribbons rubbed his face. "I don't know."

"Are you sure you don't have it?" Toni said.

"No, of course not."

"Could the secretary have it?"

"I can ask her. But I can't imagine why she would take it."

"Thank you Father, but we'll ask her ourselves," Toni said as she pointed at the photograph again. "So, you have no idea where this journal is?"

"No, detective, I don't. I'm sorry.

Toni took Father Gribbons in for an extra moment.

"Is the secretary here now?" Geddes said.

"No, she's gone for the day. She'll be in tomorrow morning at nine."

"Well, we'd like to speak with her tonight," Toni said. "What's her name?"

"Juanita Perez."

"We'll need her home address and phone number," Toni said.

"Of course."

"Father, did you take anything from this office? Geddes said. "Since Father Manny's murder?"

"No, not at all. Except, of course, the folder I gave you with the letters."

"Yes, right. Besides that folder," Toni said. "Anything at all, even if it was only a pen or a sheet of paper?"

"No, detective. I didn't take anything from this office."

Toni took a long look at Father Gribbons and said, "Okay."

Then she looked up at Geddes, "Anything else for Father Gribbons?"

"No," Geddes said. "Thanks, Father."

"Thank you, Father," Toni also said.

They started to walk out of the rectory office when she turned back and said, "Father, we'd appreciate if you not call Juanita to let her know we want to talk to her."

179

"I won't, detective."

Toni and Geddes jumped into their car. Toni pulled out her iPhone and Googled Clarence Abbey whispering as she typed. "What's up with the abbey?" Geddes said, looking over at her.

"I want to confirm Gribbons was at that retreat."

Geddes raised one eyebrow.

"I mean, what's up with that Geddes?"

Toni pulled the crime scene photo out and repeatedly pointed at the red journal — clearly resting on Father's Manny's desk — like she was trying to stab a mosquito.

"This photo was taken just before we got there or after we left, right? Crime Scene was there when we got there, taking photos, right, doing their thing? After we left, the Crime Scene photographer stayed to finish up. Well, the journal is not there now. Gribbons said he didn't move or take anything, so where is it?" Toni looked at Geddes. "We don't have it."

"The secretary?" Geddes said.

"Maybe."

Toni dialed the Clarence Abbey.

Toni wasn't yet able to find out if Gribbons had spent the whole weekend at the Clarence Abbey from the monk she'd spoken to. She needed to speak with the abbot who wasn't available but would get back to her.

CHAPTER 22

It was all done with empathy and efficiency. Liz was brought
into a white, chilled, bright room; it contained a body in the
center draped with a white sheet. Ryan guided Liz to the side
of body, holding her shoulders from the back. The N.Y.P.D.
detective (permanently assigned to the morgue) lifted the
sheet from the face of the deceased and asked if she knew this
person.

Liz stood still, stared at the disfigured face for several
moments, then when recognition set-in, a sound—a whistling
sound—started from someplace deep, and rose up like a tea
kettle coming to a boil—until she shrieked and reached for her
sister's body; her knees buckled. Ryan caught her before she
dropped to the cold, white, tile, floor, and held her tight, her
suddenly deluged face buried in his chest, as she
uncontrollably shook; wailed and shook. Ryan held her up as
if she'd suddenly been struck paraplegic.

After Toni and Geddes paid a quick visit to the apartment of
Mount Carmel's secretary, Juanita Perez, only a few blocks
away, they were on their way back down to Manhattan.
Juanita claimed to have no idea where Father Manny's red
journal was. She claimed to not know Father Manny even had
a red journal in his private office. They were headed to the
Medical Examiner's office to take a look at the M.E. and
toxicology reports for Father Manny and Samantha Cohen.
When they entered the air-conditioned lobby, out of habit,
Toni scanned the framed black-and-white photographs of
former New York City Chief Medical Examiners lined up on
one of the walls. The more recently appointed medical
examiners—in colored photos on the opposite wall—didn't
interest her.

Each time she entered the lobby, she'd particularly make a point of looking at the photo of Dr. Charles Norris, the recognized pioneer of American forensic toxicology, appointed in 1918. She'd always been struck by the passion of his gaze. He was evidently a man on a mission. It stirred something inside her. Forensic science had come a long way thanks to Dr. Norris, she thought.

After flashing their gold shields at the uniformed cop assigned to the glass-encased reception desk, and continued past, Ryan, and a wearied Liz Rivera were headed in their direction on the way out. Ryan reluctantly made a brief introduction.

Toni took Liz's hand. "Mrs. Rivera, I'm very, very, sorry for your loss. I'm the detective responsible for finding who killed your sister."

"Oh, Thank you, detective" Liz said. "Oh, you're the detective that spoke to my sister about Father Manny. I found your card in her apartment."

"That's right, I'm investigating Father Manny's murder too," Toni said, and looked to Geddes, "and this is Detective Geddes."

"There's a team of my detectives working Samantha's case, Liz," Ryan said, giving Toni a tough glance. "Detective Santiago and Detective Geddes are only two of them."

"I'd like to speak to you sometime when you're up to it," Toni said, without looking at Ryan. "I know this is a terrible time for you."

"I've already spoken to Mrs. Rivera," Ryan said. "I don't want her to have to repeat herself."

Ryan took Liz's arm to continue out.

"Oh, I don't mind, Ryan," Liz, said, looking up at him.

"Whatever I can do to help find Samantha's killer I'll do." Liz then looked back at Toni and said, "We can speak now, detective, or if you like we could speak at my sister's apartment, I mean her former apartment, I mean where my sister lived." Liz's head drooped.

Toni gently squeezed her arm. Liz looked back up at Toni with brimming eyes. "It's on 57th and Sutton Place. Ryan is dropping me there now."

"Yes, I know," Toni said. "That'll be fine. Say in about an hour?"

"Yes, okay, in an hour."

"Okay, Liz, let me get you home," Ryan said and took her arm to leave but then turned back to Toni and Geddes with a hard look and barely whispered, "I'll be right back. Wait right here."

Toni watched Ryan put Liz in the department car and step back up into the building, pull her and Geddes a few steps down a hallway out of cop's hearing range.

"What are you doing here?" Ryan said to Toni.

"We came down to see Father Manny's M.E. and toxicology report." She lied. She had every intention of reviewing Samantha Cohen's report too.

"Didn't I tell you that I'd take care of those reports?" Ryan said trying not to raise his voice.

"You didn't say anything about Father Manny's report," Toni said. "You only said Cohen's report."

"I don't want you speaking to Mrs. Rivera without my permission, you understand?"

"Before I couldn't speak to Samantha Cohen without your permission, and she's dead. Now I can't speak to her sister."

Ryan looked at Toni for a few moments.

"Effective right now, you're off the Manny Gonzalez and Samantha Cohen homicides. You understand that Detective Santiago. Effective right now you're off those cases," Ryan said. "Now, I'm heading back to the office after I drop her off. I want you both back in the office too."

Geddes said, "All right Loo, you got it."

Toni didn't respond and gave Ryan a dead stare. "What about Mrs. Rivera, she's expecting me."

Ryan didn't reply and said to Geddes, "Stay with her."

183

Geddes was following Ryan out the door but Toni wasn't. Geddes looked back.

"Where you going, Toni?" Geddes said.

"I've got to use the head, damn-it."

Toni stayed in the ladies room a while.

"What was that all about?" Geddes said when Toni stepped out of the ladies room.

"I don't know. He's got a bug up his ass about something," Toni said and started to walk away.

Geddes loosely held her by the arm. "What do you mean he's got a bug up his ass? Did he tell you he'd take care of the reports?"

"Relax, Geddes," Toni said and looked down at his hand on her arm. Geddes let go.

"What do you mean relax, Toni? Did the lieutenant tell you he'd take care of it?"

"Yeah, he did," Toni said. "And I don't give a crap."

"What? What the hell are you saying?"

"They're my cases!" Toni shouted up into Geddes's face on her toes, extended like a ballerina, then strutted down the narrow hallway that led to the string of deputy ME offices. She didn't look back.

Geddes stayed put for a few extra seconds.

Toni's voice bouncing off the walls.

"What do you mean I can't see the reports? They're my cases, damn it. Wasn't I at the crime scene? Wasn't I at the autopsy? They're my cases."

When Geddes got to the office doorway, Toni was leaning into the Asian M.E., inches from his face, gripping the armrests to his rolling desk chair. The M.E. was leaning as far back as he could, eyes and mouth open wide like he was about to get a root canal. Toni gave the chair a shove and the M.E. toppled to the floor.

"I gave a copy of the reports to Lieutenant Condon," the M.E. said. "He said not to discuss the findings with anybody else. He's your commanding officer, isn't he?"

"Yes!" Toni shouted, picked the M.E. up from the floor, planted him in his chair like he was a Geisha girl, picked up his glasses, attached them to his face, then summarily turned and brushed past Geddes out the door.

"If Lieutenant Condon says I can discuss it with you I will, detective. Just get his approval."

Toni's marching steps landed solidly on the black linoleum floor and echoed back.

Geddes's leaned against the doorframe of the M.E.'s office without moving. "Uhhhh, ohhhh," Geddes uttered.

It was a silent start to their drive back to the Bronx from the Medical Examiner's office on East 25th Street up First Avenue. As they approached the intersection of E. 54th Street it was hard not to notice the bold green and white letters spelling out "Starbuck's" spread across the building on the corner.

"How 'bout a coffee?" Geddes said pointing at the Starbuck's on his side of the avenue. Toni didn't answer him, but pulled over and double-parked in front of the place. A red Toyota Corolla — following them from the M.E.'s office — pulled over too.

Geddes jumped out of the car without asking what she wanted. She grabbed her notepad and began to jot down some of her thoughts.

Toni pulled out her iPhone and called the main number for the M.E.'s office and asked for the Forensic Biology department. She hoped Ryan (or the deputy M.E.) hadn't gotten around to telling them not to give her any information. The Lab gave her what they had without a problem. Ryan missed that step.

Since she couldn't see the full M.E. report, she at least wanted to know, first, if Forensic Biology was able to attach the lipstick left on the coffee cup in the rectory kitchen to anyone through the Combined DNA Index System (CODIS.) It came back without a Hit.

And, second, was an identity attached to whatever DNA material Crime Scene investigators collected in Father Manny's office. The latter was just as important to Toni as the lipstick. She thought that whatever DNA material was left, even if — as yet — it could not be connected to a person, would eventually turn out to be the killer.

And, as it turned out, there had been a strand of hair collected from Father Manny's office floor that they'd originally thought was unidentified, and not connected to any of the rectory staff, i.e., Father Gribbons, or, any of the investigators that entered the office, i.e., Bronx Homicide or Crime Scene. But additional follow-up connected it to the hair sample the lab had on file for Lieutenant Ryan Condon

When the hell was Ryan in Manny's office, Toni wondered. He wasn't there the day of the murder when Crime Scene would've picked-up the strand. Maybe Ryan's strand of hair fell to Manny's office floor on some prior visit.

Her iPhone then rang. It was the from the Clarence Abbey.

Geddes jumped back into the car about ten minutes later with her Tall Pike black coffee — which had always been her Starbuck's drink of choice in the two years they'd been partners — and a Venti Caramel Cocoa Frappuccino — with whip cream — which had always been his. They pensively sipped their coffees, eyes fixed at the windshield up canyon-like First Avenue.

Toni watched multiple colors of traffic zigzag past them. The ratio of yellow cabs to other vehicles was easily two to one. It was a little like a Jackson Pollack painting, Toni thought, in which he simply had more cans of yellow paint to splatter.

She raised her eyes up a few blocks to 59th Street and the recently renamed Ed Koch Queensboro Bridge built in 1909. She watched the traffic go across into Queens, and had just captured a glimpse of the Swiss-made cable car heading in the same direction before her view was obstructed by the building line.

"I just got a call-back from the Clarence Abbey."

"Oh, yeah, the abbot," Geddes said. "What'd he say?"

"Father Gribbons left Saturday night."

"Ah, huh. Well, there's probably simple explanation for it."

"You think so," Toni said. "That's almost 36 hours from the time he left the abbey to his getting back to the rectory early Monday morning."

There might be an explanation, she thought, and she'd be all ears to hear it, but whatever he was engaged in had to be pretty heavy for him to lie to the police in the murder investigation of a fellow priest. That's serious stuff. She needed to find out where he was from the time he left the abbey, and if he was anywhere in the area of Mount Carmel when Father Manny was killed.

"I want to talk to the secretary again," Toni said, "but first I need to make a stop."

"After we check in with the lieutenant, bulldog."

She made the right turn on East 57th Street disregarding Geddes's reminder — and drove in the direction of Sutton Place, which was the next block over. They were about halfway down the block from Samantha's apartment building.

"Where you going? You taking the FDR?"

"Nope," Toni said as they approached the building.

"Then where are you going, Toni?" Geddes said, raising his voice. "We got to get back to the office. You got it? That's insubordination. We'll both get suspended."

Toni continued down 57th Street without speaking.

"You can't talk to the sister now," Geddes said.

Toni was mute.

187

"We can't go to Cohen's building now," Geddes repeated. "We got to get back."

"You don't have to come, Geddes. I got to see the sister," Toni said, as she was about to double-park on the curbside of Samantha's building. "After I speak to her, you and I got to talk."

Geddes ran his hands through his hair.

At that moment, just before Toni was about to shift the car into park, her driver side window shattered with a blast that forced her to hit the gas and pull the steering wheel hard to the left. Their vehicle soared over the double yellow lines; sideswiped several cars before it crashed into the light pole on the north side of the street directly across from the Sutton Place apartment building.

The solid foundation of the light pole didn't budge one inch. The front of the Bronx Homicide unmarked car folded into a perfect V around the pole, which triggered the siren to blare in the constant mode, resounding throughout the entire privileged neighborhood. New York City Police Detective Antonia Santiago was unconscious; her head slumped over the steering wheel. New York City Police Detective John Geddes's head struck the windshield.

When Ryan approached the foot of the Willis Avenue Bridge at East 125th Street (to cross back over into the Bronx) he was about to switch back to the Bronx radio frequency when he heard the Citywide dispatcher broadcast shots fired at East 57th Street and Sutton Place. He made a hard stop and pulled the car over at the foot of the bridge.

The City-Wide dispatcher continued to relay information: "Be advised ten-fifty-three…vehicle accident…confirmed shots fired at East Five-Seven and Sutton Place…possible police officers involved."

Sixty seconds later the dispatcher announced "First unit on the scene reports confirmed police officers down, Five-Seven and Sutton Place! Be advised confirmed police officers down...Five-Seven and Sutton Place!"

Two minutes passed, "Be advised two detectives unconscious Five-Seven and Sutton Place. Emergency Service responding, EMS responding, Manhattan South Detectives responding.

Three minutes passed, "Be advised...detectives involved...Bronx Homicide...unconscious, possibly shot, Five-Seven and Sutton Place. Being transported to New York Hospital."

Ryan held the steering wheel tight with both hands, head leaning down against it. His cell started to ring. He raised his head slowly, yanked the car into gear, flicked on his lights and siren, made a vicious U-turn and exploded back down the FDR Drive.

CHAPTER 23

Jeremiah Francisco twisted awake again. Though his vertical blinds were drawn, bright sunlight squeezed underneath. Lying on his back, he became consumed with gawking at the whirling ceiling fan in his bedroom. He alternated fixing his sights on the center, which produced a blur of fluttering; then tried to follow one blade of the fan around-and-around-and around. That he could not do very long without feeling he would be flung out his fifth-story window. He would return his fix on the center until the moment he was stable, only to get back to following the single blade until the point of being flung again.

This went on for hours. Laboriously he tried to piece together bit-by-bit what had occurred Sunday night. Then sudden banging on his apartment door snapped him out of his fixation.

He swung his legs over the side of his bed slowly and sat without moving. The thumping at his door would not stop. He then stood up and wobbled down his narrow hall, touching the walls with both hands to balance his way.

It then hit him who could be banging on the door, and he was right. Waiting were a sergeant and lieutenant from Internal Affairs. He'd been due back to his precinct at 8 a.m. and his digital clock read: 6:07 p.m.

They entered his apartment, demanded his shield, I.D. card, and firearm. All he had to give them was his shield and I.D. card. He didn't offer an explanation for his missing Glock. He was told he was suspended without pay pending termination after a department trial for being A.W.O.L. and for failure to safeguard his firearm.

Ryan got back to his office late. It was after 2 a.m. He'd been at the 57th Street shooting scene since that afternoon. Toni and Geddes remained unconscious at New York Hospital.

He'd directed a canvass of the area for any witnesses, but nobody had any idea where the shots had been fired. Nor was there any physical evidence discovered such as spent cartridges on the street, sidewalk or rooftops of the surrounding buildings.

The Crime Scene Unit and the Medical Examiner's office still needed time to collect more information before they arrived at a theory as to the origin of the shot. Furthermore, although the round pulled from Toni's shoulder and the unmarked car was nine-millimeter, there was as of yet no weapon to compare it against.

The only piece of information that seemed certain — based on the available eyewitnesses interviewed — was that only two shots were fired.

His chair squeaked when he leaned back and took a swig from the can of Sprite he'd grabbed on the first floor of the precinct before he went upstairs. He stood up, walked to the coat tree and pulled from inside his suit jacket pocket Toni's notebook and placed it in the center of his desk. The first unit at the shooting and crash scene had handed it to him. The uniform said he'd found it a couple of feet away from their car in the middle of the street. " 'You couldn't miss it, Loo,' " he said. "It landed on the double yellow lines.' " The white, lined, scribbled pages had been faced down on the pavement.

He leaned forward on his elbows and looked down at the mangled pad. Toni had printed on the cover of it with a black marker. It read: *Det. Santiago, shield # 664; Bx. Homicide #147, Location: Mount Carmel Rectory; Deceased: Gonzalez, Manuel.*

He then slowly flipped through the first few pages that had basic information like her time of arrival, and who were the first officers on the scene.

There was also a rough sketch of the scene that indicated where she saw the body when she arrived, and the layout of the location. The Crime Scene detectives would have provided all of that in their report, but Toni preferred to have something in her pad anyway. Making her own sketch helped her to memorize the scene. Something she'd picked up from her father.

He came to several pages with bullet statements or questions in Toni's dashed off handwriting such as *Ryan knew Samantha Cohen? Who's he trying to protect? Is he involved in their murders?...Father Manny...S.C???????* Alongside that, she wrote, "*No way, no way, no way, can't be, can't be, can't be!!!*"

He then noticed a notation that she'd been down to Communications to listen to the park 911 call, followed by another notation that she and Geddes were at the M.E.'s office. She wrote, "*What is his problem! He's withholding info from me. Why!!!!! He's involved for sure, but how????? This is not good!!!!*" He then noticed another notation, "*Jeremiah Francisco, Orphanage, Putnam, Franciscans.*"

Where did she come up with that name? Her notations were saturated in ink; she'd run over and over the letters with her pen in deep thought.

"Putnam Franciscans Orphanage," Ryan whispered and closed Toni's pad slowly as if the pages had weight. He stayed in that position fixated on the cover of Toni's notepad. She was one damn good detective. It would have been just a matter of time before she figured out he'd been with Samantha the night she was killed. She would've have gone over his head, and who could blame her. What he was trying to conceal would have exploded in his face. He was very lucky he'd been given her notebook. If it had landed on the desk of Chief Buddy King, his misguided attempt to get to the truth his way would've collapsed.

He swiveled around in his chair to his personal, two-drawer file cabinet behind his desk and secreted Toni's notepad in the bottom drawer to the rear, and pulled out Father Manny's red journal. He opened it again. The journal was almost entirely filled with reflections on such things as the Holy Trinity and scripture. It appeared to Ryan that Manny sometimes used his personal journal to prepare for homilies. That he would commune with God by writing in his journal. There were no personal references to persons or places except for the very last entry. It had been underlined,

" 'Must finally tell Ryan and Samantha. Jocelyn must understand.' "

Two days later Toni stirred in her hospital bed. She'd opened her eyes slowly and looked up to a bland, white ceiling. What time was it? She wondered. Is it daytime or nighttime? She couldn't figure out it was 3 a.m. Sunday morning. It was so quiet she could just hear the low hum of the dim fluorescent light on the wall behind her head that brought much of what was in the room into hazy view.

She looked high above her feet and noticed the green, digital squiggly, horizontal lines, and numbers of the heartbeat machine hanging from the ceiling, against the opposite wall. She could hear the steady, reassuring sound of beeps. There was a T.V. set hanging adjacent to it.

She twisted her head to the window side slowly and looked out. It was dark outdoors. She had a partial, blurry view of the series of white headlights and red brake lights flowing up and down the FDR Drive. She was alone in the room, tubes attached to both arms. She looked at the door of the room and could see the partially angled profile of a uniformed police officer sitting outside the door. Although she was too foggy to identify the color of his uniform, she could briefly capture the silhouette of a newspaper he was reading and the Glock on his hip.

She then tried to raise herself up but a harpoon-like pain fired through the entire left side of her body. She bit down on her lip, but she didn't scream. She was thirsty. Careful not to dislodge any of the tubes she gingerly crossed her right hand to her left shoulder where the pain originated and felt a mound of bandage. What the hell happened? She wondered.

She started to drift out again fighting to stay alert. She was barely able to scan the room in a desperate effort to stay awake. She wanted to call the officer. She wanted to ask him a question, but she could not find the strength to get her voice to utter any words. Her eyelids began to lower; she lifted them up with all the will she had, but they lowered again. Her eyes closed.

Before she was out again, in a fragile whisper she said, "How is Geddes?"

Monday morning, Ryan was on his way back to the 51st Precinct. He'd received word from the court that his request for Samantha's rape case folder be opened was approved. The court clerk had emailed the order direct to the 5-1 Squad and the folder had been pulled.

"You want me to bring it up to you, Loo?" the 5-1 detective said.

"No, I'll come down. Thanks."

He could've also had one of his detectives pick up the folder and bring it up to Bronx Homicide, but he felt oddly bound to spend more time in the detective squad office in the 51st Precinct. The precinct in which he'd grown up, the precinct in which he'd met and had come to love Manny and Samantha, the precinct in which they were both murdered.

When he walked into the 5-1 Precinct Detectives squad room, he was greeted by the three detectives working the day-tour and was told the folder was on Lieutenant Hullihan's desk. He thanked the detectives, stepped into the squad commander's private office, and closed the door behind him.

He was again struck with the odor of cigar smoke. Bill Hullihan enjoyed an occasional Cuban cigar, and nobody seemed to have gotten around to letting him know about the "No Smoking" policy in department buildings.

He stood over the desk and looked down at the blue case folder not able to sit and open it right away. The office ceiling light produced more illumination than he wanted, so, he stepped to the wall and flipped the switch off. He went back to the desk and turned on the fluorescent desk lamp that fired an umbrella of contained light on the desk. It was as if he didn't want to be seen reading the details of Samantha's first calamity.

He remained standing and gaped at the standard case folder label with its entries:

Date of Occurrence: August 7
Time of Occurrence: 2200-2400
Location of Occurrence: Mount Carmel Park
Crime: Rape/Assault
Victim: Samantha Morales, age 20
51 Pct./Complaint #   2379
51 Det. Squad #1023
Perpetrator: M. Iglesia
Arresting Officer: Santiago, J. 51 Pct.
Detective Assigned: Schimmel

He finally sat down and leafed through the folder. It was about two inches thick. Every possible rape-case document was packed into it. The top two-thirds were a collection of fill-in-the-blank forms, as well as an assortment of typewritten narrative reports and handwritten notes. It opened with the standard Complaint Report prepared by Toni's father, the same complaint report Toni had seen at One Police Plaza the day before.

Ryan hadn't given that a second thought. It hadn't occurred to him for a second that Toni's father had taken the initial report and made the arrest. In a department of over thirty-five thousand cops, detectives, and bosses, you'd expect more than a few Santiago's' (past and present) to make an appearance on the job, and Sergeant Tazzo hadn't mentioned Toni's telling him her father took the initial rape report.

The folder included evidence vouchers for Samantha's blouse and skirt, principally her underwear, which contained evidence of the assailant's discharge, and the rape kit. It had all been turned over to the 5-1 detectives for submission to the police lab after the hospital's emergency room doctor completed her physical examination of Samantha. Then a collection of long, detailed reports, followed with the results from the lab, and the Crime Scene Unit.

None of those reports gave him what he most wanted to know.

What he wanted was the arrest report. He wanted to know about M. Iglesia. He continued to trudge through page after page of documents. He came across the interview of the doctor at the hospital who examined Samantha. Then he came to the arrest report.

According to the report, she'd been heading home from work when accosted by her attacker in the park. A prior arrest of Iglesia by P.O. Santiago for public intoxication in the park (hours before the rape) exposed Iglesia as a suspect. Joe Santiago picked Iglesia up and brought him to the hospital for a show-up, but Samantha couldn't identify him.

He looked at the caption, Name of Perpetrator, and it had the same entry: M. Iglesia.

"Didn't anybody write first names back then?" he whispered in frustration.

He then shifted his attention for the address: 475 Crimmins Avenue. He sat up straight, "That was Manny's address. This guy lived in Manny's building," Ryan whispered. So, the rapist was a neighborhood guy.

Ryan figured Manny must've known him. And wondered if he'd known him himself, or had ever come across him in the neighborhood. He closed his eyes for a moment and pressed his temples hard with his thumbs. He looked for the entry with a description of the perpetrator: Male, Hispanic, 6'2", 275 lbs. big mutt, he thought, and another ache pierced his heart for Samantha. He looked for a photo of the perp.

Normally there would have been one attached to the arrest report — not the official arrest photo taken at Central Booking, but a simple Polaroid shot taken at the precinct by the arresting officer. He rifled through the whole package of paperwork for a photo but didn't come up with one. Maybe the photo had been removed since the records had been sealed.

His chest began to cave in as he again imagined the scene of her assault in Mount Carmel Park, by such a big, sick, low-life. He placed his forehead down on the desk, into the middle of the folder, and kept it there. His eyes were closed shut; his hands clenched between his legs as if in prayer. After a few moments he raised his head slowly, grabbed the folder; suit-jacket, and left.

CHAPTER 24

Ryan arrived at the Franciscan orphanage grounds about one hour after Father Joseph Egan called the Bronx Homicide Squad. It was fortunate Egan called when he did. Tracking down the orphanage was next on his list.

While Ryan had been focused with anticipation over what the friar would tell him about Jeremiah Francisco, the scenic drive up was not wasted on him. Cruising up the winding tree-lined road of the Saw Mill River Parkway to the orphanage was welcomed. He could've traveled with the windows sealed tight and the air-conditioning blowing, but he chose the forest-scented air of the parkway to course through the wide-open interior of the unmarked department car. As he cruised in a state of anxious delight, he imagined the gusting breeze purging the barbaric events of the last few of days.

When he pulled off Route 9 and coasted through the wide-open gate and under the iron lettered sign that read, "SUFFER THE LITTLE CHILDREN TO COME UNTO ME," he sensed the peace that such a place could give, and felt an unexpected and surprising touch of thankfulness that Jeremiah Francisco had been raised there.

He deliberately drove up the ascent of twisting blacktop, carefully scanning one side of the road to the other, taking in the white and gray statues of various shapes and sizes of Jesus Christ, the Virgin Mother, St. Francis, and other saints, as well as the collection of residential structures generously spaced amongst the wild foliage.

Most of the buildings were freshly painted white wood of one or two floors with black roofs, but as he reached the summit of the mountain he came to a different kind of architecture: a seven-story beige brick, modern, dormitory-style building he estimated to be about the width of one city block. It regrettably reminded him of police headquarters. It seemed to him that that sterile brick building did not belong on that mountain.

Father Egan, a plump friar, who appeared to be in his mid-seventies, greeted Ryan in the lobby. He was in sandals wearing the customary brown garb of a Franciscan: a hood neatly hanging from the back of his garment, a white rope-like belt around his waist, and a crucifix around his neck. His hair was pure white and he had bright blue eyes and rosy cheeks. It struck Ryan at how similar the friar's rosy cheeks looked to those of Pope John Paul II.

Early in his career, Ryan had been part of the Pope's security detail on one of his rare visits to New York and had the opportunity to shake his hand. Actually, as Ryan recalled the experience, it wasn't really a handshake; it was more of a hand-hold. When the Pope left the residence of St. Patrick's Cathedral that morning, he held the hand of each officer within arm's reach, and extended his blessing to the rest, before he climbed into his Pope-Mobile and made his way to Central Park where thousands fervently waited for him on the Great Lawn. What is it, Ryan wondered, about rosy cheeks and a life devoted to the love and service to God and man?

Egan escorted Ryan to an office down a long hall. The hall was draped with a string of framed group photographs almost exclusively of jovial Franciscans taken over many decades.

"Thank you for reaching out to us, Father. I know this isn't easy for you."

"Of course, Lieutenant, this is a very tragic thing that has happened. Very tragic."

"Yes."

"You know my father was a New York City police officer?" the friar said as they walked down the long white fluorescent-lit hall.

"Is that so? When did he retire?"

"Oh, it was many, many years ago. He was a lieutenant just like you," the friar said, looking back at Ryan with a hearty grin.

"How about that?"

"Yes, he was a policeman for almost forty years, and both his sons became priests," Egan said with a wide smile. "What do you suppose that means?"

"It means he must've been a very good father, Father."

Egan looked back at Ryan again with a twinkle in his eye and said, "That he was. That he was."

When they got to Egan's office Ryan found it tranquil with a nice floor lamp that delivered a warm yellow light in contrast to the fluorescent hall lighting they had just come through. Ryan scanned the wide ceiling-high bookshelves with not a space for one more book. A crucifix hung on the wall behind the desk, and there were other symbols of the Catholic faith generously displayed. The friar offered Ryan the simple loveseat opposite his own single seat.

"I appreciate your coming up here so promptly, lieutenant. After I'd seen the news reports about Father Manny I knew I needed to speak with someone in the police department."

Egan explained that he'd learned about Father Manny's murder on the evening television news a few days before.

"I was terribly shocked to hear such news."

The friar had known Father Manny for over twenty years. He said he'd come to meet him while Manny was still at the seminary. Manny had contacted the orphanage with the wish that his order adopt a newborn child.

"We didn't normally adopt newborns, you understand, lieutenant, but, of course, we would always assist in finding the child suitable adoptive parents. So his wish for my community to adopt the infant ourselves was very unusual. But Father Manny had been very insistent. He'd explained that the mother had been raped, which was very disturbing to hear, but that she could not bring herself to abort the child, which, of course, we were extremely gratified and heartened by."

Ryan nodded.

"And it was clear she could not bring herself to keep and raise the child. Father Manny and Jeremiah's mother insisted the infant not be turned over to a family but raised at the orphanage itself. They believed the child's only hope to overcome the darkness in which he was conceived was to be raised under a penetrating barrage of God's light through a religious order. So we agreed. But Jeremiah, of course, never knew."

Egan continued that he was assigned to act as his primary parent.

"You raised the child yourself, Father?" Ryan said.

"Well, no, not exactly. I was the child's primary guardian, but all the other friars and nuns chipped in. Which they were more than happy to do. He was a beautiful child. Jeremiah's mother asked us to name him."

The friar continued that they named the baby Jeremiah after the Old Testament prophet and gave him the last name of Francisco in honor of their order's founder, St. Francis of Assisi.

"Did you know the mother's name?" Ryan said, with hesitation.

"Oh, yes. Her name was Samantha Morales," Egan said. "She was only twenty years old when she had Jeremiah."

Ryan looked away and out the window, which faced the back of the building. On the top of the mountain, overlooking the valley and a series of mountains was a perfect replica of the Vatican's Pieta by Michelangelo. His eyes locked on it.

"Are you okay, lieutenant?"

"Ahh, yes, yes, Father," Ryan said having trouble getting his voice back. "Ahh, did you know…"

"That Samantha Morales is dead?" Egan interjected.

"Yes. I learned of that from the news too. The poor child; very sad."

Ryan remained silent and looked back out at the Pieta: The Virgin Mother holding her limp, dead, son on her lap.

"Lieutenant."

"Ah, huh, what did he think happened to his parents all those years?"

"We told him that his parents had been killed in a car accident in Virginia. Father Manny somehow created a newspaper article to support it when he got old enough to understand. You must understand we did lie to the boy, but it was to protect him."

Ryan didn't respond noticing a red bible and a hardcover copy of the Catechism of the Catholic Church resting to the side of the friar's desk.

"Tell me more about Jeremiah. How long did he stay here?"

"He remained here until he graduated from high school, about five years ago. But there was a turning point in his life when he first began high school. I and the other friars always thought he would follow in our footsteps and join our community. That is what we hoped."

"Well, when he began high school he developed a strong interest in your department: the N.Y.P.D."

"Is that right?" Ryan said and immediately wondered where this would lead.

"Yes, that's correct. He'd received a police badge in the mail one day. He never knew who sent it to him."

"Excuse me?" Ryan said. "He received a badge. You don't know the badge number, do you, Father?"

"I will never forget it, he showed it to me enough times, badge number 6-7-0-2."

"Oh God," Ryan muttered under his breath and abruptly sat up very straight, unable to say anything more.

"Well, right after Jeremiah graduated from high school, he moved to Manhattan and entered the John Jay College of Criminal Justice. We arranged for him to live at a Franciscan house on West 31st Street while he completed his studies. You know that college, don't you, Lieutenant?"

"Yes, I know it very well," Ryan said, still dazed to learn that it was to Jeremiah who Manny sent his duplicate shield. He'd given it to Manny years earlier when he'd been promoted to sergeant as a gift.

"He joined your department's Cadet Program at John Jay College, which worked out well for him because the department paid half of his tuition."

"Yes, right, Father. I know the program," Ryan said, a little scattered. "Did he complete the program? Did he graduate?"

"Oh, yes. B.A. in Criminal Justice, summa cum laude. He was always a very bright boy."

"Did he go into the academy?"

"Oh, yes," Egan said looking up at Ryan. "He graduated in December. He's been a police officer since then, about eight months now. He's in a precinct in Manhattan. Maybe you've come across him; he's a tall, handsome young man."

Ryan shook his head.

"Lieutenant, you should know that the day before Father Manny was killed, I received a call from Jeremiah—

"What?" Ryan said, feeling disoriented. "What did you say?"

"Jeremiah called me the day before Father Manny was killed. He was very angry that we had lied to him about his parents. You must understand, lieutenant, we were trying to do what was right for everyone, for him, for his mother."

"What else did he say?"

"He was very angry at his mother too for giving him up for adoption."

"How did he find out about it?"

"I have no idea," Egan replied. "I was shocked when he called and brought it up."

Egan explained that Jeremiah told him he intended to speak with Father Manny and then two days later he learned of his murder, that's when he became terribly fearful that Jeremiah was involved. Then Egan learned that Samantha had been murdered.

Ryan suddenly stood up and looked down on the portly friar.

"Father, I need to see him right away."

Ryan took Jeremiah Francisco's telephone number and address from the friar and left.

Ryan flew south on Route 9 to get back to the Bronx. A battering rain blanketed the parkway. Ryan's mind was racing as fast as he was driving. The thoughts flashed by as rapidly as the trees he was blowing past.

Why would Manny do that? Why would he send this particular kid his cop shield?

Ryan groped to grasp what was becoming more and more obvious.

He reviewed some of what he knew again. Samantha had been raped. She turned the child over to the Franciscans to raise because the child was the offspring of the rapist. Did Manny know who the rapist was? Did Manny know who the father was?

And that cop that thought he and the guy talking to Samantha outside Mount Carmel Park the night she was killed looked like him.

Ryan thought about what Manny may or may not have known over the years. And whatever he did know, his closest friend, Father Manuel Gonzalez, had never shared any of it with him.

"Why?" Ryan asked himself again.

Looking into the windshield with the wipers flapping away sheets of rain, working hard to lessen the blur of the white and red lights on the parkway ahead, he whispered the question he sensed could be true.

"What if he's my son? Is that possible?" He rubbed his eyes, then stayed quiet for at least another bucketing mile until he whispered, "Is that why Manny sent him my shield? Because he knew Jeremiah was my son?"

Ryan needed to get on his Blackberry to notify Sergeant Tazzo that there was a rookie cop named Jeremiah Francisco who could have killed Manny and Samantha. He needed to give the sergeant a list of things that he knew needed to be done: contact Operations at One Police Plaza, find out what precinct Francisco was assigned, get a photograph of him, find out if he was working and, if not, when his next scheduled tour would be, confirm his home address and have a couple detectives sit on it, contact Internal Affairs.

That's what he should do. Yet he couldn't. He just couldn't. He couldn't risk where that would lead. So, he had to keep Jeremiah Francisco to himself, at least for now.

CHAPTER 25

By Monday afternoon Toni was sitting up on the edge of her hospital bed. She was dressed to leave: jeans, running shoes, and a plain white V-neck t-shirt. There was a blue sling on her left arm, the white strap around her neck.

The night before — when she was finally out of the stupor she'd been in for two days since her surgery — the doctors told her she was very lucky. The .357 bullet that pierced her shoulder stopped hard when it flattened against the shoulder bone. They were able to remove it without complications.

Just after breakfast, she'd gotten a call from Ryan. He wanted to bring her home. She had zero interest in being picked up by him. She told him she'd already made arrangements to be taken home, and that if he didn't explain how he was tangled-up with Father Manny and Samantha Cohen, she'd have to go over his head. Ryan didn't answer, so she hung up.

A few hours later, there was a knock on the room door. It was Sergeant Tazzo. Her first question was how was Geddes?

That's when she first learned her partner had been so severely injured that he'd been unconscious and listed in critical condition up to only a few hours earlier. He'd finally been upgraded to serious-but-stable because he'd regained consciousness. She was relieved to know he was doing better, but to hear he'd been critical the last few days shook her up. Tazzo explained that Geddes had suffered a severe concussion when his head hit the windshield. He was lucky his head didn't go through it. Toni's eyes watered.

"It's my fault," she said, shaking her head.

The room was quiet for a few seconds.

"Toni, you've been suspended."

Toni didn't reply at first then in resignation and said, "I see."

"What were you doing in front of the Cohen building?"

Toni squinted at Tazzo through swollen, bloodshot eyes and remained silent.

"Condon thinks you were there to interview Elizabeth Rivera. Didn't he tell you were off both homicides?"

"Why, Sarge? Why was I pulled off those cases?"

"I don't know why," Tazzo said, with open palms and a shrug. "But that's not the point. The lieutenant had his reasons. Did you plan to interview her?"

Toni remained silent. She didn't need a union rep. or an attorney to advise her that she should keep her mouth shut.

After several long moments, Tazzo looked away and Toni said, "Am I being served with department charges?"

"I'm sorry, Toni," Tazzo said and handed her a document from the department prosecutor's office. "You're being charged with insubordination. You're suspended pending a department trial."

Toni was dropped off at her Riverdale apartment by Shaft. He walked through the apartment, checking closets, her balcony, kneeling down to look under Toni's bed. Toni didn't want to discuss the details of her suspension, and Shaft had enough sense not to ask.

"Why don't you have the uniform in the radio car sit on your door here, Toni?" Shaft said.

"I don't want to alarm my neighbors. And I sure don't want another cop inside my apartment either. I'll be fine."

"Well, you've got to screen your visitors yourself then."

"Yeah, I know."

Shaft soon left. But not before making sure the portable radio personally assigned to suspended Detective Toni Santiago was transmitting and reminded her not to hesitate to radio the cop parked in front of her building if she felt even a trace of trouble.

"Even suspended cops get protection," Toni said, as she walked Shaft to the door. "How about that."

"You got my cell on your phone, right?" Shaft said.

"I do."

"Anything you need, Toni, call me."

"Thanks, Shaft."

As soon as the door closed behind him, Toni slogged through her apartment checking for herself with her slung arm, opening, and closing, kneeling and standing, groaning and grumbling.

She then called her aunt and asked for her bulldog to be brought up.

"How are you, my child?" her aunt said, as Toni let her in.

"I'm okay, *Tia*," Toni said, and bent down to hug her wiggling dog with her one good arm, but Vita wouldn't stay still trying to slobber Toni's face. She was a virtual whirling dervish.

"You didn't bring all the flowers, my child," her aunt said. "They were so beautiful. Your friend should've brought them to you."

"I left them for the nurses, Tia."

"Ahh, okay. And how is John doing? Still getting better?"

"Geddes is good, Tia," Toni said. "I think he's going to be okay."

"Good, Good," her aunt said and stepped into the kitchen. "I'll make us a pot of coffee."

Toni went over to her dining room table and sat down to go through her mail. With one hand she leafed through a pile of charity envelopes: Christopher and Dana Reeve Foundation; National Police Officers Memorial Fund; PBS television and NPR radio stations; ASPCA. She was a soft touch for charities and they knew it. She pulled out her bills: American Express, Con Edison, Verizon, and a vet bill. She placed them off to the side.

A few minutes passed and Toni's aunt stepped out of the kitchen and handed her a cup, and sat down at the dining room table. Toni did the same and sat there for several seconds looking out her window.

Vita climbed up from the outside of Toni's leg without invitation, rested her head, and panted with excitement. Her two muscular arms and upper body rested on Toni's thighs; she felt her dog's comforting warmth. Toni stroked Vita's brown and white coat, not thinking or seeing much of anything, but that didn't last long.

She whispered at the window, "I screwed up big-time."

"Is there anything I can do, my child?"

Toni didn't reply at first then repeated, "I screwed up big-time, *Tia*, and almost got my partner killed."

She dropped her head a few moments with that recognition then straightened up again.

"Why did I have to interview Elizabeth Rivera? Why did I have to do it then? If I hadn't driven down 57th Street to the Cohen's building Geddes wouldn't be hurt. What a screw-up I am. Was it worth it? Hell no! Why do I have to be so damned stubborn? Why couldn't I just follow orders? Why am I always such a stubborn bitch?"

Her aunt watched Toni for a couple seconds with a warm smile then said, "I wouldn't say always, my child."

Toni turned back to her aunt and smiled, but then her eyes began to well up; her head dropped again; one fist clenched to her forehead.

After several moments Vita poked the knuckles of Toni's fist with her flat face. Toni raised her head slowly. She lifted her dog and held her tight against her chest. Vita's breathing rumbled in her ear. She then put her down.

"Who took that shot at us, *Tia*?"

Her aunt didn't respond. Her aunt knew her statement did not necessarily require a response, so she sat there and listened with complete attention.

"Who didn't want me to talk to Elizabeth Rivera, *Tia*?" She said and paused, "Besides Ryan Condon?"

She wiped her eyes with the back of her hand. Her aunt handed her a tissue.

"I can imagine the picture Ryan had painted for the brass downtown. " 'I told her to stay away from that apartment building but she disobeyed my order. If she had listened to me, Detective Geddes would not be in serious condition and Santiago would not have been shot.' But what reason could he give the brass to explain why he didn't want me — the case detective — to speak to the deceased's sister."

"I just made chicken and rice, your favorite, my child. Would you like me to bring some up for you?"

"I'm not hungry, *Tia*, but thank you."

"My child, you must eat."

This kind of exchange with her aunt had been going on since she was a little girl.

"Okay, *Tia*, thank you."

Soon after her aunt went back downstairs, Toni's apartment bell buzzed. She looked at the intercom and could see a male with a delivery of flowers. As soon as she buzzed him into her building, she went to her bedroom and grabbed her two-inch .38. Actually, it was her father's .38: left for her when he died. Her automatic and shield had not been returned after being released from the hospital due to her suspension. The department didn't know about the .38.

The purpose of having a radio car with one officer fixed in front of her building was to provide a rapid response should she radio for help. She was not just a suspended cop, but the victim of an attempted murder. And, in any case, she knew help could only come if she had the chance to reach for the radio.

When the flower guy arrived at her door, she opened it wide and kept it that way with her leg.

210

"Put the flowers on that table," she said, pointing at the dining room table where she had all her mail scattered. Vita escorted the flower-man, grunting as she sniffed his legs. Toni never closed the door, her revolver pointed down behind her leg.

"That five-dollar bill on the table is for you."

He gratefully took it, and she promptly locked the door behind him. She placed the .38 on the table and pulled the small card attached to the paper wrapping. It read:

Dear Detective Santiago:

I was very sorry to hear what happened to you, and your partner. I pray you both get well soon. You're both in my prayers. I would like very much to speak with you about something whenever you're feeling up to it.

Sincerely,

Liz Rivera

Her aunt returned with the chicken-and-rice in a plastic covered container when her phone rang.

"You want me to get that for you, my child?"

"No, thank you, *Tia*, I'll come down to see you later," Toni said and trudged to her cell as her aunt rubbed Vita's head, and closed the apartment door behind her.

The cell was on the coffee table in front of her sofa. She was anxious, figuring it could be Ryan.

"Yeah."

"Detective Santiago," a female voice said.

"Yes."

"I hope I'm not disturbing you? It's Liz Rivera."

"Liz Rivera," Toni repeated. "No, Mrs. Rivera, of course not," she said, sitting down on her sofa to take the call.

"How are you?" Liz said.

"I'm fine. I'm fine. Thanks for asking, and thank you for the beautiful flowers. That was very thoughtful of you, but you shouldn't have gone through the trouble. I mean, you have so much going on yourself."

"Oh, no, it was the least I could do. I called the hospital many times the last two days to find out how you both were, but they wouldn't give me any information. And Ryan would only say you were both doing better, but wouldn't give me any details. I found out you were discharged today."

"Well, thank you very much," Toni said.

"I was so shocked when I heard what happened to you and Detective Geddes," Liz said. "How is he?"

"I think he's going to be okay."

Toni pushed herself up from her knee with her elbow and stood carefully, but still felt a shot of pain pierce her left, slung arm. With the iPhone in her hand, she walked onto her terrace, which overlooked the Hudson River to the New Jersey shore. Her glance captured two jet skiers rushing up the Hudson; two expanding V's gushed from their sterns. Then one suddenly accelerated directly in front of the other, and the V's became one.

Liz said, "You know, I can't shake the feeling that there's a connection between what happened to you and Detective Geddes and my sister's murder. Do you think there's a connection?"

"We don't know at this point, but I promise you it's being looked into."

"I mean you were attacked right on my sister's corner."

"Yes, I know. But we can't jump to any conclusions about that. There may or may not have been a connection. I'm sure Lieutenant Condon has a team of detectives working to identify your sister's murderer and who fired the shots at us. And if there's a connection they'll figure it out."

"Were you on your way to see me?'

"I'd rather not say."

There was silence.

"Ryan hasn't told me very much."

"Well, I'm sure he will when he can," Toni said, not at all certain of that.

Toni said, "How are you doing? I know it's been a terrible time for you."

"Yes, well, it's been very hard. Today is the last day of my sister's wake and tomorrow will be her funeral. You know, Detective, my sister had so many friends. I had no idea how loved she really was," Liz said softly.

"I knew she was highly thought of by the partners in her law firm, but I found out for the first time that she did pro bono legal work for a senior citizens' organization in the neighborhood where we grew up. I knew she volunteered some of her time, but I didn't know how involved she really was."

"In the South Bronx?" Toni said.

"Yes. She did quite a bit of personal injury work for them. That was my sister's specialty."

"Yes, I knew that," Toni said, and drifted back to her sofa.

"Oh, yes, my sister was one of the best." Liz's voice cracked. "But she did other things pro bono, like some housing work, or just standard things like drawing up wills or just helping them to fill out forms that had nothing to do with anything legal. My sister's wake — over the last two days — has been overflowing with senior citizens, all of whom barely speak English or can't speak any English at all. It's been very emotional."

"I can understand that," Toni said and remained silent to give Samantha's sister a moment to collect herself.

"Many of the old men and women watched us grow up and knew my parents."

"Really?" Toni said. "Are your parents still living?"

"Yes, well, my mother is. My father died some years ago. You know, my mom still lives in the building where we were raised on Cedar Avenue."

"Really?" Toni said again. "Right by the park?"

"Yes. Samantha and I tried to move her out to someplace nicer and safer many times, but she didn't want to go."

"How old is she?"

"She's eighty-one and still has a very sharp mind."

"It must be so hard for her, too."

"Yes, yes, it is," answered Liz. "But she's a very strong woman, my mother."

Toni started to again dwell on Samantha Cohen's murder. She thought of Liz Rivera losing her sister in such a vicious way. Toni knew what losing someone to violence was like; the awful and sudden void it left. But she didn't know what it was like to have a person you loved, so intimately sullied and savagely murdered. What the killer must've put her through, Toni thought, for her to of looked so annihilated. The brutal blows delivered; the shots fired; the unrestrained desecration of her body; those horrible mental images of her sister's isolated and helpless predicament.

Yet, there she was on the phone, pressing her. It was evident to Toni, as polite as Liz Rivera was, that she was a force to be reckoned with in the pursuit of her sister's killer. Toni felt only admiration for Liz and silently hoped Samantha had plunged into unconsciousness early in the attack.

"Mrs. Rivera—

"Please call me Liz."

"Okay, Liz, if you wouldn't mind, I'd like to attend your sister's funeral tomorrow."

"Of course, I'd appreciate your being there very much. But are you sure you would be up to it? I mean you just got out of the hospital," Liz said with genuine concern.

"Oh, I'll be fine. Where's Samantha's service taking place?"

"Our Lady of Mount Carmel," Liz said.

Toni found that odd but didn't think she gave that indication.

"You're probably surprised to hear that, since what happened to my sister was so close by, and, well Father Manny's—

"No, I can understand that. It was your childhood parish, wasn't it?"

"Yes, it was. And she was always very fond of it, especially of Father Manny. My sister loved Father Manny, you know. It's just, I don't know how to say it. Just terrible what's happened to my sister and her friend."

Toni remained silent.

"Could there be any connection between Father Manny's murder and my sister's, do you think?" Liz said. "Is that possible, Detective?"

Toni remained silent for a couple of moments and said, "Anything's possible. I promise you if there's a connection, it'll come out." Toni paused. "Liz, I don't know if anyone informed you that I've been suspended?"

"No, I didn't know. Suspended?" Liz said. "But Why?"

"Well, I can't get into that. I just thought you should know that someone else has probably been officially assigned to your sister's case, and Father Manny's case. I don't know who that is, but Lieutenant Condon can tell you."

"Does your suspension have anything to do with my sister's murder investigation?"

"I'm sorry, Liz. I can't get into that."

Now Liz remained silent.

Toni then said, "You said in your note with the flowers that you wanted to speak to me about something. Was there anything else?"

Liz did not respond right away.

"Yes there is, and I don't care if you are suspended, Detective Santiago, I want to tell you something. There's something odd about the evening before my sister died. I mentioned it to Ryan, but I'm not sure he heard me or maybe he didn't think it was important."

Toni suddenly straightened her back. "What is it?"

"Well, when I came to my sister's apartment the following day — the day after my sister was killed — I thought I picked up an odor in her bedroom — something different."

"How was it different?"

"Well, like somebody else had been there. Like a man had been there. There was a smell of a man's cologne or aftershave or something."

"I see," Toni said with complete attention.

"Not only that, but the sheets had been messed up more than I think Samantha would have them. I wanted to mention it to you when you stopped by but then —

"How so exactly?"

" — well, I mean my sister only used one side of her bed as far as I ever knew. We once talked about it some years ago when she was first divorced. She couldn't sleep in the middle of the bed. She always slept on the side closest to the door. And whenever I came for a visit or she came to visit me in Florida she only slept on one side of the bed," Liz said. "And detective —

"Yes."

" — the sheets smelled like sex."

"Liz, was your sister dating anyone?

"No, not as far as I know. And I was up for a visit only two weeks ago and she didn't mention anybody. My sister hasn't been with anybody since her divorce. So, I can't imagine her bringing anyone home to stay over, especially since she had her daughter," Liz said. "Am I making sense detective?'

"Yes you are," Toni said. "Liz, have you changed the sheets?"

"Yes, I have, but I haven't washed them."

"Good, good." Toni could not help expressing some excitement.

"Oh, good, did I do the right thing? You know each time I thought about just throwing them in the wash I would stop. I told Ryan about the sheets, but he said it was okay to wash them. But every time I thought about it I would stop myself."

"Good, good, Liz. If someone else was in your sister's bed the night she died, we need to know who that was. It may have nothing to do with your sister's murder, but we have to find out who that was. There should be some DNA information our lab could pick up."

"Well, I have the sheets in a shopping bag in her closet."

"Good. I'll arrange to have them picked up," Toni said, disregarding—not forgetting—that she was under suspension.

"Okay, I'll keep them for you."

"Liz, do you know if Samantha had any other children?"

"Yes. She had a son. Ryan asked me about it too a few days ago."

"He did?"

"Yes, I told him Father Manny had helped find a home for the child," Liz said. "I told him the child was named Jeremiah Francisco. He was conceived when my sister was raped. Did you know about that?"

"Yes, I did," Toni said. "What time is the service tomorrow?'

"Nine o'clock."

"I'll be there," Toni said. "And if there's anything I can do for you, don't hesitate to call me, even if you just need someone to talk to, okay?"

"Okay, thank you, Detective Santiago."

"And, Liz."

"Yes."

"Please call me Toni."

As Toni tried to figure out how to arrange to have those sheets picked up and tested by the lab, she called the Franciscan Orphanage in Putnam County to speak with the Father Joe Egan. The Father Egan mentioned in the letters.

When she got off the phone with Father Joe, she couldn't move. The Friar assumed she'd called as a follow-up to Ryan's visit. He mentioned that Ryan had taken Jeremiah's contact information before he left.

She needed to find this Jeremiah Francisco, offspring of a rapist, possessor of a Glock, and could very well be the drunk ripped off by Mateo Mateo in that East Harlem dive bar the same night Samantha was found dead.

She sat on her sofa in a bit of a daze at first. She couldn't believe what she was about to do. She was sure that if her father had been alive, he wouldn't have suggested she show up at a murder suspect's home—while under suspension. The conditions were not ideal: being solo, injured, and of all places his apartment. But in her gut, she felt her father would've taken the risk, to get to the truth. So that was that. She would do what needed to be done.

She left for the address she'd pulled from her iPad when she and Geddes had left the rectory with the letters. She needed to talk to this rookie cop directly before Ryan got to him if he hadn't already. Her investigative juices were flowing again. Self-pity was not her way, at least not for long. She would find this kid, and one way or the other he would answer her questions. But it had to be done right away.

She knew she had to be careful as she left her apartment building. She had to get into her car and pull out without alerting the cop in the radio car out front. He could not see her leaving.

218

The reality she believed she was up against was that Ryan was somehow involved in the two murders, and that's why he obstructed her investigation. But she also reminded herself that she didn't know what role the rookie played in all that had happened and had to be careful.

Before she'd left her apartment, she'd placed the two-inch .38 in a gym bag, grabbed the police radio and the flowers she'd received from Liz Rivera, and walked out with Vita on her leash.

Toni turned the corner from Eastchester Road down the service road of Pelham Parkway to Jeremiah's six-story elevator apartment building. She took it nice and slow in case she spotted Jeremiah coming or going, except, she realized she didn't know what he looked like. She took it slow anyway. Somehow she sensed if he were a killer she'd know it.

His building was at the very end and passed an old age home on the corner followed by two other postwar brown brick apartment buildings that were identical to Jeremiah's. When she jumped out of her car, there was a terrible pungent scent in the air that she and Vita couldn't help noticing. They both sniffed the air in an attempt to figure out its source.

"What the hell is that, Vita?"

Toni buzzed the apartment bell for J. Francisco, apartment 5C. She had to buzz again. There was a camera looking down on her from the upper corner of the vestibule. She carried the flowers Liz had sent to her. Vita was sitting like a statue outside the door, out of the camera's view.

"Yes," a male voice answered.

"Flower delivery," Toni said.

She had her long, black hair up in a baseball cap. It took a moment before he buzzed her in. She stepped into the lobby, called for Vita, who dashed in after her.

When she stepped onto the elevator up to the fifth floor, it again occurred to her she needed someone to pick up Samantha's bed sheets and bring them to a lab, but what lab and who could she trust? Would Geddes have helped her? If she told him what she was thinking and doing, would he have helped? She didn't know. And it didn't matter. Geddes was in the hospital because of her and that recognition made her shake her head again.

CHAPTER 26

Toni pushed the doorbell. Jeremiah opened the door and held it. Toni handed him the flowers, the .38 pointed at his chest with her slung arm.

"Step back," she said.

Jeremiah let the door go with resignation in his eyes, turned his back to Toni, and took several steps in. Toni switched the .38 to her good hand and gave it a flick, "Inside."

Vita and Toni muscled their way in. She watched the broad back of the handsome six-foot-two Jeremiah step into his apartment and was directly taken aback when he turned and she got a long look at his face.

"What's your name?" Toni said.

"Jeremiah Francisco," he said, standing perfectly still, cradling the flowers. "Where do you want me?"

Toni still caught-up by what she thought she was seeing; untangled her tongue and said, "Go over by the table, by that window; put the flowers there."

Jeremiah walked deliberately to the dining room table, put the flowers down, and stood motionless. Toni still pointed the gun at his chest. She didn't lower it.

The heat in the apartment was stifling.

"Don't you have AC?"

"Oh, sure," Jeremiah pointed to it. It was in the wall under the living room window next to the radiator.

"Well, put it on," Toni said. "You don't want to kill the flowers, do you?"

Jeremiah pushed the button and stood back up straight with his hands down his sides. The rush of cold air started to spread out.

"All right, interlock your hands, and put them behind your head," Toni said. "And don't move."

She then dragged one of the chairs at the table across his wood floor and put it next to the apartment door.

"Slowly take your shirt off," Toni said.

221

He cautiously brought his hands down from his head and unbuttoned his long-sleeved, white collared shirt, which was rolled up at the cuffs, and took it off. He had a white tank top on underneath. He looked at her and made the motion to place it on the back of the chair. She nodded and he did.

"Now raise your t-shirt and slowly turn around."

He did as he was told and she very carefully perused his rippled stomach and naturally tanned back in a pair of belt-less jeans.

"Okay, put it down. Empty out your pockets, right there on the table."

Jeremiah wore brown boat shoes without socks.

"All right, step away from the table."

Toni again eased her revolver into her left slung arm. She knew she wouldn't be able to use that arm but would have no problem bending her trigger finger to deliver a bullet into his chest if he made one stupid move. She walked to the table.

"No wallet?" she said.

"It's in the bedroom."

"Take a seat."

She transferred the gun to her right hand.

"Vita, come here." Vita immediately gave up the sniffing and sat at Toni's side, facing him.

After Jeremiah sat down, Toni tossed him a set of handcuffs.

"Cuff yourself to that radiator."

Jeremiah did what he was told.

"I want that cuff nice and snug. But don't cut off the circulation," Toni said. "Now, let me hear some clicks."

Jeremiah clicked the handcuff tighter to his wrist.

Toni lowered the gun to her side, index finger inside the trigger guard. There were about twenty feet between them. Toni paced the living room looking around as if she was going to buy the place.

"Where's your gun?"

"I lost it."

222

Toni squinted at him.

"Do you know who I am?" Toni shouted from his narrow hallway, ducking into his bedroom and closets, bathroom and cabinets for a quick search. No gun.

She returned to the living room, trudged over his one area rug and absently studied the rug's colored squares and diamond shapes: blue, maroon, orange. Her mind spun with scenarios over how things could develop. She passed his copy of Norman Rockwell's "Runaway" above his pseudo fireplace — back and forth — as if she was picketing.

"No, no, I'm sorry I don't," Jeremiah said. "Are you on the job?"

Vita's head and body lay flat on the wood floor at the apartment door with her hind legs extended behind her as bulldogs do. The dog's eyes moved following Toni's movements as if watching a mechanical metronome. She was fully awake; yet, a rumbling, bulldog snore filled the room. "Toni Santiago, Bronx Homicide," Toni said, and paused, giving Jeremiah an opportunity to think about that. "You don't know why I'm here?"

Jeremiah didn't answer at first. "You're working the Father Gonzalez murder?"

"Right you are."

There was silence for a few moments.

"So you're on the job?" Toni said.

"Yes?" Jeremiah said. "Well, not very long, I've only been out of the academy a few months."

"I'm going to ask you again. Where's your gun and shield?"

"I lost my gun."

Toni squinted at him again.

"I've been suspended for going AWOL and for losing my gun," Jeremiah said. "Internal Affairs came here a little while ago and suspended me. They took my shield."

"How'd you lose your gun?"

223

"I'm not sure. I went to a bar and got pretty drunk. When I made it back home I didn't have it."

Toni's eyes focused. So it was Jeremiah's gun Mateo Mateo ripped off in the men's room of that bar. And, it was Jeremiah's gun that was used to kill Father Manny. She stayed silent for a few moments looking at Jeremiah's face, sizing him up, mannerisms, profile; she wondered again if what she was thinking was possible.

"All right. Now, let me tell you something. We got your Glock and the dupe."

"Who had it?"

"None of your business. What's important is that Ballistics tested that Glock and it was the gun used to kill Father Gonzalez."

He was quiet.

Toni just watched him for a few moments in silence.

"You need to talk to me," Toni sat down, leaned back in the chair she'd placed by the apartment door, the .38, and Vita still pointed in his direction.

What Jeremiah hadn't noticed was the digital recorder secreted in the flowers on the table, next to the radiator he was handcuffed to. Toni had flipped it on as soon as he buzzed her into his building.

After a long pause, Jeremiah said, "I'll tell you how it happened."

Toni looked at him then asked, "All right. Before you get started, I got a question: Do you have family on the job?"

"No, I don't"

"All right, go ahead. I'm all ears."

He said he'd received an anonymous letter at his home that informed him for the first time that a Father Manuel Gonzalez had been responsible for turning him over to the Franciscan orphanage when he was an infant, and that his mother was alive.

"When did you receive it?"

"Day before I went to see him. Saturday."

"Day before he was killed?" Toni said.

Jeremiah nodded and continued.

He'd always thought it was Father Iglesia who brought him to the orphanage. Jeremiah explained that he'd first met Father Iglesia when he'd just turned seven. It was Father Iglesia that told him his parents had been killed in a car accident not far from Georgetown, Virginia. Years later, when Jeremiah was in high school, Father Iglesia produced a short local newspaper article that reported the details of the accident. The headline read, "NY COUPLE KILLED IN CAR ACCIDENT; WIFE PREGNANT; BABY SAVED."

"Did the article identify the victims?"

"No."

Jeremiah explained that the article said the police would not reveal the identity of the victims until the next of kin had been notified.

"So you didn't know your parents had been killed in a car accident until this Father Iglesia showed up at the orphanage to visit you?'

"That's right," Jeremiah said. "I knew they'd been killed in an accident, the Franciscans had told me that but told me they didn't know the details. Father Iglesia showed up with the details."

"So when you got this anonymous letter, you always assumed your parents were dead, it was the first time you learned your parents were alive?"

"Right," Jeremiah said. "Well, at least my mother. The note didn't say anything about my father."

"Okay, just your mother," Toni said. "And that Father Gonzalez at Mount Carmel knew all about it?"

"That's right."

"Didn't you ever have any curiosity about your parents after Father Iglesia had shown you that Virginia press clipping? I mean…you didn't even know their names. Weren't you curious?"

225

"Yes and no," Jeremiah said. "All I can say is there was a part of me that wanted to know, but there was also part of me that felt if I went after more information, I might regret it. I can't say why I felt that because I was—at least—I thought I was convinced that they had been killed in an auto accident. I mean, I believed what the friars told me, and when Father Iglesia showed up and confirmed it, I just let it rest. I guess I thought there was no point. Except, there was something in the back of my mind that wasn't so sure."

"All right, go ahead," Toni said.

Jeremiah continued that he'd arrived at Mount Carmel to attend the 11 a.m. mass. He had called the rectory first to find out which Sunday mass Father Gonzalez would be the celebrant. So he showed up at the mass and watched the back of the priest as he approached the altar and when he turned to face the congregation he was shocked to see it was Father Iglesia, or whom he believed to be Father Iglesia.

"Wait a minute!" Toni said. "You're saying Father Gonzalez is the same priest who visited you at the orphanage when you were a kid and identified himself as Father Iglesia?"

"That's right."

"Father Manny Gonzalez, pastor of Mount Carmel?"

"Yes."

"The murdered priest?"

"Yes."

Jeremiah said that it just blew his mind that this priest—whatever his name was—had lied to him that way. That he'd told him his parents were dead when they weren't. That he'd deprived him of the truth his whole life and the chance to know his parents.

"How could a priest do that?" Jeremiah said.

Toni didn't answer.

He'd always believed his being turned over to the Franciscan Orphanage in Putnam County was God's hand at work. But, always a part of him, etched into his heart, was the notion of rejection; the belief his parents didn't want him. It made no sense, of course, since he'd been told his parents had died in a car accident.

So, as he grew up he was never told the truth. The Franciscans must've thought they were protecting him. They were all trying to fill the role of father and mother to him and the other orphans, and he was grateful. They couldn't bring themselves to tell him his parents had not wanted him.

"Maybe they never knew the truth," Jeremiah said. "Maybe that's what they were told."

"Maybe," Toni said. "Maybe not." Toni didn't want to bring up the letters between Father Manny, his mother, and Father Egan.

"Well, the truth was my parents hadn't been killed; that my mother had given me away; that I was the product of rape." Jeremiah shook his head. "This news blew me away. I just sat in a bar and poured the booze down my throat."

At the mass, as he listened to Father Gonzalez speak of Jesus' teaching of honesty and purity he'd become enraged. Enraged by how Father Manny Gonzalez had deceived him; enraged by the sham.

"What a miserable hypocrite! Jeremiah said.

He knew real well another one of Jesus' central teachings was forgiveness. That we should forgive when we are wronged. That we should forgive seventy times seven times. That we should turn it over to God's judgment — not our personal judgment — when we've been harmed; that we should make peace with our brother. But he was so outraged to learn he'd been brought into the world that way, he just wanted to run as far away as he could get.

"I want the rapist's blood bled out of me," Jeremiah said

Toni looked at him for a few extra moments.

227

"Do you still have the note?" Toni said.

"Yes. It's on top of my bureau in the bedroom."

Toni went to the bedroom and returned with the envelope and note. She noticed it had a Bronx postmark with the same zip code that covered the Mount Carmel Church area. Toni read the typewritten note out loud:

Dear Jeremiah,

Wouldn't you like to know what really happened to your parents? Wouldn't you like to know who your mother is? Wouldn't you like to see her? Sure you would.

Go see Father Manuel Gonzalez at Our Lady of Mount Carmel Church on E. 138th Street, in the Bronx. He is after all the person that took you away from your mother and dumped you in that orphanage when you were only two days old.

He has all the answers you need.

Good Luck

P.S. Did you know that you're a product of rape?

Toni then looked back at him. Who was living in that area at the time it was mailed besides Father Manny? Then it hit her. Father Gribbons. Could he have mailed that letter? She'd never had a chance to ask him where he'd gone after he'd left the Clarence Abbey Saturday afternoon. It was soon after she'd found out he hadn't spent the entire weekend at the abbey that she and Geddes had been shot at. She needed to confront Father Gribbons. But what possible motive would Father Gribbons of had to send that letter?

Jeremiah continued that he went to talk to Father Manny. He wanted information. He wanted an explanation. He'd gone to Mount Carmel to demand both. After the mass, he watched from across the street and waited for him to be alone. He saw a few parishioners enter the rectory and stay throughout the afternoon, and when they left, a few others came in the early evening."

"So what did you do?" Toni said. "You waited outside and then what?"

"From the street I could see the lights in the dining room on so I walked into the alleyway along the side of the rectory, and could see Father Iglesia sitting at the dining room table having a cup of coffee with a woman."

She must've left the lipstick on that rectory coffee cup, Toni thought.

"What'd she look like?"

"I didn't get a good look. I only took a quick glance. Long red hair, maybe in her 40s"

"Would you recognize her if you saw her again," Toni said.

"No, I doubt it. I looked at her quickly. I just saw her profile," Jeremiah said. "Anyway, I got frustrated waiting; it was already almost nine o'clock. So I got this idea to climb up the fire escape in the back of the rectory, find his office and wait for him there. I deliberately wanted to shake him up," Jeremiah said. "I wanted to shake him up bad."

Toni looked at him in silence and waited.

"When I got to his office, I had no trouble finding it. His name was on the door. I had nothing better to do so as I waited I started to go through his files thinking there might be something about me in one of them. See what I could find out. I didn't know if he'd go to his office — after the woman left — or go right to his bedroom. I figured in case he came to the office, I'd kept my Glock on the desk so I could get and keep his attention. Anyway, I searched the drawers," Jeremiah said.

"Did you intend to kill him if he walked in?"

"I'm not sure if I could, but I was very upset at that moment," Jeremiah said. "And I figured the Glock would keep him from moving a muscle as he explained to me every detail of what he knew about my parents and my adoption, and why he lied to me all these years." Jeremiah paused. "He was no longer a priest to me. He was just another man."

Toni remained silent and waited for Jeremiah to continue.

He said he'd found a yellow folder in the bottom drawer in the back that contained letters from his mother to Father Manny when he was at seminary. Regular correspondence over whether she would abort him or have him. He found out that Father Manny had been very helpful to his mother.

"I hadn't even known my mother was still alive, and now I had her name. It was a lot to take in."

And it confirmed for him that he had been conceived as a result of her being raped. He explained that when he read that, he lost it, and didn't remember much, except he started to storm out, planning to hit a bar in East Harlem.

"It was then I could hear loud yelling, a woman's voice, almost a scream, but not like a scream of distress but…

Toni cut him off. "Who was screaming—the redhead?"

"I guess so. I don't know for sure. I went to the door, opened it a crack. It sounded like the woman was pleading with him."

"What was she saying? Could you make any of it out?"

"It sounded like she was saying, 'Please don't Manny, please don't do this.' But I couldn't hear any answer."

Who was that woman? Toni wondered.

"So, what did you do?" Toni said.

"I left."

"How'd you leave—the front door?"

"No, no. I went the way I came, down the fire escape."

"Was the redhead still there when you left?"

"I don't know, I think so."

But before he made it to the bar, he remembered — in his rush to get out of the rectory — that he'd left his Glock on the desk and had to turn back. He'd decided to just knock on the front door of the rectory and confront Father Manny. When he got back, he found the front door open. He walked to the kitchen thinking he should start there and found his bloody body layout in the kitchen. Jeremiah said he then rushed upstairs to the office, grabbed his Glock, which was still on the desk, and blew back out through the front door.

"So what are you telling me," Toni said, locking his eyes, "that you don't remember shooting him in the face?"

Jeremiah looked at Toni in silence.

"I don't blame you for thinking I killed him, but I didn't. It happened the way I said it did. He was dead when I came back."

"And the Glock was exactly where you'd left it?"

"Yes."

"On the desk?"

"Yes."

Toni considered what he said.

"Ah huh," Toni said. "What did you do next?"

"I went to a bar in East Harlem to get drunk," Jeremiah said. "On One-hundred and Fifth and Second."

"You say you ran out of the rectory, got in your car drove off and came back because you knew you left your Glock on the desk? Is that right?"

"Yes."

"Where were you when you realized you'd left your Glock?"

"I'd just gone over the Third Avenue Bridge into the Manhattan. I then shot over to First Avenue and flew over the Willis Avenue Bridge back into the Bronx."

"How long do you estimate it took you to make that trip and back?"

"It's hard to say, twenty, twenty-five minutes maybe."

"Was there any traffic?" Toni said.

"No, not really."

"Then, it was five minutes to get over the one bridge, five minutes to get back over the other bridge: So we're talking about ten minutes tops?"

Toni wondered if anybody could have gone in after Jeremiah, potentially shot Father Manny with his Glock, returned it to the desk and got out without Jeremiah seeing him.

"Yeah, I guess so," Jeremiah said, "but, oh yeah, I forgot, I didn't have any money so I had to go to an ATM first."

"You mean before you remembered you'd left the Glock, you hit an ATM?"

"Yes, right.

"Where was the ATM?"

"A hundred-twenty-fifth and second. I didn't have enough cash on me to drink the way I planned to, so I stopped at the ATM. When I got back in my car that's when I knew I left my Glock."

"That would've taken you ten minutes at least."

"I guess so," Jeremiah said.

Toni just looked at Jeremiah carefully, her eyes unconsciously squinted. She wondered if he was trying to hint all along that someone else must've shot Father Manny since he'd claimed he'd forgotten his gun for at least twenty to twenty-five minutes before he made it back and thought the added piece of information about the redhead's pleas would put off any notion of his involvement. She wondered if this Jeremiah was slick enough to try and lead her down, "Bogus Alibi Road."

"You got an ATM slip?" Toni said.

Jeremiah froze and looked at Toni in a bit of a daze.

"Yes, yes, I must have a slip in my wallet. I mean I don't remember grabbing the slip, but I must've grabbed it." He reached into his back pocket for his wallet but then gave Toni a blank stare.

232

"Yeah, right, you're wallet's in the bedroom," Toni said. "If you don't have it, and you were there like you said, the bank will have you on video. Right?"

"Yes, right," Jeremiah said, with wide eyes.

"Now, what about your Glock? What did you do with the Glock?"

"I had it in my inside jacket pocket. I had a blazer. It must've have been stolen while I was in the bar."

"What about the shield?"

"The duplicate shield? That was stolen too," Jeremiah said. "Internal Affairs has my real shield and I.D. card."

"Yeah, the dupe."

"It was stolen when my Glock was stolen. I kept them both in the blazer."

Toni looked at Jeremiah for an extra second, ashamed of the flare of disgust she felt for this rookie cop as if she hadn't known other good, stand-up cops, who did stupid things too in a state of intoxication, including her.

"What's the number of your real shield?" Toni said.

"Two-three-two-six."

"What about the dupe?" Toni asked. "Do you remember the dupe's number?"

"Yes, of course," Jeremiah replied. "Six-seven-oh-two—

"Why do you say, 'Yes, of course?' " Toni asked with steady eyes.

" —I had that shield a lot longer than my real shield."

"Where'd you get the dupe?"

He said he would never forget the day he anonymously received duplicate shield number 6-7-0-2 in a small box at the Franciscan orphanage. It was the summer after his first year in High School. It also had a Bronx, New York postmark. He'd opened it slowly, and there was a note he didn't read at first but saw the shining police shield # 6-7-0-2.

He held the shield in the palm of his hand and slowly glided his fingers over the numbers, over the raised letters like he was reading Braille, "City of New York Police" and over the raised, official, New York City seal: the figures of an Indian and a Dutchman separated by the shield with a windmill enclosed. He read the note: "This is a duplicate New York City police shield. It is the symbol of authority carried by the thousands of professional men and women—past and present—who have chosen a life of service as police officers."

It was after receiving the shield that he took an interest in the New York City Police Department. He soon learned much about the rich history of the department. It was then he'd found his calling to pursue a New York City police career and not the religious life.

"Don't you have any theory why you got the dupe?"

"No, not really," Jeremiah replied. "I didn't know anybody on the job."

"Does the name Lieutenant Ryan Condon mean anything to you?"

"Lieutenant Ryan Condon, no, no, I don't think, does he work in Manhattan? Wait," Jeremiah stopped. "Wait a minute, isn't there a Lieutenant Condon, yeah right, he's the C.O. of Bronx Homicide? I've seen his name in the paper. Is he your boss?"

"Yeah, he is," Toni said, and looked carefully at Jeremiah. "Have you ever met him?"

"No, I never have. Not that I remember anyway."

Toni's mind locked into intense thought. Jeremiah, a possible suspect in Father Manny's murder, was the son of Samantha Cohen who was also murdered.

"Did you ever get to meet your mother?" Toni asked

"I know my mother was murdered, Detective," Jeremiah said, holding her gaze. "I saw it in the paper. And you want to know something else? I was with her in Mount Carmel Park the night she was killed."

"What?" Toni blurted and her index finger found its way back inside the trigger guard of the .38.

"Yes, right. I called her. I got her home number from the priest's Rolodex and called her. She agreed to meet me at Mount Carmel Park."

"You were with her in Mount Carmel Park the night she was killed?" Toni said, unable to disguise her alarm.

"Yes," Jeremiah said, "I was."

They sat silently for several moments locked in an intense gaze.

"That's a recurring thing for you isn't it?" Toni said. "You just happen to be with murder victims just before they're murdered?"

Jeremiah remained silent.

Toni spoke up again. "It was your idea to meet at the park?"

"Yes."

"Why?"

"Because I wanted her to show me where I'd been conceived." Jeremiah's shoulders and head shifted down a notch. "But you have to know that I wasn't high on booze or in a blackout or anything the night she was killed. I had a conversation with her in the park and left her there alive

"So she was alive when you last saw her; that's what you're telling me?"

"Yes. That's why I'm glad you're here."

"Why?" Toni leaned forward. "Why are you glad I'm here?"

"Because I want to help you find my mother's killer."

There was a long pause.

After Samantha finished telling Jeremiah the details of how he was conceived, as terrible as it was, there was still a deep part of him that didn't want to ease her suffering; that didn't want her to reconcile with him. There was a deep part of him that refused to admit her humanness. He said he was horrified to hear what had happened to her. Yet he couldn't get past the illusion that a mother's love can overcome any heinous obstacle. But, his mother's love could not.

"I still couldn't forgive her," he said shaking his head. "And yet, another part of me wanted to forgive her. I wanted to hold her and cry with her and say I believed she loved me, and explain honestly that I was just heartbroken she couldn't have kept me," Jeremiah said. "So, without saying a word I walked away from her. I left her in tears at the park."

There was one other thing she wanted to tell him, but he wouldn't stop to listen. He'd heard enough. He said that when he strutted away from her, he didn't expect her to stay on the bench in the middle of the park where he'd left her. He thought she'd follow in his direction back to her car after a second or two and drive off. But when he got back to his car, parked in the bus stop, she was nowhere in sight.

"I looked over to her car still parked on the street, then looked back into the park and could then just barely make her out slowly walking on the center path to the exit. It was then I climbed into my SUV and drove off."

"So why the hell would I let you help me?" Toni finally shot back at him.

"Because you can use my help, and I must help find my mother's killer detective," Jeremiah said. "And I know you're suspended too."

"Ah-huh," Toni said, recognizing that her suspension must've made the news.

"I must help find my mother's killer, Detective Santiago," Jeremiah said. "If I'd forgiven her, and we walked out together, and I put her back in her car, she'd still be alive. Please let me help you."

236

"No way I'm letting you get involved in this," Toni said. "I shouldn't be involved in this."

"I have to make this right."

"You're too close to this, Toni said. "No way I can trust you."

"Yes, I am too close. Someone is following my footsteps and killing people once I turn my back. Whoever is doing this took away a mother I had already lost once, and took her away for good this time. So, yes, I'm too close and I shouldn't be involved. But as you said, neither should you. And the truth is I'm already in the mess. But I have to make this right."

Toni was silent.

"We both have to make it right," Toni said.

"Yes."

"You know before this is over we're both gonna get fired," Toni said. "You sure about this?"

"Yes," Jeremiah said. "I'm sure."

It was early evening when Toni offered to make them each something to eat. He didn't have much in his refrigerator but a few single wrapped slices of American cheese, a half a loaf of whole wheat bread, a two-percent container of milk which expired the day before, and a jar of Kosher pickles with one sorry looking pickle floating like it was being preserved for laboratory study.

She made a couple grilled cheese sandwiches and kept him handcuffed to the radiator as they ate. They were even: both had only one arm to eat with. They didn't speak.

What a bizarre situation she found herself in, she thought, as she watched him chew. She couldn't help noticing he chewed with his mouth closed and used his napkin after each time he took a swig from the glass of milk she'd given him. Apparently, the Franciscans had taught him manners.

"So you want to help me find your mother's killer?" Toni said with a tilted head.

"Yes."

The prime suspect in the murder of Father Manuel Gonzalez wanted to help her. This suspended rookie cop who had lost his gun in a drunken stupor in a bar, the one used to kill Father Manny, wanted to help her. This suspended rookie cop — as if she should talk — who could have been the very last person Samantha Cohen saw alive, and, could be, in fact, her murderer as well, wanted to help her. She took a long swig from her own glass of milk and watched him carefully.

"Where's your wallet exactly?"

"It's on top of my bureau, in a silver dish."

Toni needed to see that ATM slip. Before she could put any trust in him she had to see that slip. See if he was on the level about it. She knew that by getting the ATM slip it gave him a potential alibi, but it also put Jeremiah within a short distance of the shooting scene.

That was a decent piece of incriminating evidence, especially since there was not one witness who saw him going into or leaving the rectory. It was hard for her to think he would be so stupid as to volunteer the slip unless he had, in fact, been straight with her about it.

Toni told Vita to stay, as she slipped to the bedroom and grabbed the wallet from the silver dish on his bureau. The rim of the silver dish had the following words engraved into it: THIS TOO SHALL PASS. And the wallet had praying-hands across the front of it.

"Geez," Toni whispered.

Toni sat back down by the front door in the living room and worked her way through the few slips secreted on one side of the wallet: a pink Memphis Cleaners slip for two uniform shirts and two uniform pants; one Duane Reade credit card slip; and there it was, a sky-blue ATM slip for the JP MORGAN CHASE bank on E. 125th Street and Second Avenue that put him dead center at the ATM location during the time the M.E. estimated Father Manny had been shot.

She knew, though, that the estimated time of his being shot was broad — a two-hour period — and could not be more exact. So he still could have shot the priest, gone to the ATM, and returned to get his gun. But the ATM slip did seem to show that he was definitely not at the rectory during some fragment of the time-range in which the shooting had occurred.

What then circled around in her mind was information from the Crime Scene Unit's report of Father Manny's murder scene. They had two sets of footsteps soaked in blood: a size-11 boat shoe, and a size-7 running shoe.

But it was not just the different shoe sizes that had Toni's attention. Or that the size-11 left tracks entering and leaving the rectory, but that the size-11 didn't casually walk out, but bolted out. Made evident by the distance of the strides between each step.

That must've been Jeremiah, Toni figured. On the other hand, the strides between each step of the size-7 were very short. He was in no hurry. His tracks went one way, and that was out.

"Take off one of your shoes," Toni said.

Jeremiah did and held it in his hand.

Toni pointed at the shoe in his hand and said, "Get the shoe, Vita,"

Her bulldog barreled over to Jeremiah, grabbed the shoe and brought it back to Toni.

"Good girl," Toni said and rubbed her head.

Toni looked at the sole of the shoe. "Looks like dry blood to me."

What then got her thinking was that duplicate shield again — number 6-7-0-2 — that had been sent to him at the orphanage when he was a kid. The same shield number Ryan carried as a cop.

But there was something else coming back to gnaw at her. She wondered if what she was thinking was possible. Is Ryan Jeremiah's father? Did Ryan rape Samantha twenty years ago? Is that possible? That would sure explain his interference. But is that possible? Could the Ryan Condon she thought she knew do such a thing?

If the department ever found out what she was doing with Jeremiah, she'd get fired for sure. But what other choice did she have? She couldn't take the chance of turning Jeremiah over to Ryan. Despite his story, there was no logical reason for her to believe that Jeremiah was not Father Manny's killer, and Samantha Cohen's, for that matter, since he'd been at both crime scenes before they ended up dead. But, she just believed him.

The truth was she liked Jeremiah. She looked into his eyes and what looked back at her were not the eyes of a killer—she'd looked at enough sets of murdering eyes before. What she saw, when she looked into Jeremiah's light, brown eyes, were the eyes of a wounded human person. He had the same look in his eyes she perceived she had in her own.

Toni then said to Jeremiah, "Do you have a valid driver's license?"

CHAPTER 27

The sun was setting when Toni and Vita walked out of his apartment building behind Jeremiah. They made a left in the direction of her Jetta, halfway down the block. He was no longer handcuffed. She had to get Jeremiah out of there. She knew it was just a matter of time before Ryan managed to I.D. Jeremiah and showed-up at his apartment with the troops. She knew she'd caught a break getting to Jeremiah before Ryan did. But she hadn't thought through where she would take him? For a minute she thought she could ask Samantha's sister Liz to let them stay with her on Sutton Place, but there were too many eyes in that building and she wasn't ready to spring Jeremiah on her — the nephew she'd never met.

Just as they got to the car, she finally took notice of that progressively horrible stench filling her nasal passages again.

"What is that smell?" Toni said, looking up and down the parkway, leaning down to cup her nose and mouth with her slung arm.

"Oh, that's the horse stable on the corner, behind my building. You can just about make out the stable fence at the very end. Can you see it?" Jeremiah pointed in that direction. "It's always worse in the evening."

"In the Bronx?" Toni said.

"Oh, yeah. As far as I know, there's only one other stable in the Bronx, if you don't count the stables in the Bronx Zoo," said Jeremiah.

"Lived here most of my life and never knew there were horse stables around," Toni said.

"I read in the paper this stable won't be around much longer. The property's been sold to an apartment developer."

"Good," Toni said, then tossed him the keys to her Jetta. "All right. Jump in. Behind the wheel."

Jeremiah did, followed by Vita, who leaped into the back seat, and Toni, who took the front passenger seat.

"Listen, if anybody asks, your name is Christopher DeStefano, Chris. Got it?" Toni said.

"Who's Chris?"

"Nobody you know. Name of a Marine from Montana I used to know," Toni said. "Got it?"

"Uh oh," Jeremiah murmured.

Just as they were pulling out, a tall man in his forties, in a lightweight beige suit and tie, holding a portable police radio, was approaching the front door of his building.

"What?" Toni said and stiffened. She followed his line of vision to the front of his building. "Is there somebody at your building?"

"Yeah, I think so," Jeremiah said. "Looks like a detective to me."

"I knew it!" Toni said. "It was just a matter of time."

She concentrated on the man too. He looked in their direction as they slowly inched down the service road of the parkway. The detective then stopped cold in front of Jeremiah's building and turned back at them with laser beam-like focus.

Toni shouted, "Stop!" They were only about five car lengths from where the man was standing.

Jeremiah hit the brakes hard, causing the screech of burning rubber on the blacktop, even at their crawling pace.

"No! No! No!" Toni repeated as she scrunched down as low as she could in her seat. "That's Condon. Lieutenant Condon. Get out of here!"

With that order from suspended Detective Toni Santiago, suspended rookie Police Officer Jeremiah Francisco swung the car in the only direction he could to avoid driving past Ryan and jumped the curb barreling through the neatly cut grass divider between the service road and the main road of Pelham Parkway. Kicking up grass and dirt he left a trail of perfectly parallel tire marks and a curtain of dirt that carried far enough to cover the three horses in the nearby stable.

He tumbled onto the main road and took off in the direction of the Bruckner Expressway. Within minutes Jeremiah managed to get them completely out of the area.

"Is he chasing us?" Toni screamed, as her head bounced up into the underside of the dashboard.

"No, no," Jeremiah said. "I'm sure he isn't. I looked in his direction real quick as we took off; he didn't budge. He just stood there and watched us. He just watched us take off."

"Damn it!" Toni was rubbing the top of her head.

"You okay?"

"Yeah, yeah!" Toni snapped from under the dashboard. "Damn it! I knew he'd find out where you live."

"I guess he knows about me," Jeremiah said as he continued to accelerate, now comfortably cruising south on the Bruckner Expressway.

"Yeah, I'd say that's confirmed," Toni said, and finally sat up. "Man, we just made it. A few more minutes and he would've had both of us. All right we're going to my place. Looks like you'll be staying with me for a few days."

Toni sat there quietly and stared out the windshield. She wondered if Ryan had seen her in the Jetta. "Man, am I crossing the line," she thought, then figured, if he'd seen her, she'd find out soon enough.

"You all right?" Jeremiah said and looked over at her.

"I'm good," Toni said, without looking back at him.

"Oh, no," Jeremiah said in resignation.

"What?" Toni said, then the sudden yelp of a police car siren ratcheted-up her feeling of dread.

"We're getting pulled over," Jeremiah said. "A radio car is stopping us."

"Damn, damn," Toni said. "Is it marked or unmarked?"

"It's marked. Looks like Highway One."

"Damn," Toni said again.

The officer announced over the radio car's speaker system, "PULL OFF AT THE NEXT EXIT…WILLIS AVENUE!"

"What do you want to do?"

"What do you mean, what do I want to do? Exit at Willis Avenue like he said. I'm not going to take a radio car on a chase. It's over. That's all there is to it. Lieutenant Condon must've recognized my car or caught my plate. He must've put it over the air."

"Too bad were both suspended," Jeremiah said. "No I.D."

Toni gave him a crooked look, "I don't think I.D. would help under the circumstances."

The highway cop approached the Jetta cautiously in his calf-high black leather boots and sparkling gun belt: firearm in his grip but holstered. Toni told Jeremiah to keep his hands on the steering wheel, and she put her unslung hand on the dashboard.

The officer approached the driver's side window and said to Jeremiah,

"You know why I stopped you, don't you?"

As Jeremiah fumbled to reply, the cop looked over to get a better look at the passenger.

"Hey!" the officer shouted with a big smile. "Toni Santiago. Is that you?"

Toni's head snapped in the direction of the driver's side window. She observed a massive African-American highway cop with Colgate white teeth leaning in. She could see her slung-armed little-self sitting innocently in the passenger seat, reflected back at her in the officer's mirror sunglasses.

She replied with genuine excitement and relief, "Hey, Vernon George, how's it going?"

38,000 cops in the five boroughs of New York City, she thought, and how many could one cop know personally? A couple hundred, maybe.

"Good, good, Toni. How are you?" Vernon said and pointed at her sling. "I read about you and your partner. How's the arm? You took a shot, didn't you?"

"I'm all right, Vernon. It went in and out."

"Good, good," Vernon said.

Vernon George had worked in Manhattan North Narcotics with Shaft and Toni. He was a six foot seven Haitian, weighing in at almost three hundred pounds. Toni loved his strong voice and Haitian Creole accent. He sounded like the Lion King.

Whenever they needed to execute a search warrant and a door separated them from the druggies and drugs, Vernon would take the door, no problem. He wouldn't even use the battering ram.

"How's your partner?" Vernon said. "What's his condition?"

"Stable, Vern," Toni said. "Thank God."

"Yeah, thank God."

Toni pointed at Jeremiah. "Vernon, this is my friend Jeremiah."

Vernon shook Jeremiah's hand and told him to put his wallet away. After he and Toni shared a few more words, he told Jeremiah he'd stopped them because their left taillight was out.

"Oh, sorry, Vernon," Toni said. "It's my car, I didn't know it was out."

"No, problem, *senorita.*"

Toni explained to Jeremiah that she and Vernon had been in narcotics together.

Vernon said to Jeremiah, not knowing or caring if he was a cop or civilian, "Toni was the ice-woman. Never got rattled. Gun to her head a few times as an undercover and never lost her composure. She was frigid. I mean frigid."

Jeremiah looked at Toni with admiration. Little did they know at the Narcotics Division that after each of those episodes, without fail, she would coolly excuse herself, swagger to the division's ladies room and vomit.

"How you like Highway?" Toni said.

"Good, it's a good detail. I like working alone. Just the road and me. The bosses are good too. As long as you're where you're supposed to be, and don't do any slumming, they don't bother you. But you know how it is, every once in a while there's a knucklehead thinks he can park a marked radio car in front of his bimbo's place for three hours like nobody will notice."

"Yeah, there's always one or two," she thought if he only knew.

"You guys have an I.D. on the shooter?"

"No, not yet," said Toni. Thinking wouldn't, Vernon, be surprised if he knew that the shooter could very well be sitting between her and him at the moment. "I'm out sick, but I know the squad is on it."

"Sure, right," Vernon said. "Well, take care of yourself, Toni. If there is anything I can do, you know where to find me."

"Thanks, Vernon. You take care, too. Really good to see you."

"Likewise, and don't forget to get that tail light fixed," he said, all teeth.

"You bet, officer," Toni returned the huge smile.

The highway cop gave Toni an informal salute, stepped to the rear of the Jetta and slowed down traffic so Jeremiah and Toni could get back on the expressway.

They traveled silently for several long minutes, both trying to come down from the rush of adrenaline they'd felt moments before. Jeremiah drove as far south on the Bruckner Expressway as possible, which eventually swung around and up like a horseshoe and fed into the Major Deegan heading north.

Taking the highway from his place on Pelham Parkway in the northeast Bronx to her place in the northwest Bronx was not the most direct route, but since Ryan had them in view the shortest route to her place was not the priority when they'd taken off.

Jeremiah broke the silence. "Detective Santiago. You don't have to do this. There's no reason for you to lose the job over this. My career hasn't even begun so it doesn't really matter. I appreciate your giving me a chance to help you, but there's too much at stake here for you."

A couple of moments passed before Toni peeled her gaze from the windshield and looked at him.

"I'm not doing this for you. I'm doing this because I have to do it. I can lose everything whether you're involved or not. If you want out, I still can't let you go. Not yet anyway. So you decide what you want to do."

"I don't want out."

"All right then," Toni said. "That's settled."

They kept driving in silence.

As they cruised up the Henry Hudson Parkway, blocks from Toni's apartment building, she finally turned to him again and said, "Since we're in this heap together, you should start calling me Toni."

They made it to her Riverdale apartment without any more interceptions. Toni directed Jeremiah to park behind her building, which he did, and they used a back entrance to get inside the building as well. Toni wondered again if Ryan had caught a glimpse of her in the car. She stepped out onto the balcony to see if the radio car—posted for her protection—was still downstairs. It was. It didn't look like the cop assigned to the car had any idea she'd been out, or, that the cop had been alerted. She had to assume Ryan didn't see her when they took off from Jeremiah's street.

Toni made a fresh pot of coffee. There was no point in handcuffing Jeremiah. She had to trust him and that was that. After Vita slopped up some water from her bowl, she curled up in her basket.

So Ryan almost made it to Jeremiah before she did, which didn't surprise her. But what didn't make sense was that he showed up alone. What was that all about? If he'd been genuinely working the case, and wanted to nail the killer, why would he show up alone at Jeremiah's doorstep?

Toni took another long look at Jeremiah.

Does Ryan know Jeremiah could be his son? Toni wondered. Has he always known about Jeremiah?

How could he not know? she thought. If he were Samantha's rapist, he'd have to have known that Samantha had the kid. At least Father Manny would've told him. And that would possibly explain why Samantha made reference — in one of her letters to Manny during her pregnancy — that she had known it wasn't easy for Manny either. She knew that Manny was terribly disturbed by what his dear childhood friend, Ryan Condon, had done. Is that possible?

She handed a cup of coffee to Jeremiah, who was sitting on the sofa. She chose to sit at the dining area table.

"So, how does Lieutenant Condon know about you?" Toni said. "Any ideas?"

"No, I don't," Jeremiah said. "I mean I suppose he could have seen the department FINEST message that I was suspended.

"Maybe," Toni said. "Tell me about your conversation with your mother in the park."

CHAPTER 28

The night of Samantha's murder, as Jeremiah had demanded, she'd walked through the park with him and reconstructed the horrific events of that night over two decades before.

She'd been walking home from her summer job—at a woman's clothing store off East 149th Street and Third Avenue, about a mile from her street around Mount Carmel Park.

It was a little after 9 p.m. when she arrived at the entrance to the park. Normally her boyfriend would've met her, and they'd walk through the park together, but he'd gone away that week with his family.

"Did she say who the boyfriend was?"

"No, I'm sorry," Jeremiah said. "And I didn't ask."

Even though walking around the park instead of through the park added six blocks to her walk home, that's what she'd planned to do. But when she got to the north entrance on 149th Street where her boyfriend would normally be waiting for her the thought of taking the chance took hold. She knew to walk through the park at that hour alone was a bad idea, but after almost ten hours at the store mostly on her feet that day, and the over half a mile she'd already walked, she'd convinced herself she'd make it without any trouble. After all, she'd thought, it was a summer night and there would be people in the park late, including the occasional police car slowly cruising the asphalt path.

Finally, she considered that it was a straight, flat, wide-open boulevard-like path that only ran—from the north to the south entrance—six blocks.

When she entered the park, a nice cool breeze accompanied her at first. She was moving at a steady pace down the open path wide enough for four cars to drive side-by-side. The path was lined with benches and full overhanging trees. Some of the park lights were lit, but not all. To the west were rocky hills; to the east were basketball and handball courts and then the baseball field itself that continued to the south end of the park.

She remembered thinking how much quieter the park seemed that night than usual. The night-lights of the baseball field that were often on, and created such a glow that they illuminated well beyond the boundaries of the field, were off. No one was playing on the field that night. She'd seen one teenaged couple leave the park at the north entrance where she entered, but by the time she had walked halfway through, she had not caught a glimpse of anyone else.

The ball field was so desolate she'd imagined that only minutes before she'd walked in, the park had been brimming with activity, but for some inexplicable reason, everyone had been evicted. Like a plague announcement had been made or something. Even the gentle breeze that had been present when she entered had moved on. The trees had assumed a stoic demeanor, fixed in place from trunk to leaf.

It was then she noticed a large figure on the other side of the park benches coming over the top of the hills from the west. She tried not to stare but kept walking. To her surprise this person called out her name and started to try and catch up with her. She didn't recognize the voice. She looked again and saw the big, dark silhouette rapidly stumbling down the hill.

Without stopping she asked who it was, but the figure didn't answer. She started to walk faster but was having a hard time with her heels. She could then hear the figure grunting as he ran to catch to her, and she started to run too, but could not find her voice to scream. Within seconds he'd caught up to her. She was struck by the intense odor of booze coming from him first; then he grabbed her shoulder.

"Hey, Samantha," he said.

His speech was slurred. Samantha swung around facing him, about to swing at his head and eyes with her pocketbook and kick at him, even though he towered over her. His eyes were red and glossy.

"Oh, hi, hi..." Samantha said with terror in her eyes, "...I didn't know it was you. You scared me."

Even though he was intoxicated, she felt relieved that someone she'd known from the neighborhood—the younger brother of a dear friend—was walking with her.

"Where you coming from?" he said, having trouble walking straight but with a huge smile, the smell of booze and perspiration gushing from his pores. There was such a strange sound to his voice. So different from the gentle voice she had heard whenever she would run into him with her friend.

"Work," Samantha said as she started to walk at a steady pace again. "I work at Gilda's on Third Avenue."

"Want to sit down for a while? Enjoy the smell of the trees for a while, look at the moon," he said, keeping pace with her, looking down into her blouse.

Samantha began to feel alarmed again, "No...no...thank you. I got to get home. I'm already late. My father and sister are probably out looking for me right now." She started to pick up the pace.

"What are you walking so fast for?" he said, grabbing her by the forearm. She fleetingly looked down at the huge hand that completely engulfed her forearm. Her forearm looked like a child's in the mouth of a wolf.

Samantha told Jeremiah that she had tried to yank her wrist out of his grip and leaped to get away but he held it tight, twisting her arm back. She screamed as piercing pain shot through her arm and back, shocking her. As he started to drag her, she kicked at his groin and wrenched her wrist out with all the force she could and broke away, but only managed a few strides before her heel snapped and she tumbled down hard to the black, tar, path, striking the side of her face and head.

She vaguely remembered being hauled up like a rag doll, his massive arms wrapped under her armpits, and across her chest, dragging her past the benches and up the hill. Her toes and feet were dangling about a foot off the ground.

She tried to scream in her dazed state, but he cupped her face with his massive hand and continued to sweep her up and over the hill. She remembered tearing her face out of his nasty palm and biting down on his forearm with all the might she had, but it had no effect. He did not even flinch. It was like biting into a piece of oily leather. It happened so quickly.

He lifted her petite frame up onto his shoulder, and for a flash she was face-to-face with the bright, full moon that broke through a brief crack in the clouds. But the darkness sealed the gap again, as if annoyed by the sudden escape of light, and resumed its dominance.

He pressed her up into the air, spun around a few times like a professional wrestler, and slammed her down on the ground like a toy. Her already pulsating head and face collided with the dirt and grass at the bottom of the hill. She was semi-conscious when he invaded her.

Hours later, she was discovered by the police semi-conscious in the park and taken to the hospital. The physical examination conducted at the hospital showed she had in fact been brutally raped, receiving substantial external and internal injuries.

Later that night, at the hospital emergency room, two police officers — whom she then learned were the same two officers who'd found her ragged body hours earlier — brought her attacker in for her to identify. Standing with the attacker was his half-brother, her dear friend. She didn't identify him to the officers. To her knowledge her friend arranged to have her attacker committed to a state mental hospital where he's been ever since.

"Who was her friend?" Toni said.

"I don't know," Jeremiah said. "She didn't say."

Toni sat in deep thought trying to take it all in.

Jeremiah took a slow, deep sip of his coffee. He then stood up, walked to the living room window with his mug and looked out to the north and south stretch of the Hudson River shoreline, abundantly shaded with trees. The setting sun delivered a bright glow over the muster of living green.

"This is beautiful view you have here," he said looking back at Toni with a moist face.

"I like it."

"It reminds me of the orphanage where I was raised," he said. "At the top of the mountain at the orphanage there's a sculpture replica of Michelangelo's "Pieta" and next to the sculpture — imbedded in this massive rock — was a big, majestic cross."

Toni listened.

"You know, after Internal Affairs suspended me, I finally asked myself, 'What would the Master have done?'" Jeremiah said.

"What master?" Toni said with a furrowed brow.

Jeremiah smiled. "What would Jesus Christ have done? That was a question the Franciscans suggested I ask whenever I thought I just could not forgive. What would Jesus Christ have done?"

"Oh, that Master," Toni said, feeling her face heat-up for not knowing whom Jeremiah was talking about.

"The answer was clear. The Master would've forgiven my mother. It was at that moment I knew what I needed to do. I needed to find her and forgive her. But now it's too late. I had my chance and squandered it."

Toni stayed silent.

Jeremiah returned to the sofa. They sat quietly for a few moments.

"You notice I have a Rockwell too," Toni said and pointed to it hanging on her wall. "The Runaway."

Jeremiah looked up. "Yes, very nice."

There was also an old framed black and white photograph of a male uniformed cop rested on the mantle of the fireplace, next to the Rockwell.

"Is that a relative?" Jeremiah said as he pointed at it.

The police officer was in a posed position, apparently taken at a studio. He was dressed in the old winter blouse and the traditional choker collar with two straight lines of glittering parallel brass buttons that extended from the collarbone to the waist.

"Yes. That's my grandfather."

"Your grandfather," Jeremiah said. "Very distinguished-looking man. In photos at the Police Museum, I always found the choker winter blouse the sharpest of the uniforms. Too bad they were phased out."

"Yeah, I agree," she said. Her face lit up with humble pride. Her eyes unexpectedly became a little misty. "But you have to change with the times."

"When was that taken?"

"The early fifties."

"Wow, no kidding," Jeremiah said. "And his granddaughter followed in his footsteps."

"Well, more like following in my father's footsteps," Toni said. "He was on the job too."

"No kidding, Jeremiah said. "Your father too, is he still on the job?"

"No, no. He retired a few years ago and died soon after that."

"Oh. I'm sorry to hear that, Toni."

It was the first time he called her by her first name. It startled her a bit to hear her first name coming from his mouth.

"If you don't mind my asking—what was the cause?"

Toni didn't answer at first. She wondered whether it was a good idea to tell him too much about her background.

"I apologize. I didn't mean to get so personal," Jeremiah said.

"That's all right. My father was killed by a hit-and-run driver."

"What?"

Toni nodded.

Jeremiah leaned forward and said, "I'm sorry to hear that. Very sorry to hear that."

"Thank you."

They remained silent for several long moments—each taking deep sips from their mugs.

Jeremiah put his cup down. "Toni, who'd the driver turn out to be?"

"What driver?"

"The one who struck your father," Jeremiah said. "He was collared, wasn't he?"

"No, no. He wasn't. No idea who he…" then she thought to include the female sex, "…or she was. The driver was never identified."

"I'm really very sorry to hear this."

They continued to sip their coffees in silence.

"It must be very difficult," Jeremiah said. "I mean it must be very difficult not knowing who took your father's life. It must be very difficult living with that."

Toni was struck by how sincere Jeremiah appeared to be. As if he knew just how she must feel. But of course he must know, she realized.

"Well, what you've lived with is very difficult too. Not knowing who your parents were for most of your life," Toni said.

"When did your father enter the department?"

"The early eighties."

Toni went into her father's background some. That he'd done twenty-eight years in the department and retired a first-grade detective from the Major Case Squad. She shared with him some of the cases he worked on, which Toni could see he'd genuinely found riveting. She then brought up that her father — then Patrolman Joe Santiago — had found his mother in Mount Carmel Park after she'd been raped as a girl.

Jeremiah's eyes opened wide. "What?"

Toni nodded.

Jeremiah dropped his head and closed his eyes for a few moments as if in prayer or meditation.

"You all right?" Toni said. She waited for him to say something but he continued to face the solid black area rug under his feet; coffee mug suspended in his hand.

Toni took his mug and went to the kitchen. "How about I make a fresh pot?"

Over the following couple of minutes, no words were exchanged. The only sounds in Toni's apartment were those created by her preparing coffee and Vita's snoring.

"Thank you," Jeremiah said when she handed him another cup. He took a long sip from the mug and placed it on her all-glass coffee table. "Did you ever talk to your father about that day, the day my mother was attacked?"

"No, I never did. I was only a little girl when it happened and he never brought it up, even when I was older."

Toni explained to him that her father's only involvement was taking his mother to the hospital and taking the initial report as far as she knew. She reminded him he wasn't a detective at that time. Her father was then a uniformed cop.

"How'd you find out he found her, Toni?" Jeremiah said. "I mean if he never discussed it with you?"

"Well, that was a fluke," Toni said. She told him about the *Daily News* headline her father had kept in a shoebox with other newspaper articles and mementos of his police career. And, that she followed-up on the article by pulling a copy of the initial report from the Criminal Records Division at headquarters.

"Were there any follow-up reports at headquarters?" Jeremiah said. "You know, DD 5's. That's what they're called, aren't they? The detective follow-up reports."

Toni paused for a second, taking in this troubled suspended rookie cop who seemed to have picked up a few things in his short time in the department. He'd probably still not yet laid eyes on an actual prepared detective DD-5 report in his short career but learned such a thing existed from his academy training.

"That's a good question," she said. "There weren't any in the database, which is unusual. There definitely was a follow-up investigation by the detectives, but there was nothing on file. The only thing that I can figure is that the court directed the department to expunge the reports from the case file. And that only very rarely happens."

"So the records were removed?" Jeremiah said.

"Maybe."

"I guess there was nothing else in your father's shoebox"

Toni stared at Jeremiah blankly. She hadn't taken the time to go through the box. She'd been caught up in the excitement of having discovered the *Daily News* article, and left it at that. But then her eyes opened wide and she jumped from her seat at the dining room table too fast, which caused a piercing pain to shoot through her slung arm.

"Ahh!" Her knees buckled and she eased down to the carpeted floor, doubled over, as if in a call to prayer.

Jeremiah jumped off the sofa too and kneeled down with her; gently wrapping an arm around her back. "You shouldn't have jumped up so quickly."

"No kidding, Sherlock!" Toni gasped, still doubled over. "Damn this hurts."

Jeremiah held Toni until the pain started to ease.

Toni then raised her head slowly and came face-to-face with Jeremiah's eyes, and her heart tweaked. That feeling startled her. They looked at each other for several moments. The two of them locked in each other's sights; she couldn't turn away. Toni knew she needed to let go of his gaze, but she just didn't want to: there was something deeply comforting in his eyes.

When the phrase, 'The eyes are the window to the soul' flickered through her mind it gave her such a scare she snapped her head up, jumped up from the carpet and blurted, "bull-shit!"

Jeremiah didn't move from his kneeling position and looked up at her with a blank stare.

"Let me get my father's shoebox," she said and took off for her bedroom closet just as suddenly as she had a moment before.

"AHHHH!" she yelped again, as she dragged herself to the bedroom. "DAMN IT!"

CHAPTER 29

After a few minutes, Toni went back to the living room. She was glad she'd never had a chance to put back all the shoeboxes she'd pulled down the last time to get to her father's box. It would have been tough to pull them down with one arm in a sling. She would've needed Jeremiah's help, and, for some reason, she wouldn't have wanted him to see how neatly organized and clearly marked were her boxes and boxes of stacked shoes.

She put the shoebox on the dining room table and eased the lid off. Jeremiah had begun to step over to the table to help her look through it.

Toni waved him away. "I'll do this myself. Please stay there. If I come up with anything, I'll let you know."

"Of course," Jeremiah said, and went back to the sofa.

Toni slowly went through the things in her father's shoebox. The last time she'd breezed through it and stopped as soon as she came across the *Daily News* headline about the rape. This time she carefully looked at each item like an archaeologist.

She'd gotten through a dozen or so other news articles he'd saved, none of which had anything to do with the park rape. She placed each article and item neatly on the table next to the box. At the bottom of the box, she'd discovered he'd chronologically stacked each slender Activity Log he'd used during his twenty-eight-year police career.

She pulled out one at a time and stacked them on the table as well.

"Are all your father's activity logs in there?" Jeremiah said.

"It looks that way," Toni said, without looking up at him.

She knew Jeremiah was thinking just what she was thinking: If her father had saved the activity log in which he'd made entries on the night of Samantha's rape, it could have information that will lead to the murderer.

She carefully pulled out one at a time. The sky blue, serial numbered. rectangular activity logs each had the standard blocked title, "NEW YORK POLICE DEPARTMENT," and also printed lined references that required filling in:

RANK_____

NAME_____SHIELD #_____

DATE OPENED_____; SUPERVISOR SIGNATURE_____

DATE CLOSED_____: SUPERVISOR SIGNATURE_____

She dug to the bottom of the box and pulled the first fifteen logs prepared during her father's first five years in the department, and went through them fast, scanning the dates each book was opened and closed. She'd begun to hum. It was a habit of hers whenever she'd felt herself getting a bit too excited.

"Is that the Marine Corps Hymn?" Jeremiah said.

"It is."

"Are you an ex-Marine?"

"Former Marine," Toni said. "Yes."

A few more moments passed.

"Here it is!" Toni couldn't help blurting as she waved the activity log like a winning lottery ticket.

The activity log had been opened on July 6th and closed on December 21st. She flipped through the pages, briskly looking for the beginning of the August 7th entry. She found it.

The beginning of his shift entries read as follows:

Weds. August 7, Tour 1600x2400//Assign: Sector A; RMP#1923;

___

Meal: 2000; Roll Call: Sgt. Gannon; Partner: Ptl. Manley, shield#2352;

Weather: 88 degrees/clear; Veh. Inspec: Gas, ½ tank; Lights/Siren, operational; Floor/Back seat searched, no contraband."

During the course of the first four hours of his tour, he and his partner had handled a variety of assignments ranging from several gun-runs to taking a report for a purse snatch and another for a Bodega robbery, as well as taking a sixteen-year-old teenager in labor to the hospital, and transporting a fourteen-year-old juvenile (arrested by another officer) to the Spofford Youth Detention facility for possession of a loaded gun. The arresting officer went to the Bronx Family Court to draw up the official complaint.

At 2020 hours they'd returned to the 5-1 precinct area after dropping the juvenile at Spofford. Toni noticed that instead of taking their meal in a restaurant or the station house, they'd decided to take it in Mount Carmel Park. When she was a uniformed cop, she'd often choose to eat outdoors in the radio car too. And if it was a hot summer night, the park was always her first choice. Plus you never knew what you might stumble upon in the park.

Her father's next entry was case-and-point:

2055 hrs: Intox. M/H; observed open container (bottle/Qt. Bacardi Rum);

Walking erratically; raised door to antiquated City fallout shelter and descended.

U/S officer and partner followed. Observed candles; table, cot, chair, etc.

Stopped, questioned and frisked male. No weapons found. Male

Transported to 51 Pct, arrest-Cr. Tres. Milton Iglesia, age 16, 6'3", 260 lbs.

2115 hrs: Next of kin notified. Manuel Gonzalez, age 19, step-brother.

2140 hrs: Manuel Gonzalez arrives 51 Pct (Seminarian, St. Joseph's

Yonkers.)
2225 hrs: Compl Rep Prep. Cr Tres/Closed;
  Arrest Voided- Authority Sgt. Gannon.
  U.F. 250, Stop Question and Frisk Report
prepared;
  Juvenile released to brother: Manuel
Gonzalez.

"Holy shit!" Toni said.

"You find something?" Jeremiah said.

She didn't answer.

Toni then came across all the entries her father made three hours or so later that had to do with the rape of Samantha Morales. It started with their sector being called to Mount Carmel Park by the precinct captain to conduct a search for a missing person toward the end of their shift at 2340 hours:

0030 hrs: Semi-conscious, abused body of Samantha Morales discovered
  behind rock, Mount Carmel Park.
  0033 hrs: Victim trans to Jefferson Hosp via radio car. En route
  sobbing semi-conscious state victim blurted following: "I couldn't
  fight him. I don't know why he did this to me. He was drunk. I couldn't
  stop him. He was too strong for me."

Toni's father made the next entry:
  Asked victim recognized perp? Victim nodded barely. Victim semi-conscious.

Toni then came upon a note scribbled on the back of one of the log pages that indicated her father and partner went to Milton Iglesia's apartment to question him. When they knocked on his door, Manuel Gonzalez told them that his brother had gone back out shortly after the officers had released him to his custody. The seminarian—who was one hundred pounds lighter and several inches shorter than his brother—had a bruised face and bloodied nose.

Toni's father and partner (joined by Manuel Gonzalez) returned to the fallout shelter and found Milton Iglesia lying on the cot intoxicated with his pants undone and his tank top shirt torn and bloodied: a bite mark on his arm.

They took him into custody and transported him to Jefferson Hospital for a show-up.

0150 hrs: Show-up of Milton Iglesia to victim, Samantha Morales.

Vic regained consciousness. Vic would not confirm/deny Milton

Iglesia assailant. Vic eyes opened wide when she looked at Iglesia;

Then looked at Manuel Gonzalez and said, "Oh, Manny," and began to

sob. The seminarian repeatedly said he was sorry.

"Holy shit!" said Toni again.

CHAPTER 30

Toni woke up first. It was early Tuesday morning, only a little past 6 and she showered, careful not to get her mound-of-bandage wet, making sure the bathroom door was locked. She went to the kitchen to put on a pot of coffee. She peeked into the living room through the counter opening and saw Jeremiah was sound asleep on her sofa; he'd fallen asleep with the T.V. set on; doused in its flickering, blue and white glow.

There was a white-haired priest on the screen giving a talk from his desk: maybe from a rectory somewhere. Is this Jeremiah for real or what?

He'd been watching the Eternal Word Television Network station. She didn't know anybody that fell asleep to a Catholic channel instead of a late night movie, Jimmy Farrell or Stephen Colbert. He was partially covered in the multicolored knit blanket she'd handed him. Her mother had made it for her when she was only three.

Toni could not help contemplating Jeremiah's appearance. He had a peaceful face. He was on his back with his hands neatly interlocked on his chest. Even while he slept he kept a gentleman's appearance, and with a silent chuckle, she wondered whether he ever snored.

Her sofa was not long enough to handle his length, so his legs were raised at an angle and rested on the opposite armrest. His jeans had partially risen, which revealed his tan, hairy ankles. She recalled that he didn't protest when she handed him her childhood blanket. He just thanked her politely and said good night. If only she were ten years younger, she fleetingly thought.

The blanket covered only from the middle of his chest to the middle of his calves, the essential zone of coverage for most men. Toni had come to recognize that men were as concerned about being covered while they slept as women, particularly when they were on someone else's sofa.

The last thing they wanted was the invariable hardness that resulted from an overloaded bladder — in most cases — to astound their host.

Suddenly, he stirred and Toni was so startled he might catch her gawking that she pivoted abruptly. Her slung arm swept the glass coffee pot from the counter, which soared and crashed onto the kitchen floor.

"AHHHHHHHHHHHHHHH!" Toni screamed in agony.

Jeremiah and Vita blazed into the kitchen. He held her around her shoulders as Vita tried to lick Toni's face.

"What happened?" Jeremiah said, rubbing his eyes, still wobbly from his deep sleep.

"Shit! Shit!" was all Toni could utter, not only because of the pain that riveted her nerve endings but because she was too embarrassed to come up with some explanation for how she'd managed to whack the coffee pot off the counter. She certainly couldn't admit she'd been watching him sleep and had been innocently thinking about his potential hardness. It wouldn't matter that she was merely taking into consideration how the distended bladder of a male had a direct effect on that specific part of their anatomy.

Jeremiah swept up the kitchen floor and made the pot of coffee himself, using a small aluminum pot, eventually handing her a steaming mug, and, after asking for permission, jumped into the shower himself, while Toni took Vita for a quick walk, and dropped her off with her aunt.

Two hours later, after a couple more cups of coffee and a toasted English muffin with butter and strawberry jam, a banana, and a glass of orange juice apiece, they were cruising down the tree-lined, panoramic, Henry Hudson Parkway in Toni's VW Jetta en route to Samantha's funeral mass at Mount Carmel.

Toni knew it was risky continuing to travel in her Jetta, but what choice did she have? They couldn't use Jeremiah's SUV figuring Ryan would have the plate, make and model, for sure. Sometime the evening before, she'd even taken the step of calling Sergeant Tazzo and telling him she wanted the uniformed cop pulled off her building. She knew the department's policy was not to force protection on anyone — cop or not.

Tazzo insisted she keep the portable radio, which she did. Before she jumped in the shower that morning she looked out her bedroom window to see if the radio car was parked out front, and it wasn't.

"Good," she said, under her breath.

Toni and Jeremiah had talked until almost 3 a.m. At times she'd thought she'd tell him about his remarkable resemblance to Ryan Condon, but she couldn't bring it up. She couldn't even bring herself to let him know that his mother had a daughter. That he had a sixteen-year-old half-sister out there. If he'd asked about Samantha having other kids, she would have told him. But it just didn't seem like the right time to pass on that information, and, if she had, how would that have helped with her immediate predicament?

Most important to Toni was to get to Samantha's funeral to pay her respects, number one; then speak to Liz Rivera and arrange to get those soiled sheets to a lab. Except, she hadn't figured out where she would send the sheets when she got them. And not only that: She wanted to have a discreet talk with Father Gribbons if the opportunity were there. She had a lot on her agenda.

They'd arrived a few blocks from Our Lady of Mount Carmel Church about forty minutes after leaving the Riverdale area.

She knew it was risky bringing Jeremiah along and understood Ryan would be there, but she had to keep Jeremiah close. Except, she couldn't take the chance of his being spotted. Ryan had to have Jeremiah's I.D. card photo, so she told Jeremiah to drop her off around the corner from the church.

"I want you to stay in the car," Toni said as she twisted around to the backseat to grab her small black purse. Even though her arm was in a sling, she couldn't bring herself to attend the mass without a purse.

"That dress looks very nice on you," Jeremiah said, and looked away.

"Thanks," Toni said and took a quick glance at him.

"I hope you don't mind my saying so."

"No. Thanks, I appreciate that," Toni said and felt a flutter in her stomach.

She'd decided to wear a black one-piece dress instead of a black pants suit. She wondered what that was all about. Although the sleek dress wasn't suggestive at all, she knew she looked pretty good in it. It captured her solid, shapely figure nicely, and fell just right on her athletic legs. There were a number of other outfits she could've worn, that didn't make her appear quite as radiant, but she'd chosen that dress because it was completely appropriate for a funeral mass.

Did she want Jeremiah to see her legs in heels, she wondered, as she turned the corner to the church.

"Nahhhh," she answered herself, shaking her head. She couldn't bring herself to think she was wooing him. Was she?

As she'd approached the front of Mount Carmel, she could see Sergeant Tazzo smoking a cigarette, at the bottom of the steps to the church, talking with three detectives from her squad. She walked in their direction. When she made eye contact with them, they peeled away, and up the steps, and into the church, except for Tazzo.

"How you doing, Toni"

"What was that all about, Sarge?" she said as she watched the backs of her colleagues continue up the steps.

"They'll get over it," Tazzo said. "Everybody's a little uptight right now."

"They're holding me responsible for Geddes?" Toni said. "That's it, isn't it?"

Tazzo pointed at her with the cigarette, "How's the arm?"

"Better," Toni said as she continued to watch their backs.

"You know Geddes's back home?"

"I know," Toni said. Her eyes welled up. "I spoke to him."

"What are you doing here anyway? You're out sick. You're supposed to be home nursing that arm."

Toni was deep in thought, looking past the sergeant, she then registered his question. "Cohen's sister called me, asked if I would come."

They stood silently watching the numbers pile into the church to pay their respects to the late Samantha (Morales) Cohen. It wasn't the usual crowd you'd find at a predominantly Latino church service in the South Bronx. The street was lined with limousines—and not just the limos assigned to the family— but limos waiting for those who'd known Samantha Cohen, attorney-at-law, professionally, and, maybe, lived in the Sutton Place area.

Our Lady of Mount Carmel Roman Catholic Church was only a block from the number six—Pelham Bay—subway train, which made it a snap to get to-and-from the Upper East Side, but her colleagues and neighbors chose not to take the fifteen-minute subway ride up to the South Bronx.

Intermingled with all the suits were the locals in their humble black dresses with black kerchiefs over their heads and the men in their short sleeve, dark *Guayaberas*. They'd all known the Morales family and knew Samantha as a bright, spirited, pretty Latina as she was growing up. There was also a large number of former clients she'd represented pro bono and members of their families who came to pay their respects.

"Life delivers some curveball stuff sometimes," Tazzo said. "Who would've thought the day after she came by the office to see the boss, she would be killed. Right?"

Toni's head almost exploded with that information. It took all the self-control she could muster not to snap her head to the sergeant in a glower. *Nobody told me that!* — echoed through her mind.

"Right, Sarge," Toni said, with just enough resignation in her tone.

Tazzo tossed his cigarette. "Looks like it's about to start. We better get inside."

As they went up the steps Toni said, "Is the lieutenant inside?"

"Yeah, he is."

After the mass, Toni stood in front of Mount Carmel at the top of the steps alone. She watched the casket as it was placed into the hearse. She turned and noticed Father Gribbons speaking to an elderly Latino couple in the rear of the church. After another minute, the couple stepped out of the church and Gribbons stepped back inside. Toni followed him.

"Father Gribbons," Toni called out.

Gribbons was walking down the side aisle of the church, in the direction of the sacristy. He stopped and turned.

Toni stepped up to him.

"How are you feeling, detective?" Gribbons said, pointing at her slung arm. "I was so sorry to hear about what happened to you and your partner."

"Thanks, Father," Toni said. "Father, before we got shot, I heard from the Abbot at the Clarence Abbey. He told me that you left the abbey Saturday night."

Gribbons was silent.

"Where did you go when you left the abbey, Father," Toni said. "You told us you didn't get back from retreat until early Monday morning. About six-thirty. So, where were you really when Father Manny was shot?"

Gribbons finally got his voice. "I've been told that you're suspended, detective."

Toni paused for a moment and took Gribbons in.

"You sure you want to play it that way, Father?" Toni said. "If you want a non-suspended detective to ask you that question, I'll just mention it to Sergeant Tazzo on the way out."

Gribbons' face turned red.

"This is very hard for me, detective."

Toni waited.

"I was with the secretary of our church, Juanita Perez," Gribbons said.

Toni waited for more, but Gribbons stopped.

"And?" Toni said.

Gribbons remained silent.

Finally, it occurred to Toni what he was getting at.

"You and the secretary are a—

"Yes," Gribbons cut Toni off.

Toni took that in.

"Did Father Manny know about that?" Toni said.

"No, no, he didn't."

"Because that would give you a pretty good motive to kill him if he was about to expose you."

"No, no, it wasn't like that at all," Gribbons said.

"And it also gives you a pretty good reason to steal his journal if you knew he'd written something about it."

"Father Manny was like a brother to me. I could never

hurt him, no matter what. But I don't believe he knew about us."

Toni looked at Gribbons long and hard.

"I hope you're not lying to me again, Father," Toni said.

"That's the truth, detective," Gribbons said. "And that aberration in my life is over."

Toni held the priest's eyes for a long minute.

"Okay, Father. If that's the truth, you're secret is safe with me," Toni said. "God knows, we all have our share of aberrations."

"Thank you, detective. Thank you."

"But if you're lying, you know you're toast."

"I fully understand. That is the truth, detective."

"All right, now, I'm going to ask you one more time. Did you take that journal?"

"No, I did not."

"But you were the only person in his office after Crime Scene took the photos I showed you."

"Well, yes, from the parish, but, no, I mean, I wasn't the only one in that office."

"Juanita already said she didn't go into his office," Toni said.

"I mean, Lieutenant Condon, of course. Lieutenant Condon went into Father Manny's office."

"What?" Toni said. "When?"

"You didn't know that?" Gribbons said. "Last Monday, after I spoke to you and your partner, and I told you that Father Manny was a good friend of the Lieutenant Condon, and you both left, remember?

"Yeah."

"Well, he came by that afternoon to look around and went up to Father Manny's office."

Toni stood there without a word for a long moment.

"Did you go to Father Manny's office with the lieutenant?"

271

"No, he asked me to wait downstairs."

So that's what Ryan was up to while she and Geddes were wasting time waiting on Ernesto Cruz to show-up at the Upper Westside SRO, she thought. He must have Father Manny's journal. And he has it for a reason.

She again started to wonder about another thing. How is it that the strand of hair that Crime Scene picked-up was identified as Ryan's? Ryan wasn't in Manny's office until after Crime Scene had finished up.

Toni stepped back out of the church and watched Liz Rivera. She was standing only a few feet from the family limousine with her mother, and a beautiful teenager in a simple one-piece black dress. The visitors that couldn't join the procession to the cemetery offered their condolences, returned to their vehicles and left. Others joined the procession for the drive to the cemetery and waited.

Toni approached. The moment she made eye contact with Liz, she broke away from the others.

"*Un momento, Mama,*" Toni could hear Liz say, then Liz put her arm into Toni's good arm and walked to the rear of the limousine.

"Thank you so much for coming, detective," Liz said and hugged Toni.

"I'm very sorry for your loss, Liz."

Liz then waved the beautiful teenager over to them.

"Please, Liz, it's Toni"

Liz nodded, with a smile.

"Toni, this is my niece, Vanessa, my sister's daughter."

Toni took Vanessa's hand with both hands. "I'm so very sorry for your loss, Vanessa. So, very sorry."

"Thank you," Vanessa replied with a nervous smile. Her eyes glossy. Her cheeks looked like they'd been smudged with tomato paste. Red and raw from prolonged crying.

Liz told Vanessa to get in the limousine with her grandmother, and that she'd be there in a second.

Liz then hugged Toni again and whispered in her ear, "I have something to tell you. The bed sheets are being analyzed at a lab in New Jersey."

"Are you kidding me?" Toni said with surprise but maintained the hug.

"No, no. I went on the Internet and found a lab in New Jersey that does work for the State Police there. They seem very professional. They sent a lab technician to the apartment to pick it up. The DNA results I've been told will be available by tomorrow."

"Excellent," Toni whispered. "Excellent. Okay, call me as soon as you have the report."

"You can count on it."

As Toni continued to hug Liz, whose back was then facing the church, she spotted Ryan, talking with Tazzo on the steps.

"I've got to go, Liz. But as soon as you get the results and I come up with a suspect's DNA to make a comparison, I'll reach out to you."

Liz released the hug but held one of Toni's arms as she began to step away. "Toni, after the cemetery service, there's food waiting for our friends and family at my sister's apartment. Could you come?"

"Will Lieutenant Condon be there?"

"Yes, he said he would come by."

"I'm sorry, I can't. I'm technically supposed to be home. Call me when you get the results." Toni pulled away and moved at a steady pace.

As soon as Toni turned the corner, she looked back and could see Ryan breaking away from the crowd, walking in her direction. She snapped her head up and down the street from left to right like an owl but couldn't spot her silver Jetta.

"Where the hell are you?" She whispered and kept walking fast, afraid to stay on the corner and let Ryan catch-up to her.

Jeremiah suddenly pulled up and flung the passenger side door open, and she jumped in.

"Make a U-turn, and get out of here!" Toni shouted.

Jeremiah spun the car around like a stunt driver and was gone.

"What's wrong?" he said as he kept his eye on the road, cruising through one intersection after another. Thankfully the lights were green for several successive blocks.

"Where the hell were you!" Toni yelled. "Didn't I tell you to wait right there!"

"I went into the church." Jeremiah calmly said.

"What!"

"Yes." Jeremiah directly said and kept driving. "She was my mother."

"But what if Lieutenant Condon had seen you?"

"I had to take that chance."

"You had to take a chance! You had to take a chance!"

Jeremiah didn't reply.

Toni fixed an intense gaze on him for a few long moments; then looked away. There was silence for several blocks.

Jeremiah spoke up, "What happened?"

"Lieutenant Condon was trying to catch up to me," Toni said. "That's what happened."

"Oh," Jeremiah said as he screeched, making a turn and heading in the direction of the Major Deegan Expressway.

Toni turned her body to face Jeremiah. "Don't pull that on me again. No more surprises. You got to be straight with me about what you need to do. If you pull something like that again we're finished. You understand?"

"I'm sorry Toni. I didn't plan on it. It was just that after you jumped out, I just had to be there too. I'm sorry. It won't happen again. I promise."

Toni didn't respond.

She sat still in the car in a dazed state, in deep thought, eyes fixed on the road ahead but not seeing the road at all.

She wondered how she could get her hands on a sample of Ryan's blood or saliva or something?

CHAPTER 31

Ryan stood at the corner looking up and down the street but there was no sign of Toni. She must've jumped into her car and taken off like a shot. He couldn't blame her.

He slowly walked back to the front of Mount Carmel Church and thanked the two uniformed cops standing out front for providing outside security during the mass. Even though the service wasn't for a government official or police officer, he'd made arrangements with the precinct to assign a couple of cops in anticipation of the turnout. It was the least he could do for the family.

Sergeant Tazzo approached him after the uniformed cops pulled away in their marked radio car.

"Loo, we got something on this Milton Iglesia."

Ryan took off his sunglasses.

"Turns out he was released from this home for EDP's in the Adirondacks early the same day Father Manny was killed. State Mental Health told us he was directed to the same S.R.O. on the Upper Westside, same S.R.O. we picked up Ernesto Cruz in front of."

"Hmm."

"Trouble is he hasn't been around for the last couple of days. I got a couple of guys sitting on it."

"All right, good," Ryan said. "Send somebody down to the D.A.'s office to get a search warrant for his room. If he doesn't show up by midnight tonight, go in and search the place."

"You got it."

"I got a feeling he isn't heading back to the S.R.O. though," Ryan said.

"Probably not."

"All right, Vic, I'm heading to the cemetery. Let me know when you got the background on that rookie, Jeremiah Francisco. I've been invited to Sutton Place after. You can get me on my cell."

Ryan headed to his car.

Jeremiah took the Cross-Bronx Expressway heading west in the direction of the George Washington Bridge and turned off on the northbound Henry Hudson Parkway back to Riverdale. They approached the toll to get over the Henry Hudson Bridge back into the Bronx.

Toni watched the tollgate go up and blurted, "Wait a minute!"

"What, what?" Jeremiah looked over at her. "What's the matter now?"

"Where's my iPhone?" she said to Jeremiah as if he would know.

She grabbed her purse from the back seat and dug her cell phone out, pulled up her telephone directory and scrolled down to Liz R. and dialed. The phone rang and rang.

"Pick up, pick up," Toni muttered.

"Hello," Liz Rivera answered.

"Liz, don't say anything. Just listen and answer yes or no. This is Toni Santiago."

"Yes."

"I know you're on your way to the cemetery. Sorry, I didn't think of this outside the church. I know your mother and Vanessa are sitting next to you. I hate to bring this up now but it's very important that I ask you to do something."

"Yes."

"Don't be alarmed with what I am about to say, and try not to jump to conclusions. I just need you to follow up on something so that we cover all the bases, and only you'll have the chance to get it done. Do you understand?"

"Yes."

"Liz, when Lieutenant Condon comes to your home after the service at the cemetery…"

"…Yes."

"I need you to keep some item that he puts his lips to a glass, fork, spoon. Then I want you to put it in a clear plastic baggie and get it over to that lab in Jersey. I want the lab to compare the DNA removed from your sister's bedroom sheets with Lieutenant Condon's DNA. Do you understand?

There was silence.

"Liz, are you there?"

"Yes."

"Liz I know this is a shock. If it turns out there's a match, all that means is that your sister and Lieutenant Condon had been intimate the night she was killed. It doesn't mean he's her murderer. Do you understand?

The silence remained.

"Liz?"

"Yes."

"I know this is hitting you from left field —

Toni could overhear Liz's mother ask, "Who's that, *mija*?"

"Just a friend, *Mama*."

"Liz, I just found out that the day before Samantha was killed, she came by Bronx Homicide to see him."

"Uh, huhhhh."

"All right. Will you do that?"

"Yes."

"And not mention it to anyone else, including your mother, husband — "

"Yes."

"Okay," Toni said and tapped end on her iPhone.

Pensively she put her phone back in her purse, keeping it on her lap, her open palms resting down on it, like she was holding down a jack-in-the-box, and resumed her fixed, fully absorbed view of the road. All she could see were the blinking, vertical white dashes on the blacktop ahead as Jeremiah drove.

They traveled in silence for a few more minutes or so when Jeremiah said, "Can I ask who you just spoke to, Toni?"

"What?" Toni twisted her head to face him, shaken out of her mental state. Then it struck her. "Ahhhh, no," she blurted.

In her urgency to speak to Liz and tell her to get a DNA sample from Ryan, she'd forgotten that Jeremiah would hear her conversation.

"Who were you talking to, Toni?"

They traveled in silence for a few more minutes as Toni got her thoughts together. Jeremiah momentarily looked over to her, standing by for a reply.

"I was talking to your mother's sister."

Jeremiah turned to her again. "My mother's sister?"

Toni nodded.

"My mother's sister. That must have been the woman sitting in the first pew at the church. It just never occurred to me she was my mother's sister." Jeremiah stopped himself. "Do you know if my mother had other kids?"

"Yes, she had a daughter."

"Really? How old is she?"

"Sixteen."

"Is that right. That means I have a half-sister. A sixteen-year-old half-sister. What's her name?"

"Vanessa."

"Vanessa," he repeated under his breath.

"I saw her too, right, at the service?" Jeremiah said momentarily taking his eyes off the road to look at Toni.

They kept driving in silence. Toni kept checking him out. She could see he was deep in thought, looking out onto the blacktop of the expressway.

Jeremiah then abruptly turned back to Toni. "So what's this about Lieutenant Condon?"

"I suspect Lieutenant Condon was with your mother the night she was killed."

"What?" Jeremiah said. "Where?"

"In your mother's apartment on Sutton Place."

"Why?" Jeremiah said, switching his view back and forth from the road to Toni. "You mean before she met me over at the park?"

"Yes, I think so."

"Why do you think that?"

Toni didn't answer at first. She wondered if it was the right time tell him what she'd been thinking. But what choice did she have? She and Jeremiah were in it together, and she had to tell him what was on her mind.

"Your mother's sister had suspected someone had been in your mother's bed the night she was killed."

"What does that have to do with the lieutenant?"

"Your mother and the lieutenant grew up in the same neighborhood. They dated. They were a couple then."

"Is that true?"

"Yes," Toni said, "it is."

Toni was struck by Jeremiah's measured seriousness. How he shifted from what appeared to be a gentle, thoughtful soul who could not act in any other way into a person whose mind would focus and operate in a laser-like fashion. Not that he appeared threatening to her in any way. He reminded her of a distinguished senior judge who asked the right questions absent emotion, but in a very interested and concerned manner to get to the truth.

"Jeremiah." He turned again to look directly at her.

"I think Lieutenant Condon's your father."

For a moment Jeremiah looked at her with a blank stare; then he frowned; looked back to the road; then back at Toni; then suddenly sped up out of the left lane; into the middle lane; into the right lane; pulled off the next exit and onto the service road; slid to within an inch of the curb; came to a swift controlled stop; put the car in park; twisted in his seat to look at her directly.

"What are you talking about? I'm..." Jeremiah swiped his face with his hand. "I'm the product of a rapist, you know that!"

"I know this is a shock, but I don't think you are."

"But why, why don't you think I am?" Jeremiah said with more excitement than Toni had seen before, but she still didn't feel at all threatened.

"Because I can hear his voice in your voice," Toni said. "I mean you sound just like him. You even have some of his mannerisms. It's kind of surreal."

Jeremiah was speechless. Toni felt his look meant he was wondering if she had all her marbles.

"Listen, I think your mother and the lieutenant dated around the time you were conceived. You're about the right age for that to be possible. But what really convinces me you're his son—" Toni stopped then slowly and softly said, "Because, Jeremiah, you are the spitting image of the lieutenant. I'm not kidding. You two look so much alike, it just can't be a coincidence. I know it's a shock. But—"

Jeremiah cut her off. "Come on, Toni! How could that be possible? I mean, so we look alike. A lot of people look alike who aren't related."

"Yeah, I know. I kept telling myself that too. But I think there are just too many things coming together here to pretend there isn't something up," Toni said. "I mean…you're the spitting image of him."

Jeremiah was quiet.

"You've never seen him, have you? I mean aside from in front of your building yesterday. You couldn't have gotten a good look at him when we bolted out of there."

"No," he said. He shifted his gaze back in the direction of the windshield.

"He was in the church. I guess you didn't notice him." Toni placed her hand on his shoulder. "Well, if you had, I don't think you'd doubt it."

They sat there without speaking. Toni was deaf to the rumbling traffic whizzing past them at sixty-plus M.P.H.

Toni then said, "But there's another thing that makes a connection between you and the lieutenant."

Jeremiah turned to look at her without responding and waited for her to continue.

"You know that shield you got as a kid, the dupe," Toni said. "What's that number again?"

Jeremiah looked at Toni for a moment and slowly said, "6-7-0-2."

"And when did you receive that shield?" Toni said. "Do you remember?"

Jeremiah again slowly replied as he held her gaze, "The summer after my first year of high school."

"Well, that was the same summer Lieutenant Condon was promoted to sergeant," Toni said and waited for the lights to go on in his eyes.

Jeremiah didn't speak for several long moments, then his eyes widened and he said, "The lieutenant's white shield was 6-7-0-2?"

"You got it."

They did not speak. They sat quietly consumed by the whooshing sound of traffic.

"But there is one final thing. There was a strand of hair that was picked up from Father Manny's office. The DNA in that strand of hair we thought was the killer's, but, the DNA came back to Lieutenant Condon. Except the lieutenant didn't go to that office until after Crime Scene left the office," Toni said. "Do you follow what I'm saying?"

Toni waited.

"You're saying that the DNA is so similar to the lieutenant's that the lab made the mistake of thinking that it was the lieutenant's, but it's really mine?"

"Yes, that's what I think happened."

"So the lieutenant raped my mother?" Jeremiah said. "Is that what you're also saying?"

Toni twisted in the passenger seat to face him again. "I don't know about that. That's hard for me to wrap my head around," Toni said. "But I don't know."

"If I'm his son, do you think he knows?"

"I don't know that either," Toni said. "I'm sorry."

After several minutes of quiet, he leaned his head against the steering wheel and kept it there. Toni embraced him.

CHAPTER 32

Before Ryan entered the lobby of Samantha's Sutton Place apartment building he took a quick look through the window to see if either the doorman or concierge were the same two on duty the night he'd been there with Samantha. They weren't. When he walked into the lobby, he scanned the different CCTV cameras affixed to different ceiling corners. Something he'd hadn't given a thought to doing when he'd shown up there the night she was killed. The cameras had every piece of that lobby area covered, all the way up to the elevator banks, and inside each elevator too.

Ryan made his second appearance ever at Samantha's Sutton Place apartment.

As soon as he entered that lamentable space his chest tightened. Liz approached him directly and thanked him for coming.

She offered Ryan something to drink, but he declined and told her that he couldn't stay long. Liz then offered him something to eat.

"I'm not hungry, Liz, but thank you."

He looked around. Some of the people were sitting and eating and talking, wrapped around the dining room table. Others were on the sofa and chairs in the living room holding their plates with one hand, scooping their food with the other or opted to place their plates on their tightly squeezed legs and use both hands.

He remembered how he and Samantha deeply kissed, on the very sofa that was being used by others to consume a meal in her memory.

"We have all this food, Ryan," Liz said, with a warm smile as she swept her hand to the dining room table that held a catered, buffet-style variety of salads, breads, cold cuts, and hot food. Two male and female servers, wearing white collared shirts and black vests, were serving behind the stretch of food.

"Please have something to eat Ryan," Liz said. "I want to speak with you. I'll just be a minute. I need to attend to a few of my other guests first."

"Of course, Liz. Go ahead. I'll have something."

Liz excused herself, and Ryan grabbed a plate. He let the servers put a few Swedish meatballs and a scoop of tortellini salad onto it, found himself a chair in the corner away from anybody else, and planted himself.

Another server roaming the apartment swept by him and offered him something to drink. He accepted a can of Coke, and she came back with it in a glass.

Samantha's ex-husband approached Ryan. "Is there anything else you need, Lieutenant?"

"No, thank you. I'm all set."

"May I," Mr. Cohen motioned to the seat next to him and sat down.

"Sure," Ryan said.

"It was a very nice service."

"Yes, it was," Ryan said.

"I think Samantha would have been pleased.

Ryan nodded.

"Thank you again for coming."

He couldn't help but wonder what it had been like having Samantha as one's wife: To wake up with her day-by-day; to come home to her night-after-night; to breathe her in every day of his life. It was a life he'd never known and would never know. His heart burned yet again with that certainty.

He wondered if they'd ever had together what he and Samantha once had: That God-given something that cannot be faked or recreated. It's either there or it isn't. If his love for Samantha had not been returned, then he possessed no more than he'd had all those years: a sandstorm of obligations with no glimpse of heaven.

And to think that one, violent, aberrant, act drove them all into that desert and robbed the potential for true loveliness from all of their lives.

"I thought you'd want to talk to me eventually."

"Sure. But there's no rush. I know you had a good relationship with Samantha. You had an amicable divorce."

"Yes, that's true."

"So I thought you had enough going on with the shock of her death, dealing with your own grief, and taking care of your daughter."

"I appreciate that, Lieutenant."

"In the next week or so I'll send one of my detectives to your office to take your formal statement. Are you okay with that?"

"Of course, that'll be fine. May I ask, has there been any progress with the investigation?"

"We have a number of solid leads, but I can't discuss it right now."

"I understand. I'm sure you'll let us know as soon as you make an arrest."

"Yes. You can count on that."

The ex-husband stood up, shook Ryan's hand and stepped away.

Liz sat next to him soon after.

"Ryan, has there been any progress?"

Ryan promptly put his fork down on his plate with a couple tortellini attached and wiped his mouth with a napkin.

"Yes, Liz, there has been progress. We do have a couple of leads, but I'm not at liberty to discuss it right now. I'm sorry."

"I see," Liz paused.

"I'm really sorry, Liz, but I need to get going," Ryan said, and started to stand, holding his glass and plate. "Thank you for inviting me. Samantha had a beautiful home."

Liz didn't rise and held his forearm.

"Ryan, had you seen my sister after she stopped by your office?" She said looking up at him.

He looked away and over her shoulder, out the vast living room window, down to the East River, and noticed an oil tanker. He was seized with the memory of another oil tanker he'd briefly watched troll up the river as Samantha embraced him from behind the night she was murdered. After they'd made love—before he raced out her door.

"Ryan?"

It was such a contrast to the one he'd noticed on the night they were together. It was a similar red-and-black oil tanker that time too, except that one was empty, seemingly suspended above the dark river, heading south toward the Atlantic. That night he could easily see twenty or more feet of its black bottom, and there was no escorting tug: it didn't need one

"Ryan?"

This tanker had a bright red tugboat pressing it north toward the Bronx. It was carrying a full load. Its bottom was sunk deep into the river. Barely a sliver of its black bottom exposed. It was as if Samantha's intense, abundant spirit had been poured into the tanker and was being carted away.

"Well, Ryan," Liz pressed him.

He finally sat back down.

"Why do you ask?"

"I don't know, I just thought that since my sister stopped by your precinct to see you, maybe you both agreed to meet again later," Liz said. "After all you hadn't seen each other in so many years."

Ryan's mind started to flicker with responses; they came so fast it was like flashbulbs popping off in his head. Popping thoughts that momentarily blinded him. He couldn't admit the truth. The truth that he'd been with Samantha the night she was killed.

He had no doubt that if Chief King knew he was not only Father Manny's personal friend but Samantha Cohen teenage boyfriend, King would have no choice but to heave him off the case. And he just could not be taken off this case.

"No, Liz, I didn't see Samantha after she came by the office."

Ryan held her gaze until Liz's husband called for her and she excused herself again. Ryan rose from his chair. Liz stepped to the front door and with her back to him stood with her husband and another couple.

Ryan walked into the kitchen and started to place his glass and plate in the sink.

"Please, Ryan, you're my guest," Liz said and grabbed the plate and glass. "I'll take that!"

It seemed to Ryan she'd dropped into the kitchen from the ceiling. Only a moment before she'd been talking to that couple, seemingly unaware of his movements, and, the next moment, she was in the kitchen with him.

"That's not necessary, Liz," Ryan said, as several of the other guests drifted into the kitchen and placed their plates and glasses into the sink.

Both maintained their hold of the glass and plate and held each other's gaze for an extra moment.

"Please, Ryan, you don't have to do that. Let me have it."

Ryan released his grip. "Of course, Liz, thank you."

288

Liz placed his glass on the center of his plate and slid it away from the others. "I hope you'll be able to share with me the progress you're making sometime soon."

Ryan walked to the front door to let himself out, and Liz followed.

He grabbed the doorknob, turned back to Liz and said, "I'll be in touch when I find Samantha's killer. And I will find him. I promise you that."

CHAPTER 33

Toni and Jeremiah were on the elevator of Toni's Riverdale apartment building.

Her aunt opened the door slowly, and Vita shot up at Toni, wiggling with excitement.

"*Hola, Tia,*" Toni said, kissed her aunt on the cheek, and bent down to rub Vita's gyrating head and body.

Her aunt looked down at her with raised eyebrows. "You have a visitor, my child."

Toni stood up and looked past her aunt and into the apartment. From the front door, she could see into the living room and the kitchen, but nobody came into view.

"*Donde esta, Tia,*" Toni whispered to her aunt.

The toilet flushed and they both turned their heads down the apartment hallway in the direction of the bathroom and her aunt whispered, "*En el bano.*"

Just as Toni asked who it was, in a whisper too, Ryan stepped out of the bathroom.

Toni spun around and slammed the door right on Jeremiah's face.

"What are you doing here?" Toni said.

"Can we talk?" Ryan said and thumbed in the direction of the kitchen.

"I'll be in the bedroom, my child," her aunt said and took Vita with her. "You call me if you have trouble."

"Thank you, *Titi.*"

Toni marched into the kitchen, turned, one arm still in the sling, the other on her hip. "What's there to talk about?"

"I know you've got some ideas about me."

"I do?" Toni said. "Like what?"

Ryan walked over to the kitchen window and looked out. Toni followed him with her eyes.

Ryan turned. "Toni, there's a lot I haven't been able to tell you. I needed some time to sort things out. I'm trying to get to the truth here. And to be honest with you, I've been in shock with all that's happened."

"Oh, yeah? Why are you in shock?"

Ryan paused before answering. "I can't get into it right now. I just need you to trust me."

"I see you can't get into it right now. How about I get into to it right now? How about you explain what you were doing in Samantha Cohen's apartment the night she was killed?"

"You saw the CCTV?"

"Does that matter?" Toni said. "What were you doing there?

"That's none of your business."

So he was in Samantha's apartment the night she was killed and probably in her bed, she thought. She got him to slip there.

Toni watched Ryan move to the living room; she followed, not letting up. "How is it that you were at mass the same day Father Manny was killed and you were with Samantha Cohen the same night she was killed?"

"What are you trying to say?" Ryan said, raising his voice.

"Let me ask you something else there, lieutenant. How is it your cop shield ended up in the hands of that drug dealer?" Toni said. "Why didn't you just acknowledge it when I brought it up to you and Tazzo? How do you explain that? What are you trying to hide?"

Ryan repeated with resignation, "It's none of your business."

"Who raped Samantha Cohen twenty years ago?"

Ryan was silent.

"Did you rape her?" Toni said.

"Are you out of your mind?" Ryan said and started to walk to the apartment door.

291

"What about Milton Iglesia?"

Ryan stopped, turned, and stepped back up to Toni. "How do you know about him?"

"Did he rape Samantha?"

"I want to know right now how you know about Milton Iglesia!" Ryan said, looking down on Toni, pointing his finger in her face. "Right now!"

Toni stood up on her toes and thrust her face into Ryan's finger.

"Get your finger out of my face."

After a few long moments, Ryan put his hand down.

"I told Tazzo my old man took the original complaint on the rape," Toni said. "He didn't tell you?"

Ryan stayed silent

"Anyway, what I didn't know — when I first saw the complaint report — was that my old man suspected Milton Iglesia was the rapist. I went through my father's Activity Log. He made a notation that he picked-up Milton, and brought him to the hospital for a show-up, but Samantha wouldn't I.D. But his notes seem to show that she recognized him."

"Who's Milton Iglesia?" Toni said, knowing he was Father Manny's brother, but she wanted to see how Ryan would respond.

"I can't say, Toni."

"They're my damn cases!"

"No, they aren't!" Ryan blasted back. "Not anymore they aren't."

"Oh, yes they are! You think 'cause you suspended me that I'll let this go. You know me better than that. There's no way I'll let this go until I find out who murdered Manny Gonzalez and Samantha Cohen. You got that?" Toni said. "And if I find out you were involved, you're going down."

Ryan looked at her in dead silence, looked down at his feet, looked back up at Toni and said, "If you interfere with this investigation —

"What...I'm already suspended. What are you going to do, re-suspend me?"

"I will lock you up. I will lock you up for obstruction. You understand that!"

"You're the one obstructing asshole!"

Toni's aunt suddenly appeared in the living room, holding back a growling Vita on a leash. "Are you okay my child?"

Toni paused, locked on Ryan's eyes and whispered, "How did I ever come to admire you?"

The instant Ryan was out of her aunt's apartment, Toni flung herself into the hallway like she was tossed on stage. She felt almost sure he'd left. She'd heard the elevator door open and close. She swiveled her head from side-to-side, down the length of the hallway, looking for Jeremiah.

Jeremiah had secreted himself in the stairwell. He'd had a clear view of her aunt's apartment door through the window of the stairwell door. From a bent position—which exposed only the top of his head and eyes—he'd watched Ryan Condon barge out of the apartment and jump on the elevator.

Jeremiah threw the stairwell door open and rushed into the hallway.

"Let's go!" Toni said as she pushed past Jeremiah into the stairwell Jeremiah had just come from. "Forget the elevator!"

"Where are we going?" Jeremiah shouted as he stayed with Toni in her dash down the stairs. She took two steps at a time; still in a dress and heels.

"We're tailing Lieutenant Condon!" she yelled back at Jeremiah as she consumed another flight of steps.

Jeremiah didn't say a word and bounced down the staircase on Toni's tail shaking his head. They blasted out the rear of her building and Jeremiah jumped behind the wheel of her Jetta. Toni jumped in the back seat.

"There's less chance he'll pick up the tail if he doesn't see two heads in his rear-view mirror, and I don't think he could make you from the car."

Jeremiah was having trouble getting the key into the ignition.

"GO, GO, GO! He's gonna get away!"

"How close do you want me to get to him?"

"Just move it!" Toni screamed.

Toni and Jeremiah tailed Ryan down the Henry Hudson Parkway to the Cross Bronx Expressway heading west in the direction of the Whitestone and Throgs Neck bridges to the Northeast Bronx. Ryan bypassed the exit that would've led to the Bronx Homicide office.

"Where do think he's heading?" Jeremiah said.

"I don't know," Toni said, peaking over Jeremiah's shoulder from the backseat.

Ryan pulled off at the Country Club Road exit.

"It looks like he's heading home," Toni said.

They watched Ryan as he pulled into the driveway of his home in Throgs Neck from a half-block away.

"Once he heads into his house, I'll get out and see what he's up to," Toni said.

"How?" Jeremiah said, with wide confused eyes.

"Maybe I can see through one of those windows," Toni said and shot out as soon as Ryan stepped inside.

"Be careful, Toni."

"Just stay in the car."

Toni carried her heels as she slid along the cement walkway on the side of the house. All of the windows were closed, and the curtains blocked her from seeing inside until she got to the back. There was a dining room in the back. One of the two dining room windows was open a few inches, and the white, sheer curtains were drawn back. She kept her head low, peaking just above the windowsill.

Ryan walked into the dining room with a bottle of Budweiser. He took his suit jacket off and placed it on the back of one of the eight chairs at the dining room table, loosened his tie, then sat at the head of the table. He stared at the label of the Budweiser bottle, gripping it with both hands as if he were contemplating Proverb 23:19-21 *"Hear thou, my son, and be wise, and guide thine heart in the way. Be not among wine-bibbers; among riotous eaters of flesh. For the drunkard and the glutton shall come to poverty: and drowsiness shall clothe a man with rags."*

He leaned back and took a long pull from the bottle. When his head came down, Jocelyn was sitting at the other end of the table.

"Geez, you scared the crap out of me!" Ryan said.

It scared the crap out of Toni too.

Toni thought the dining room was empty. She hadn't noticed Ryan's wife slip into a chair at the long table.

Jocelyn didn't speak. She was wrapped in the same baggy work shirt she'd worn the day Toni and Geddes had notified Ryan of Father Manny's murder. It was still too big for her.

"You want a beer?" Ryan said, lifting up his bottle to her.

"No thank you."

"I thought you were teaching after school today," Ryan said.

"Yeah, well, I canceled it. I took the afternoon off. I was kind of tired."

Ryan noticed a bandage wrapped around her left hand. "What happened to your hand?"

Jocelyn casually raised her hand to look at the bandage herself and said, "Battle wound. One of my challenging little girls bit me as I was trying to keep her from beating up a challenging little boy."

"You need to get a shot," Ryan said, and started to get up. "I'll take you to the doctor now."

295

"Already done," Jocelyn said. "Relax. Enjoy your beer."

Ryan slowly eased back into the chair.

"All right, that's good," Ryan said. "So what's up Joss?"

"You tell me," Jocelyn said with squinted eyes.

Ryan didn't answer. They sat in silence gazing at each other for a few moments. Toni's heart rate picked up.

"What are you doing home?" Jocelyn said.

"I wanted to grab a shower before I go back," Ryan said and took another sip from his beer. "The humidity is killing me."

"So, you attended Samantha's funeral?"

Ryan didn't reply at first, then said, "How'd you know that?"

"I know my husband."

Silence.

"So," Jocelyn said, leaning forward, hands clasped together like she was leading an inquiry. "Is there a connection between Manny's and Samantha's murders?"

Ryan paused before answering: sitting back, arms extended to the bottle in his grip resting on the table.

"It's possible. We don't know that for sure, but it is possible."

"Don't you think that's strange, Ryan?"

"Yes, I do think it's strange."

"I wonder if it has something to do with the past," Jocelyn said with her head tilted.

Ryan didn't reply, held his beer, and looked at his wife.

What did she know about their pasts? Toni wondered. Did Jocelyn know Samantha had been raped twenty years before? Did Jocelyn know about Jeremiah? Had she had any conversations with Manny about it? Did she know who the rapist was? Did she know who killed Father Manny and Samantha Cohen?

Jocelyn continued. "Well, they grew up in the same neighborhood, went to the same church and park, and they knew each other. Just like you."

Ryan remained silent.

"Can I ask you a question?"

"Sure."

"When was the last time you saw Samantha alive?"

Toni's pulse quickened.

"I saw her a couple of days ago. She came by the squad to speak to me the day after Manny was killed. She wanted to know how the investigation was going and if there was anything she could do to help."

"Was there?" Jocelyn said.

"Was there what?"

Jocelyn's brow furrowed. "Was there anything she could do to help?"

"No there wasn't, but I told her I'd let her know when we made an arrest."

Jocelyn stood up slowly and walked to the sidebar of the dining room, picked up the framed photograph of the two of them holding each other on a sunny day, taken on a sailboat on the Long Island Sound, ten years earlier. They were all smiles. She gently brushed the glass of the framed photograph with her fingertips.

"Had you seen Samantha before she came to visit you at the precinct?"

Ryan evenly said, "I hadn't seen Samantha since we were all kids, Jocelyn."

Again they silently looked at each other.

"Does Chief King know you dated Samantha when you were kids?"

Ryan took a breath. "No. He doesn't."

"Shouldn't you let him know?"

"I don't think that's necessary," Ryan said. "At least not now."

297

"Haven't you told me it's your policy to pull any of your detectives off a case if you find out they have some personal connection to the victim?"

Toni watched Ryan hold his wife's gaze, but didn't answer.

Jocelyn's face became flushed and seemed to lose its shape.

Toni could see her eyes tear up as she looked down on Ryan.

"Okay, well, I've got to go to *Stop & Shop*, pick up a few things for dinner," Jocelyn said and planted the framed photograph on the table, within the sidelines of his extended arms, between his beer and his face. Ryan didn't move.

Toni looked at Jocelyn Condon carefully: Tall, long red hair, with lingering beauty. And her eyes: kind, devoted, wounded.

"Wait a minute, red hair," Toni murmured. The woman sitting with Father Manny before he was shot had red hair according to Jeremiah.

Jocelyn turned to head out of the dining room but then turned back to Ryan.

"When Samantha went to see you at your office, was that the last time you saw her?"

Toni waited for the answer to that one too.

"Yes," Ryan said.

Toni whispered, "You lying creep."

She watched them both in silence until Jocelyn stepped out.

Toni then watched Ryan's head drop, arms still extended, holding the beer, facing the framed photograph, until the engine of Jocelyn's car turned over. Then, finally, he pulled his arms in and planted his face in his hands. After several long beats, he stood-up returned the photograph to the sidebar, then leaned his eyes into his fists like he was looking into a microscope for several more long beats, grabbed his jacket from the back of the chair and walked out of the dining room.

Toni bolted for the Jetta and Jeremiah.

"Follow her!" Toni yelled, and Jeremiah pulled out. "Did you see her before she got in the car?"

"Yes, I did."

"Is she the redhead you saw talking to Father Manny in the rectory?"

"Could be, but I can't be sure."

Toni wasn't sure it was a good idea tailing Jocelyn. Maybe she wasn't the same redhead. Maybe they should still be tailing Ryan to see what he does next. But she had to make a choice, and her gut told her to track Jocelyn for a while.

Jocelyn took off down the Bruckner Expressway. Toni figured she'd be traveling to the *Stop & Shop* off Tremont Avenue, blocks from her home if she were really planning to go to a supermarket, Toni thought, but when that exit approached she went past it and continued south. After two miles, she exited at 138th street and cruised in the direction of Mount Carmel Park.

"Look at this?" Toni said, totally intrigued.

Jocelyn pulled up to the north side entrance: the very same entrance Jeremiah and his mother had entered the night she died.

"What's she doing here?" Jeremiah said.

"We'll see," Toni said in a whisper trying to contain the exhilaration she was feeling.

Jocelyn Condon remained parked for close to an hour. She didn't get out of her car.

"You think she's waiting for somebody?" Jeremiah said.

"We'll see."

If Jocelyn were waiting for somebody who could that be? And if she wasn't waiting for somebody, what was she doing at the park? Toni wondered. Why did she come to the park, to begin with, and then just sit there motionless?

Suddenly a coarse male voice asked, "Waiting for somebody?"

Toni and Jeremiah snapped their heads in the direction of the voice. A massive man stood at the driver's side of the car, but their focus was on the deep dark tunnel of the long-barreled revolver pointed at their faces.

CHAPTER 34

Liz Rivera returned to Samantha's apartment about 8 p.m. She felt grateful the service at Mount Carmel had been so beautiful. Flowers had clouded the church. The altar was inundated with various colors and smells; even the walls on both sides of her and Samantha's childhood parish were lined with flowers from the altar to the rear.

Liz felt Samantha would have loved the fact that the immense floral appearance was compounded, not only because of the deluge of flowers sent in her memory but because her flowers had been combined with those sent two days prior in Father Manny's memory. Liz was grateful Father Gribbons chose to leave Father Manny's flowers out until after her sister's service.

Liz had seen her husband and two daughters off at La Guardia Airport to return home, but she came back. She needed to stay. Samantha's daughter was with her father. Vanessa and her father had insisted Liz stay with them at his apartment on East End Avenue, but she'd convinced them she would be okay. The caterer had done a good job of cleaning up. She looked forward to being in her sister's home alone. She was not frightened. It brought her comfort.

She took a long, hot bath, which Samantha often did. Liz herself had not done so since she was very little, and even then, she always shared it with Samantha. She generously poured the bubble bath (which her big sister always had an ample supply) into the rushing hot water. She sat on the toilet seat cover and watched the steam slowly expand and thicken — until she could barely make out the bathtub itself — before she eased herself in.

When she made it to the living room, she was snuggly wrapped in one of Samantha's thick, white, terrycloth bathrobes. She settled into her sister's chaise lounge, brought her legs up under her, and sipped on a steaming mug of herbal tea as she scrolled through photographs Samantha had kept on her iPad.

She started with several photographs of Vanessa being cradled in Samantha's arms in her hospital bed when she was born. Vanessa looked like a little alien with closed eyes, a scrunched face, and a patch of straight, black hair down her forehead. But Samantha clearly felt differently, holding her baby girl, cheek-to-cheek, with a smile that split her face from end-to-end in a glitter of perfect, white teeth.

Yet Liz again detected just a hint of sadness fused with the apparent joy in Samantha's beautiful dark eyes. Ever since the rape, there'd always been a hint of sadness swimming in her sister's eyes. The iPad screen protected the images of the new mother with her newborn child from Liz's tears. She wiped the screen with a tissue and closed the iPad. Another bottomless sob began.

When she finally looked up — through a blurry view — she noticed her iPhone vibrating on Samantha's desk. The phone hadn't rung; she'd forgotten to take it off mute. She rose slowly, eased herself to the desk, and listened to the voicemail message.

"Mrs. Rivera, this is Tom Manley over at Integrated Labs. Just want to let you know that we completed the DNA comparison. The DNA from the sheets and the glass is positively from the same person. Please give me a call when you get a chance; let me know where you want the report sent. You have my number. Thank you."

"Oh my God" Liz whispered. "Ryan."

She sat down at Samantha's desk and listened to the message again. She could hardly believe her ears. Ryan had been in bed with Samantha the night of her death. She immediately dialed Toni's home number. There was no answer. Liz left a message for her to return her call at Samantha's apartment or on her cell phone. She didn't leave any details. She then dialed Toni Santiago's cell phone.

"Hello…" Then silence. The fleeting connection was lost. Liz tried Toni's cell phone again and it went directly to voicemail.

A little bewildered, Liz didn't leave a voicemail message. She pulled the iPhone away from her ear and looked at it suspended in her hand as if there might be some explanation written outside of it. She tried again and decided to leave a voicemail after all.

"Detective Santiago…ahh…Toni, this is Liz Rivera. It sounded like you picked up but then we lost our connection. This happens with my cell phone too every once in a while. Anyway, would you please give me a call when you can? I have some information from the lab. Thank you." She hit the red 'end call' icon.

After absently sitting still at Samantha's desk for sixty long seconds she then sent Toni a text, "Toni please call me. Urgent. Liz…I hope you're okay."

Toni and Jeremiah sat still as the big man paced back and forth in front of them with the .357 revolver in his hand. She could hardly believe where they were. After he'd forced them both out of her Jetta, he'd directed them into Mount Carmel Park.

Toni had turned around and asked the big man, "Where are you taking us?"

The big man casually responded by tapping Toni with the barrel of the steel revolver on her forehead, which caused spots to flicker before her eyes and inspired a fast bump to rise.

"No questions."

Toni didn't respond. She was too busy holding her head, but Jeremiah did.

"You do that to her again, and I'll shove that pea-shooter up your fat ass!" Jeremiah said. "You got that?"

The big man smiled. "Oh, a Hero, I'm so scared. Walk, hero."

The big man walked them into the center of the park, over a hill and forced them to climb down into a fallout shelter. It was about thirty feet from where Samantha's body had been discovered behind the glacier rock.

When Toni and Jeremiah landed on the concrete floor of the shelter, they were stunned to see an actual park bench up against one concrete wall where they'd been ordered to sit.

"Mother of God!" Toni murmured, when she first saw the bench, wondering how on earth it had made it down into the shelter.

It had the usual series of long one-by-two horizontal wood strips — for the seat-and-back — painted in pealing park green. Even the three concrete slabs — shaped like a chair — to support the wood strips — were still attached. The slabs looked to have been yanked out of the park walkway; rusted metal tendons still stuck out of it, which elevated the bench about a foot above the floor.

It reminded her of an old Jack Nicholson film she'd seen on Netflix, "One Flew Over the Cuckoo's Nest." There's a scene where a massive Native American psychiatric patient at a state mental hospital manages to yank out of the floor a sink — pipes and all — and throw it out the window. Toni shuddered at the thought that the big man had that kind of strength.

She then noticed brown boxes stacked against one wall marked, "CIVIL DEFENSE SURVIVAL RATION CRACKER CONTENTS 40 ½ POUNDS...DATE OF PACK 1962" and another stack of boxes were marked 1957.

Toni then remembered another article her father had saved. It was an old article published in the *New York Times* about a fallout shelter under the Brooklyn Bridge. Toni vaguely remembered the article saying something about the Cold War, and that historians believed the 1957 dated provisions found under the Brooklyn Bridge were in response to the Russian's launch of the Sputnik satellite, and the boxes marked 1962 were in response to the Cuban Missile Crises.

Toni felt a sudden thrust of gloom with the thought of where they must be. It had to be the same fallout shelter her father had picked-up Milton Iglesia after Samantha's rape twenty years prior.

Is this guy Milton Iglesia? He seemed about the right age. He looked to be in his mid-thirties, which would make him a juvenile of about sixteen when the rape occurred. If he was Milton Iglesia, she wondered if he was their shooter. Did he kill his brother—Father Manny, and Samantha?

But the other question most ricocheting inside the interior wall of her brain was: Where the hell was Jocelyn Condon?

CHAPTER 35

Sergeant Tazzo was sitting at his desk in the Bronx Homicide office sipping on a stale Dunkin Donuts coffee he'd brought in hours before from the shop a block from the precinct. (Starbucks, his coffee of choice, hadn't gotten around to setting up shop in that section of the Bronx.)

He'd just taken a call from the commander of the Manhattan South Homicide Squad. The lieutenant said he'd been notified that the license plate of a car Bronx Homicide had submitted for input to the Real Time Crime Center database at headquarters had come up with a match.

As it turned out a car that had been at the scene of a cold case homicide out of the Manhattan South Homicide Squad, had also been parked in the area of Father Manny's homicide scene in the Bronx: within two blocks of Mount Carmel Church.

"What kind of case you got, Loo?"

"Unsolved hit-and-run: retired detective. Happened about three years ago. Crossing Third Avenue and East 5-0 about 3 a.m. and got slammed. He was intox. No witnesses.

"Joe Santiago!" Tazzo blurted.

"Yeah, right. You knew him?"

"Yeah, well, not exactly," Tazzo said. "He was the father of one of our detectives."

"Oh, right, Toni Santiago," the lieutenant said. "I talked to her a lot for about a year after her dad was killed. I didn't know she was in Bronx Homicide. Last I knew she was still in Manhattan North: the two-three."

"Yeah, she's been here about two years," Tazzo said, took a sip from his cold coffee and started to think out loud. "So the same car in the area of her old man's hit-and-run was in the area of our priest homicide."

"What kind of homicide did you say?" the lieutenant said.

306

The question broke Tazzo's spell. "Oh, yeah, it's heavy, Loo. You probably heard about it. Priest, Father Manuel Gonzalez; Mount Carmel."

"Oh, sure, right," the lieutenant said. "How's it looking?"

"Just starting to pick-up, I think," Tazzo said. "Whose the plate come back to?"

"A senior citizen out in Nassau County. We talked to her three years ago. Turned out her daughter borrowed her car the night of the hit-and-run. We talked to her too. She was at La Maganette, popular Latin restaurant, and bar.

"Yeah. I know the place," Tazzo said.

"It was diagonally across the street from the hit-and-run scene. We didn't talk to her as a suspect, just as a potential witness; she didn't see anything. She said she was in the restaurant when it happened," the lieutenant said. "My guys should have taken a look at the car at the time, but their heads weren't thinking suspect. We need to talk to her again."

"What's her name?" Tazzo said.

"Hold on a second," the lieutenant said with sudden urgency in his voice.

Tazzo could hear the lieutenant talking to a few people in the background. Multiple muffled voices. He then got back on with Tazzo.

"Listen, gotta run. Looks like my guys have somebody barricaded in his mother's apartment—took her hostage. I got to get over there," the lieutenant said. "I'll send the case folder up to you."

"Appreciate it, Loo."

"Listen," the lieutenant quickly said, before he hung up, "both squads should send a detective out to the island to interview the daughter. Let me know when you want to do it."

"Will do, Loo," Tazzo said. "I'll talk to my boss and get back you."

Jeremiah's hands had been tied behind his back and attached to the bench with twine. Since Toni's left arm was in a sling, the man had tied only her other arm to the bench.

The concrete floor had splotches of brown dirt and grass scattered around. There was a grimy green military-like cot up against the other side of the shelter. Black stains appeared on the taut green material as if someone regularly used it to wipe their hands after changing a car's oil. The shelter stank of urine.

With a quick scan, she saw that the big man used the corner as a urinal. He had all of Mount Carmel's green to piss on, and he chose to piss in his cave. A twenty-three-year-old Mount Carmel church calendar hung on the other side of the shelter for the month of August.

"For Crissakes!" Toni whispered to herself.

Is it possible nobody's been back to this shelter since the rape two decades ago? It struck her this would have been a typical way for the City to handle it. They were notified to seal the shelter twenty-three years ago, not bothering to clear out what was down there. Just follow orders and seal it. So it was sealed.

But somehow Milton Iglesia — if that's who paced before them — found his way back in and now used it to hold them hostage.

Ryan made it back to the office still thinking about the conversation he'd just had with Jocelyn at home. Tazzo followed in right behind him, leaving his shrimp lo mein to get a little colder.

"Jeremiah Francisco is missing in action, Loo. Internal Affairs was at his place earlier and suspended him. I sent two guys up to sit on his apartment."

"Suspended for what?" Ryan said.

"AWOL."

"You got a photo of him?"

"Right here," Tazzo said and handed it to Ryan.

308

As soon as Ryan looked at the photograph his heart started to race. His face started to heat up. It was his face at Jeremiah's age. Then a sudden sharp pain nicked his heart. He recognized that while Jeremiah had his facial features, he had Samantha's dark eyes.

"Loo?" Tazzo said, breaking Ryan's silence. "He looks a lot like you."

Without raising his head Ryan said, "He's my son, Vic. The son I never knew I had."

They were both quiet for a few moments.

"Does the chief know?" Tazzo said

Still fixated on the photograph of Jeremiah, it took a few seconds for him to look up.

"Vic, I need a favor."

Tazzo was silent.

"I need you to keep this to yourself, at least for now. I know I'm putting you in a bad spot. The shooter could be my son. But if he's the shooter, I need to bring him in. Can you understand that?"

"What are we talking about here?"

"We're talking about getting to the truth without anybody else getting killed," Ryan said.

Ryan watched Tazzo trudge over to his office sofa and drop into it. Tazzo stared at the floor for several long moments, scratching and rubbing his forehead.

"I got to ask you a few questions, Loo?"

"Fire away," Ryan said.

"Why didn't you want Toni to pick up the CCTV tapes from Cohen's building?"

"Because," Ryan said, and paused, "the tapes would show me visiting the apartment the night she was killed."

"Is that true?" Tazzo said.

"Yes," Ryan said. "I was there, we had sex, and I left."

"So, you've had a thing with Cohen for a while?"

"No," Ryan said. "I hadn't seen her for over twenty years until she showed-up here after Manny was killed."

Ryan waited.

"What about the 911 tapes? Why didn't you want Toni to pick them up?"

"I just wanted to get to that caller before she did. I had this feeling I might know who the caller was, but I wasn't thinking straight.

"Who'd you think it was?"

"I can't say, Vic. It was a stupid thought. In retrospect, it was a mistake. It only made Toni more suspicious. I overreacted."

Silence.

"Listen, Loo, we go back a long time. I owe you a lot," Tazzo said. "You were a great help when I had to put my oldest in rehab. I can never thank you enough for giving me the time I needed to deal with it. And if I were in your shoes, I'd do the same thing, but —

Tazzo stopped.

"I know it's a mess Vic," Ryan said.

Long silence.

"Listen, Loo, I don't think for a second you're involved in anybody's murder, but this is tough."

"I know it is," Ryan said.

"Listen, I gotta go with my gut on this," Tazzo said.

"So, I'll stay out of your way for now, but wherever the chips fall, Loo. If your son's the shooter, you got to bring him in. There's no getting around that. I'll do everything I can to back you up. But you got to bring him in."

"I fully understand that Vic," Ryan said. "I appreciate it."

"All right. All right, "Tazzo said and rubbed his forehead again. "Let me tell you what else is cooking. We did a search warrant at the S.R.O.: Milton Iglesia's place.

"I guess he didn't show up either."

"No, he didn't. Nowhere to be found. We did the warrant. Looked like he had no intention of coming back. The one closet and the dresser drawers were all empty." Tazzo placed a newspaper article on Ryan's desk for him to see.

"There was only this *Daily News* article on Father Manny's murder."

Ryan browsed the article a couple seconds; then his head shot up.

Tazzo said, "Yeah, I know, two cops are mentioned in the article and they're both underlined. You and Toni."

"Get on the phone; call Toni at home; let her know!"

"I just tried. No answer," Tazzo said. "I tried her aunt's number too. She lives in Toni's building, you know; takes care of her dog. The aunt said Toni had been there a little while ago but left without saying where she was heading, but left in a hurry."

Toni must've gone out the door as soon as he left her aunt's apartment. But where would she go? Ryan wondered.

Tazzo said, "Too bad she wanted the uniform off her building."

"Did she keep the radio?"

"Yeah, she did. That's all she wanted. We tried to raise her on the air but she didn't answer. Maybe she doesn't have it with her."

"Call Communications. See if they can track the location of the radio's GPS."

Tazzo went for Ryan's office door. But he turned back suddenly and pointed at Ryan's desk before he stepped out and said, "Loo. The photo of that juvenile rapist is on your desk. The judge signed the order."

Ryan looked down at the two-inch thick brown folder with the bold, black letters, *"Family Court, Juvenile Records Section,"* in the top left corner. Addressed to *Lt. Condon, Commanding Officer. Bronx Homicide Squad.* On the bottom right corner were the words, *"Personal and Confidential."*

He turned it over and tore off the wide, clear tape that sealed the envelope. He yanked the paperwork out, which was held together with a long Acco fastener.

The top cover sheet was titled "Juvenile Status Report," and in black, bold letters the name, "M. Iglesia." He quickly leafed through the rest of the paperwork for the arrest report.

Finally, at the bottom of the folder, he found it — the arrest report with a black and white photograph attached.

Ryan drew the photograph closer, then suddenly dropped it on his desk and leaned back in the chair, making a crow-like sound. He gripped both armrests as if he was on a set of parallel bars. His forehead erupted in beads of sweat, and his pulse quickened. He then leaned forward to look down onto the rapist's face again.

"This is too much!" He shouted as he looked into the dark, familiar, mentally disturbed eyes of Manny's half-brother, Milton — the rapist. "This is just too much!"

Tazzo rushed back into Ryan's office. "What's up, Loo? You all right?"

"Text this photo to everybody — this is who we're looking for."

Tazzo looked at the photograph and back at Ryan.

"He raped Samantha Cohen years ago and maybe killed her and Father Manny," Ryan said. "He's Father Manny's EDP half-brother."

"No kidding," Tazzo said as he looked at the photo. "Lousy photo though."

"He's only sixteen there. Now he's about forty. Get a current photo of him from the place he just got cut loose from," Ryan said. "See if they can email it. If they can do it right away, wait until you get it then give it out. Send it to Manhattan detectives, too."

"You got it, Loo." Tazzo said, and made it to the door but turned again. "Loo, listen, forgot to mention. Got a call from Manhattan South Homicide. Turns out a car parked in the area of Father Manny's church — the night he got shot — had been parked in the area of the hit-and-run of Toni's old man three years ago."

"What?"

"Yeah. I'm waiting on the case folder. Don't have much just the car was registered to an old lady on Long Island. We don't have a plate, or name yet. Turns out her daughter had the car the night of the hit-and-run. She didn't see anything."

"What?" Ryan said again. "Car kills Toni's father in Midtown and ends up around Manny's church. What the hell is that?"

"Yeah, I know," Tazzo said.

"All right, Vic," Ryan said. "As soon as the folder gets in, run that Long Island plate against the plates canvassed on Sutton Place."

"Right, will do," Tazzo said, as he started to leave Ryan's office. "Wouldn't that be something if the same car shows up around Cohen's murder too."

Ryan stood for a few seconds, feeling a surge of adrenaline. He absentmindedly looked down at his desk again at the collection of reports, but then got focused.

In addition to Milton Iglesia's juvenile records, Father Manny's, and Samantha's case folders, each containing separate volumes of follow-up reports, were on his wide desk.

He opened each of the folders and spread out the reports.

He first noticed Father Manny's autopsy report and realized he'd never had a chance to read it, with all that had happened since his murder. When he'd been down to the ME's office, and had that confrontation with Toni, he'd only taken a look at Samantha's report. All he expected to see was that a bullet pierced his friend's face in medical examiner terms.

313

But he flipped through it anyway and saw a line on the last paragraph of that last page that corroborated what Samantha had told Toni, and what he later learned from Samantha directly: that he'd had pancreatic cancer that had furiously metastasized.

He then noticed a Communications Division request form slip out of Samantha's case folder. It occurred to him that it must be for the recording of the caller who notified 911 about discovering Samantha's body in the park. He inserted the CD into the Mac disc drive on his desk and listened.

When he heard the caller's voice his whole body went cold.

"It can't be," he whispered. The voice was slurred. She sounded intoxicated.

He played it again.

"Operator 272, where's the emergency?" the 911 operator answered.

"There's a woman in Mount Carmel Park..."

"Yes, what about the woman?" The 911 operator asked.

The slurred voice said, "...she's dead, I...I think she's dead."

"Where exactly in the park is the body?"

No answer.

"Hello, ma'am, are you there, ma'am?"

"...she's behind a big rock."

The line went dead.

Ryan sat in a daze then shook his head at hearing the caller's voice. "You're losing your mind, Ryan. You're losing your mind."

Ryan stood up from his desk, grabbed his jacket, and walked out.

"Vic, I'm heading to Santiago's apartment. See if they're any signs of foul play. You can reach me on my cell."

"You want somebody to drive you?"

"No," Ryan said and left.

Unbeknownst to Ryan, when he left his office, Liz Rivera was on her way up on the executive elevator at One Police Plaza to meet with the Chief of Detectives.

CHAPTER 36

Ryan had to stop by Toni's aunt's apartment first to get her keys before he got in.

He looked around and nothing seemed out of the ordinary at first. There was no sign of any struggle. His attention drifted to the dining room table, where he saw all the blue activity logs piled up. He looked at the cover of the one on top, and it had Toni's father's name. In fact, they all had his name.

He pulled Joe Santiago's decades-old log for the year and month Samantha had been raped.

He read through the entries Toni had mentioned.

Somehow it brought him comfort to know that it was Toni's father who'd discovered Samantha in the park, and it was Toni's father who'd taken her to the hospital, and it was Toni's father who'd locked up her attacker. He didn't know Joe Santiago, but he knew his daughter, and that somehow brought him some comfort.

Then he came to the fallout shelter entry.

"A fallout shelter?" he whispered. "Holed up in a fallout shelter."

Ryan's cell phone rang. The caller I.D. showed it was his office.

"What's up?"

"Loo," Communications just called," Tazzo said. "They tracked Toni's radio. They say it's on East 149th between Jackson and St. Ann's Avenue's."

"The north side of the park," Ryan said.

"Yeah, I know. Maybe she's sitting in a car there or something. Communications says the radio is stationary. She's not moving," Tazzo said.

"What's she doing there?" Ryan murmured.

"Loo, another thing. Just got a call from a captain down at the Chief of Detectives office. The chief wants you down there forthwith. And Chief King called too. Asked where you were. He said he'd been ordered down to meet with the Chief of D's too.

"The captain say what it's about?"

"No. Just said to reach you wherever you are and direct you downtown forthwith."

Ryan stood in silence for a couple of moments. He sensed that somebody got to the Chief of Detectives. His first guess would've been Toni, but her police radio signal was coming from the park. Whoever it was dropping the dime on him, he really couldn't blame.

But what then cut him deep was that he'd never had a chance to give his former partner, Chief of Bronx Detectives, Buddy King, a heads-up. That Buddy was getting blind-sided by the Chief of Detectives all because he'd put his trust in Ryan.

"Crap" he muttered.

"You there, Loo?"

"Yeah, Vic, I'm here. All right, I'm heading down there. And just for the record: if it's about this case, I won't mention anything about our arrangement. Not a word."

"I appreciate that."

"Now, listen to me. I found something at Toni's apartment," Ryan said. "Long-story-short. Toni has her father's activity logs. There's an entry that her old man collared Milton Iglesia for the rape in the park."

"In the park?" Tazzo said. "Toni mentioned her old man had taken the complaint report that night but I didn't know her father made the collar."

"He did," Ryan said. "He collared him in an old fallout shelter in the park."

"A what?"

"A fallout shelter, the city built a few during the Cold War," Ryan said. " Now listen, I got the feeling that Milton Iglesia could have Toni in the shelter. We can't reach Toni on the radio and we know he's out there somewhere and he knows who she is based on that newspaper in his SRO. I just got a hunch Toni and Milton crossed-paths."

"You could be right."

"Get the cavalry out to the park right now. Notify the Bronx Task Force. We need a lot of uniforms to sweep the park to find that shelter. See if anybody's still around in the Parks Department. Make sure you get Emergency Service out there too with the big lights. It'll be dark as hell in the park. Notify Aviation too."

"Yeah, right, but it's a lot of ground to cover."

"Tell them to start from where Samantha Cohen's body was found by that rock and work out from there," Ryan said. "You got it?"

"Got it, boss."

"Now, listen. You don't know this yet, but I'm going to the park first before I go downtown. I'll call Chief King to give him a heads-up."

"I don't know if that's a good idea, Loo."

"Vic, listen to me. Toni's probably with this sick dude. I can't go downtown now. I'm just telling you so you don't race out the door and head to the park yourself. Somebody's got to stay at the office to handle whatever comes in," Ryan said. "Got it?"

"I got it, I understand."

"All right, I'm out of here."

Toni had dropped into a dream. She was in a swimming pool. It was the parks department pool in Mount Carmel Park. She'd never swum in that pool but had once been there to interview a college-aged lifeguard who'd witnessed a shooting in his project-building lobby on East 137th Street a couple years earlier. Crack dealer-on-crack-dealer.

She was treading water desperately trying to keep her head above it. Her legs were heavy as if something or someone were pulling on her ankles. In the dream, she couldn't swim. Loud explosions then started to erupt all around her. Half the pool would empty with each barrage. She tried to look around her, fighting to clear her eyes, nose, and mouth of the water, fighting to breathe, but couldn't see what was causing it. It felt like depth charges were being tossed at her but from where? She was completely unmoored.

She slapped the water, tried to swim away from the explosions but they were at her feet. Crushing blows blasting her around like a toy. She didn't know how much longer she could keep fighting; gasping for breath, water blasting all around her.

She then went under; she didn't think she'd get her head up for even one more breath, but she managed to get her beaten arms and legs up just enough to lift her face up when she saw what was causing the explosions. Father Manny was calmly walking around the pool in his black suit and white collar with Jeremiah's Glock automatic firing shots at her one after another after another.

She believed it was Father Manny, but she couldn't see his face. Somehow the priest's head was twisted one hundred eighty degrees around, and Toni could only see the back of his head. The back of his head with red, white, and green soupy brain membranes dripping out from the back of it.

The pool walls began to compress, Father Manny continued to fire, Toni frantically tried to avoid being shot, blast after blast, flapping desperately, ducking into the water to avoid the shots, choking, forced to come back up, waves of water everywhere; she couldn't breathe, smaller and smaller the pool became, there was less and less room for her to get away.

The walls were only a couple of feet from her when Father Manny's head suddenly turned and his face was melting. She could smell his burning flesh. He was being burned alive.

"Ahhhhhh!" Toni screamed from the bench. Her black dress and the pillowcase over her head and face were saturated with sweat.

"What!" Jeremiah screamed back at her. "What is it?"

Ryan's Blackberry rang.

"Yeah!" Ryan yelled above the wailing siren.

"Loo, listen, just want to give you a heads-up," Tazzo said. "Just got the case folder from Manhattan South Homicide. The car parked at the hit-and-run in Midtown and by Mount Carmel Church was also parked in the area of the park when Cohen was killed,"

"Can you believe it," Ryan said.

"Yeah, and it also came up in the area where Toni and Geddes got shot on Sutton Place."

"What?"

"Yeah."

"What kind of car?"

"Red, 2008 Toyota Corolla."

Ryan felt that freeze come over him again, just as it had when he listened to the 911 tape.

"Who's the car registered to?"

"Senior citizen in Valley Stream. Couldn't reach her on the phone. Spoke to Nassau County P.D. They're going to take a ride over and ask her a few questions for us. Name's Madeline Hart."

Ryan punched end and changed direction.

Just over six hours had passed since Toni and Jeremiah had been abducted. They were still tied to the shelter's park bench.

Milton had placed two foul pillowcases over their heads. Toni's covered the swelling, bruising, and trickle of blood that had already dried caused by getting cracked across the face by Milton with the .357. The case over Jeremiah's head, however, did nothing to hide the bullet that pierced his calf.

Milton's direct reaction—when Toni asked who killed Father Manny and Samantha—had rocketed him into a state of rage; which followed with his cracking Toni; which drove Jeremiah to make a doomed, emotional attempt to lunge for the gun head first; which cost him his left calf muscle.

Toni's head hung down. It was pitch black. She had no idea if Milton was still in the fallout shelter with them at that moment or they were alone. She'd lost consciousness after he'd struck her.

"Oh, wow, what a nightmare," Toni murmured. "Jeremiah, are you all right?"

"Yeah, yeah, I think so." Jeremiah had trouble getting his voice to work again. Their throats were so dry. "I think so. Are you all right?"

"Yeah, I'm all right, I think we're alone," Toni said as she tried to look through her pillowcase, but her view was a shroud of darkness.

"Yeah, I don't hear anything," Jeremiah whispered.

After several long beats, Toni whispered, "He really cracked me with that Magnum. Knocked me completely out; I think he broke my cheekbone; I probably have a concussion. I can't see you; I have something over my head."

"Me too. He shot me after he hit you, then hit me across the head a few times with the gun, too."

"What!" Toni hissed, which made her head ring. "He shot you? Where are you shot?"

"My calf; I think it went in and out."

"That creep! That damn creep!" Toni said. "How's the bleeding?"

"I think it's clotted. At least I hope it is. I can't see it or feel it."

"We've got to get out of here!" Toni said.

"It's all right, I think it's going to be all right," Jeremiah said. "We'll figure something out."

"It is not going to be all right. We've got to get out of here. He's going to kill us for sure," Toni hissed again.

"Yeah, right, yeah, ah," Jeremiah moaned. "Oh, God, this hurts."

CHAPTER 37

Within minutes Ryan had blasted through the front door of his Throgs Neck home. It slammed against the wall, causing the wall mirror by the door to shake. It was just past 10 p.m.

He stopped and shouted, "Jocelyn!" There was no response. "Jocelyn!"

Still no response.

He looked up and shot for the staircase to the second floor, taking three steps at a time. Barreled into their bedroom and yanked the door to his closet; dropped to his knees onto the wood floor.

He tapped hard on the code to his gun safe with his sweaty hands — 6-7-0-2. The safe didn't open. He'd always kept his two other handguns — the Glock and .357 Magnum — in his safe at home. He, himself, always preferred to carry his two-inch, five-shot, .38, on his hip at work. He'd never felt he needed the sixteen-shot Glock. And the .357 Magnum was a gift from Chief King when he was promoted to lieutenant. He never carried it. But what nobody ever knew — including Jocelyn — was that he also always carried a non-department authorized tiny .22 automatic, wrapped in a handkerchief, in his back pocket, with his comb.

He slowed down; tapped in the code again, dread building with each tap.

The safe clicked open. Ryan slapped the thick small door aside, took a breath, and slowly put his hand in. He could feel the felt material on the bottom of the safe. It was empty. He leaned down sideways, like he was trying to look under a car: still empty. His body erupted with heat.

"Missing something, Ryan?" Jocelyn said, pointing his Glock at his face.

Ryan lost his balance, toppled into the safe, and looked up at his wife. There was dead silence. Ryan slipped into agony over what had now become clear to him: that somehow Jocelyn had been behind all the carnage.

Ryan stood up slowly.

"Jocelyn. Give me the gun."

"No, I think I'll hold onto it a while longer."

"Jocelyn. Listen to me. This has to stop. There's been enough killing," Ryan said and stepped closer with his hand out. "Give me the gun."

"Uh, uh. Don't move another inch closer, my good and faithful husband, or I'll put you down just like all the others. It doesn't matter to me," Jocelyn said. "Not anymore it doesn't. Now you go back downstairs."

Jocelyn flicked at the door with the gun, and Ryan stepped out of their bedroom. Jocelyn followed him down with the Glock pointed at his back. She directed him to his study and ordered him to sit behind his desk. She then told him to pull out the extra set of handcuffs in his desk drawer and cuff himself to the arm of his big leather chair. She then carefully walked behind him, kissed the top of his head, and gracefully pulled his .38 from its holster on his hip.

"Why, Jocelyn, why would you do this?"

"Because I love you, Ryan Condon, with all my heart. I vowed never to let anyone interfere with us. Not anyone."

"But why, Jocelyn? Why Joe Santiago? What did he have to do with this? How could he interfere with us?"

"Ryan, there's so much you don't know. And I did my best to protect you, but that ex-detective was going to press for that ancient rape case to be re-opened. I couldn't have that. He couldn't leave well enough alone," Jocelyn said. "He told Manny he planned to press the prosecutor's office to re-open the case, and where will that lead? That would lead to you."

"But why?" Ryan said. "Why would that lead to me?"

"Come on Ryan, why do you think? DNA," Jocelyn said. "After they tested the DNA everyone would know that Milton wasn't the father, but you were. Which Manny always knew anyway."

"But a DNA test could only lead to me if my DNA was tested against the kid's"

"Which is exactly what would've happened," Jocelyn said. "You really think that if that case was reopened and, you know — that tramp — she would have to be contacted, right? I mean she's the victim. Well after they confirmed that Milton was her rapist, I have no doubt in my almost childbearing mind that she would have finally wanted to have Milton's DNA compared with the kid's. She'd finally want to be sure Milton was the father."

"How do you know about Milton, Jocelyn?"

"How do you think? Manny told me. I knew about Milton for years, but it was when Manny told me Milton was getting released from that place, that I decided I'd get him to help me straighten a few things out, so, I met him at the bus when he arrived at Port Authority. I've been managing him ever since. He's got the mind of a child."

"Did you shoot at my detectives, Jocelyn?"

"No," Jocelyn said. "But I directed it."

"What does that mean?"

"Milton shot at them," Jocelyn said. "I overheard a few of your conversations on the phone. I know that female detective was becoming a nuisance for you and could become a nuisance for me, so I gave the order. But, unfortunately, he's not as good a shot as I am."

"How did Milton know they would be at Sutton Place at that time? Ryan said. "Was he waiting for them or tailing them?"

"I was tailing you, and Milton was tailing your detectives in my mom's car," Jocelyn said with a smile. "When you left the medical examiner's office with the tramp's sister, I followed you to Sutton Place and watched you drop her off. But as it turned out Milton called me to tell me that that female detective and her big partner stopped at a Starbuck's, but then pulled up on the tramp's Sutton Place block a few minutes after. That's when I told Milton to take a shot at them."

325

Jocelyn was pacing the study like she was in a courtroom making a summation to a jury.

"Anyway, back to the tramp," Jocelyn said. "She was only twenty when it happened. Right? Now she's a grown-up woman and a lawyer too, right? This would have jogged her to take that step. You know she would've taken the next step. I'm a woman, I know."

Jocelyn finally slipped into another leather chair in the study, crossed her legs, leaned forward, arms comfortably crossed on one knee, gun still pointed at Ryan, like it was on a tripod.

Ryan mulled over Jocelyn's farfetched belief that the possible testing of Milton's DNA—against the two-decades-old rape kit's contents—could lead to him. And, that that farfetched belief was the catalyst for all the murders.

"How did Manny know?" Ryan said.

"By the time the kid turned about five, Manny could see you in his face. He knew his brother wasn't the father, and that he wasn't the kid's uncle," Jocelyn said. "The same day he recognized that he called me to let me know."

"Have you ever seen the kid, Jocelyn?"

"No, I have not!" Jocelyn said. "I don't want to see the face of the tramp's kid!"

There was silence for several long beats.

"And why didn't Manny tell me? I mean—" Ryan stopped himself short when it occurred to him that Jocelyn must've pressed Manny to keep his mouth shut.

"That's right. Manny didn't tell you because of me."

Ryan held Jocelyn's eyes as he took that in.

"But how did you know what he was going to do, Jocelyn?"

"Manny told me that old detective went to see him. He knew somehow that Milton was getting released. He was going to see to it Milton's DNA was tested against that old rape evidence." Jocelyn uncrossed then crossed legs again and continued.

"Supposedly he always regretted he hadn't put Milton in jail overnight when he arrested him for being drunk in the park. He knew that if he'd kept Milton overnight, your tramp girlfriend wouldn't have been raped."

"Manny told you that?"

"That's right. According to Manny, it worked on this old cop for twenty years, — can you believe it?"

Toni bit down on her lip hard as she pulled her wounded left arm from the sling and yanked the pillowcase off her head. She then untied the knot attached to the bench, eased up and yanked the pillowcase off Jeremiah's head.

"For crying out loud, Jeremiah," Toni said. "Your face and head are blown up like a balloon. How many times did he hit you?"

His face was in a frozen grimace, eyes almost swollen shut, squinting tight, face stretched-out like the 1893 Edvard Munch painting "The Scream."

"A few," Jeremiah mumbled.

Blood was sneaking from his wound, rolling down his leg. Toni looked around the shelter from side-to-side, and spotted a grimy hand-towel resting under Milton's cot, and grabbed it, took a half-second to look at it, "Crap," she said and flung it across the shelter

"Ah, Toni. We're in rough shape."

"Yeah, we're a sight. New York's Finest. Three good arms and three good legs between us," she said. "We got to get out of here before they come back."

They both looked up at the door.

"I know, Toni, but I can't get myself up that ladder. There's just no way. And I don't think you can handle—

"Yes, I can buddy. I'm going to strap you on my back and we're climbing that ladder."

"You can't Toni."

With staccato-like timing, she snapped, "Yes—I—can!" and held his eyes for an extra moment.

Toni then untied Jeremiah's hands from the chair and helped him stand up when the sound of an avalanche shuddered above the shelter door.

"He's back," Toni muttered and put the pillowcase back over Jeremiah's head and over her own.

Ryan looked at Jocelyn's movements carefully and wondered how he could get the gun from her, but cuffed to that heavy, leather, chair, he knew he wouldn't get far. And he couldn't conceive of pulling the .22 from his pocket that Jocelyn had missed. He couldn't imagine for a second that he could shoot his wife.

Ryan remained silent for a moment.

"Did Manny know you killed the detective?"

"No, no, of course not," Jocelyn said, with a wave of her hand, sat back and crossed her legs again. "I never told him. He just thought, like the others, that some car hit him and left. Manny never knew I was the driver."

"Jocelyn, this has to stop. I'm so sorry for how I've hurt you. But this has to stop."

"Oh, Ryan, don't be ridiculous. It's too late to stop. I've got one more thing to do: just one more thing," Jocelyn said. "You know, I thought I could trust Manny. I thought he'd always help me protect our marriage. I thought he would take that knowledge about that kid of yours to the grave with him. But I found out I couldn't trust him."

"Jocelyn please."

"Did you know he had terminal cancer, Ryan?"

"Yes. Yes, I did."

"Yeah, his body was ravaged with cancer cells. But I just can't figure it out. If they're going to die, why can't they just die? Why do they have to destroy other people's lives before they go?"

It cut right through Ryan to hear Jocelyn speak of Manny in such a hateful way. How did he not see her psychosis coming on? Over the years he'd become very skilled at picking up on her behavioral changes, and getting her to the doctor before it got out of hand.

"But how?" Ryan said. "How could Manny have hurt us?"

"A few weeks before I shot him, he invited me to the rectory. He told me about his cancer and that he had a few months. Then he tells me it was wrong to have kept the truth from you; about you being the father of that kid," Jocelyn said. "Can you believe it, after all these years? And I couldn't change his mind. He just kept saying I was a strong enough to handle it, and that you deserved to know you had son, and that that bastard deserved to know too.

"So, I wrote the tramp's son and told him he could find out about his real parents from Father Manny. I hoped he'd be so upset he would blow Manny's head off. But it didn't work out that way, and the truth is I always knew I'd have to do it myself. But fortunately, Ryan, I didn't have to use your gun. Somebody else left a gun, so I used it."

"Where?" Ryan said. "Where'd you get the gun?"

"Manny's office," Jocelyn said. "After I got through my head that Manny wouldn't change his mind. I asked to use the bathroom, but I didn't go to the bathroom. I snuck up to his office. I knew he'd kept a file on the tramp and the kid somewhere in the office. I thought after I killed him, and your detectives showed up later and did their search, without the file, they'd have nothing much to connect to the tramp and her kid and you, but I couldn't find it."

"And the gun?" Ryan said.

"I found the Glock resting on Manny's desk."

"And you shot him when you came back downstairs?"

"That's correct Lieutenant," Jocelyn said, with a smirk. "And you know what he had the nerve to say before I shot him?"

Ryan stayed quiet.

" 'Mercy'," Jocelyn said. "He said 'Mercy' before I fired."

Jocelyn jumped up from the chair.

"How dare he! How dare he ask for mercy! What about him having mercy on me! After all, I've been through. What about mercy on me!"

"What did you do with the gun?"

"I put it back on Manny's desk," Jocelyn said. "I took my time about it too. I felt calm. Almost free. I'd taken care of what needed to be taken care of and just took my time going back up the stairs and placed it back on his desk. And took my time going out the front door."

"Jocelyn, this has to stop. Please stop."

Jocelyn screamed at him like she was firing a Taser with her eyes. "It'll stop when I say it stops!"

There was silence. Several minutes passed before Jocelyn started to pace again and spoke up.

"You, know, Ryan, I should've known, when we were young—when you cheated on me—it wouldn't work. I imagined in time it would pass. But you never got over her, did you?" Tears started to slowly run down Jocelyn's cheeks. "It never really did, did it? Over twenty years of marriage and you were still in love with her."

Ryan dropped his head and then raised it slowly. "I'm so sorry, Jocelyn."

"Yeah, me too. We were more like brother and sister than husband and wife, weren't we?" Jocelyn said, stopped pacing, and looked at Ryan.

"Yeah. But all I can say is that I have loved you with all I got. There was not a day since the day I met you that being with you didn't make me feel blessed. Truly. Even with how much I resented you for what you did with that tramp, I felt blessed. You were truly the one for me."

Ryan was silent.

"Jocelyn, please let me help you. You're just not well right now. You can't be held responsible for all that's happened. I'm responsible. We'll get a good lawyer. You'll get the help you need."

Jocelyn wiped her face with one hand and continued to hold the gun with the other.

"What? And spend the rest of my life in jail. No, sir. It's too late for that. And there's nothing wrong with me. I did what needed to be done, and I'd do it again to protect what we have. I'm just sorry you figured it out. I just have one more thing to take care of, then, whatever happens, happens. I should've taken care of it years ago."

"What one more thing?" Ryan asked with squinted eyes. "What do you mean?"

Jocelyn ignored his question.

"You think I didn't see you go to your tramp's house?" Jocelyn again raised her voice.

"You think I didn't see you go to the tramp's Sutton Place building? Oh, I saw you, Ryan. You thought I was at my mother's. But I wasn't. I followed you right to her building. Right to the slut's fancy building."

"Not bad, huh? I tailed you and you didn't know it. You see: I've been listening all these years to my cop husband. You know what I mean. Listening to you I learned how to tail somebody without getting noticed. And, of course, how could I not pick-up a few things about guns."

Ryan stayed quiet.

"Anyway, we both know what you did, don't we, Ryan, you and your girlfriend in her Sutton Place pad? I guess I was never enough for you," Jocelyn said. "I couldn't give you a child so I was just never enough for you."

"It wasn't that Jocelyn," Ryan said. "I'm so sorry."

331

"Now, I ask you, Ryan, what would you expect me to do? After I ran down that detective and shot Manny to protect our marriage? You think I'm going to let your childhood slut jeopardize what we had? No way, *senor!* I was so upset watching you leave her building. Ryan, I couldn't move. I just sat in the car; I didn't know what I would do. I even went to a Seven-Eleven and brought back a few beers, went back and just stared at her building. I sat there in the car drinking beer after beer just like you, Ryan, and you know I'm not a drinking woman. You know I had to be pretty upset to drink, don't you, Ryan?"

"Jocelyn please."

"Then providence arrived and she walks out of the building and drives up to your old neighborhood. How lucky could I get! Late at night she decides to head up to the Bronx, and meet some guy. Probably to buy drugs." Did you know that, Ryan?"

"No," Ryan said, but realized that must've been Jeremiah.

"That's right, Lieutenant Ryan Condon, N...Y...P...D..., your precious tramp leaves her apartment in the middle of the night to buy drugs in the old neighborhood."

Jocelyn circled Ryan at the desk and placed her hand on his shoulder.

"Anyway, after the drug dealer left, she decided to stay in the park. Can you believe it, Ryan? At night she decides to stay in the park. I guess she'd lived on Sutton Place too long and forgot what it takes to survive in the Bronx. And here I am a Long Island girl and I have better sense than that. Jocelyn said and pressed the Glock into the back of his head.

"Well, I hope you don't mind, too much honey, but I put one of your bullets into her head. That's right, from your gun. One of your bullets pierced her slutty skull—from this gun right here in my hand," Jocelyn said and pressed the gun harder into the back of Ryan's head. "How do you feel about that?"

Ryan couldn't speak; his head dropped.

"Get your head up!" Jocelyn shouted.

Ryan raised his head slowly. "And you made the 9-1-1 call, Jocelyn?"

"Heh, how about that? I'm impressed. You recognized my voice from the tape. And I thought I did a good job of disguising it. Anyway, yes, that's right, I called 9-1-1. I was a little concerned that some meddler would come across the body and tamper with it. I didn't want that. I wanted you to find her just the way I left her. And you did find her just the way I left her, didn't you, Ryan?"

He did not respond.

"You were in shock, weren't you, Ryan? Images of your precious Samantha shot in her head have been dancing in your head ever since" Jocelyn said. "Haven't they!"

"Jocelyn. Listen to me. This has to stop."

Jocelyn looked at Ryan for several long beats, went up to him, put the gun to his head, then slowly leaned down and kissed him, long and hard, almost with violence. Without another word she then stomped out of the study.

CHAPTER 38

Ryan heard the front door slam and Jocelyn's car start-up. He started to drag the leather chair he was handcuffed to from the study and out the front door of their house.

He'd left the department car running. Jocelyn hadn't touched it. He stretched to the ignition and cut off the engine. On his key ring, he'd always carried a handcuff key. He un-cuffed himself and left the chair on their front lawn.

She needs to do one more thing, she said. What one more thing?" he wondered.

Then it hit him. She means to kill Jeremiah. And if Toni's in the way, she'll be killed too. In her bizarre state of mind, she didn't want the product of his infidelity to live on any longer. Something that she said she should have done years ago. Did Jocelyn know about his fling with Toni? Where would Jocelyn think to look for Jeremiah? Does she know Toni could be at the park?

Ryan punched Jocelyn's cell phone number, listed in his contacts: "Wife, I.C.E." He got her voice mail.

He put the car in gear and tore off for Mount Carmel Park. He had to stop Jocelyn from killing Jeremiah and Toni. If he did nothing else in his rupturing life, he had to stop that.

Ryan blazed with the siren blasting and lights flaming down the expressway. His mind was momentarily captured in imagining how different all of their lives could have been if he'd had more courage. But he hadn't had courage. What he had was weakness and selfishness, and he knew he was now paying for a lifetime of deficiencies.

The destruction of the past few days was his fault; he knew that in the deepest part of his being. He stunk, and now Toni Santiago's life was in danger again, and so was the life of the son with whom he'd never had the chance to be a father. Ryan reached Buddy King on his cell phone.

"What the hell is going on, Ryan?" King said.

"My wife is involved in the murders."

"What? Jocelyn?" King said. "What are you talking about?"

"I can't lay it all out for you now, Buddy," Ryan said. "The bottom-line is Jocelyn's behind the hit-and-run of Toni's Father —

"Joe Santiago?"

"Yes," Ryan said. "She's also behind the murders of Father Manny and Samantha Cohen."

"But why?" King said. "How do you know this?"

"She just told me, and I think she's on her way to a fallout shelter in Mount Carmel Park where Toni and maybe my son are being held?"

"A what?" King said. "You're what?"

"A fallout shelter," Ryan said. "My son."

Ryan continued that Toni had suspected him of having some involvement in the murders.

"Are you involved, Ryan?

"No chief."

Ryan continued that Toni couldn't be located; that her police radio was tracked to a street outside Mount Carmel Park, which he was heading to, and not One Police Plaza as they spoke.

"No, you're not!" King shouted.

"Buddy. You know I'm done. You know that. I know that. My only hope is that Jocelyn doesn't kill Toni or my son. I believe they're together".

"How do you know that?"

"When I went to get Toni's keys from her aunt to get into her apartment, she told me Toni was with a young guy who looked a lot like me, and he fit the same description of the person seen by the sector team outside the park talking with Samantha the night she was killed. I think they're together. So I'm heading to the park."

"No, you're not, absolutely not! You're off this investigation effective now! Do you understand me?"

———

"I'm really sorry about this, partner. You know where to find me."

"Ryan, don't—

Ryan hung up.

CHAPTER 39

The door to the fallout shelter opened and Milton descended the wall-ladder, followed by Jocelyn Condon. Milton pulled the rope attached to the door above them shut. The space again relied on the light of only a single 40-Watt bulb.

They looked down onto Toni and Jeremiah. Milton tore the pillowcase off Jeremiah's head and pressed the Magnum under his chin forcing his head back like he was cattle. "How's the leg Hero?"

Jeremiah looked up at him with blinking eyes and kept quiet. Milton slapped the pillowcase three times across Jeremiah's swollen face then spiked it onto the ground.

Milton bent to Toni, yanked the pillowcase off her head, and shoved the Magnum under her chin. "I'm tired of waiting."

The corners of his mouth were caked with milky, white spittle.

"Give me the gun, Milton," Jocelyn said. "Sit down."

Milton turned it over, stepped to the corner of the fallout shelter and sat on a green recliner with chunks of material missing: like it had been chewed up by a battalion of carpet beetles. He leaned back and the footrest rose with him, levitating his bulky legs. Toni and Jeremiah were forced to look at his grizzly face through his spread-open legs as if through two field-goal uprights.

"Detective Santiago," Jocelyn said, and gestured with the gun in her direction as if she were pointing a Bic pen, "we keep running into each other."

"Yes," Toni said.

Jocelyn looked at Jeremiah. "Looks like my friend Milton had to get your attention. Look at that face. Like you have Bells Palsy."

Jeremiah didn't reply.

"And who are you?" Jocelyn said.

Toni blurted, "Oh, he's my friend. "

Jocelyn looked back at Toni with a glare. "Did I ask you that question?"

"No, you didn't."

"Then why did you answer for him?" Jocelyn said as she stepped closer to Toni.

Jeremiah spoke up. "That's right. I'm her friend. My name's Chris, Christopher."

Jocelyn stopped her advance, but maintained her focus on Toni for a few extra moments and eventually looked back at Jeremiah.

"Chris what?" Jocelyn said.

"DeStefano," Jeremiah said. "Christopher DeStefano."

"You look familiar to me."

Toni's was focused on Jocelyn, but then turned to take a longer look at Jeremiah's disfigured face, then back at Jocelyn when it struck her: Jocelyn must've have seen Jeremiah at some place and time, but just didn't recognize him.

Milton smiled from the recliner and said, "You mean like girlfriend, boyfriend?"

Milton's smile was disturbing to look at. He was missing his two front eyeteeth that gave Toni the strange feeling that he'd been deliberately defanged, as with snakes to remove their venom. What was left of his teeth looked rusted.

"Yes, that's right," Jeremiah mumbled. "She's my girlfriend."

"Well, too bad for you there, Chris-my-boy, that you were with your sweetheart," Jocelyn said.

Jocelyn circled around Toni and Jeremiah and continued.

"You didn't think I saw you and your boyfriend sitting in your little car on our street?"

"No, I didn't," Toni said.

"Next time you're spying on somebody, maybe your driver should remember to turn the headlights out in the daytime. It kind of stands out."

Toni did not respond.

"And I let you follow me right to where I wanted you," Jocelyn said. "Right into Milton's hands. You made it easy for us. Now you can't interfere with what needs to be finished."

"What needs to be finished?" Toni said.

Jocelyn ignored her. "You know, I've got to give you credit, you're like a bulldog. You don't give up," Jocelyn said. "After you were shot I thought you'd stay out of the way. But here you are, apparently suspended from the NYPD, wearing a sling, and still trying to play detective."

"You shot at us?" Toni said.

Jocelyn ignored Toni's question again and shifted the revolver from one hand to the other.

"All right, Milton, stay here with them," Jocelyn said. "I'm going to go and find your son."

"Milton's son?" Toni said.

Milton shouted. "His name is Jeremiah Francisco. He's Samantha and my son."

"Samantha Cohen?" Toni said, pretending not to know. Milton stood up and looked down on Toni. "You're surprised, right? Everybody was surprised. You're like everybody. Nobody knows we loved each other. Just like you are with him. We loved each other. And she had my son."

"All right Milton," Jocelyn said, patting his shoulder.

"I didn't know Samantha Cohen had a son," Toni said.

"That's Samantha Morales!" Milton shouted.

"Yes, Samantha Morales," Toni said. "I'm sorry, Milton."

Jocelyn glared at Toni. "You didn't know Samantha had a son? What kind of detective are you?"

"Finding out if she had a son wasn't important to me. I was trying to find her killer."

Jocelyn kept her gaze on Toni.

Toni said to nobody in particular, "Whenever I'm burdened with something for a while, it helps to admit my part, whatever it is. It's the only way I can get a little peace."

"I bet you do," Jocelyn said.

———

Her words hit Toni like a smack. Did Jocelyn know she'd had sex with her husband?

"I want my son, Jocelyn," Milton said. "I'm tired of waiting."

Jocelyn looked at Toni for a few moments more then turned to Milton and said, "Stay here with them. I'll find Jeremiah."

She handed the .357 back to Milton and climbed up the ladder.

When Ryan pulled up on Mount Carmel Park, there was a massive N.Y.P.D. Temporary Headquarters bus parked on the opposite side. One patrol car after another swooped in and stacked behind the other like a cross-country freight train. Cops piled into the park. Flickering lights bounced everywhere.

As they broke for the park the rattling of equipment on their gun belts: handcuffs, flashlights, keys, crackling portable radios, made it seem like some kind of tribal ritual was about to start. People on the street stopped cold: Women pulling shopping carts home stopped; kids texting on their iPhones stopped; fruit and ice vendors stopped. Traffic came to a standstill, car windows zipped down and tenement buildings windows zipped up sacrificing all their A/C in their space to watch the spectacle.

Ryan then spotted Toni's VW Jetta surrounded by the blue-and-white patrol cars. He turned the steering wheel hard, and bounced up over the curb and barreled into the park down the wide blacktop. The same blacktop that Samantha had been accosted years before. He broke to a hard stop, jumped out of the car and made a quick scan.

Jocelyn had only been gone fifteen minutes when Milton suddenly jumped up from the recliner. "I want my son!" Milton yelled, losing his footing and pounded his ass on the dirt floor, but sprung back up before either Toni of Jeremiah knew what had happened.

"I want my son!" Milton yelled again. His voice assaulting the dense walls of the shelter.

They sat lifelessly and fixated on the sounds of the burly madman as he waved the Magnum around like he was conducting the New York Philharmonic. They'd pretended to still be tied to the bench.

Milton looked down on Toni for a few moments, then started to pace.

Toni and Jeremiah looked at each other with calculation in their eyes.

"Where is he!" Milton screamed back at Toni. "Where is my son! You know where he is!"

"I don't know, Milton." Toni calmly replied. "I'm sorry, but I don't."

"I WANT MY SON!" Milton shouted again, punching the Magnum at them with each syllable. Then he stopped. Disgust painted across his face. He turned abruptly and stepped away to his favorite corner to urinate. Milton switched the Magnum to his left hand and hung it down at his side; he unzipped with his right and looked up—as if to the stars—and let out a roar.

Toni gave Jeremiah a quick glance then blasted off the bench and barreled her one good shoulder of her 120-pound frame into Milton's lower back. Milton's massive body slammed into the moist wall he'd been marking, but he didn't drop the gun. Simultaneously Jeremiah bounced over on one leg and when Milton twisted to look over his right shoulder down onto Toni, Jeremiah surged up under Milton beefy arm and got a trap-like grip on the Magnum.

CHAPTER 40

The cops tumbled into three ranks to get instructions from the uniformed sergeant directed to conduct the search for missing Detective Toni Santiago.

"Get them out there, Sarge!" Ryan yelled as he leaped over the park benches like he'd so often done as a rookie. Bolted up the rocky hill on instinct. He didn't know where the fallout shelter could be, but he was driven to the area where Samantha's body had been found. He froze on that now hallowed ground and took in the park slowly doing a three-sixty, stepping off and started to sweep his legs over the grass like he was kicking a soccer ball.

When he got to the other side of the massive rock he spotted something odd. There was a square patch of grass that was much darker than the grass surrounding it. He rushed to it and dropped to his knees. There was a pull-up handle secreted in the grass patch. He swept the grass away from the handle, and there was a door. No more than three feet in diameter.

He put his ear to the door. He could hear thrashing and yelling. "Get the gun, get the gun!" He recognized Toni's strong voice. "Don't let him go! I'm trying!" He yanked the door open and two cannon-like shots rang out.

Ryan pulled out the .22 and dropped down into the hole.

There was just enough light—he spotted Milton with the .357 in his hand. But another man was dangling from Milton's arm, trying to strip it from him. He realized it must be Jeremiah, his son. Toni was desperately trying to pull one of Milton's bulky legs out from under him with one good arm.

"Milton, drop the gun!" Ryan shouted.

Milton turned without hesitation and fired another round. Ryan could hear it whiz by his ear.

Ryan returned fire: Two rounds into Milton's chest.

Toni and Jeremiah dropped off; landed on their backs, onto the cement floor, and tried to back out of the way, kicking and pushing away in the dirt.

Milton stopped, ripped open his shirt and looked down at this chest. Lowered his gun hand but did not drop it. He was still erect. "I want my son!" he bellowed like a wounded bear. His loud voice cracked.

"Drop the gun, Milton; don't make me do this."

Milton slowly raised the gun again.

Ryan fired two more rounds again into Milton's chest. Milton lowered the gun and again looked down at his chest, but still, he did not drop it, and slowly started to raise the gun and pointed it at Ryan. Ryan fired the final round to his head, exactly where a priest would have placed a black cross of ashes. *"From dust, you came, to dust you shall return."*

Milton stood with wide visionless eyes for a moment, then went down with a thud like someone had taken a machete to his overstuffed legs.

Within seconds ESU heavy weapons cops in black military gear dropped into the hole, turned Milton onto his stomach, handcuffed him even though he was seemingly dead. They then cleaned and wrapped up Jeremiah's leg to stop the bleeding and put a fresh bandage on the healing wound of Toni's slung arm.

Toni muttered to Ryan, "Your wife was here."

"I'm sorry Toni."

"Me too," Toni said.

After they were patched up enough, Jeremiah and Toni climbed onto the backs of two ESU cops and they were carried up and out of the shelter. Ryan climbed out on his own power.

Other Bronx Homicide and Crime Scene detectives climbed into the hole to secure the crime scene and document the details. They would wait for the medical examiner to pronounce Milton DOA before removing the body.

———

343

Two NYPD helicopters were fluttering above with their disk-shaped spotlights painted over them all. Toni welcomed the circling hot air.

John Geddes got to the scene and knelt down to Toni as she was being put on a stretcher.

"You okay, partner?" Geddes said

"Yeah, yeah, I'm good John," Toni said delighted to see him. "How are you?"

"I'm good, I'm good," Geddes said. "Let's get you out of here."

Toni held Geddes's arm. "See how the boss is doing. He's got something to tell you."

Geddes stood up and approached Ryan, "How you doing, Loo?"

"All right, Geddes. I'm glad you're here. You know my wife?"

"Yes, sir."

"My wife is wanted for the murder of Father Manny and Samantha Cohen," Ryan said. "I already notified Chief King.

As soon as Ryan finished giving Geddes that instruction, he'd spotted Jocelyn atop the glacier rock. The same rock where Samantha's body had been found. She was stretched out in a prone position, his Glock in her hand, punched-out and down in the direction of Toni and Jeremiah strapped down to stretchers and about to be put on an ambulance.

"No, Jocelyn, don't!" Ryan yelled and waved his arms as he jumped in front of Toni and Jeremiah when a shot rang out, striking him in the stomach. Another shot followed, hitting him in the shoulder spinning him around and dropping him to the grass.

The helicopters shifted their spotlights to Jocelyn, illuminating her atop the rock, she jumped up straight. The two compounded beams of illumination made her look like she was being struck by lightning.

She started to fire insanely into the blinding light of the choppers. As if she was firing directly into lighting. The ESU cops on the ground opened up on her with M-16's firing multiple shots. The storm of bullets held her riddled body upright. When the firing stopped, her body toppled forward off the top of the rock landing in the dirt and grass — the same pathetic dirt and grass in which Samantha's body had been discovered days before.

"No! God! No!" Ryan struggled to lift himself up and crawled to her, through the grass, and moist dirt.

He scooped her into his arms, holding her tight, blood pouring from them both, her head hanging back as he rocked her, "Oh, God! My wife! My wife! My poor wife! Forgive me! Forgive me! Please forgive…" In mid-sentence, he fell forward, over her.

A circle of blue uniforms enclosed husband and wife in silence.

They were both dead.

EPILOGUE

Four days later.

Toni stuck her head inside the open door of Jeremiah's hospital room. "Can I come in?" There was a young nurse taping a fresh bandage onto Jeremiah's bullet wound.

"Oh, of course," the nurse said with a warm smile, as she pasted the last strip of tape, and pulled the sheet over Jeremiah's leg.

Two bouquets of flowers rested on the windowsill overlooking Columbus Avenue's afternoon gridlock. Toni recognized her flowers, a collection of yellow and white daisies. And the other she figured was from the Franciscans at the orphanage. A collection of sunflowers with a miniature wooden statue of St. Francis hanging off the side of the vase.

"I'll be back," the pretty, young, nurse said with a warm smile. "Enjoy your visit."

Toni could not help watching the nurse leave the room. Immediately she recognized the nurse was no more than twenty, twenty-one. At that moment, Toni felt ancient.

"You doing all right?" Toni said. "You need anything?"

"I'm doing good, thanks."

Toni looked at the Franciscans flowers, "From your hooded friends?"

Jeremiah looked at the flowers too. "Yeah, yeah. From Father Egan and the other friars. They invited me to heal-up at the orphanage when I'm discharged."

"Nice," Toni said. The mixture of fresh flowers with the assorted aromas of a hospital room always brought her a trickle of comfort. Fresh flowers make everything better she thought. They should have flowers in the medical examiner's autopsy room, massive quantities of flowers.

Jeremiah was sitting up in his white hospital smock, clean-shaven, but you couldn't miss the bruising on his face, arms and hands from the waltz he and Toni had been in with Milton Iglesia. Nor could you miss the healing bruises on Toni's face.

"How are you doing, Toni?"

"I'm good."

"And Vita?"

"She's good. She's with my aunt."

"Catching up on her snoring?"

"Yeah, she is." Toni drifted from the foot of Jeremiah's bed to the side. "Listen, Detective Geddes will be up in a minute. He's been assigned to make an official notification to you on behalf of the department."

"Oh, right, of course," Jeremiah said, with resignation.

She took his hand and squeezed. "I'm very sorry about your father, Jeremiah."

"Yes, thank you, Toni. I appreciate that. I'm just sorry I never really knew him. And his wife." Jeremiah pursed his lips. "Heartbreaking stuff."

"Your father was a great cop," Toni said. "We owe him our lives."

Jeremiah nodded but remained silent.

"Were you able to find out if he ever knew about me?" Jeremiah said.

"Doesn't look like he did. At least, not until the last couple of days," Toni said. "Pulling all the pieces together it looks like only his wife and Father Manny knew about you, and your mom. And, of course, Milton, but he thought he was your father."

"Right," Jeremiah said and flicked away imaginary specks from his sheet.

"We're pretty sure that Father Manny knew you were not Milton's son. He probably figured that out the first time he saw you. And the fact that he sent you Ryan's cop shield, I think it means he knew there was a definite connection between you and your father. Maybe it was Father Manny's small way of trying to help you to have some connection with him."

"Yes."

Again they were quiet.

"Were you able to figure out who shot at you and Detective Geddes?"

"It looks like it was Jocelyn or Milton," Toni said. "The round pulled from my shoulder matched Lieutenant Condon's .357 which—as far as we could tell—they'd had in their possession throughout the whole thing."

"I'm sorry about your father, Toni," Jeremiah said. "I hope knowing how your father died brings you some peace."

"It has, I guess. I am proud of what he was trying to do. He was trying to amend for a serious error in judgment. I guess all those years how he handled Milton and the rape of your mom worked on my old man. With all my dad's imperfections, he tried to make things right. I'm grateful he died trying to do the right thing."

There was silence again.

Then a solid knock on the open door and Geddes strutted into the room. "How you feeling, Francisco? How's the leg?"

"Not too bad, detective." Geddes shook Jeremiah's hand. "It's healing up pretty good. They say I'll be able to run again in six months or so."

"Good, good. Good news." Geddes said and looked over at Toni for a moment. The recognition of how close a call it was for the two of them was swimming in their eyes."

"All right, let's get down to some business, "Geddes said. "Jeremiah I've got some information I need to give you officially."

Jeremiah and Toni listened.

"Here's the deal. All the department charges were dropped."

Jeremiah raised his eyebrows.

"Here's the way the job sees it. Your Glock was stolen. Maybe you weren't fit for duty, but anybody can forget a jacket in the bathroom."

"But not with a Glock in one of the pockets," Jeremiah blurted.

Jeremiah glanced at Toni, who maintained her focus on her partner. But she peripherally caught his glance.

"Yeah, well, whatever," Geddes said. "Anyway, you didn't know what they'd use it for. It was bad judgment, but it sure was not criminal, so that's that. As to your shield, well, it wasn't a real shield anyway, and it wasn't even the shield number assigned to you. The truth is the availability of your Glock or that duplicate shield is not what led to the loss of life here. Sadly, that would have happened anyway. And the truth is that you acted heroically to protect the life of another police officer." Geddes tilted his head to Toni.

"And since you had not been terminated at the time of your heroic action but were only on suspension, you were still a police officer," Geddes said. "Therefore, you were wounded in the line of duty. So in the department's infinite wisdom, you were reinstated. But, unfortunately, since you have a permanently disabling injury you are being retired. You've been awarded a disability pension."

Jeremiah sat with eyes wide: speechless.

"It's a small pension," Geddes continued. " But what do you expect after only a few months on the job, but it's something. And you get your good-guy letter. You're being honorably retired from the department."

Jeremiah did not speak. Looked to Toni back to Geddes, back to Toni and back to Geddes.

"I don't know what to say."

"Is that acceptable to you?" Geddes said.

"Yes, yes, Sir. Of course."

"Good. All right. I've got to go," Geddes said and took Jeremiah's hand and shook it again. "When you're well enough, get down to the Pension Section to sign the paperwork. And you might want to pay Chief King a visit. He was a good friend of your father's. You may want to thank him."

"Yes, Sir. Thank you."

"Good to meet you, Jeremiah. If there's anything I can do for you, don't hesitate."

He then looked at Toni. "You need a ride? You leaving with me?"

"No, I'm going to stick around a little longer."

"All right, I'll give you a call later."

"Okay, Geddes."

Toni's gaze followed Geddes's back on the way out; she then turned to Jeremiah.

They just looked at each other without speaking for several moments.

"So, how's it feel to be a retired cop with a pension for life?"

"Well..." Jeremiah breathed a long sigh and took Toni's hand. "Toni, I don't know what to say. I can't thank you enough. I mean, if you told them all that I told you, this wouldn't be happening."

"I don't know what you're talking about," Toni said with a twinkle in her eye, but then paused and added with all sincerity, "I don't believe I'd be alive if you hadn't been with me."

They held each other's gaze.

"So what do you plan to do with yourself Mr. Retired Police Officer?

"Well, I've had a lot of time to think about things. Especially lying here."

"Of course," Toni said.

"Well, I've decided to enter the seminary. I'm going to be a Friar. A Franciscan Friar."

Toni looked at Jeremiah for a long moment without expression then she smiled and nodded, pulled her hand out of Jeremiah's and said, "Of course."

She stepped away and back to the foot of his bed, and turned away to the door with cheeks and ears that had suddenly become beet red.

"Oh, for crying out loud, I almost forgot. Listen, there's a few people who want to meet you." Toni slipped out of the room.

One minute later, Liz walked in with Jeremiah's sixteen-year-old half-sister, Vanessa. Toni remained at the door.

Vanessa approached the foot of the bed in an adorable yellow summer dress. Jeremiah and Vanessa looked at each other for several moments without speaking. They realized at the same moment that they each had their mother's eyes.

"Vanessa?" Jeremiah said.

"Yes." She stepped to the side of Jeremiah's bed, leaned down to him, rested one side of her face to his chest and wept.

Jeremiah held his little sister tight.

Toni stepped out and closed the door.

THE END

"For surely I know the plans I have for you—to give you a future with hope."

Jeremiah 29:11

Made in the USA
Lexington, KY
30 November 2018